SWEETEST REVENGE

EDWINA FORT

SWEETEST REVENGE

Kaleb &
Monica's Tale

Published by Griot's Garden Publications

Griot's Garden Publications

2533 Bert Kouns Ind. Lp.,203 #187

Shreveport, La 71118

Griotsgardenpublications.com

Sweetest Revenge/Edwina Fort. – 1st edition ISBN

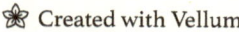 Created with Vellum

PROLOGUE
MONICA

I sat on the basketball court bleachers forcing myself not to pull at the little skirt that barely covered my butt. I was going to lose my nerves. What I was attempting was so far past crazy I began to doubt myself.

Oh goodness! If I was caught my Nana would never see me again! My death would probably be bloody and painful! I couldn't do this! What was wrong with me? I was getting ready to get myself killed!

I stood clutching my book bag to my chest which had enough rock cocaine in it to get me sent to prison for a long time. But then a memory of my big brother by one year, Man-Man, surfaced. He was smiling down at me as he handed me one of Nana's honey buns that were stashed up high in her closet. She thought we didn't know about them. She busted us and he took all the blame. Boy, Nana tore him up!

I eased back down to the bleachers, remembering why I was doing this.

My brother was dead! Murdered!

And the man responsible was down there standing on the sideline, larger than life, watching his younger brother play in a four-on-four hood tournament. Although this event was big in the hood, and Rasheed, his younger brother was something of a hood legend, being the biggest and most violent drug dealer on this side of town, the groupies were not here to see Rasheed.

No, they were all here to see Kaleb. If Rasheed was the prince around these parts, then Kaleb was the king, who rumor has it, was not only the power behind Rasheed, but also had his hands in everything from prime real estate to being the money behind several big named record labels here in the Chi. But what he was known for was The King and Sons' Classic Car Restoration Shop.

The story goes, their father, whose name was King, was this big-time drug dealer in his day. And to hide all the money he had coming in, he opened a classic car restoration shop in downtown Chicago. Anyway, the shop got so big it is said that it was bringing in just as much money, if not more than his dope empire. Needless to say, King did well with the business.

Kaleb however, has taken it to another level. Their shop had become the place to take your classic car amongst our people, and not just hood rich folks either. Big time rappers have shot their music videos at the shop. They rapped about driving their fresh whip off the lot. Hell, even the mayor joked about having to leave a press conference early, because he was going to pick up his '69 Cutlass that had been restored at The King and Sons'. They say the waiting list is like eight years out to even get a quote.

Hmm! Yeah, the women were not here like this to see Rasheed. He was a regular on the block. His older brother was not. So, when-ever Kaleb was spotted in the neighborhood, folks surrounded him as if he was a king. And tonight, there was going to be a party at his place. So yeah, the chickens were out.

I looked around at all the women who were here dressed like I was, hoping to be picked by one of the party promoters, who believe it or not, were moving around the park handing invites to certain girls. Certain girls that looked like they were down for whatever. Pretty girls. Scantily dressed girls. And they were cheesing and smiling as if they had just won the damn lottery.

Silly women!

I on the other hand, was dressed like a whore because I was getting ready to bring down the untouchable. And trust me, being dressed in a mini-skirt that left most of my legs and thighs exposed, and a crop-top that exposed my stomach and hung low on one side exposing my shoulder was not easy. And to top it all off, I was not wearing a bra. I let my long locs fall to cover the side of my face.

I'm not going to lie. I was hiding behind them, letting my body do all the work for me.

Hell yeah, I was ashamed that I was using my body this way. I could only imagine what my Nana or big sister Stormy would say if they saw me dressed this way.

Come on, Mon. Remember, you're just playing a part. This is not real. It's acting. I told myself.

And like Madame Queen, the woman who had been my acting coach for the last ten years had always said, "To convince the world that you are a certain character, you must first convince yourself." Today, I was not Monica. Today, I was Toya, hoochie mama extraordinaire. A gold-digger, whose every dream would come true if only Kaleb, Drug Lord, King Pin, would just choose me to come to his big party tonight. And as I watched his goons continue to move around the crowd giving exclusive invites, I almost threw up in my mouth.

I just wanted this to be over. I had to get revenge for my brother. I could not let his death go without somebody paying for it. Then I can have peace. Then I can focus on graduating high school in a few months, and then on to Juilliard. I had been accepted there on a dance scholarship. My Nana was sad that I was going to be moving to New York, but she was thrilled about me being accepted at Juilliard. She herself has been one of the first black women to dance on Broadway behind the late, great, Ms. Janet Collins, who had in fact been the very first black prima ballerina of the

Metropolitan Opera House. Her and my Nana were my role models.

I too wanted to dance on Broadway. Ever since I was a little girl, it had been my dream. Before Man-Man got turned out to the streets, he would help me practice by lifting me high in the air, twirling me around in my little tutu. I had hoped that he would one day come back to us. That he would turn back into the Man-Man me and Nana loved instead of the gangster he was so determined to be. I used to tell Nana that it was just a phase, and he would snap out of it and be normal again.

But he never will. He will never do anything else, because he was dead. I angrily wiped away the tears that began to well up in my eyes.

No! I will not cry! I will not!

Instead, I will get revenge for my brother. And then I will leave town and become a prima ballerina like my grandmother.

I looked back down at the man who was responsible for the death of my brother, and pure hatred shot through my veins. He had messed with the wrong girl's brother. And if it was the last thing I do, tonight, he was going to pay for it!

However, later that night I found myself in a bit of trouble. Everything had gone so smoothly at first. While most of the girls at the park had been loud and obnoxious to get noticed, I had taken a different approach for two reasons. First and foremost, I was terrified and ashamed of showing off so much of my body! The last thing I wanted to do was to draw too many eyes. I just needed to draw the eyes of those that mattered, Kaleb's goons.

The second reason was something Madame Queen had always told me. "You don't have to be loud to be noticed. In fact, use your body language to speak. Speak with the arch in your back, the curve of your hand, the grace in your step, the swan-like dip in your neck. Let your grace speak for you. It is more noticeable than any voice."

And so I did. I sat there reading a book, not speaking to anyone.

4

Every now and again I would flip my hair. When I reached for my water bottle next to me to take a sip, I curved my palm so that my long slender fingers gracefully lifted the bottle to my lips. When I drank, I sat straight up with just a slight arch to my back. I elongated my neck as the cool water ran down my throat, and then when I was done, I licked my lips.

Seconds later, I had my invite. I was handed a card with the address to Kaleb's Gold Coast penthouse condo by some guy that was very proud of his looks. I know this because every now and again he would stop and take a selfie of himself talking to someone, or shaking their hand or something. And he was proud of his car. He made sure everybody knew he was driving the candy red Lexus. Every now and again he would point his keys toward it and click a button to turn it on.

"Got to keep the air conditioner blowing, you know what I'm saying!" he would say to whoever was standing by him before laughing and looking around the park—probably trying to make sure everybody was watching him. Anyway. The clown handed me the card, and instructed me to give it to the guards in the downstairs lobby of Kaleb's condo.

"You need a ride boo?" he asked. I flinched.

"Oh no, I can get there. Thank you for the invite though!" As he made his way back down the bleachers, I breathed a sigh of relief.

Now that I was in, my plan was to fade to the background while I try to find a place to plant the drugs. I know you're wondering about the drugs. And to make a long story short, I found them in my brother's room. I know my brother sold this crap for Rasheed and Kaleb, so I figure I will just return their product and just maybe, make an anonymous call to the police, saying that a white woman was about to be murdered by a group of black thugs while at the same time making sure the drugs were somewhere that the police could see.

I know the white woman part was low. But hey, it will get the results I needed for this to go off as planned.

When I got to the penthouse, I was pleased to see that the place was packed, which was perfect. I found a seat in a dark corner where I could go unnoticed while I staked out the joint. Kaleb's penthouse was huge, I mean life of the rich and famous huge. I sat in what I assumed was the parlor, which was good, because it kept me close to the front door and it opened into the rest of the condo, giving me a great view of the sunken living room. You had to walk down a few steps to go into it. Wait staff came in and out of the kitchen. There were a full bar and a DJ table. One whole side of his place was glass windows. Outside of them was a big pool area with an Olympic size pool. There was a full bar out there as well.

The other women that had been invited were doing their jobs fabulously. They were all dressed in tiny dresses and high heels. I kind of felt underdressed. Most of them had gone home and changed into something far more glamorous than what they had been wearing at the park earlier. I still wore the tiny jean skirt and crop top that I was going to burn on my grill after tonight. Oh well, I wasn't here to be noticed at this point.

I heard a girl scream by the pool. Some guy had snatched off her bikini top and tossed her in the water. Oh, my goodness! I held my breath, waiting for her to emerge from the water and yell, "Rape!" Except when she came up, it wasn't her bare breasts she was squalling about, it was her hair.

Em, Em, Em...

Welp! So, like I was saying with all that kind of activity going on, who would pay attention to little old me in a dark corner, right? Right.

Okay, so this is where things started going wrong. You see, I had planned on being out of this place by now. But neither Kaleb nor Rasheed was here, and timing was everything. I needed to plant the drugs at the right time and make my call. Hopefully when they find Man-Man's drugs they will go ahead and search the premises for more drugs. Now granted, from what I've researched on Kaleb, he's nobody's dummy. So chances are he won't have any drugs here at his house. But I bet he had a gun or two. Plus, Man-Man had enough drugs to put anybody away for a good while. I don't care how it happens, just as long as the bastard goes to jail. Him and his psychotic brother.

The guy that had given me the invite sat down on the wide circular chair next to me. I had to force myself not to stiffen at his nearness. I was playing the role of a whore after all.

"The book reader," he said leaning in close to me. He had on so much cologne I almost choked. I smiled at him.

"Yep, I like to read," I told him, wishing he would just get up and leave me be.

He held up his hand and one of the serving girls came over carrying a tray with two shot glasses of alcohol on it.

Oh crap! I was getting ready to panic.

"Thank you, baby," he said to her as she put the glasses down on a table next to us. When she turned to leave, he smacked her on her butt. Goodness, what a savage!

"You drink Tequila, boo?" He turned to look at me while handing me one of the glasses. "It's Patron; only the good stuff for the sexiest girl at the party." Everything in me screamed for me to say, "No," but I would draw too much attention to myself saying no to a drink. With a very forced smile on my face, I nodded.

"Oh, yeah, I like Patron," I told him. He smiled before he turned his glass up and swallowed the contents in one swoop. Oh crap. I have never drunk a thing in my whole life. Oh crap! "I am playing a part," I reminded myself, before I lifted the glass to my lips and duplicated his action.

I almost died! As the fiery liquid washed down my throat, I began to choke. It was taking everything within me to keep it down. Oh goodness! It was horrible! I'm pretty sure I just drank rubbing alcohol.

"You okay, boo?" The creep said, patting me on my back. I nodded.

"Yeah!" I croaked. "It's just been a while."

"Girl, the way you took that, it looks like it's been never." He frowned at me.

Even though it almost killed me, I forced myself to stop choking. The last thing I needed was for this guy to start asking questions. The less anybody knew about me here, the better. Tonight I was supposed to be a phantom.

The drink was beginning to warm me up on the inside. I took my foot and scooted my backpack underneath the chair out of sight. The alarm system was going off inside my head and I didn't know why.

"So," he said, putting his arm on the chair behind me, "what's your name, boo?"

What is with this guy and the "boo" thang? I cleared my throat.

"Toya," I said, clearing my throat again. Something was wrong. I was beginning to feel warm on the inside, and my throat felt scratchy. It was probably just the shot. I guess that's what it was supposed to do. I mean why else would anybody drink such vile tasting stuff?

"Toya. Em, that's a pretty name, just like you." He put his hand on my thigh, and for the third time tonight I almost threw up.

"Thank you," I said, turning to look around at the other party goers. "Please leave!" I screamed in my head. I began to fan myself with my hand. Somebody must have turned on the heat, because it was really getting hot in here.

"I was thinking me and you can get out of here and go for a little drive in my Lexus." He winked at me, and oh my goodness! I could not stop the laughter that erupted from my mouth. I don't know why, but that wink coupled with his words was hilarious.

"What's so funny?" he asked.

"You, boo!" I told him, before I erupted into another fit of laughter. This dude was trash and so was his game. Dang, was I drunk? Why did I just find that so funny? Was it possible to get drunk off of one shot?

"Can you get drunk off of one shot?" I asked him. He smiled then, very wickedly.

"Yep, if it's Liquid Ex." I frowned at him.

"Is that Tequila?" He shook his head.

"Nope." Those alarm bells were getting louder.

"What is it then?"

"It's new... just hit the streets." My eyes widened. Oh no!

"Don't worry, baby. It's just a little something to help you loosen up a bit, that's all." He opened his mouth to say something else to me, but right then the front door opened and Rasheed walked in. Behind him were several guys that I had seen standing with Kaleb. Either they were his main boys or maybe even his bodyguards. Behind them walked in Kaleb.

My breath stalled in my throat. I don't know if it was because of the drugs or just the general impact of seeing this man up close for the first time, but it felt as if I had been sucker punched right in the stomach. You see, I had not gotten a good look at his face earlier.

What a face!

He was extremely good looking, in a very rugged kind of way. He was good looking without even trying. He wore his beard low as if it hadn't been cut in a few days. However, his fade looked fresh as if it had been cut today. He didn't have a friendly face. You know the kind that welcomed people to approach you?

His face said loud and clear, "Don't mess with me, because I'm not in the mood." He frowned. In fact, he looked as if he was irritated with us all.

That, added with the fact that he was big. I mean *really* big. He wore a button-up shirt with the top three buttons opened that gave a sneak peek at the immense chest underneath it. The material hugged his arms just enough to see that they too were gigantic. He could probably snap me in half like a twig if he chose to. And him being dressed in all black—black jeans, black shirt, black Gaiter boots—only added to the fear I was feeling right now.

This fear I couldn't blame on the drugs. If anything, the drugs were keeping me from getting up and running for my life. I have a confession to make. I may have a slight problem of getting an idea in my head and running with it before I could think it all the way through. My Nana and Stormy say my little condition was probably going to get me in trouble one day. And I think that today just may be that day.

I am so stupid! Why did I just assume that Kaleb was going to be like Rasheed? Yeah, Rasheed scared a lot of people on the streets because he was a murdering thug. Him, I could have handled. But this force that was his older brother was a different story. He was... dangerous. I felt way out of my element. He was above anything I had ever encountered. Power and experience just seemed to radiate from him. Everybody felt it. I could tell by the way they all stared at him with a look of awe on their faces.

And to top it all off, I had been drugged. Even as we were speaking, I could feel it making changes to my body, or at least how I felt about my body.

The shame I had felt earlier for exposing so much skin was gone. And although I know I was afraid right now, my brain wasn't sending the proper signals to my body, like..."Run!"

"Welcome home, Boss," the man who had been sitting on the couch next to me said, getting up to approach the group. His voice boomed over the music so that all of us that sat in the front parlor heard.

"Jamie, I don't need you to welcome me to my own home," Kaleb spoke sounding tired. His voice was deep and raspy.

"Sit your goofy a$$ down!" Rasheed said shoving Jamie in the head, causing a bunch of people to laugh. "Why do you keep this chump around?" he asked his brother. Kaleb chuckled, shaking his head a bit. As the men passed me, I prayed to Stormy's God, Yah, that I went unnoticed. My heart was beating so loud in my ear it was louder than the music. I wanted to fan myself because I was extremely hot now. I could feel beads of sweat pooling up on my temples, but I sat perfectly still as not to draw attention to myself.

But right as he passed, Kaleb looked down at me. At first his eyes just seemed to skim over me. I was just about to exhale when they flew back to me. And Oh! My! Goodness! He stopped dead in his tracks and turned to look at me fully. The heat had turned into an inferno! I was burning alive!

Please floor, just open and swallow me, this chair and my brother's drugs through you. I began to breathe heavily. At least it seemed like it to me. My chest rose and fell with each panic breath I took. *This was not the plan! This was not the plan!*

"You the shorty with the book," he said, and a quiver went through me as his deep voice washed over me. I almost moaned. His voice felt so good. What the world was happening to me?

I just froze in fear. If Madame Queen could see me now, she would shake her head and say, "Well, you were born to be a dancer. This acting thing just comes in a strong second to that." I opened my mouth to speak but nothing came out. I don't know if it was the drugs in my system or just the power that seemed to ooze from him, but I felt terrified. Having his full attention was like having the attention of an oncoming, speeding Mac-truck. I bit my lip, more nervous than I've ever been in my life. His eyes lowered to my mouth.

"Boss, she ain't nobody. I brought her here for me. *This* is what I have for you," Jamie said turning to gesture towards two very voluptuous women dressed in brown bikinis that matched their brown oiled up bodies perfectly.

Dang! They looked like two bars of chocolate. The mouths of Rasheed and the other men that came in with him fell open as the women approached Kaleb. They both wore inviting smiles on their faces as their hungry eyes took in all that was Kaleb. Kaleb looked at them for a minute. His eyes slowly traveled up their bodies and back down again. I eased my hand down on the side of the chair and pushed the bag back to the wall so that it could not be seen at all. My heart was racing so fast I was finding it hard to breathe. I needed to get away from this force that was Kaleb.

I eased to my feet. While everybody's attention was on the two chocolate drops, I would just ease myself out of this situation. With my head down, I quietly slipped away. I had taken five, maybe six steps when I felt a strong, warm hand come around my waist and palm my flat, bare stomach.

Oh! I closed my eyes as a feeling I had never felt before shot through me. Oh! What was happening? I think I was feeling pleasure; pure, intense pleasure. How could this be? How could I feel pleasure for a man I hated? He pressed his front so close to my back I could feel the outline of his strong body.

"Where you going, Shorty? I'm not finished talking to you," he spoke quietly, his lips brushing my ear as his deep voice and warm breath caressed my lobe. I closed my eyes and suppressed a moan that tried to escape my lips. It had to be the drugs. Oh no! That jerk slipped me a Mickey!

"I..." my voice quivered as I spoke. I cleared my throat. "I was just going to get some air, that's all," I told him.

"Good idea. Let's go together." He took my hand and began to pull me across the huge parlor. With panicked eyes, I looked back at Jamie. I would rather deal with him and his buffoonery over this power force any day.

"Boss, what's up?" Jamie yelled after us. Kaleb came to a stop. As he inhaled, his nostrils flared and the muscle ticked in his cheek. He didn't turn around. He just stood there for a few seconds, breathing angrily while staring straight ahead. Right then, two of the big goons that had come in the door with him, stood from where they had been sitting with a girl on their laps. Rasheed, who had been whispering something in one of the chocolate drop's ears, stopped and approached Jamie.

"Man, what the hell you just say?" he growled at Jamie, who now wore a look of terror on his face.

"Nothing. I just wanted to tell the boss to enjoy my treat to him." Kaleb grunted then continued walking. I was doomed. He led me through the crowd and up the sleek stairs that sat in full view of everyone. I let my hair fall to cover my face, so embarrassed. Everyone was looking at us. Some of the women looked as if they wanted to claw my eyes out. I wanted to beg someone to take my place. Please!

Two big men with guns sat in the open space that was at the top of the stairs.

"Boss," they said as we passed. Kaleb didn't speak. He just slightly nodded his head. We walked down a long, dark hallway, passing a few rooms to a pair of wooden double doors at the end of it. He opened one and pulled me through it.

And yes, he was pulling me because I was dragging my feet.

"Umm, I should go back to the party," I told him, trying to pull my hand out of his. I couldn't even pretend that I was not afraid, and yet the drugs were making me feel something else. I was trying to fight them, but the feeling was getting stronger and stronger.

"Naw, Ma. I ain't in the mood for all that out there. It's been a long week, and I just want to chill with you, okay?" I opened my mouth to say, "Not okay," but then I got my first view of his room and my words just seemed to die away. Just like the rest of his place, his bedroom was humongous and very masculine. On his big bed was a very plush looking black comforter with matching pillows. All the furniture was made of mahogany wood.

His room smelled like him; a mix of his spicy cologne and soap, and maybe even laundry detergent. He walked to a pair of glass double doors that were across the room and opened them to a beautiful modest size balcony.

"Wow!" I said as I crossed the floor with feet that seemed to have a mind of their own. He had the most amazing view of the lake.

"Best place to get some air." He spoke so close to my ear I jumped. I didn't hear him come up behind me. I walked away from him to the rail and looked out across the dark lake. The gentle breeze felt so good blowing against my warm skin. I held my head back and let the wind blow my locs around my body and face. It felt amazing. I closed my eyes and moaned as the wind caressed my skin that seemed to be inflamed ever since Kaleb first looked at me.

Giving in to the caress of the wind was all the drug needed to take over. I could no longer fight it. I wanted to feel good. I wanted to dance.

And as if on cue, the DJ began to play something slow and sensual. I lost track of reality. In my mind, I was dancing in the night, in the streets of Paris or across the sands of Arabia. I was slightly aware of Kaleb watching me. He felt like a king and I his harem girl, dancing for his pleasure.

He sat on the edge of his bed and watched me move through lowered lids. I can tell he liked what he saw because of the hungry look on his face. Funny, his look didn't repulse me like it should. No, quite the opposite. It made me feel good, sexy, and empowered.

I went up on my toes and came down in a simple balance, which is a rocking sequence of three steps.

"You're a ballerina," he stated quietly as if he was speaking to himself. I stopped dancing and looked at him.

"You don't know me," I laughed. "I'm the phantom of the opera." One of his eyebrows lifted.

"The opera?" he asked, his deep voice washing over my body, causing everything within me to want something I had never wanted before. Well, at least not like *this*.

"And where is this opera?" I opened my arms wide.

"Here." His gaze lowered to my stomach and probably the underside of my breasts that I was revealing with my raised arms. He licked his lips, watching me like a wolf watched a small deer. I snatched my arms down and laughed.

"You look hungry," I told him. Slowly he nodded.

"I am, baby. I want to taste you so bad it's taking everything within me to keep my hands to myself right now." I closed my eyes as pure uncut pleasure shot through me at his words.

"How old are you?" he asked. I opened my eyes and looked at him.

"Eighteen."

"Damn, you're young," he said looking miserable. I giggled.

"How old are you?"

"Twenty-nine. I'll be thirty in a few months." I shrugged my bare shoulder.

"Why does my age upset you?"

He shook his head. "I don't mess with young women. They get attached because I make them feel something they have never felt before. Next thing you know, they're in love and don't know how to go home when it's time."

I lifted one side of my mouth in a grin. "Baby, you ain't never got to worry about me falling in love with you. And as far as going home, that sounds like a great idea. I'll just let myself out." I turned to head for the door. Damn, that was easy.

I had only gone a few steps before I found myself lifted off my feet and into a pair of strong arms. My startled breath whooshed out my body. I looked at him in shock. He smiled at me.

"I see you a sassy young lady. What's your name?" he asked, carrying me back to his bed. I was so befuddled by suddenly being in his arms that I opened my mouth and uttered the truth.

"Monica!" I closed my eyes as soon as my name escaped my lips. Damn it!

"Well, Monica, if I don't have to worry about you falling in love, then I want a taste."

When we got to the bed, he tossed me in it. I giggled, trying to fight my way out of the plush blanket. Before I could, he was on the bed. He wedged his big body between my legs and was holding himself up over me with one hand. His other hand was coming towards my face. I laid there paralyzed. I know I should be stopping him. My mind said I should. But my body... my body wanted to know how it felt to be touched by a man.

And I ain't gon' lie. The fact that this powerful man was looking at me like that... like I was something he craved... He lifted a finger to my lips and gently rubbed across my bottom lip.

"So soft," he whispered. "Can I taste you?"

Say, No! Say, No!

I slowly nodded. *What am I doing?* I thought, as he slowly lowered his head. When his lips first touched mine, it felt like electricity. I inhaled. He lifted his head, looking down at me. I touched my lips with fingers that shook as I stared up into his searching eyes. He had felt it too. His eyes fell on my lips and he lowered his head again, but this time when he took my mouth, he ravished.

Oh! Goodness! He was so hungry, I—

I clutched his shirt in my fist, trying to hold on for dear life.

"You taste so good... so sweet," he said low in my ear before his mouth was on my neck.

His big palm lay flat against my belly, feeling each quiver he caused to go off there. Slowly his hand lifted, and with it, my shirt. He broke his lips away from mine and looked down at my flesh he had just exposed. He moaned.

"Beautiful, baby," he said, before he slowly lowered his head—

Okay, yeah. So, I'm going to do a little editing at this point. But for the sake of my story, I'm going to fill you in on a little more detail. At one point, at that very moment he made me a woman, a look of utter surprise crossed his face when I screamed out in pain.

"You're a virgin?" he whispered. His surprise turned into confusion. His confusion turned into a look of utter... possession?

"You're a virgin," he whispered in my ear as he slowed down, and then very gently continued to awaken my body in a way that will forever ruin me to the touch of any other man.

Now, I want to say that after we finished I felt ashamed and got my clothes and left. But then I would be lying. We made love two more times before we both passed out in an exhausted sleep.

When I woke up, I was in bed alone. I sat up and looked around the dark room confused.

Where was I? For a moment, I was completely lost. And then the last few hours came back to me. And yes, for the fourth time that night, I felt as if I was going to be ill. I scrambled out of bed.

"What have I done?" I whispered as I quickly put my clothes back on. Oh, man! This was not good. This was not good! I stopped when I looked down at the condom wrapper on the floor.

One wrapper!

My hand flew to my mouth. Oh, goodness! One wrapper!

The last two times we made love had been unprotected.

No! No!

Okay. Get it together, Mon. You need to get out of here! Yes, that's what I needed to do. I had to get out of here. Now was not the time to think of anything else outside of getting revenge for Man-Man and getting on with my life. I had to see this through. I had already botched it something terrible. And I had to move quickly before that bastard came back.

I eased the bedroom door open, listening. It was quiet. It sounded as if the party had died down.

Okay, you can do this!

I took a deep breath, then walked out of the door and down the long hallway. I didn't even look at the men that were still in the opening before the stairs. I just quickly made my way down them. There were only a few stragglers still here. Kaleb stood with his back to me out in the pool area talking to a few guys. What a bastard. He was probably telling them he was ready for me to be out of his bed. I almost laughed out loud. You don't have to worry, Mister. After today, you ain't gon' never see me again.

I made my way back to the parlor. I could see that my bag was still under the chair I sat in earlier. Quickly, I pulled it out and carried it across the room to a closet that I had scouted out and figured would be the perfect place for the cops to find dope.

With hands that shook, I took out the drugs and stashed them on the top shelf. And then without looking back, I slipped out the front door.

An hour later I stood outside with the small crowd that was forming and watched as the police came out with a handcuffed Kaleb as well as a few other people. Unfortunately, not Rasheed.

But I was fine with that. Like Bob Marley said, "I shot the sheriff. I don't need to shoot the deputy." I pulled out one of Man-Man's Cuban cigars, his prized possession, that he had more than likely stolen. And as the police car that carried Kaleb rolled past me I lit it, and put it to my lips. When his angry eyes connected with mine, I winked at him with a smirk on my face.

Got you, bastard!

Chapter 1
I WANT MORE

MONICA

2 Years Later...
  Life has a way of turning sharply and going in a different direction than where you were steering it. And no matter how hard you slam on the brakes and try to turn the wheel back the other way, your life continues down a road in which you never wanted it to go. I could say that I'm bitter. I could say that I'm kicking myself over and over for the mistakes I've made. But the truth is, I don't have time to dwell on the past, because my present day is very demanding and very needy. And it's my responsibility to feed her.

"Bye, baby. You be good for Nana," I said, taking my two-year-old daughter, Eve into my arms and hugging her tightly.

"I come too," she said, beginning to get herself worked up I exhaled, putting her down on her feet. I hated working so much! I was a horrible mother! My baby missed me so much. It broke my heart each day I had to pry her little arms from around my legs.

"Not this time, baby. Mama got to go to work. When I come home I will bring you a freeze-pop back." She pressed herself up against my legs. She wasn't having it.

"Nooooo!" she started to whine in her little toddler voice. I held back tears. I was under so much pressure I thought that throwing a tantrum sounded good right about now.

"Baby, please! Mama going to bring you the red one like you like," I told her, my voice quivering slightly. How had I come to this? I had so many dreams. I wanted to do so many things. I never imagined I would be flipping burgers for a living, and when I wasn't doing that, I was frying chicken down at Chucky's Chicken Shack. I worked at The Burger Joint every day from 10:00 AM to 4:00 PM. Then, I came home to have lunch with my baby and Nana before I caught the bus to work at Chucky's from 6:00 PM to midnight. This was my daily routine except on Wednesdays. That's when I get a break and could do what I love. I picked up teaching Nana's dance class down at the center since she hasn't been feeling up to leaving the house these days.

Oh God! What did I do to deserve this?

"Pease, Mama! Net me go wit you." I squeezed my eyes shut.

You can't give up! You can't give up!

Your Nana and your baby girl are depending on you.

"Come on now, Eve," Nana said while walking slowly through the kitchen door. It pained me to see her like this. All those years of dancing had taken a toll on her body. She once walked with the grace of a swan. For as long as I can remember, she instilled in me to glide instead of walk. Now she walked hunchbacked with a cane —arthritis being her constant tormenter.

Thank God for Stormy. She had gotten one of her friends SaafiYah to make a liniment for Nana and it worked like magic. But my Nana was too proud to keep asking for refills. She hated bugging Stormy more than anything because she had already done so much for us and the center. If not for her, both the boarding house and the center would have been long gone by now. Nana hated feeling like a burden. And so did I, which is why I worked the way I did. I had to make sure our bills were paid and that we could afford the little food we had.

"Mama!" Eve yelled out as Nana pulled her away from my leg.

"Go on, child. This baby will be okay. I'll put one of her movies on...works every time." I kissed my grandmother on her cheek.

"Thank you, Nana. I'll bring home some burgers for lunch, and I'll stop by the store to get some things to make chicken salad for dinner." She nodded while holding back Eve, who was now in full tantrum mode.

"Mama love you, baby," I said to my screaming little girl. I had to hurry and leave the house. Oh boy! That tore me up every day. As I stood at the bus stop waiting on the 14, I couldn't help but reflect over my life and how drastically it had changed over the last couple of years; how drastically it had changed after that night.

I had been on top of the world back then. I had brought down the man responsible for my brother's death. I had been accepted into Juilliard. My grandmother had been so proud of me, and that was all that had mattered. My brother had brought her so much grief. I needed to do the opposite and reverse the damage her constant worrying about him had done to her. And for a moment I had, by being a straight-A-student and graduating as valedictorian of my class.

Oh yes! I had been on top of the world. But it crumbled right under my feet when my actions that night caught up with me. I walked across the stage three months pregnant. And of course, when I called my counselor at Julliard and explained the situation to her, in hopes that they would hold my scholarship, she pretty much told me, "Tough break," and that they would be giving the scholarship to someone else. I begged her with everything I had, ensuring her that I could be a mom and a student at the same time. I'll never forget what she told me.

"Monica, I'm really sorry. It's just that there are so many young talented people waiting to fill that spot. And we have found that single parents cannot set aside the time needed to pass your cour-ses. I am so sorry. You were so talented. It really is a waste." So careless she was in flushing my dreams, my goals, and my aspirations down the toilet.

I struggled with my feelings toward the child I carried in my womb during pregnancy. This was my enemy's child. I debated whether or not to get an abortion. But then I thought of my mom and how hard she worked to take care of me and my brother. She could have aborted us. Like me, she had dreams of following in my grandmother's footsteps. Instead, she got pregnant with my brother, then me shortly afterward, and ended up dancing on a pole because she chose our lives over her dreams.

It wasn't this innocent baby's fault that I made some very dumb decisions. Why should she have to pay with her life? So, I chose to have my enemy's child, and it was the best thing I have ever done. I can't imagine my life without Eve. She's the smartest, prettiest baby in the world. And she wants to dance just like her mama. For a two-year-old, she was pretty good at it. I always took her to class with me on Wednesdays.

I didn't make it, but I was determined to make sure she does. If it's the last thing I do, I was going to see to it that she made it all the way to the top.

After leaving The Burger Joint, I took the bus to the grocery store and grabbed a few items—mainly salad. I felt horrible because money was so tight we ate a lot of burgers and fried chicken. But I made sure to serve veggies with every meal. When I got home, I made a chicken salad and put it in the fridge for their dinner, and a garden salad to go with our burgers. After putting Eve in her high chair, I plopped down in the chair across from hers and rested my head against my palm.

"You tired, baby?" Nana asked. I could hear the strain in her voice. She was so sick. I was so worried about her. I sat up straight in my chair.

"Heck naw! These little jobs ain't nothing," I lied.

Like Stormy was so fond of saying, I was as tired as a Hebrew slave—the ones that were in ancient Egypt and those that were here in America today. But my granny didn't need to know that.

"You a good girl, baby...taking care of your old grandma like you do." She picked at her salad. I frowned at her.

"You not hungry?" I asked. She shook her head.

"I ain't had much of an appetite as of late."

"That's it, Nana. I'm taking you to the County on Wednesday." I put down my fork and handed Eve her sippy cup.

"Pss! Child, I ain't going down to that county hospital to wait eighty years for some white man to pick and poke at me. I'm just fine."

"Yeah, but you're not just fine. At least let Stormy's friend, SaafiYah come and see you." She waved her hand.

"Mon, I'm old. *This* is what old age looks like. We don't need to bother Stormy and her family no mo'." She stirred some honey into her tea. "Shew, that man of hers already coming out of his pocket to feed the kids now that the damn government done got rid of our lunch program." She began to cough, reaching for her napkin.

"You have any idea how much that cost?" she continued when she could speak again.

"If not for Stormy and Solomon, this house that my husband built for me with his bare hands would be gone. They paid the taxes on this place for the next ten years. I can't keep asking those folks for stuff." She began coughing again because she was getting herself worked up.

"Okay, Nana—Just calm down. We don't have to ask them for no mo' money. I make enough to handle things around here." I lied again. My Nana's precious home was deteriorating around us. Everything was wrong with it. It needed a new roof, pipes, and floors. I didn't even know where to begin. I had gotten a book on plumbing from the library and was trying to do some of the work myself. I wasn't making much progress though.

Leaving out for my second job was always easier because I

would give Eve a bag of animal crackers when it was time. That, plus Sesame Street made for a clean getaway, free of tantrums. I exhaled when I got off the bus in front of Chucky's. Chucky paid in cash. The pay wasn't bad either. It was two-hundred and fifty dollars a week, which was awesome. However, Chucky was an old pimp or something and thought he was God's gift to women.

"Monica, bring yo' fine a$$ in here and make me some money!" he said as soon as I came into the kitchen.

Dang! It was going to be a long night.

I locked the doors as soon as twelve o'clock hit. Twenty minutes later, I was at the bus stop. I hated being out this late. This was such a bad neighborhood. And the only folks out this hour were either high, drunk or both. I tightened my grip on my book bag straps. None of these bastards better try to mess with me tonight, because my feet hurt bad and I wasn't in the mood. They were going to get cussed out for real.

A black Cadillac truck with darkly tinted windows pulled up in front of me, cutting off my view from the rest of the street. Oh! I really wasn't in the mood for this. I tossed my long locs over my shoulder and craned my neck to see if the bus was coming. I'm telling you, this fool better be ready to take, "No," for an answer. No, I didn't *have* a man. And no, I didn't *need* a man. And *hell* no, I wasn't looking for a friend. The back door opened and a giant of a man stepped out.

I was so caught up in trying to comprehend just how big he was that I didn't notice the two men quickly approaching me from behind. By the time I saw them it was too late. They moved so fast I could barely catch my breath. I opened my mouth to scream, but a rag was quickly stuffed in it before they roughly wrapped duct tape around my mouth and head, it pulled viciously at my locs. I went to swing, but the big guy caught my hand and turned me so that both were behind my back then quickly secured a plastic tie around them, pulling it tight. I screamed into the rag from the pain, but it did no good. My mouth was tied so tightly that only a muffled

scream came out. In front of me stood the two men that snuck up
on me. I saw now that they had been in separate vehicles. I was
trying to see if I recognized them from around the hood. If you saw
one thug, you'd seen them all. I kicked out at the one that wore his
hat cocked to the right. My gym shoe caught him right in the shin.

"Bi***!" He hissed before he punched me in my mouth. I
flinched from the pain while trying to fight unconsciousness.

"What the hell you doing?" the big guy said, shoving the man
away from me.

"This bi*** kicked me!" he snapped, shoving the big guy's hand
off him.

"Let's go. We don't have time for this!" another man yelled from
the front seat of the Cadillac truck.

Then everything went black as one of them put a dark sack over
my head. The breath was slammed out of me when someone put
their shoulder in my stomach before lifting me. I went wild, trying
to wiggle out their grasp. But seconds later, I was being put into
what I was sure was a trunk. I brought my legs up to try to keep the
trunk from closing. Someone roughly grabbed my legs, bringing
them together, before tying my ankles together with another plastic
tie. Then they threw my legs down and slammed the trunk.

Oh! My! God! I was being kidnapped! My heart pounded so
hard in my chest—I was having a hard time breathing. I had never
been so afraid in my life. I was getting ready to die or worse! I was
getting ready to be raped or sold into slavery! Nana was always
watching the news. She was just saying yesterday that there had
been an increase in black women and girls being kidnapped and
sold as sex slaves. Oh, no! Oh, no! I was getting ready to be sold as a
sex slave! And then a thought crossed my mind that made me
freeze in terror.

Organ harvesting!

Nana said that they were kidnapping black people for their
organs as well. Tears came to my eyes. I was screaming so much my
throat got sore. I could feel my wrists being scrapped raw from

where I pulled against the plastic tie trying to break it. I didn't care about the pain. I just wanted to be free. I thought about Eve and Nana—They needed me! I could not die! Who would take care of them if I died?

We drove for about thirty to forty-five minutes before the car came to a stop. I was so scared I was shaking. I still couldn't breathe and my busted lip felt swollen and sore. The trunk opened, and I was roughly lifted out of it and stood upon my feet. My teeth began to chatter. Dear Yah, help me! I prayed to Stormy's God because she said that he had saved her life. So maybe he could save mine right now!

The bag was yanked off my head. I blinked, trying to take in my surroundings. Judging by the tools and smells of oil and gasoline, I was in a warehouse or a garage. It was full of classic cars. I continued scanning the place while trying to catch my breath until my eyes landed on the face that haunted my dreams. I sharply inhaled, feeling as if the wind had been completely knocked out of me.

Dear Yah! It was Kaleb!

He smiled wickedly at me from where he stood surrounded by his men. The giant that had stepped out of the Cadillac was next to him. Amazingly, although the man was clearly bigger than him, his girth was not enough to overshadow Kaleb's might. Just like the first time I saw him, power seemed to radiate from him. He wore it well. There was no question who was king here. Dressed in all black again, he sported jeans and a t-shirt that lay on his muscled chest just right; showing that he was very well built underneath his clothes. And like the first time I saw him, he wore a pair of black boots on his feet. Unlike the first time, he now sported a full beard on his handsome face.

So many questions raced through my mind at this moment.

When had he gotten out?

How had he gotten out?

The last I heard, he had been facing twenty years for tax

evasion or something like that. It was a little unnerving that none of the drug charges stuck. Still, I was thrilled to learn that they had found something to get him on... and for twenty years. That made it all worth it for me. Of course, I heard that through the grapevine. Not that I didn't do all I could to get better information. It's just that some were hard to come by, even when calling and pretending to be an attorney interested in the case.

His eyes slowly raked down my body. He lifted his hand and someone yanked the tape from behind my head. I closed my eyes, flinching as the tape was snatched off my sore mouth, my wound being reopened in the process. The man from the front seat came around and took the cloth out of my mouth. I sucked in my bottom lip to feel how much damage had been done to it. Oh! Yeah, it was definitely busted. I looked at the punk who hit me, and for a moment, anger took over my fear. However, the fear quickly rushed back in when Kaleb began to move towards me. His eyes narrowed on my lips.

He lifted my face with his finger, looking at my busted lip.

"Who hit you?" he asked quietly. His deep voice was so deadly. I was so scared with him being so close to me... and touching me, that for the life of me I could not speak. He turned around and looked at his men.

"Who hit her?" His deep voice filled the huge garage. The thug that hit me stepped up.

"I-I did, K," his voice shook a little. Kaleb looked at him for a minute before he held his head back and laughed. It was something about that laugh that was bone chilling. And I wasn't the only one who thought so either, because all his men, except for the giant, began to fidget—especially the guy who hit me.

"K, she kicked me!" The man said trying to explain his actions.

"Aww... She kicked you?" Kaleb cooed as if he was talking to a small child. He slowly walked towards the now very nervous man, who began to frantically look around at the other men for help.

"Kaleb. Man, I'm sor..." he began. But before he could finish,

Kaleb moved quickly, grabbing two mammoth-sized wrenches from a nearby table. What he did with them next caused me to open my mouth with a scream frozen in my throat as I stared in horror. He brought one wrench up with a mighty blow, catching the man with such force underneath his chin he flew up in the air, before he came down with the other wrench on top of his head, causing his dead body to crash to the floor with his head split open from the impact.

Kaleb threw both wrenches down on the lifeless body, hard.

"Kick *that*, punk!" he said to the body, shaking his head.

And it was right then that I realized that I was dealing with a cold-blooded killer. When he looked back at me, that scream escaped. I turned and tried to run, remembering too late that my ankles were tied. Another scream escaped my throat as I tipped over, getting ready to hit the floor. Because my hands were still tied behind my back, I couldn't bring them out to try and stop my fall.

The giant reached out and grabbed my arm, preventing my fall, but leaving me slightly suspended in the air from where I still tipped forward.

"Where you going, baby? I was just getting ready to invite you to dinner," Kaleb said, coming to stand in front of me. He wrapped one arm around my waist and snatched me up against him. The breath slammed out of me from the impact of our bodies suddenly coming in contact.

"Surely you won't be so rude as to leave without first having dinner or even saying goodbye." The anger that came from his eyes was real. Oh, my goodness! What had I done, getting entangled with this maniac? I licked my dry lips and winced when my tongue came across my wound. His eyes followed before he slowly lifted me up his big body, bringing my mouth close enough for him to gently kiss my wound. A quiver shot through my body...I sucked in my breath, taken off guard by my body's response to his soft caress.

"I'm sorry about that," he whispered before he gently kissed it one more time. "A man that hit a woman ain't sh**..." I could tell that he meant what he said.

"Even a treacherous woman—that will give a man her virginity, to set him up, and get him thrown into prison," he continued just as quietly, still holding me close. I opened my mouth to say something to defend myself. I thought about lying and acting as if I had no idea what he was talking about, but then I remembered what I had just witnessed. He had brutally killed a man, yet as easily as one would put on a pair of shoes.

"I..." I began, but I was so scared I couldn't think of what to follow that with. I'm sorry, perhaps?

"You... what?" he asked as his eyes raked over my face. I felt as if he could see into my soul.

"Come on... beautiful little liar. Surely you can bring something through those treacherous lips of yours." I was shaking so bad I think my teeth were chattering.

"Have dinner with me." He spoke softly, his hungry gaze still on my mouth.

"I don't want to," I managed to get out barely over a whisper. His gaze left my mouth and slowly traveled up my face to my eyes before going to my hair, my nose, and my neck. The way he looked at me made me remember that night... how he had touched my body... how he had kissed my body. It made me remember how he had taken me over and over—awaking my body to the pleasure of a man's touch without mercy. It made me remember how I had begged him to let me rest because I felt as if I would die if he caused my body to shatter one more time. Only for him to show me that...no...I would not die.

"I insist," he spoke suddenly before letting my body slide down his until my feet were once again planted on the floor. Then he squatted down right in front of me. My breath froze in my throat because his face was so close to my center. I closed my eyes, too afraid to look down to see what he was doing. Was he going to rape me? Oh, my goodness! Was he going to rape me in front of all his men?

But seconds later, I felt the tie give way around my ankle. I exhaled. He stood looking down at me as he used the knife he had used on the tie around my ankles to cut the one around my wrists. The way he watched me as he did it let me know he was aware of my thoughts.

There was activity going on around us, but I couldn't look away from his gaze. I rubbed my sore wrists. He took a few steps back and I blinked twice, seeming to come from under whatever power his gaze had just had over me. I looked around and saw several wait staff setting up a table for two. His men were gone. I frowned turning where I stood. They were all gone and had taken the body of the guy who had hit me with them. There was no evidence that he had ever been there... not one drop of blood.

What the world?!

My gaze flew back to Kaleb who stood there smiling at me as if he could hear my thoughts. Oh, man! I had to get away from him. He held too much power over me.

I had convinced myself that the only reason that night had happened the way that it did was because I had been drugged, and if it were not for the drugs, I would have never given myself to him. But now I know that I had lied to myself. When he held me in his arms, and his gaze...he had the power to make everything else just disappear.

"Please, sit," he said holding out one of the chairs at the beautiful table for me. I stood there wondering what I should do. I looked around. The big garage was now empty. It was just me and him. Where had the wait staff gone? I bit my lip and flinched from the pain. Goodness! I forget it was damaged, but I was so nervous I didn't know what to do.

"Come on, sweetheart. Have a seat." He spoke softly, but there was something in his voice that said his patience was wearing thin. I inhaled and slowly walked to the chair. After I sat, he gave my chair a little push up to the table. Then he reached past me, taking the metal dome off my plate before he turned and handed it to a waiter that seemed to just appear out of nowhere. Then he walked around and took his seat in the chair across from mine. The table wasn't that big. So when he sat, I felt his long legs open to the side of both of mine.

"I don't know about you, but I'm starving." He removed the dome from his dinner and handed it to the server. Another server came to the table with a bottle of wine and poured us both a glass. Another came and placed a glass of brown liquor on the table by Kaleb's wine.

"Would you like something else besides the wine? I'm a cognac man myself," he said as he picked up his fork and knife and began to cut into his steak. The server stood waiting for my answer I shook my head.

"No, thank you." My voice was hoarse from all the screaming I had done tonight. The server nodded and disappeared as quietly as he came. I looked across the table at Kaleb with my hands in my lap.

"Aren't you going to eat?" he asked, putting a piece of steak in his mouth with his fork. I shook my head.

"I'm not hungry."

"Did you eat some chicken?" he asked with a grin on his face, his gaze falling to my Chucky's Chicken Shack shirt. Wow, look at that. The killer had jokes.

And let me tell you, had I not just witnessed him kill a man effortlessly with two big King Kong sized wrenches, I would have given him a piece of my mind for teasing me about my job. I nodded instead.

"Yeah, I ate chicken." I saw no need to pretend that I was happy to be here. He paused in eating to look at me with those dark eyes of his. I tried not to squirm underneath his gaze. When he looked at me like that, it made me feel aware... that yes, I was sitting here in my Chucky's Chicken Shack uniform and that it had been a while since I touched up my locs, and I probably looked as haggard as I felt.

"You sure?" he asked. "These are Mama Rita's steaks." Oh, man! For the first time, I looked down at my plate. Mama Rita's? Everybody in the hood knew about Mama Rita's steaks. It's just that you had to be hood rich to buy one. Right then, my stomach let out a crazy growl.

Well damn, thanks, stomach.

"I guess I could have a little taste," I told him picking up my knife and fork. You see, I had a Mama Rita's steak once. Stormy had treated me to lunch at Mama Rita's restaurant, and I promise, it was the best thing I ever tasted in my life. The knife slid smoothly through the meat. I cut a small piece and using my fork, put it between my lips, careful not to touch the sore one.

Oh! It just melted in my mouth.

"Mmm!" I don't know if I moaned out loud or to myself, but dang! This steak was fire! You can taste the char-broiled, buttered, garlicky goodness in every bite. I cut another piece. I don't know the last time I ate something so tasty. He joked about me eating chicken, but it was the truth. I ate fried chicken every day.

I cut another piece and lifted the steak to my mouth. Right then, I looked across the table and froze when I saw him staring back at me. The look on his face was all kinds of inappropriateness.

"What?" I asked, before putting the steak in my mouth.

"I see you found your appetite." I shrugged, cutting another piece of steak. Who was I trying to impress? Who knows when I'll get another Mama Rita's steak?

"Only a fool will let a Mama Rita's steak go to waste," I told him around a mouth full of steak. He nodded.

"You ain't lying. For two years, I sat in prison counting the days to my release, for two things: one of which was a Mama Rita's steak." Something in his voice made me lose my appetite. Here it is. We have come to the turning point of our meeting. I lay my knife and fork down on the table before picking up my napkin and gently wiping my mouth. Carefully, I placed it on the table and after taking a deep breath, I looked over at him. He too had stopped eating, and his angry gaze washed over me like an inferno.

"And the other?" I asked. He grinned slightly, and it gave me chills.

"Well, you see, the other thing I wanted more than I wanted this here steak... the other thing I dreamed about every night." He paused for just a moment before he continued. "I couldn't wait until I was free...so that I can get my hands on you." Pure rage came from his eyes at that moment, I did what came natural, which was to run. Quickly I stood. But just as quickly, he grabbed my wrist, pulling me back down and halfway across the table so that our lips were almost touching. My wine and water glasses crashed to the floor. I winced from where he was grabbing my sore wrist.

He turned to look at my wrist and for the first time noticed they were red from where the tie had rubbed them raw. Slowly, he brought my wrist to his mouth and softly kissed where it hurt. I almost moaned. Every time his lips touched me my body had a startling response. Then he turned and looked back into my eyes, his angry gaze reminding me that he was a killer.

"You took two years from my life. Why?" he growled through clenched teeth. I flinched from the force of his anger.

"What did I do to you? Who sent you after me?" The muscle ticked furiously in his cheek. Tears came to my eyes. I was so taken back by his anger the only thing I could do was cry.

"Answer me, damn it!" he yelled at me.

"You killed my brother!" I yelled at the top of my lungs. A look of shock crossed his face. He loosened his grip on my wrist and I snatched away from him, falling back into my chair. He sat back in his chair frowning at me.

"Who is your brother?"

"Man-Man," I told him rubbing my wrist.

"Man-Man?" He looked confused. Right then, pure hatred washed over me. This bastard!

This bastard didn't even have the decency to remember my brother! I stood angrily.

"Sit down, Monica!" he said heatedly.

"No! I'm leaving. We're done here." He moved then, bringing his fist down so hard on the table that almost everything on it crashed to the ground.

"Sit down!" he roared.

I ain't gon' lie. He just scared the hell out of me. I sat, looking up at him with wide eyes.

"We are not done until I say we are." Each word he spoke was accompanied by a finger jab on the already weakened table.

"You are responsible for me losing two years of my life rotting in jail. The only reason you ain't dead now is because I want something from you in exchange for the time that I lost." I swallowed, my throat suddenly going dry.

"What do you want?" My question was barely over a whisper. He sat back in his chair, resting his elbows on its arms while crossing his hands in front of his mouth. He looked off into the distance and chuckled.

"For so long I fought a battle in my head debating if you were even real." His deep penetrating gaze came back to me. "You see, your lips had been the sweetest I had ever tasted. What are the odds of sipping such nectar right before my world begins to crash in around me?" His finger slowly rubbed across his bottom lip as he spoke.

"A lot of things have changed in my life over the last two years, but one thing has not. In fact, it has only grown with each passing day."

I swallowed again, "What's that?" I asked but was terrified of the answer. He moved suddenly, sitting up in his chair and coming to the edge of it, bringing him closer. He leaned on the table.

"My hunger for that nectar." He grinned so wickedly my breath got caught somewhere between my throat and my lips. His eyes lowered to them.

"I...want...more..." He spaced those three words, emphasizing each syllable.

"You took two years of my life. In exchange, I want two years of yours. You will be at my beck and call. I work hard and I need someone to look after my basic needs."

"Basic needs?"

That devious grin grew on his face. "You know, a good meal, a nice warm body in my nice warm bed, and full access to that sweet nectar." I frowned at him.

"It sounds to me like you need to find yourself a wife." I intentionally used the "W" word. Madame Queen said that was the quickest way to get a man to run for the door. Yet that grin was still there on his face. It had not faltered.

"You know what? You're right. That's exactly what you'll be for the next two years." My mouth dropped open. Umm, that was not the way he was supposed to respond.

"Man, you tripping!" I told him. "I got responsibilities. I got bills. I can't just drop everything and cater to you!" I didn't care if I was talking recklessly. At this point, I didn't care if he picked up one of those giant wrenches and split my head open the way he had done that poor bastard earlier.

"Yes, you can. And you will. You're done at the Chicken Joint and the Burger Shack, at least for the next two years. However, if you do a good job and be a good girl for daddy, I'll leave you straight so you won't have to go back to work again if you don't choose to."

I narrowed my eyes at him. "It's the Chicken Shack and Burger Joint!" I corrected him, not caring if I sounded petty. He chuckled.

"It doesn't matter."

This Mutha Foster! How damn dare he talk to me like I'm some whore! First, he kills my brother...then acts like he doesn't remember. He seduces me and gets me pregnant—destroying all my dreams of dancing on Broadway. He gets his punk self out of jail eighteen years early. He kidnaps me and then turns around and demands I be his paid whore for the next two years.

"And if I say no?" I asked. He chuckled again.

"Oh, that's simple. I destroy you and all those you hold dear." I nodded. Yep, I pretty much knew he was going to say something like that.

"Okay. Well, what choice do I have?" I told him. But you see, I had already started planning. No, I couldn't beat him strength-wise. The man was a brute. And no, I didn't have an army to go to war with him. I had something far deadlier. You see if nothing else I am astute. And astute people always find a way to fight back.

He narrowed his eyes at me.

"Do you know why I approached you that night at the party?" he asked. His question caused me to pause. It is something I have been wondering about for two years. For the life of me, I couldn't figure it out. I by no means was the star of the party. In fact, I hid so deep in the corner I was surprised he had seen me at all. I shook my head.

"I saw you at the park, and although you put on a fine show, that isn't what I noticed about you." He leaned close again. His deep gaze doing that thing it did, making me feel as if he could see... me.

"I saw your fear. I saw that you were uncomfortable dressed the way you were. I could smell your innocence. I knew that you were unlike any other girl there, and I had to see for myself. I had to see if you were as innocently sweet as you looked." He sat back in his chair.

"I see your brain working, Mon. You have got it in your mind that you're going to fight me." He smiled. "I welcome the challenge, sweetheart." He stood and crossed the space between us. Bending down, he wrapped one arm around my waist, pulling me up out the chair.

"But you should know, I will not be denied what I have come to crave." His eyes fell to my lips and he dipped his head and kissed me gently, being very careful of my hurt lip. I did groan then I couldn't help it.

"Come on. Let's get you home." Panic shot through me.

Home!

Eve was at home. Oh, my goodness! I couldn't let him find out about Eve! Oh God! Why hadn't I thought about this till now? If he found out about Eve, he would have even more control over me. He looked down at me, reading me like a book. Damn, I needed to be on the lookout for that trait of his. He was good at it.

"Umm, I don't need you to take me home. I can just take the bus." I was trying to sound normal and not let my panic bleed through. He looked at me for a minute before he chuckled.

"Yeah, right," was all he said, still chuckling as he took my hand and began to lead me to the only car there that wasn't a classic. In fact, it wasn't a car at all. It was a Land Rover. He opened the passenger door and I got in. My mind raced, searching for a way out as he walked around the truck and got into the driver's side. My mind raced as we drove. It was racing so much—I didn't realize he had not once asked me where I lived. Yet here we were, pulling up in front of my house.

Now that I thought about it, he knew a lot about me, including where I worked. He killed the engine.

"Can I ask you something?" I said without turning to look at him. I stared straight ahead.

"Yep," he sat back in his seat.

"How come you know where I live and where I work?" he didn't say anything. I turned to look at him then, his intense gaze penetrating through the darkness of the truck. He grinned at me in the wicked way he does.

"I know everything about you," he spoke quietly. I looked at him, schooling my features, being very careful not to give away my hand. He didn't know everything about me. I knew for a fact he was unaware of Eve. If he had known of her, this night would have gone completely different.

"Hmm," I reached for the doorknob, but I had one more question before I left. "How did you get out?" I knew my question was borderline rude, but I didn't care.

"Out of prison, you mean?" I nodded. He smiled.

"I had a damn good lawyer."

Chapter 2
MONICA

I laid in my bed the next morning staring out the window. I was in trouble and I didn't know what to do. I tried to convince myself that last night had not happened. But then my phone that was on the nightstand next to the bed rang. I frowned as I picked it up. I didn't recognize the number. At first, I thought that it was one of my kids from the center.

"Hello." I gently rubbed my finger across the small cut on my lip that had gone down significantly since last night.

"How did you sleep?" That deep voice almost made me drop the phone. Dang it! How did he even get my number?

"Like a baby," I lied. He chuckled.

"I'm glad to hear that."

"Why are you calling me?" I wasn't even going to pretend to be cordial with him.

"I just wanted to let you know that today I will be getting my own breakfast, but I am going to need lunch. You can bring it by the shop." I sucked on my teeth.

"I told you I have responsibilities, and I don't have time to play the role of yo' mama. Get your own lunch!" I hung up the phone. I put my hand on my chest. It felt as if my heart was trying to run away from my body. What had I just done? *Yeah, I guess I told him. I was a real tough guy... on the phone.* I laughed at myself.

My phone rang again. I stared at it, waring with myself. I could just ignore him. Eventually, he'll have to stop calling, right? Or I could block his number. Yeah, I'll do that! I picked up my phone.

What are you doing? I shook my head. That was the dumbest idea. What if he came over here? What if he saw Eve? What if he hurt Nana? I answered the phone.

"Hello," I spoke in a kinder voice. Fake, but kinder.

"Did you just hang up on me?" he asked. I shook my head.

"No, man. My phone lost the signal. Don't be paranoid." If it killed me, I had to try to stay on his good side until I found a way to get rid of him. My mind raced for a solution to this problem. He chuckled.

"Monica, Monica, Monica. I see you're going to be a handful," he exhaled.

"Yeah. So, maybe you should rethink this irrational idea you have of, of..." I couldn't even say the words out loud.

"Of what?" he asked. Mmm! His deep voice was wreaking havoc on me. It reminded me of...

Focus, Mon! You were talking your way out of this, remember?

"You know what I mean. I don't have to say it!" I was so glad he couldn't see me blushing.

"Come on, Monica. You're a big girl. Say it." He was enjoying the fact that he was making me uncomfortable.

"Umm... No, I won't say it! BUT, going back to what you said about me being a handful, you're right. My Nana tells me that all the time. And I'm way younger than you. What are you? Like 40, 45?" I smiled. *That was a good one, Mon.* If I could give *myself* a high five I would. He chuckled again.

"Not quite. But what's your point?"

"Well, my point is, I am young. And I remember you saying something about not hooking up with younger women. I just turned twenty-one. Don't put yourself through that. Go with your first mind. Surely at forty-five, you do *not* want to deal with a twenty-one-year-old." He chuckled again.

"Quite the contrary, sweetheart, I not only want to deal with you, I want to make love to you over and over again until you beg me for mercy... real pretty... like you did that night." My mouth dropped open. I took the phone from my ear and stared at it. I couldn't believe he just said that to me.

"Umm... I, umm..." Damn! I was tongue-tied.

"Relax, Monica. I know about your daughter." My heart stalled. I mean, it *literally* stalled.

"You do?" My question came out barely over a whisper.

"Yeah, I do. Where's her daddy?" His question caught me completely off guard.

"He... He died. Yeah... in a motorcycle accident."

"Sorry to hear that." He didn't sound sorry in the least. It sounded like his attention was somewhere else. I could hear someone in the background talking to him.

"Hey. Look, you sound busy. I'll see you around sometime,' I was so ready to get off the phone with him.

"I need the white walls for the 62'. You're going to have to order more," he spoke to whoever it was that was there with him.

"Monica, you'll see me today. Bring lunch and your daughter so I can meet her," he said to me although he was still talking to the other person.

I was about to have a panic attack. *Think, Monica. Think! Remember your improvisation exercises with Madame Queen. You can do this. Just breathe and let it flow.*

"Kaleb, I don't think that's a good idea. Eve is a little sensitive... you know, with just losing her dad and all."

"Oh! He just died?"

"Yeah, just a few months ago." See? This is the problem with lying. You tell one, you got to tell a hundred. Goodness! And why did people have to ask questions when you were lying? It seemed like I got myself deeper in the muck the more I spoke.

"Did you love him?"

"Who? Eve's dad?" *Yikes!!!* "Not at all." Now, *this* I could say truthfully. I couldn't even bring myself to tell *that* lie.

"Good." That was his only response. I frowned again. I could have kicked myself. The one time I told the truth, I should have lied. If I loved this mystery man, *that* would be a reason for Kaleb to leave me alone, so that I could mourn. Damn!

"I can respect you not wanting to introduce me to your daughter right now. But you're going to have to do it eventually. She's going to see me a lot. So, she might as well get used to having me in her life."

Oh, hell no! Not if I can help it, potna!

"Why don't we just get used to each other first?" I needed to buy some time to figure a way out.

"That's fine. We'll do it your way, for now. As for lunch, I would like it homemade. I don't eat from any restaurant but Mama Rita's. So, whenever you can't prepare food, just go there and pick us up something. I don't eat pork, shellfish of any kind, or catfish. I'm a steak and potatoes type of guy. So, if you stay in that general area, you can't go wrong with me."

"Brother, I work at The Burger Joint and Chucky's Chicken Shack. I cannot afford to feed you, and I sure can't afford Mama Rita's!" This dude was crazy.

"No. You *used* to work at The Burger Shack and Chucky's Joint." I rolled my eyes at him butchering my jobs' names. I was beginning to think he was doing it on purpose.

"Don't worry about money, shorty. I got you."

"Kaleb, I don't feel comfortable with that."

"I don't care. I'll be sending someone to scoop you up in a few hours. Be ready." The phone went dead. I stared at it, dumbstruck.

"Mama!" Eve yelled, opening my door and running across the floor in her little onesie. She clutched the cover and pulled herself up in my bed before collapsing in my arms. I laughed as she began to bury herself in the covers. This was her morning routine. She did it every morning at seven o'clock whether I was up or not. She was my little alarm clock.

I ran my fingers through her soft hair. She looked so much like Kaleb, but prettier and smarter. I had to keep him away from her no matter what. He was bad news. He would destroy my baby with his life of drugs, guns, and only Yah knows what else.

I needed to call Marge at the Burger Joint and Chucky to request a couple days off while I sort this mess out. By then, I should have rid myself of Mr. Man. I wasn't worried about my jobs. I was in good with both of my bosses. They will always take me back.

I spoke with them both and assured them that I was alright. Well, assuring Marge was easy. But Chucky suspected I was leaving him for another man.

"Chucky, I just need a few days off. I'll be back."

"Monica, with your fine a$$, some nigga done came and scooped you up, didn't he?"

"No, Chuck. I just need a few days off," I repeated as I looked through my closet for something to wear.

Eve was sitting on my bed taking all my stuff out of my book bag.

"Monica, you know... the offer is still on the table. Let Chucky be your sugar daddy. Baby, you ain't ever got to work another day in your life!" I laughed.

"Bye, Chucky!" I said before hanging up on him. He was ridiculous. That brother was stuck in the movie, *Super Fly*.

Okay, so what was I going to wear? I didn't want to wear anything too nice, because it would make it seem as if I was interested. I wanted to wear something that said I was serious... something that said, "Don't mess with me. I'm a prude." Ah-ha! I had the perfect idea. I needed to borrow an outfit from Nana. I scooped up Eve and headed downstairs to her room. She had given the master bedroom to me long ago because she couldn't take the stairs anymore.

Our house was huge. My grandfather built it with his bare hands. When Nana returned to Chicago after her career in New York ended, she got with the city and began the center. My grandfather was the janitor there at the time, and he was in love with her. Now Nana had a little money, which intimidated him a bit. So, he decided to build her a house. And boy, did he build it—eight bedrooms in total. When the house was done, he brought her to it and proposed to her.

She asked him why so many rooms. He said it was for all the children they were going to have. But he died shortly after Nana got pregnant with my mother. Between the center and this house, her money went fast. So, she turned it into a boarding home. This worked well for a while. Now it needs so many repairs, we simply can't attract any more business. She was keeping up with repair costs at first. But my brother got arrested a few times and posting his bail had depleted us.

I had so many dreams of making it big and fixing up my grandma's home for her. I know it must grieve her beyond anything I can imagine, seeing the house that the love of her life built for her just disintegrate before her eyes. I'm not going to give up though. I've got a few repair books and I am going to do the best I can to get this place back into shape.

When Eve and I walked into Nana's room, she was sitting in her chair with a horrified look on her face while staring at the news. I rolled my eyes. My Nana and her news. I sat on the bed sitting Eve next to me, who instantly headed for the nightstand.

"What's wrong now?" I asked her. She slowly turned away from the news to look at me, putting her hand to her chest.

"Child, these folks just said it was a hole in the sun." Her eyes were as wide as saucers. I chuckled.

"So, what's the big deal?" I shook my head at her. I was going to have to forbid her from watching the news.

"What's the big deal!" she screeched. "You know what's wrong with you young folks? Y'all stupid. The whole world is crumbling around y'all, but y'all ain't noticed' cause you too busy snapping selfies." I laughed.

"Not me, Nana," I kissed her loudly on her cheek. She batted me away. "I'm too busy taking chicken orders and flipping burgers." That made her laugh.

"I've come to borrow clothes." She frowned at my statement.

"From who?" she asked, looking confused. I laughed.

"From you." Her eyes narrowed.

"Monica, what are you up to?" I put my hand on my chest while batting my eyes.

"Why, grandmother, whatever do you mean?" I laughed at her suspicious look as I hopped up to look through her closet.

"I know you. You're up to something." I shook my head as I carefully looked through her things to find the perfect look.

"Nana, you shouldn't say things like that about me!" I halted my search on a high neck black dress that would literally cover me from chin to ankle.

"Perfect!" I said excitedly, taking it out the closet to hold it in front of me in the mirror.

"What you want to put on that old ugly thing for? I knew it was ugly when I bought it in the '40s!" Nana cackled from her chair. Even Eve, who had gotten a hold of Nana's teeth paused to look at me with a frown on her little face. I smiled at them both.

"I've got a job interview," I said before I took down one of her old hat boxes and pulled out an old brown church lady hat that would be perfect with this dress. Nana frowned.

"Child, are you trying to get the job?" She scratched her head.

"Not at all," I answered. With the dress draped over my arm, I went to her jewelry box and picked out a pair of earrings and a long string of pearls. Just because I was going to be dressed like a 1940's prude didn't mean I couldn't do it in style.

"Oh, okay," she said, nodding.

"Lil girl, leave my teeth alone!" she screeched at Eve, who

dropped the teeth back in what we called 'teeth juice,' before sitting back in the bed like she hadn't been touching them at all.

"You betta leave Nana teeth alone. You know she don't play about them," I jokingly scolded Eve, while picking her up and heading to the kitchen. I sat her in her high chair and gave her a bowl of wheat circles before putting on a pot of coffee for Nana. Then I cut her and Eve up some fruit.

"Aren't you eating?" Nana said, sitting down at the table in front of her bowl.

"Naw, I'll grab something later." She shook her head.

"You need to take better care of yourself. Breakfast is the most important meal of the day. You always say you're going to grab some later, but I know you never do." I nodded. Nana gave the same speech every morning. I just wasn't a breakfast person.

"I love you, Nana," I told her, kissing her cheek before I headed back upstairs to get ready for my important so-called job interview. The first thing I did was draw a nice hot bath. As I soaked, I thought about my game plan for Operation: Unattract. The idea was for him to take one look at me and say, "Oh, I'm sorry. I've made a huge mistake."

Honestly, I didn't know why he was attracted to me in the first place. Guys like Kaleb didn't tend to go after the loc wearing, cultural type. They went for the Cover Girl, runway model type. And trust me, Kaleb could have any woman he wanted. He was fine, paid, and a boss. Women went crazy over men like him.

But not girls like me. No. We were into the intellectual type: the poet, the deep thinker. I mean, don't get me wrong, I know I'm pretty, but I'm "Average Joe pretty," not "King pretty."

When I finished bathing, I moisturized my skin well with mango butter. Then I went to my lingerie drawer and grabbed a plain pair of bra and panties. But I put them back. I figured if I was going to be dressed exceptionally hideous on the outside today, underneath I was going to be fabulous.

"Hmm... which pair should I pick?" I eyeballed my vast collec-

tion. Okay, confession time: I have a secret. I may have a little addic-
tion to buying sexy underwear. I don't know why either. Nobody
ever sees them but me. I have never even been with another man
besides Kaleb.

Yet, I enjoy wearing lingerie underneath my clothes. I don't
know what it is about it. Hmm... today I was pulling out the big
guns. I went to my closet and hanging there was a purple set that I
splurged twenty bucks on. Now I know some of you are frowning
saying, "Twenty bucks?" But let me tell you, that's an arm and a leg
for me.

I stood in the mirror admiring myself in my beautiful bra and
panties before reaching for the black dress. An hour later, I had
become a school teacher from the 1940s. I chuckled as I scanned my
reflection in the mirror from head to toe. I looked ridiculous. I
tightly wrapped my locs into a low bun and topped my outfit off
with the huge church lady hat that had lost its shape decades ago.
Plopping it on my head, it drooped so low it covered the top portion
of my face. To finish the look, I threw on a pair of Nana's old
eyeglasses.

Since the dress fell to the floor, I sported my Adidas. Hours
later, I rejoined Nana and Eve downstairs. They both paused for a
moment to look at me before erupting into laughter. I smiled.
Perfect!

For Kaleb's lunch, I grabbed the leftover chicken salad and
peach cobbler I made yesterday out of the fridge, spooned them
into separate Tupperware bowls so they wouldn't spill, and stuffed
it all in a bag.

"Steak and potatoes kind of guy..." I mumbled, "I got your steak
and potatoes, in this here chicken salad."

If this dude thought I was going out my way to cook for him, he
had another thing coming. Imagine me cooking for my enemy. Ha!
He had the wrong girl. I threw what was left of some salad dressing
along with a fork in the bag. I didn't try to arrange it nicely either.
Then I made lunch for Nana and Eve.

An hour later, I looked out my window and saw that black Cadillac truck sitting outside. I exhaled. Okay, it was game time. But it took me a little longer to pry Eve's arms from around my legs today.

"Baby, mama will be right back!" I told her.

"No, mommy. I come too!" she wailed, which crescendoed into a scream when Nana grabbed and held her back so that I could get out the door. Goodness! That really broke my heart. When I came out the door, the giant stepped out the passenger side of the truck. I slowly approached him, having mixed feelings. The last time I saw this guy, he was kidnapping me.

I looked up at him. He frowned as he took me in. However, he was a professional, because if he thought I looked odd he didn't say anything.

"Good afternoon, ma'am," he said as he opened the door for me.

"You know, after you kidnap someone, certain pleasantries just seem silly. Don't you think?" He chuckled.

"I guess you're right. Name's Tiny." My mouth dropped open. Did this giant of a man just tell me his name was Tiny?

"Tiny?" I asked. His chuckle turned into a laugh.

"Yes, ma'am."

"Okay, Tiny. Enough with the ma'am stuff. You can call me Monica." He nodded.

"Okay, Monica." I climbed into the back seat.

"Name's G," the driver said, who was also the driver yesterday.

"Hey, G. I'm Monica." He saluted me through the rearview mirror and pulled off after Tiny got all eight feet, four-hundred pounds of himself in the truck. My phone dinged in my bag. I took it out and discovered that I had a text.

Kaleb: I'm starving
Me: Eat then
Kaleb: I will when you get here

```
Me: Maybe I won't come
Kaleb: Lol, you're coming
Me: You sound so sure of yourself
Kaleb: I'm sure cause my men are bringing
you
Me: Maybe I'll run away from your men
Kaleb: Then I'll come find you wherever you
go. There is nowhere you can hide from me
```

I stopped texting and stared at the screen. How in the world was I supposed to respond to that? This man was a psychopath. I had to get away from him. He was psychotic and dangerous, and he had it in his head that he and I were getting ready to be an item. What kind of man went to prison for two years and came out desiring the one that set him up to go?

Right then, a thought came to me. What if this was a setup and he had some elaborate plan of getting back at me? What if he was going to torture me slowly for the next two years? What if he was going to try to make me fall in love with him then break my heart?

I looked out the window as we drove. I had to end this somehow. I prayed my outfit would repulse him enough to lose interest. If not, I would just have to turn up the pressure. One of the things I loved about myself is that I wasn't a quitter. If one door closed, I just tried another. Kaleb was the drug dealer who had my brother murdered, and I had to get away from him... no matter what.

We pulled up in front of the shop today. It too was full of cars—some that needed work and some that were ready to go. I wondered if they all belonged to someone or if he sold some of them. Tiny got out of the vehicle and opened the door for me.

"Just go in. The boss is expecting you," he said. I nodded and walked towards the door. They pulled off as soon as he got back in the truck.

"Wow," I said under my breath as I entered. Yesterday, I had been in the back where they worked on the cars. The front was nice. It was a showroom and put my question of whether he sold some of these cars to rest. I was no expert on classic cars, but these looked *really* nice... and expensive. I walked towards the reception-ist's desk.

A pretty brown skinned girl wearing blond weave and tons of makeup sat there speaking on the phone and typing on her computer at the same time. She did a double take when she looked up and saw me.

"Emm, Emm!" she said, taking in my outfit. Her whole face frowned up as if I stunk. Then she must have remembered she was talking on the phone because she had to apologize to whoever it was she was speaking to.

"No, Mrs. Durby, I wasn't speaking to you. I just mistyped. So yes, your husband's car will be finished and delivered to your home at the time we discussed. He's going to be so surprised! Yes, ma'am. I will definitely give you a call when it's in route. Okay, you have a wonderful day. Bye." She hung up the phone and looked up at me, rolling her eyes before she resumed typing on her computer.

"I put the Goodwill check in the mail. It should have made it to your office by now," she spoke without looking up from the computer. Now I couldn't help but wonder if she was so disre-spectful to me because she thought I was from Goodwill as if the Goodwill people that go out of their way to help the less fortunate like myself didn't deserve respect.

So, of course, I had to have a little fun with this situation. I cleared my throat, which got her attention.

"I am not from the Goodwill office, missy. I'm from the Mayor's office." My voice was laced with authority. I had to bite the inside of my lip to keep from laughing as her whole demeanor changed. She sat up straighter.

"Oh! I'm so sorry, miss. Please forgive me. How can I help you today?" I rolled my eyes at her, raising my head in the air as if I could no longer stand to be in her presence and huffed.

"You can tell Kaleb that Monica is here to see him."

"Yes, ma'am," she said jumping out her chair. As soon as she left, I erupted into laughter. That's what she got for treating Goodwill employees bad. I straightened up, raising my head back in the air when she came rushing back.

"Mr. Jacobs will see you now. Just go right through those doors," she said, pointing towards the doors she had just exited. I walked past her with my head in the air and for good measure, I gave one last huff. The poor child was sweating. My cheeks hurt from trying to keep a straight face. When I touched the doors, I gave in and let my grin free.

Goodness, some people were just easy! However, I came up short as I walked into the office. Kaleb wasn't alone. He sat at his desk speaking with a man with long locs that sat in the chair on the other side. His back was to me so I couldn't see his face.

Kaleb raised his eyes from something he was reading that the guy was showing him, and oh, man... the look on his face was priceless as he took in my apparel. His look of horrified amusement caused the man he was speaking with to turn and look at me.

"Shelomoh!" I said, recognizing him instantly.

"Troublemaker!" he responded, coming to his feet. As he took in my outfit, a huge smile spread across his face.

"What are you wearing?" he asked.

"What are you doing here?" I responded.

"I'm visiting my client." I could hardly understand him over his chuckling.

"Your client? Wait! It was *you* that got him out of prison early?" Shelomoh's smile turned really smug upon hearing my question.

"Well, you know... I do what I can do," he spoke with fake modesty.

"No!" I yelled at him. I was so mad I could scratch his eyes out. I felt betrayed. "No? That's not good."

Shelomoh frowned. I looked at Kaleb who was sitting back in his chair with his hands folded in front of his smirking face. He was enjoying the fact that I was about to have a nervous breakdown.

"What you talking about, Mon?" Shelomoh asked before his eyes widened.

"Wait a minute. *This* is the Monica you were talking about?" he asked Kaleb.

"Small world, huh?" he responded, watching us closely. I narrowed my eyes at him. Why was he studying Shelomoh and me? When he saw me looking at him, his attention came back to me fully. Instantly, I started feeling hot under this thick dress. His gaze slowly went from the hem of my dress to the top of my droopy hat. Shelomoh held his head back and roared with laughter.

"Akh. Man, I know the heart wants what it wants, but you got your hands full with this little troublemaker here. Your life won't be boring for sure. Go with Yah, brother!" he said, walking back towards Kaleb desk, who stood and came around it so that they could shake hands. But they didn't just shake hands, they brought their other arm around and embraced like I saw Shelomoh often do with the men he called his brothers.

"We still on for the Shabbat?" he asked. Kaleb nodded.

"Yep." The smile left Shelomoh's face as he looked at him.

"I'm proud of you, akh." Kaleb smiled.

"Thanks, man. I couldn't have done any of this without you."

"Naw, don't thank me. Thank Yah. Always thank Yah. We are just vessels. Had he not led me to you, I would have never known. Now it's your job to find out why." Kaleb nodded. I couldn't take it anymore.

"Oh, my goodness! Are y'all friends?" I wailed. I couldn't believe this! Shelomoh came to me and brought his hand up to ruffle my hair, but paused because of my hat.

"Ha!" I told him. He killed me doing that. I was a kid when we first met, and he ruffled his hands through my locs that at the time were short and stuck straight up on my head. That irritated me so bad that he got it in his mind to continue to do it, even though I'm a grown woman now. He chuckled.

"Go easy on him, kid," he said before walking out the door and closing it behind him. I stared after him, resenting that statement. *Me* go easy on *him*?! It wasn't *me* forcing him to be here! It was *him*. He should have told him to go easy on *me*. Chances are, he probably didn't know the details of my and Kaleb's relationship, which made me realize another thing.

I was now all alone with Kaleb and he stood behind me. Suddenly, I felt extremely nervous. I slowly turned my head to look behind me and my breath caught in my throat because he stood there looking at me with that same hunger he had in his eyes last night. I whipped my head back towards the door.

"Turn around and face me, Monica." I closed my eyes as his deep voice washed over me and down my spine. Before I came, I had given myself a pep talk—basically saying that I would come in here and be strong... that I would remember that he was the enemy... that I would repulse him with my outfit, attitude, and cold nature... and then leave, free of him. However, I had not expected him to be standing there looking edible in a light blue button-up shirt, a dark blue tie that matched his trousers and suspenders... suspenders!

Goodness! And that ensemble lay beautifully on his massive chest and arms.

Okay, Mon, you can't just stand here facing the door. You're going to have to turn. I inhaled and swirled around on one foot. Embarrassed, I closed my eyes for just a moment, because sometimes when I was nervous or not paying attention, I danced like I had just done, turning around to face him.

"I'm glad you could make it," he finally spoke. I put my hand on my hip.

"I don't recall having a choice." He chuckled and nodded his head once.

"Touché." His eyes fell on the grocery bag I held in my hand.

"Is that my lunch?" he asked. I smirked.

"Mmmm... hmmm!" I replied as I handed it to him.

"Bon appétit," I said, smiling really big at him. Chuckling, he shook his head before walking back towards his desk.

"Please, have a seat," he said, indicating the chair Shelomoh had just left. I sat, folding one of my legs up under me; a habit of mine. His eyes missed nothing. He took his time taking me in—my hat, my dress, my posture, my gym shoe that was now peeping from underneath my leg—before he sat and opened the lid on the chicken salad.

"Looks good."

He poured the dressing on it, picked up the fork and dove in. My mouth dropped. I thought for sure he was going to turn his nose up at it.

"Did you think I wasn't going to eat it?" he asked, before shoving a fork full of salad in his mouth and chewing it between his powerful cheeks.

"How do you know it's not poisoned?" His smug attitude was starting to get on my nerves. He chuckled.

"Let's just say I'm a good judge of character. You don't mind telling a lie, but you won't kill a man."

"Unlike you," I smoothly interjected. He nodded his head once.

"Touché." After finishing the salad, he opened the lid to the peach cobbler and dug in, just like he did the salad. I frowned.

"Don't you want to microwave that?" He chuckled, shaking his head.

"Not necessary. I'm easy to please. As long as the food is clean, I'll eat it. Just double what you've given me next time and I'm right as rain..." His deep gaze connected with mine. "...even if it's just thrown together," he continued, his deep raspy voice letting me know he was aware of what I tried to do. I guiltily bit my bottom lip.

"So, tell me. What motivated your look today?" I shrugged my shoulder.

"I dress how I feel." Which was true. He nodded.

"Got it." When he was finished he neatly put everything back in the bag.

"It was really good." I bit my bottom lip again because I'll be doggone if his compliment didn't just thrill me a bit.

"Did you make it?" I nodded. He smiled.

"You can cook. That's good. How is Eve?" I stiffened at the mention of my daughter.

"How do you know Shelomoh?" I asked instead. He looked at me for a minute before he chuckled and shook his head.

"He umm, showed up to visit me in jail earlier on in my case. Afterward, I fired my lawyer and hired him." I frowned.

"He just showed up out the clear blue?"

"Yeah, I thought it was strange too. So, you can imagine my surprise when looking into him led me to you." I stared at him through my grandmother's glasses.

"You know what I find strange? How it is you know so much, yet you don't know who my brother, Man-Man, is after calling a hit on him." He raised his hands.

"Nobody's perfect, Monica. I'm doing all I can to rectify that situation." Mmmm... hmm... and I'm the Tooth Fairy. I was ready to go. The outfit didn't work, so it was time to retreat and go to plan E.

I stood. "Well, I've done my job. I bid you adieu."

"Not quite." He didn't raise his voice. In fact, he spoke in a low tone that was somehow even more threatening.

"Sure, I did. You wanted lunch. I brought it. That's it!" He slowly shook his head, watching me with eyes that missed nothing.

"Naw, it's not. I'm still hungry." I held up my hands.

"Sorry. I don't have any more food."

"Come here." The look in his eyes reminded me of a tiger that had just spotted a gazelle.

"Why?" I asked my voice barely over a whisper. I swallowed. Oh, goodness! How had I survived being the source of his hunger the first time?

The drugs!! Man, I was so nervous I almost wished for them to help me through this.

"Come here around the desk."

"I don't want to." He chuckled.

"I know, but be a good girl and come anyway." He still spoke in that low deadly voice that said, *don't disobey me.* I inhaled and slowly walked around the desk to him. I stopped a few feet from him, but I might as well had not bothered because he reached out his arm and wrapped his big hand around my waist to pull me closer. I screeched when he suddenly lifted me in the air and gently placed me on the desk in front of him, displaying just how strong he was. And because he sat me right in front of him, my legs were spread on both sides of him. I pulled at the dress, trying to keep as much of my legs covered as I could. I was so glad I had worn this maxi.

"Kaleb, this is so inappropriate," I whined because he just sat there looking up at me, watching me squirm in embarrassment... and the way he was looking up at me...

He was so close and he smelled so good. And he was so big and strong, just pure power between my legs. I felt that if he touched me, he would make me melt into a puddle on the desk in front of him. He brought his hand up. I stiffened as he took off my glasses and put them on the desk next to us. Then he took off my hat. Seconds later, my bun came unraveled as he pulled out the pins and band that was holding up my mass of hair. I put my hand up to catch it, but I had way too much. So it just spilled down around my back and shoulders.

"You're so beautiful." He spoke low, and I was drowning in his deep dark gaze.

"When I first saw you in this get-up, the only thing I could think about was how much I wanted to unwrap you." He undid one button at my neck.

"I could barely focus on much else, wondering what you have on underneath this." The whole time he spoke he undid buttons. When he had reached the top of my breasts, I grabbed the dress.

"What are you doing?" I asked. His gaze raked over my exposed neck and the top of my chest. He brought his hand up and gently ran his fingers down my neck and chest where I held my dress together. He looked up at me and smiled.

"Come on. Don't be a chicken. Show me what you have on under there."

"No, Kaleb!" He sat back in his chair, giving me a little space, but not much. He put his elbow on the arm of his chair and leaned his head against a raised finger.

"You know, you play at being bold, brave, and outgoing, but you're not. Underneath all that sass is a scared little chicken." Okay, I was very aware of what he was doing. This little reverse psychology he was attempting was very immature. Yet I generally found it hard to resist a challenge. It was very astute of him to notice that about me.

I held up my head. "I ain't no chicken," I told him. He grinned.

"Prove it. Show me."

Don't do it, Monica! Don't fall for the oldest trick in the book! But there was something in his smoldering gaze. There was a real challenge there. He was curious to see if I would do it. And *that* is what made me begin to unbutton my dress. Maybe Nana and Stormy were right about me and I wasn't wrapped too tight, but him challenging me was exciting. His eyes hungrily followed my fingers as I undid each button. When I got to my waist, I stopped.

Oh, the look on his face was so worth it. He took in my beautiful purple bra like a little boy in a candy store. And for a moment, I was dumbstruck by the fact that this powerful, handsome man was looking at me this way.

"Damn, baby. You are perfect," he whispered. I bit my bottom lip. No man except Kaleb has ever seen my body, and I couldn't help but feel like no man ever would.

He sat up bringing himself closer. Our mouths only inches apart. He touched my healing scar with his thumb.

"Does it hurt?" I shook my head.

"Can I kiss you?" he whispered. Man, I was lost. It was like he held me in a trance. I remember feeling this way that night, but I thought it was because of the drugs. I nodded.

He balled his hand up in my locs and brought my lips to meet his. The first touch of our lips was gentle, just a genuine need to reconnect. But it wasn't long till he deepened the kiss. I moaned, bringing my hands up to hold on to his wrist as he devoured my mouth. He was like a fierce sea that was washing over me. At some point, he stood and lowered my back against his desk, pressing his hard body against my soft one. His hungry kiss that had left my lips swollen and slightly sore was making its way down my body.

"Uh... bruh, you need to talk to the Cubans. They won't do business with me until they hear from you!" Rasheed said, barging into the office.

Kaleb moved so fast I was confused as to what happened for a few seconds. One second I was lying on the desk lost in a haze of passion and in the next, his big arm was under me, scooping me up so that my front was pressed against his, hidden from Rasheed's view.

"Rasheed, get out!" he growled. He was so angry his body was pulsating with rage. I ran my hand down his arm, trying to calm him.

"Bruh, that trick can wait. The Cubans can't. You know they don't want to mess with me unless they know you got me covered."

"Nigga, get out of my damn office!" Kaleb yelled. Rasheed flinched from the pure force of anger that was coming from his older brother.

"Damn, man. Calm down! You got anger problems!" he said with fear on his face. Kaleb moved as if he would go toward his brother, but I clutched him tighter. Rasheed didn't say another thing. He got out of that office. For just a moment, I rested my forehead on his chest trying to catch my breath. Wow! Kaleb's anger was scary. It was like a bucket of cold water. I slid off the desk.

"Man, shorty. I'm sorry about that," he said. I shook my head, refastening my buttons. What had I been thinking in the first place?

Cubans? His brother had mentioned Cubans. Even I knew he was talking about drugs. *Good job, Monica!*

"Baby?" He tried to grab my hand. I slid it out of his grasp before continuing to button my dress. I didn't bother to do it all the way to the top. My 1940's school teacher look had been tarnished. My emotions were a wreck. How could I fall into the hands of the drug dealing murderer of my brother so easily? I was a disgrace! I was weak! I disgusted myself!

When I looked up at him, I had a new lease on life, more determined than before to get rid of him.

"I'm done here, right?" I asked, already formulating my plan B.

He stood looking at me for a minute, studying me as no one else could before he reached down to open a drawer and then pulled out a credit card.

"This is for you. Get whatever you need with it, whatever Eve needs. Pay whatever bills you have and buy food." I stared at the card.

"Kaleb, I..."

"Don't have a choice," he quietly finished my sentence for me. That really pissed me off. I folded my arms.

"So, you just gon' force me to be a criminal with you and spend drug money on myself and my child!" I spat, wanting him to know how selfish he was. He looked at me with those eyes of his that missed nothing.

"You got it all figured out, don't you?"

"Well, is it drug money or not?" I hissed. He chuckled.

"It doesn't matter. Like I said, you have no choice. The only money you are going to get will come from me. Get used to the idea. Make it easy for yourself and those you care about." I rolled my eyes. There he goes threatening my people again.

I snatched the damn card from him. Eww! I was going to make him pay for this.

"I will be having dinner at Mama's Rita's, so don't worry about me tonight." I nodded rolling my eyes. He reached back into the drawer and pulled out a set of keys.

"Can you drive?" he asked. I frowned.

"Of course." He handed me the keys.

"Come," was all he said as he headed out his office. I grabbed my things and followed. Why in the world did he give me car keys?

Rasheed leaned against the receptionist's desk flirting with her. When she saw me, her mouth dropped as she took in my hair, that was now down and falling to my waist, my kiss-swollen mouth, and my dress, that was no longer buttoned up to my chin. And I'm pretty sure I had a hickey on my neck. I bruised easily.

I couldn't resist. I stuck my tongue out at her. That's what she got for being mean. I laughed when her mouth dropped farther. But my laughter died when my eyes connected with Rasheed's. My steps slowed just a bit.

Hate! Pure hate is what I saw in his eyes. I frowned as we passed him. Kaleb put his hand on my lower back and guided me across the showroom floor.

"Hey, bruh. Ain't you gon' introduce me?!" Rasheed yelled after us.

"Nope," Kaleb responded without turning to look at him. We walked through the doors and now *my* mouth dropped. Sitting outside was a cream Land Rover that looked a lot like Kaleb's, only more feminine. In the back seat was a brand-new car seat.

"What's this for?" I asked.

"I'm a busy man. When I need my lady, I need her to come quickly. I don't have time to wait on the damn bus." He was frowning. The encounter with his brother changed his whole demeanor. He walked me to the driver's side and opened the door.

"Kaleb, I can't accept this. It's too much," I said, pleading with him with my eyes to not force this upon me.

"You don't have a choice," he told me again, still speaking in that deadly calm voice.

"Yeah! What had I been thinking?" I told him, swallowing my rage. I slid into the seat.

"Tell me, Kaleb. Do you still live in the same place you lived before you went to prison?" He looked at me for a minute before he nodded his head.

"Why do you ask?" I laughed up in his face.

"I need to know where to bring your breakfast," I lied. He narrowed his eye at me.

"Go 'head. I'll text you later," he said shutting the door. I put the key in the ignition and started it up. I didn't look back at him as I drove away. I had tunnel vision. It was time to implement Operation: Ebola. My destination... Madame Queen's costume closet.

Chapter 3
OPERATION EBOLA

MONICA

"Monica dear heart, just what are you up to now?" Madame Queen purred from her vanity table. She was surrounded by a handful of girls she was teaching how to apply make-up. Madame had successfully turned her little corner of the center into a studio that would bring everything in Hollywood to shame. At least in her mind, she had. In reality, she and Stormy were forever arguing over her budget. Madame with the air of the Queen of the Nile Valley would ask for five golden swans flown in from Paris. Stormy would bring her five paper mache swans made by the kids in the art department.

Madame would demand caviar for her post-show party. Stormy brought cookies and juice boxes. She said Stormy had it in for her because Strom thought the theater department was a waste of time and money. Madame, like my Nana, had performed on Broadway in the '30s. Madame had a slightly longer career than my grand-mother. But like most black performers of that time, she didn't make the money her white counterparts did. When her money ran out and no more work came her way, she showed up at the center and asked Nana for a job. That was thirty years ago.

If you let Madame tell it, she was responsible for the career of every actor that had come out of Chicago since then. Stormy said there was the real world that the rest of us lived in and then there was that strange thing that went on in Madame's head. If you ever want a good laugh, sit back and watch Stormy and Madame have it out. Most of the time it's because Madame has gone behind Stormy's back to talk to Shelomoh about funding something extravagant for her next stage play production.

Stormy, who was always calm of course would just shake her head and say, 'No, we can't afford to hire a professional team of stage designers... However, that would be a lovely job for the kids in the art department.' Madame's would suck in her breath as if Stormy had just called her a vile name.

"How can you speak to me this way when I performed on stage with Eartha Kent and Lena Horne?" She would elongate her neck and throw her head back as if she was, in fact, Queen of all us mere mortals.

Stormy would just shake her head, so used to the theatrics. "No, is not a disrespectful word." She would say. Now by this time, Madame is in full drama queen mode. Keep in mind when she speaks, she always over enunciates every word. Without fail she pops every P and tot every T.

"It is a disrespectful word if it means, No, I can't be all that I can be. No, my young talented pupils cannot be all that they can be. And no, I must limit myself to rags when I am worthy of riches!" She would say with her arms waving in the air, causing whatever brilliantly colored garment she was wearing to flutter around her like beautiful clouds. Because everything she did was a production.

Stormy wouldn't even look up from whatever paperwork she was going over.

"Oh Madame, no one is asking you not to do the very best you can. I'm just telling you, you're going to have to do the very best you can with the budget that was set for the play." She would speak in a sunny tone that I know grated on Madame's nerves.

"You know, young lady, I helped raise you."

"How can I forget, Madame."

"You would think you would have more respect for me." This would make Stormy look up with a sympathetic expression.

"Aww Madame, I have the utmost respect for you, which is why I haven't gotten rid of the theater program altogether. We really could use the money elsewhere." Madame would throw her head in the air as if such a thing could not be considered.

"Who knows what cesspool this neighborhood would become if not for my productions?"

I chuckled while thinking back over their arguments as I looked through the costumes in Madame's closet.

Her and Stormy's fights were legendary. And I don't know if the neighborhood would get any worse than it is right now without Madame's productions. But I ain't gon' lie, she did know how to put on a show. I always had her produce our dance recitals. During one of Madame productions was the only time there is nothing but standing room here at the center. Everybody in the neighborhood came, from the thugs to the choir and everybody in between.

However, we didn't make much revenue from any of our productions, because most people around here couldn't afford to pay more than a few dollars for a ticket.

"Little girl, I know you hear me speaking to you." She spoke while applying a layer of lipstick on her lips. When she was done, she turned around to look at me.

"I just need to borrow a few items," I told her.

"I can see that. But what could you possibly need in the costume closet?"

"This," I said holding up a white doctor's coat. She frowned, standing from her table.

"Okay ladies, go ahead and put on your foundation, applying the technique I just showed you." When all the girls were settled down in front of the mirrors she came into the closet with me.

"And just why do you need that?" she asked picking up one of my long locs twirling it between her fingers. "I know how that little

clever mind of yours work, Sweet Tart, and you're up to something."
she droned. I shook my head at her nickname for me. She had been
calling me that since I was Eve's age.

"Well, I need to convince a few people I'm a doctor." Her eyes
brightened.

"Really?" She clapped her hands together. "Well, sit-down,
child and let Madame Queen do her thing."

Okay, on a side note...

Yes, Madame is an older woman, she's just a few years younger
than my Nana, but she is the wrong one to go to if you want to be
talked out of doing something extremely dangerous and foolish.
Madame lived for adventure, even in her old age.

An hour later she was looking at me, pleased with her work.

"Now for one last step." She put a name tag on me that read, Dr.
Mitchell.

"Okay, let me hear you introduce yourself." She was in full
trainer mode now. I cleared my throat.

"Hi, my name is Dr. Rachel Mitchell," I spoke with all the flare
Madame had taught me. The smile left her face and she smacked at
my hand with her fan.

"No! Absolutely not." After an overdone eye roll, she continued.
"Remember most doctors have a confidence that only recently
came in their adult years, before that they were probably very inse-
cure. I should hear that in your tone. Not the confidence of Monica,
who has been bold and beautiful her whole life. Again, Sweet Tart,
but this time, convince me." I nodded, she was right. I cleared my
throat and tried again.

"Hi," I used my finger to push my Nana's glasses up farther on
my nose. "My name is Rachel Mitchell... Dr. Rachel Mitchell."
Madame's face brightened and she clapped her hands together.

"Yeeeeessss, Child! Yes!" I hugged her and hurried out the
center before Stormy caught me. That's the last thing I needed
right now. I had looked up the real estate company that
owned Kaleb's building. And put the address in my phone

GPS. I was surprised to see that their office was located Down Town.

Wow! This drug dealer was living the life while people like my Nana and me, upstanding hard working people could barely afford to eat.

I smiled as I pulled the Land Rover into a garage that charged ten dollars for the first fifteen minutes before charging a dollar each minute after. I shook my head. Chicago was ridiculous!

I wasn't worried though, what I had to do should only take a few minutes.

After walking into the busy high rise, I found a directory. The name of the real estate company was 7th Oasis and they were located on the 7th floor.

"Gotcha!"

As soon as I stepped off the elevator the receptionist's eyes came to me. She took in my white lab coat and my nametag.

"How can I help you?" she asked with a friendly smile on her face. I returned her smile, placing my briefcase on the counter.

"Hi," I used my finger to push up my glasses. "My name is Rachel Mitchell... Dr. Rachel Mitchell."

"How can I help you, doctor?"

"I need to speak with whoever is in charge here. I have seriously important information about one of the tenants that live in one of your buildings." My face reflected the gravity of the situation for which I spoke. Her eyes widened before she picked up the phone pressing a buttoned.

"Mr. Jenkins." She spoke in the receiver. "There is a Dr. Mitchell here to see you, sir. She says she has vital information for you." She nodded her head. "Yes, sir." When she hung up she smiled at me.

"Please have a seat, he will be out promptly."

"Thank you," I told her before taking a seat in one of the chairs in the beautifully decorated waiting room. I hadn't been sitting a minute before the office door opened and a handsome brother dressed to the nines in a three-piece suit came out the back.

"Dr. Mitchell?" he asked coming to me to shake my hand. I stood.

"Yes sir, I'm from the CDC.." I flashed my badge really quick. He blinked several times as his eyes tried without success to read the information on the badge.

"I am so sorry to bother you...but if I can have a moment of your time, I think you will want to hear what I have to say," I spoke quickly taking his mind off the fact that he never really saw the badge.

"Of course, please come into my office." I walked ahead of him into his office.

"Please take a seat." He closed the door and took his own seat behind his desk. I eased into the chair he indicated putting my briefcase down on the floor next to my leg. Then I used my finger to push my glasses up on my nose.

"I must admit being puzzled as to why a doctor from the CDC would be here in my office." I could see the confusion on his face.

"I wish my visit could have been under better circumstances... Unfortunately, this is not the case. I've come with rather dire news. We recently received word of a tenant of yours who just came back from a very long stay in West Africa." The man's eyes widened instantly.

Oh yea, this was going to be a breeze.

"He was supposed to report to the CDC as soon as he landed back here in America."

"Why?" he asked, but I could tell from his face he already knew the answer. I pushed my glasses up on my nose and cleared my throat.

"Sir, he was being treated there for Ebola."

"Whaaaaaat!!!!" I had to bite the inside of my cheek to keep from laughing at the revulsion on the man's face. I nodded.

"So, you can understand our concern, everybody that knows this man must be warned, especially those that live near him. If he comes in contact with anybody in that building, I'm afraid we may have to quarantine the whole building." He snatched up his phone.

"Gloria, I need you in here right now!" he demanded.

"Who is the person, doctor?" I picked up my briefcase and pulled out a file that I had gotten from Madame's prop closet. Then pretended to scan over it.

"A Mr. Jacobs, Kaleb Jacobs," I told him looking up from my document. The look of shock that registered on his handsome face was priceless.

"Mr. Jacobs?" he asked a little over a whisper. "Are you sure?"

I nodded, now it was time to pound this nail home. I'm sure by living in the penthouse, Kaleb was big money for this company. Shame on them for being okay with accepting dope money. So, if you're wondering if I felt bad for what I was doing to this poor sap. My answer would be a resounding no. I didn't feel guilty in the least.

"Trust me, sir, the Center for Disease Control and Prevention does not take things like this lightly. Are you aware of how quickly Ebola can spread around a city like Chicago?"

"In two weeks' time, half the population would be hospitalized fighting for their lives. In a month's time, two of every three people will be infected with the disease. I ask you, sir, does that sound like something we would not be sure about?" He opened his lips, but he could only stutter. I didn't give him time to gain control of his speech.

"I don't mean to put you in this situation. I know legally you can't evict a person because they are carrying the Ebola virus, but be warned, you should do something to protect the other tenants of that building. And unfortunately, the only true protection is to get Mr. Jacobs out of that building." I put my files back into my briefcase before coming to my feet.

"Look, can I speak to you off the record?" I asked. He nodded. "I'm sure you, being in real estate know how to skirt around the system, if for no other reason but to be a hero. The hundreds of lives that you save will be well worth it." His mouth dropped open again. Goodness, this shouldn't be so easy.

"I've taken up too much of your time, there are others that must be warned. You have a good day, sir." I turned and walked past Mr. Jenkins' secretary who was standing holding the door open for me. Her face puzzled as she wondered at the astonished look on her employer's face.

I did not break character until I was sitting inside the Land Rover.

"Yeeeeessss!!!" I did a little dance in my seat. Oh man, his look of shock was priceless. *Now what you going to do, Kaleb? You fent to get evicted from your precious penthouse.*

I felt good.

No! I felt great!

I felt so good that I went grocery shopping on Kaleb's dime. Tonight, I was going to prepare a celebratory feast for my two girls. I went to the nice grocery store, the one in Oak Park and got us some fine cuts of beef. As I walked out, I saw the Kids Corner across the street.

Hmm, The Kids Corner had some really nice clothes. I had taken Eve there a couple of times but only had enough to get her a ribbon or a pair of socks.

Y'all, as I stood there, that credit card Kaleb had given me began to burn my pocket. It was bad enough that I had brought groceries with his dirty money. I shouldn't buy clothes for my daughter with such filthy gain. Yea, that was the right thing to do. I put my groceries in the trunk, then looked over at the store one more time.

I could go and just look around a bit, do a little window shopping. It was a good day, the sun was shining bright and I had just got a bad man evicted from his house, why not? An hour later as I was heading out the store with several bags of items for Eve, I guess I could admit, I knew I was lying to myself when if first deciding to come window shopping. I justified spending this nasty money by telling myself that Eve really needed these items. In fact, I justified until my guilt melted away and my good mood had returned.

I skipped up the stairs to my house.

"Eve, look what mama got for you," I said as I threw open the door.

However, I came to a screeching stop at the sight of Kaleb sitting on my couch with Eve on his lap, talking to Nana. All the bags and I do mean all of them fell out of my hands and crashed to the floor. My heart lurched so hard in my chest it was painful. For a moment, I experienced such a high level of panic that the only thing I could do was stare at the man who was supposed to never know about Eve holding Eve. I blinked as my mind screamed for me to react, but my body wouldn't move because it was crippled in shock.

He turned to look at me with angry eyes, although he had a smile on his handsome face, no doubt for Nana's sake. No, I take that back, he wasn't angry. he was pissed. Eve looked so tiny next to his massive body.

"Why the hell are you holding my daughter?" I yelled, oh my goodness! I was so thrown off. I didn't mean for that to come out so loud, but my emotions were running crazy. My Nana's mouth fell open.

"Now just wait a minute, young lady! That is no way to talk to a guest!" I began shaking my head before she even finished speaking.

"No! No! Nana! He ain't no guest!" I cried walking to where he sat on the couch holding Eve, who was playing with his car keys. So trusting she was, sitting in his viscous arms. I had witnessed first-hand what those powerful arms could do.

"Give me my daughter, now!" I spat looking down at him. One of his eyebrows raised as he looked up at me with fire in his eyes, probably angered that I would dare speak to him that way.

"Your daughter?" he asked in that deep, low, dangerous voice of his.

"My daughter!" I reached out and gently took Eve out of his arms. I could see the muscle ticking in his angry cheek.

"Monica, why are you acting out like that? What has gotten into you girl?!" Nana was getting herself worked up.

"Nothing, Nana," I said trying to calm her. Hugging Eve close, I walked to the other side of the room. Dear Yah, I had never been so scared in my life.

"Something has gotten into you. I didn't raise you to treat guests that way!"

"I just don't like strangers holding my child, that's all!" I spoke to Nana, but I looked at Kaleb, who was having a hard time hiding his own anger.

"And he ain't a guest." I hissed.

"If he ain't a guest then who is he?" It was something in my grandmother's tone that made me look away from Kaleb and take her in. The last thing I needed right now was for her to get suspicious and start asking questions. If she knew who Kaleb really was and what I had done, she would probably have a heart attack right now.

"Nana, calm down, you don't want to work yourself up into a fit," I spoke to her, but I prayed that Kaleb had enough sense to pick up what I was throwing out.

"Don't you worry about my fits!" she snapped. "I'm trying to figure out what the world is wrong with you. If this here young man is not a guest, then who the world is he?" Kaleb turned to look up at me and blinked innocently.

"Yea, who am I?" I narrowed my eyes at him.

"A stranger! That's who he is. And you shouldn't be letting strangers hold Eve?" I hissed. It was his turn to narrow his eyes as his anger boiled to the surface again.

"Oh child, he ain't gon' hurt that baby! You know, Monica, I am extremely disappointed in you. Here this young man is our first potential border in almost two years, and you doing the best you can to scare him away." My eyes flew to her.

"What do you mean first potential border?" I shifted Eve in my arms so that she was resting on my hip.

Nana smiled folding her hands in her lap, obviously very proud of the information she was getting ready to deliver. "Well, before you came in going crazy, he was just telling me how he needed a room for a little while. Apparently, his jealous ex-girlfriend went to his apartment management building and lied to them. What were you saying, shuga?" she asked him.

He looked at me. "My jealous ex went to the management company of my building and told them that..." he paused for just a moment. "Of all things, that I had Ebola." He looked at me. "Can you believe that?" he had the nerve to ask.

Psss! Jealous ex my butt!

"No, I can't say that I do believe you," I said flatly. He nodded.

"You know, I didn't believe it at first either, but I assure you such deceit does exist." His angry gaze went from me to Eve.

"Well honey," Nana said drawing his attention back to her. "If you still want the room, we sure do have the space." I shook my head.

"No, we don't, Nana!" She frowned at me again, trying to give me the look that had intimidated me as a child.

"Yes...we...do!" she spaced each word out through tight lips.

"No...we...don't!" I responded the same way. She smiled at him and slowly got to her feet.

"Excuse me, baby, let me talk to my granddaughter in the kitchen. Her mind ain't wired right. Sometimes, I have to explain things to her, she simple..." She looked at me and jerked her head toward the kitchen. I looked down at his pleased face and I couldn't help the sneer that came on mine. Still holding Eve in my arms, I marched into the kitchen after my grandmother.

"What is wrong with you? You young fool! That man need a place to stay and we need his money!" She spat putting one hand on the counter and the other on her hip.

"Nana, we don't know him, he could be a murderer! And you just gon' invite him to stay!"

She looked at me for a minute and shook her head. "Child, this here a boarding house. We ain't known much about nobody that has ever stayed here." Yea, well she had a point. My mind raced for some excuse to give her so that she could just let this drop.

"I don't like the way he looks." I told her and I could have kicked myself. That sounded dumb even to me. She chuckled.

"I find him quite handsome myself." Then she had the nerve to blush.

"Forget his looks!" I hissed. She frowned at me.

"You the one brought up his looks." I shook my head.

"Not like that, I meant he looks dangerous. And we don't want dangerous men around Eve." I gently pulled Eve's head to rest against my shoulder and rubbed it for emphasis. The little menace popped her head back up and grinned at Nana, who waved her hand.

"That man ain't gon' harm that child. You should have seen him when he first noticed her. I thought I saw a tear in his eye. He apologized for the way he acted, said Eve reminded him of someone." She held her hand to her mouth. "I think he may have lost a child." She whispered. I blinked at her. Oh, my goodness! I was getting ready to have a nervous breakdown. This was not supposed to be happening.

"Now would you stop acting crazy and go out there and be nice, so that we can get this money?" I shook my head, no. I couldn't help it, I was freaking out on the inside. The stress of this situation was about to kill me.

"Why not!" she hissed and I could tell that she has lost all patience with me. Outside of coming clean and telling her everything, I was at a complete loss as to the reason why we should not let him stay here. I exhaled and dropped my head, defeated.

I couldn't believe this was happening. He was supposed to be busy trying to find him somewhere else to stay, not here in my living room. I looked at Eve, who was now grinning at me. I put my head against hers.

Mama done messed up now. I have led a very dangerous man to you, precious heart.

"You know," Nana spoke looking up at me with a very disapproving expression on her face. "There ain't a day go by that I don't regret letting you stay up under Queen's crazy self as much as you did when you were little, it's her fault you turned out like this." My mouth dropped open.

"And how did I turn out?"

She shook her head and turned to walk out the door back into the living room. But before she went through, she turned to look back at me. "Full of drama, just like her. Now get out here and be nice to this man, so that we can get that little extra money." She pushed through the door.

I leaned against the sink still holding Eve. How could I even begin to take her back out there? I was so busted it wasn't even funny. Good thing Nana's eyes weren't that good and she couldn't see that the child the man had lost was right here in my arms. I inhaled, considering taking Eve and just leaving out the back door. But I couldn't leave Nana in here with that maniac.

Wasn't nothing to do right now but face my trouble, there was no use hiding in here. After taking a deep breath, I followed Nana through the kitchen door.

"The rent is One-Hundred and Twenty-Five dollars a week." She was in the middle of telling him. He nodded.

"Ma'am, since it seems as if I am inconveniencing you, please allow me to pay five-hundred a week. It would make me feel much better." My Nana's eyes widened.

"We don't need your charity!" I hissed. Nana's head snapped towards me.

"Now Monica, if this man say paying five-hundred a week will make him feel better, don't you go adding your feelings to the equation. He's the guest, it's his feelings that matter, missy." She turned back to Kaleb and smiled. "If paying five-hundred a month will make you feel better, sweetheart then Nana will be more than happy to oblige you." I sucked on my teeth.

"You ain't his Nana, her name is Ms. Naomi to you!" I snapped at Kaleb. Nana reached over and grabbed his hand.

"Don't worry none about my granddaughter, remember I told you, she simple. You can call me Nana if you want to." She cooed at him. And the bastard had the nerve to look at me and smiled before he turned back to her.

"Thank you, Nana, thank you for everything." Emm, y'all don't even know how much that grated on my nerves.

"You welcome, baby." She gushed smiling really big at the fraud. Oh, my goodness, my grandmother was acting like a seventy-eight-year-old gold digger.

"Monica, go up and prepare the Blue room for our new tenant." My eyes flew to her.

"The Blue room?!" That was right across the hall from my room. I shook my head. "That's not going to work, he can have the White room." That was way at the end of the hall.

"Nonsense, the floor is damaged in the White room. Outside of yours and Eve's room, the Blue room is in the best shape." I opened my mouth to say something else, but Nana shot me a look that made me snap my lips shut.

"Bring me Eve and go on and prepare the room." She said holding her hands out for Eve. I looked over at Kaleb as I crossed the room. His angry gaze followed me. I eased Eve unto Nana's lap. But before I moved I looked my grandmother in the eye.

"I'm going to do this, but can you do me a favor and not let strangers hold my child?" I respect my grandmother, always have. But I needed her to know that I was serious. She nodded.

"Yes, Monica. Goodness!" I straightened and without looking at him again, marched up the stairs. I couldn't believe this. Why in the world would he come here? This place was a dump compared to what he was used to. Word around the hood was he and his brother had been born into luxury, their father having been in the dope game long before he'd ever thought about having children.

I opened the door to the Blue room, at one point and time it had been a real beauty. Now like the rest of the house, it was wearing down fast. It was the second biggest to my room, which would still appear tiny to him. I crossed the room and opened the windows to air it out. For a minute, I thought about sabotaging his room, but Yah knows what would happen then. Angrily I threw clean sheets on his bed. He could make his own damn bed.

"What's wrong, Monica, you having a tantrum 'cause things ain't turning out like you planned? Did your baby daddy come back from the grave to haunt you?" The deep angry voice came from behind me. I spun around just in time to see Kaleb coming through the bedroom door shutting it behind him.

Chapter 4
WHAT'S DONE IS DONE

MONICA

I whipped around.

Oh crap! He was mad!

He closed the door and just stood there staring at me, still looking so fine in his navy-blue suit pants and suspenders. His tie was long gone and the first few buttons were open on his shirt. His sleeves were rolled up, revealing his big muscled forearms. His cheek muscle was twitching so good it caused the little muscle in his temple to throb. He balled his fists up as if...as if...

"You look like you want to lay hands on me?" I said in a small voice, giving him a little smile. I held up my hands, not wanting to flash anything red in front of this bull that looked as if he was going to charge any minute.

"I do," he spoke in that low deadly voice he used sometimes that was so incredibly intimidating. My heartbeat tripled as he began to walk towards me.

"Bu—but you said a man that hit a woman ain't sh*t!" I reminded him as I went to take a step back and bumped into the nightstand...

"He ain't, which is why no matter how much I want to, I'm not going to choke you!"

"Wheew! That's good to know..." I visibly relaxed, although inside I had not relaxed one bit, because he was still walking toward me as if he was going to hurt me.

"Well, why are you still walking towards me?" I asked, trying not to let my panic bleed through my words. His smile was wicked.

"I may not choke you, but I am going to lay hands on you!" he lunged at me, but I was agile if nothing else.

Easily I dodged him, crawling swiftly across the bed. When my feet touched the floor, I flew toward the door. But for such a big guy he was fast. I made it halfway across the room when I felt a strong arm wrap around my waist bringing me to a complete stop.

"Kaleb, wait! I can explain!" I screeched.

He put me against the wall and lifted me off my feet by my collar. My toes dangled in the air. His face was a mask of rage. He was so mad he stole my breath. I had never been this close to an enraged male before. Yea, there was the couple of times my brother got really mad at me, but he was my brother, so I knew he wasn't going to hurt me.

"How can you explain? It ain't nothing you can tell me that can explain why you had my kid and wasn't going to say nothing!" His words came from between clenched teeth. He was so mad I could feel the rage coursing through his body.

"That ain't alright, Monica!"

"I know, but I didn't know what else to do!" I didn't bother lying to him. He was scaring the hell out of me. "You was in jail, I was graduating high school, my grandmother had already gone through so much with losing my brother." Tears came to my eyes and began to roll down my cheeks.

"I didn't want to put her through any more stress. It was messed up, everything went wrong for me after that night. I made a mistake, it was all a mistake...I mean Eve was no mistake, I love her...But I lost my scholarship to Julliard!" My words came out rapid and choppy.

"You, it's all about you." He dropped me to my feet and turned away from me as if he could no longer stand to touch me or look at me.

"I had a lot of things going on too before you brought yo' a** over there playing games." He rubbed his hand through his short hair and began to pace, reminding me of a caged animal.

Oh, dear Yah! Why can't this nightmare just end already? I made a mistake, I'm sorry, why do I have to keep paying for it? With hands that shook I wiped away my tears.

"You know what, none of that matter now." He turned to look at me. I still stood with my back pressed against the wall, too scared to even move.

"What's done is done, tomorrow morning we're going to city hall and getting married." My mouth dropped open. His words were like a punch in my gut. I opened my mouth to speak, but no words came out. I was so taken off guard that it took my brain a minute to comprehend fully what he had just said. And when it did, my fear dissolved like ice in an oven.

"Nigga, you crazy?" At this point, I didn't care if he pulled out that gun I knew he carried in the back of his pants and shot me. I wasn't marrying him.

For a moment, he just stood there frowning at me.

"Please!" he spat. "Get over yourself. If you think I want to marry a deceitful, lying, manipulating little girl that needs to grow the hell up for the sake of our child, you wrong."

I folded my arms insulted. No the hell he didn't just say that to me. He don't know nothing about me.

"And if you can stop thinking about yourself for just a minute and think about our daughter, you will see that it's better that her parents marry than she come up a bastard. But you so selfish it don't matter what's best for her, only what's best for you, right?"

How dare he? Of course I was not that selfish.

"I'm not selfish, I just don't think we have to marry. Moms and Dads have kids all the time without being married." Of course, I was only speculating. I never knew my dad and my mom, who died when I was three. So technically, I didn't know how well that situation worked out for a child caught in the middle.

"Yea well, I'm not doing that to my child. If something happens to me, she gets everything of mine. I worked too hard for what I got, for my only child to have to fight for what's hers."

I put my hand on my hip. Why in the hell is he standing here talking like he got a legit business?

"Look, buddy, she good. We don't need the drug emperor. You can take that with you when you go." He narrowed his eyes at me and too late, I realized it may be too soon for my lip. He slowly began to walk towards me again.

"Ol' big-brained Monica, you got it all figured out, don't you? Damn! What did the world do before you and yo' big a** brain was born?" He came to a stop right in front of me.

"You keep saying that like you innocent." My neck rolled with each word I spoke. "Your brother said y'all need to get in contact with the Cubans. Now I-." I put my hand on my chest.

"Ain't claiming to be the sharpest pencil in the box. But even I know you and the Cubans ain't fin' to get together and hand out little heart-shaped cupcakes to orphans." His nostrils flared as he looked down at me. I could tell he really wanted to lay hands on me know. And he was standing so close I could smell his spicy cologne.

"That mouth of yours." He nodded his head finishing his sentence to himself.

It was hard to discern what was in that intense gaze of his. I looked away from him and stared out the window. He was standing too close. And he was just so big and commanding. It was a bit much to be my size and try to stand up to him, not to mention the fact that he smelled so good. It was as if he had found power in a cologne bottle and sprayed it on himself.

"We don't have to stay married." He said quietly. I turned to look up at him.

"What do you mean?"

"Just a few months, long enough for me to get my affairs in

order. Get you and Eve's name on things, so that everything go to you. You a liar, but I believe you a good mother. And you'll take care of things for her."

"You talking like you finna die," I said quietly.

He gave a dry chuckle before turning and sitting on the bed facing me, his long legs spread wide as he leaned forward to rest his elbows on them. Suddenly he looked tired. As a matter of fact, he always looked tired, including the first time I had met him.

"You never know when your time is going to come, but I want to be prepared. I want Eve to be straight, just in case." I still stood leaning my back against the wall. He was so big he made this room feel small.

"How long will we have to stay married?" I can't believe I was actually considering what he was saying. The truth was I felt like crap not being able to tell people who my child's father was. But the thought of one day having to explain to Eve why she didn't have a daddy terrified me. He exhaled before laying his big body back on the bed, bringing his hands up rubbing down his face. It seemed as if he had a lot on him, and Eve and I had just complicated his life tremendously.

I stood straight up and came to stand by the bed where I could look down into his face. His hands were clasped together on the top of his head and his eyes were closed. He looked really tired.

"Kaleb..." I said quietly. His eyes opened and those deep penetrating orbs stared up at me.

"You don't have to do this, you don't have to make it more complicated than it is already. This is a huge mess. If we get married it's only going to make it worse." He sat up. His muscled body moved like a big cat.

"Naw, we getting married. Period." He looked up at me.

"Go get my daughter, bring her up her, and introduce her to her daddy." He spoke in a tired, no-nonsense way that before I caught myself, I was on the way to do exactly what he said. But wait... The marriage conversation was closed. What the world?

"Umm, you can't just close a conversation!" I said putting my hand on my hip. He chuckled.

"Sure I can, I've made up my mind." This dude was crazy.

"Yea, but it's two of us. Are you going to marry yourself?" I asked frowning down at him. He rubbed his eyes with his hands getting more frustrated with me.

"Look, Monica...I don't like repeating myself. I've made my decision. Now go and get my daughter, bring her up here and introduce her to her daddy." The frown he now had on his face was really frightening but damn that. He can't just boss me around.

"Yea, but you're not the boss of me."

He began to chuckle really good. "Oh, sweetheart! You could not be more wrong. You have to know, Eve is a game changer."

He stood and I took a step back, because yea, he's huge. He began to stalk me and I continued to step back until my back came up against the wall. He stopped right in front of me, so close that when I took a breath, my chest rubbed up against his belly. He put his elbow on the wall next to my head, his arm on the wall above my head, and then he brought his other hand up and gently took my chin in his palm. He wasn't hurting me or anything, but he was letting me know that he could.

"There is much in this world that I'm not sure of." He gently stroked my cheek. He was speaking so close to my lips that if I moved just a little our lips would touch. "But there is one thing I'm a hundred percent sure of." His eyes slowly raked over my face, taking me in so fully, my eyes, my nose, they lingered on my lips.

"You're mine." He whispered before he took my lips. My knees buckled from the force of his kiss. His mouth forced mine open and the only thing I could do was hold on to his arms as not to get swept away.

The kiss was so...so... oh goodness...

I moaned becoming consumed by his flame. His lusty kiss was causing things to happen in my belly and my girlie parts, causing all my resistance to wash away. How can he kiss me this way? I know he was my enemy, but right now, I couldn't think of why. I know I shouldn't let him kiss me this way. It was so scandalous the way his hungry mouth drew from my lips.

But I loved it. I loved what it did to my body and how it made me feel.

My fists balled his shirt up in my palms as his seeking mouth made its way down to my neck. My head fell back against the wall, as with the same force that he drew from my lips he sipped from my neck. I had to squeeze my legs together. My moans were becoming louder. Goodness, this man brought out a very primal side of me.

By the time his mouth came back to mine, I was ready, willing and able. He broke off the kiss, looking down at me breathing heavily. He was angry. He was angry that he had kissed me, angry that at that moment, he wanted me just as much as I wanted him.

"Now, for the third time," he spoke low as he used his thumb to gently stroke my sore and throbbing kiss-swollen mouth. "Go get my daughter...bring her up here...and introduce her to her father."

Well... Hmm... The only thing I could do was nod and head toward the door.

It was as I was going down the stairs that I realized two things.

One, I was screwed...and two, Kaleb was a grown a$$ man... And if I was going to get out of this jam I had successfully put myself in, I was going to have to turn my game way up. And in order to do that, I had to stay away from his mouth. It was distracting. It caused me to forget everything I should never forget. Every time he kissed me, my good sense flew out the window.

I plopped on the couch next to Eve, who was still playing with Kaleb's car keys. Nana was shaking her head at the news.

"What happened now?" I asked, but I was only halfway listening. My mind was racing. It seemed like this situation was spiraling out of control. Marriage? Hell naw! That wasn't happening. I just needed to figure out a way out of it.

85

"Girl, birds is falling dead out the sky!" I was so lost in my thoughts my Nana's voice seemed far away.

"Emm Hmm, that's good."

You see if he was just a normal guy this would be so easy, but he was a mob boss. When people disobeyed him, they showed up floating in the lake. Look at what he had done to ol' boy who had hit me. I rubbed my hands down my face like Kaleb had just done twice.

"That's good?!" Nana screeched looking at me as if I had lost my mind. She stood shaking her head.

"Child, I'm telling you, the end is here!" She picked up the remote and shut off the TV. "I'm going to lay down for a little while. I picked up those grocery bags. Looks like we gon' have a treat for dinner. Wake me up when it's done." She called over her shoulder, walking through the kitchen door to her bedroom. I frowned after her. She hadn't even asked how our guest was doing.

Hmm...

I looked at Eve, who was in baby heaven with Kaleb's keys. Every time she pressed a button the red light flashed. When she pressed the other it flashed twice.

"Eve?" I whispered looking over at her from where my head lay back on the couch pillow.

"Hmm?" she asked without even looking up.

"You want to go upstairs and meet somebody?" She looked up at me, dropped the keys and held up her arms. I smiled at her as I scooped her up.

"You the smartest baby in the whole world, you know that?" She had the nerve to nod. When I got to Kaleb's door I paused for just a moment.

Oh man! This was huge. There was no going back. Once I introduced him as her daddy, that was it. She would officially have another parent in her life. A drug selling, mob boss parent. I exhaled dropping my head.

Oh, Yah! This was all my fault. I may have just messed up my daughter's life.

I wish I could just make him go away and continue on as I was before he showed up. But there was no making Kaleb do anything unless he wanted to do it. And apparently, he took his child seriously. So seriously that he was ready to get married just so she could have his last name and not be a bastard.

"Come in, Monica, don't go chicken on me now." His deep tired voice came from the room.

I inhaled and turned the corner into the room. He was half lying on the bed like he had been earlier. When we walked in he sat up. I sat on the bed next to him with Eve in my lap. He turned to look at her, smiling down at her.

"Eve," I began, but had to clear my throat, because the lump there was impairing my speech.

"Baby, this is your daddy, Kaleb," I told her. She looked at him and smiled. And I saw him fall in love right before my eyes. He went down to one knee in front of us.

"Hey, baby," he said. Amazingly there were unshed tears in his eyes. "How are you, princess?"

Because Eve was at the stage in which she pretty much repeated everything somebody said to her. She asked her daddy how he was and then called him princess, causing his Adam's apple to bob up and down in his strong neck as he laughed at her. Then after a moment, he sobered, picking up her little hand with his finger.

"Daddy sorry." For a moment he paused, looking down at their linked hands. "I'm sorry for so many things. But mostly, I'm sorry for not being here for you till now. But you ain't got to worry about that no more 'cause I'm here now, and I'll make sure everything is all good for you, sweetheart." Eve reached for his watch that probably cost more than our house.

He held out his hands to her. "Will you come to daddy?" Eve squealed and threw herself in his arms...

Ouch! That hurt. I felt betrayed. He stood with her hugging her close. I rolled my eyes to keep from crying. He gently chucked me under my chin.

"Don't be jealous."

"Ain't nobody jealous," I mumbled.

I didn't even sound believable to my own ears. He chuckled shaking his head sitting back on the bed next to me. I looked down at my nails.

Wow! I never thought I would be here, having to share my child with another parent. Then something else came to me, something I needed to tell him before it was too late.

"Look, can you not tell my Nana any of this?"

"Any of what? That I'm Eve's daddy?" I nodded.

He threw up his hand. "Whatever, that's between y'all. You be a good girl and your secret's safe with me."

I frowned at him. "Are you going to blackmail me?"

He chuckled. "I ain't got to blackmail you, baby. You gon' do what I say on your own free will."

I couldn't help but laugh at that. "Am I now?"

He grinned returning my challenging look.

"Yep." He ran his finger down Eve's little cheek. His hand looked huge next to her little face.

"And if I don't?" I had to know. I had to know what he was going to do. "Are you going to make me disappear?"

He looked up at me then, his eyes searching mine. "Monica, you're the mother of my child, I will never hurt you." I don't know if I believed him.

"So, if you got real mad at me, I mean *real* mad. You won't have me shot."

He frowned. "Why would you say that?" he asked the question like it was something wrong with me.

"I saw you kill a man."

He nodded as if understanding my questioning now.

"Several times I have had to pay medical bills for some unfortunate girl who got on Jermain's bad side. He did a real number on a few of them. I talked to him, told him to get his stuff together or he couldn't work for me anymore. He'd clean up his act, be good for a few months, then he'd turn around and do it again. The last time he put his mother in the hospital and I put him in the bed next to her. That was his warning. When I got out of jail, he came begging me for a job. Said he was clean. I told him he only had one chance to mess up and he was out. But what did he do? He went way past messing up. He put his hands on my woman." He shook his head.

"There was no coming back from that." To hide the fact that his words made me feel all warm inside I pressed on with my line of questioning.

"So, I don't have to fear that you're going to kill me?" He shook his head at me before looking down at Eve, who was now taken with his suspenders and was slobbering over one as she tried to put it in her mouth.

"What's wrong with your mama?" he spoke to her in baby language... "No baby, don't put that in your mouth, it's nasty." He took the gold out her mouth.

I don't know, seeing this killer talk baby talk was kind of cute.

No, Monica! Get your head back in the game. Remember, this is the man that killed your brother.

Your brother!

I stood. "Okay, that's all I needed to know." I reached my hands out for Eve. She opened her arms for me and I lifted her out of his lap. I turned to walk out the room, but he grabbed my wrist bringing me to a stop.

"You think you have me figured out, but you don't. I am a very patient man. And I guarantee you I can handle anything that mischievous little mind of yours come up with." I snatched my hand from him.

We'll see. There was more than one way to skin a cat. And if this guy thought for a minute I was marrying him, he had another thing coming.

"Dinner will be ready in an hour," I called over my shoulder as Eve and I left.

Eve sat on the floor playing by my feet as I made dinner. I had a huge smile that I couldn't wipe off because I was going to get a little revenge tonight with dinner. I had only bought enough steaks for Nana, Eve and I, which meant Mr. Man was going to have to eat some left-over chicken from Chucky's.

Oh! I couldn't wait to see his face. I was so giddy and ready for this revenge that I hurried with dinner and when it was done, nearly ran to call him and Nana to the table. As I waited for them to come, I washed Eve up and sat her in her high chair.

Kaleb and Nana came in the kitchen at the same time, him through the door that led from the living room and her from her bedroom door.

"Here, baby, sit hear." I heard her tell him. I had my back to them putting the finishing touches on the dishes.

"Something smells good." His deep voice came from behind me.

"Yes, it does. We don't normally eat this good around here, but Monica brought a special meal home. I think she's celebrating a new job she got today." I closed my eyes. Goodness, Nana had a big mouth.

"Oh! You got a new job?" Kaleb asked.

"Nope! I'm celebrating *not* getting the job." I told him without turning around.

"I told you she a little off." I heard my Nana whisper.

"I can hear you!"

After I finished cutting up Eve's meat into tiny pieces, I put her plate in front of her. Once that was done, I couldn't help the feeling of glee that came over me.

Showtime!

I put on a sad face as I turned with Kaleb's plate, placing it in front of him. Then I put mine and Nana's on the table.

"Sorry, Kaleb, I didn't know we were going to have company. I only had enough steak for us. But I brought home that chicken a few nights ago, it should still be good." I pulled out my chair across from Eve and sat.

"Monica!" Nana hissed at me as if he couldn't hear her. "What is wrong with you!" She stood.

"Here, baby, you can have mine." She said reaching for Kaleb's plate.

"Oh no, ma'am! That's alright, I will eat the chicken." He said.

"Absolutely not! I insist!"

"He say he alright with the chicken!" I all but yelled at her.

What was she doing? She was ruining this for me. Do you know she had the nerve to roll her eyes at me before taking his plate and replacing it with hers? He looked down at his steak and potato before looking back up at me. And the fact that he was holding back a smirk was like the final straw.

"Why did you do that?" I asked my Nana as she sat back in her chair with the plate of old chicken. I could have screamed.

"We do not give the guest old stale food." I opened my mouth to argue with her, but that stubborn look on her face let me know it would do no good. I held my head down, feeling so frustrated I could have cussed. Now she made me feel like crap because it wasn't my enemy with the old chicken, it was my grandmother. Grudgingly, I pulled the plate away from her and switched it with mine.

"What you doing, baby?" she asked.

"I'll eat the old chicken," I said under my breath, sulking like a little girl. My Nana looked at me and blinked twice.

"Well, if you insist." She bowed her head and blessed her food, then picked up her knife and fork and dug in.

My mouth dropped. What the world? I turned to look back at Kaleb. By this time, his lips were quivering from him trying to hold back his laughter. I narrowed my eyes at him telling him he had better not let it go. And I guess that was all he could take because he burst. He held back his head and barked with laughter.

Oh! Y'all...

I can't even begin to explain the hate that was shooting through me right now. He laughed so hard tears began to roll down his cheeks. Every time it seemed as if he was going to stop, he would look at me and my angry face and start back up again.

I folded my arms shooting my Nana a glance, curious to see what she thought about this rude behavior of his. And do you know, the little troublemaker was looking down at her newspaper as she chewed as if she was so lost in the news that she didn't notice he was sitting across the table laughing his head off at me? Then I saw that she was struggling to hold back her own laughter.

I looked back at Kaleb, who was using his napkin to dry his eyes.

"Oh, Monica! I ain't laughed that hard since I was a kid!" he spoke as he tried to calm his laughter. When he had it controlled, for the most part, he picked up his knife and fork. Still chuckling he cut into his steak. He put a piece in his mouth and looked at me nodding.

"Mmm, it's really good...Juicy."

My mouth fell back open.

No...this...ni-- He burst again, laughing at my shame. I nodded, that's okay. He can laugh now. But I'm going to have the last laugh. Because tomorrow when he wakes up, ready to get married, he gon' find me gone. I call it Operation Runaway Bride.

I picked up my chicken and bit into it.

Damn it! It was horrible.

Chapter 5
OPERATION RUNAWAY BRIDE

MONICA

K aleb left out the house early the next morning. I threw back the covers and shot out the bed. He told me last night that he would be back to get Eve and me at two, which meant Eve and I had to be gone before he got back. Quickly I hopped in the shower, my mind racing. There was a part of me that said what I was doing was indeed very foolish and selfish. What if Eve needed her father in her life? What if having married parents would make life just a little bit easier for her?

But how can I marry a dangerous man like that, a man that I would always be frightened of, a man that could kill and not lose any sleep? I wanted a husband that made me feel safe, not one that made me feel afraid. I wanted a husband that I could learn from, one that can build our home, not one whose actions could tear it down. I believed that man was out there somewhere waiting for me. However, that man was not Kaleb and marrying him would be the biggest mistake I ever made in my life.

As I got out of the shower and dried myself off, I was convinced I was making the right decision. I stood in the mirror and moisturized my body. Sure, I could be making a very dangerous decision.

He said he wouldn't hurt me, but can you really believe what a mobster said?

No!

However, he could not hurt me if he couldn't find me. And because I knew myself well, I was going to need a distraction or else I was going to be worrying like crazy.

And what better distraction was there than Shante and Keturah?

I opened the door to my closet. Okay, what to wear?

Keturah was a pan-African, dead set on revolution and Shante was a straight up ghetto boo, the only revolution she was prepared to fight for was the one against the neighborhood beauty supply store for price gouging with the human hair.

Two weeks ago, I had to pull her out of the store. I thought she was going to hurt that little Chinese man. She was ready to send it up. They had raised the price a whole seventy-five cents a bag, and she was ready to throw down.

Anyway, Shante and Keturah did not get along. So unless I needed to be distracted like I needed to be today, I never tried to hang out with both of them at the same time. Keturah said Shante was the problem with the black community. Ghetto and trifling she called her. Shante said Keturah need to stop trying to get everybody to go back to hot a** Africa.

I tapped my lips with my finger... Whenever I hung out with both of them, I had to be careful to dress in a way that they could both relate to, or else they would instantly assume I was taking the side of the other. Today I had to rock ghetto boo, Afrocentric gal.

Yea!

I took down my African print wrap skirt that I got from off Madison and Pulaski, but I would shake it up by rocking my white off-the-shoulder Gucci blouse, another awesome find on Madison and Pulaski, ten dollars.

Now granted the tag on the shirt said Toms made in China,

which is probably why it was only ten dollars, but I didn't care, the tag on the outside said Gucci, good enough for me.

I piled my locs up on top of my hair into a messy ponytail, letting a few of them spill out.

Now to accessorize, I added a couple of pieces of loc jewelry and my big gold *like* hoops for my ears. I think I would go without a necklace and let the off-the-shoulder blouse do its thing. I put on my gold *like* bangles, a little lip gloss on my lips, and then my Adidas. I then headed into Eve's room to get her ready and pack her diaper bag.

She sat up in her crib blinking at me, not used to me waking her up.

"Yea, surprised you, didn't I?" I asked as I scooped her up out the bed. Today she could wear one of her outfits I got her yesterday with her little Adidas.

As I got her dressed, I went over her ABC's and her colors with her. Eve was a smart baby and the more stuff I taught her, the more stuff she learned. Her brain was a little sponge, thirsty for information. So I figured it was my job to fill it with information.

My daughter was going to be nobody's dummy. She was going to be a trailblazer like Ms. Janet Collins, My Nana, Stormy, or Mama Rita, just a few of the women I admired. I was determined that she turn out better than me, stronger and smarter. Yea! I didn't care what I had to do, I would not let her make the same mistakes I made.

By the time we got downstairs, Nana was just getting up, settling in to watch the morning news.

"Wow!! Don't y'all look pretty, where you going today?" She asked as she flipped on the television.

"Probably going to take Eve to the zoo and have lunch with Keturah and Shante." She started shaking her head before I could even finish speaking.

"You know it's something wrong with the both of them." I chuckled as I kissed her on her cheek.

"They grandmother probably saying the same thing about me." I headed into the kitchen to make her and Eve some breakfast.

"They grandmother ain't got to say that about you. *Your* grandmother say that about you!" she called from the living room. I laughed shaking my head.

I a few minutes later Eve pushed the kitchen door open and climbed up into her high chair. She looked so pretty in her little jumpsuit.

"Did you read your book for Nana?" I asked. With a grin that showed all eight of her teeth, she nodded as she began to tell me all about it in Eve language. You know, I did work a lot, so much so that I missed out on precious time to spend with my child. I thanked Yah that in spite of that, she was still a happy baby. Nana pushed open the door walking slowly into the kitchen. Her joints must be aching her today.

"How your legs feel?" I asked placing her and Eve's fruit on the table.

"My legs are just fine." Slowly she eased down in the chair. Goodness, my Nana was so stubborn. She could receive so much more help if she would just allow it.

"Maybe we should—"I began, but she cut me off.

"So it looks like our guest is an early riser, huh?" I narrowed my eyes at her. Changing the subject much?

I sighed. "Yea, maybe he had to be at work early."

"Speaking of work, ain't you supposed to be going today?" Oh crap! I cleared my throat.

"Umm, I took a few days off." She shook her head as she began to stir cream in her coffee.

"In my day, you had to show up for work every day in order to pay your bills. Good thing that young man offered to pay us a little more on the rent. And you wanted me to kick him out."

"Yea, good thing." I quickly finished making their breakfast. Rather than let Eve feed herself I fed her so that we could get out of here before Nana asked any more questions that I had to lie to her about. She was the one person I hated lying to.

"Goodness, where are you in a rush to run off to?" She asked as I finished the last of the breakfast dishes. I dried my hands with the kitchen towel.

"I told Shante and Keturah I would pick them up at nine and nine thirty."

"Pick them up?" She asked. Oh crap! The car. "Pick them up in what?" I heard her ask, but I was already out of the kitchen door with Eve. I scooped up the diaper bag and quickly slipped out the front door. Man, how in the world was I going to explain this car?

You know what? I had enough to worry about right now. I needed to just get through this day first. I'm sure I'll think of something to tell my Nana by the time I got home.

"What the hell?" Shante said as soon as she came out her front door looking at the Land Rover.

"When you said you was coming to scoop me up, I thought you meant in your grandmother's hoopty." I frowned at her.

"Girl, that car ain't worked in years."

"I know, so where the hell did you get this? Did you win the lottery?"

"Get in the car, fool! I got to go scoop up Keturah." She rolled her eyes and slid into the front seat.

"Great, now I got to listen to her talk about the damn motherland all day." She turned and looked at me as I pulled off.

"Why do you hang out with her? It's something wrong with her. She waiting on Kunta Kinte to come and whisk her away so they can live happily ever after in the bush of mother Africa." I shook my head at her.

"You wrong for that," I told her.

"Hey, baby!" she yelled back at Eve, who was enjoying her first ride in her new car seat. Just a little side note about Shante, she was always yelling. I have told her a hundred times that she was a pretty girl and didn't need to be loud in order to be noticed, but that just went in one ear and out the other, because Shante is the poster child for a Loud Woman.

"Oh, Monica please don't make me have to put up with this hot ghetto mess today, I woke up on the wrong side of the moon," Keturah said as she slid into the back seat next to Eve.

"See what I'm saying?" Shante yelled. "What the hell is she talking about? Wrong side of the moon! Heffa, you mean wrong side of the *bed*?"

"You say it your way and I say it mine, okay?" Keturah snapped at the back of Shante's head.

"Ladies, please!" I yelled at both of them. "I'm going through something and I needed both of my girls today, so can y'all stop arguing long enough to support your girl?" This got both of their attention.

"Okay, let's examine that," Keturah said sliding up in the seat till her face was right between Shante and mine.

"Let's start with where you got this nice truck from." I exhaled. Leave it to them to jump right into it. I debated not telling them, but I was so torn I needed their honest opinion.

"So y'all remember who I told y'all my baby daddy was, right?"

"Girl, we just assumed you was lying again." I hit the steering wheel.

"I'm not a liar, I'm an actor. It's a difference!" Keturah threw back her head and laughed.

"Yea, but you're a horrible actor." My mouth fell open.

"I am not, Madame Queen said—" Shante waved that away.

"Child, don't tell us nothing that cuckoo bird said. So back to your baby daddy. "

"Anyway," I said rolling my eyes at Shante's rudeness. "Y'all remember I told you it was Kaleb?" Shante starts screaming towards the ceiling.

"Monica, don't even try to tell us your crazy a** really did get pregnant by Kaleb for real!" She looked over at me, she and Keturah wore expressions on their faces as if they were waiting for me to deny it. I lifted one side of my mouth in a grin that did not reach my eyes.

"Monica!" Keturah cried with a disapproving look on her face. "That ain't cool. Girl, he is dangerous, what were you thinking?" The smile left Shante's face as she too wore a look that was akin to horror.

"Yea, Mon! That nigga a killer. What's up with you?"

"The one time y'all agree is to tell me I messed up." Shante looked back at Eve.

"Now that I think about it, she does look like Kaleb." Her eyes flew back to me.

"Not cool!" she yelled.

"Why are you always yelling?" I asked. Their response was starting to irritate me. They were causing me to see that I might have made a huge mistake by not obeying Kaleb. And come on, let's face it, nobody likes to be told that they are wrong.

"Don't try to change the subject, what he got to do with this car?" Shante came right back with. The fact that I just called her loud did not bother her one bit.

"Well, he gave it to me."

"Oh hell no! Let me out! I'm not riding around in no mobster's car!" Keturah yelled from the back seat.

"That's not the worst of it." Oh well, I was out here now. I might as well tell them everything.

"What could be worse than that?" They both asked at the same time.

I took a deep breath and began to explain to them what I had done, how I had gotten him locked up, and how he had gotten out of jail. Him forcing me to be with him to make up for the two years I had stolen from him. How I had gone down to his apartment building and gotten him evicted. How he ended up living at the boarding house. Him finding out about Eve, his demand that I be ready at two o'clock today to marry him and how I was using them as a distraction as I conveniently said the hell with him and his demands.

By the time I finished, we were standing in front of the lion's cage, where Eve was making growling sounds from her stroller.

Both of my girls just stood looking at me as if I had grown a second head.

"Say something!" I told them. I was already a nervous wreck. I didn't need them just standing there looking at me.

"You are crazy as hell?" Keturah said gaining control of herself first.

"You gon' get your fool self killed!" Shante followed.

"He said he would never hurt me." Both of them rolled their eyes at me.

"I heard that nigga took out Milo and his twin Junebug. They say he stashed the bodies in that new Central expressway ramp." Keturah and I both frowned at Shante.

"What?" I asked.

"Girl, in the cement. Them niggas in the cement. Every time somebody get on the expressway at Central they drive over them dudes." Keturah put her hands over Eve's ears.

"Don't speak of this child's father like that in front of her. That's what wrong with our children now—" she began but Shante dropped her head back on her neck.

"Aww! Don't get started with this crap! If you want to go back to Africa, fine!" She put her hand on her hip. "But you can stop trying to get me to go back to hot a** Africa."

And so they began. And I ain't gon' lie, laughing at them and the crazy stuff that proceeded to fly out their mouths served as the distraction I needed. They argued for the rest of the zoo trip, all the way back to the car and through lunch. And I'm ashamed to say that I was glad, because as long as they argued with each other, they couldn't remind me just how stupid it was to disobey a man that killed people for disobeying him, or how stupid it was to have a baby with him, tying myself to him whether I liked it or not, as if I had tried to do that on purpose.

I know it was dumb, but what the world was I supposed to do now that the deed was done? Neither of them had an answer to that question.

As I pulled away from the Lincoln Park Zoo, I saw that it was past two. I couldn't help but smile to myself. Yea, it was dangerous, but it still felt good that my plan came together.

No sooner had I thought those words, two motorcycles appeared on both sides of the car.

"What the hell?!" I cried.

This was a one-way street, but it was big enough for them not to have to be driving so close to me. Keturah and Shante stopped arguing as they realized something was very wrong.

"Oh my God, what are they doing?!" Shante yelled.

The riders were dressed in all black. Even their helmets were dark, I could not see their faces at all. I honked my horn.

"Look, there is another one!" Keturah screamed pointing in front of us.

My heart began to pound out of control. As the rider stepped on the brakes turning his bike to cut me off completely, I brought the truck to a stop.

Don't panic, don't panic! I looked back in my rearview mirror to Eve. She was out, the full day she had was causing her to sleep through this drama.

Something else caught my attention in the rearview. A black Land Rover pulled up behind us.

Oh, Yah! It was Kaleb!

He looked menacing as he drove with one hand. Our eyes connected in the mirror as he put his truck in park, mine frightened, his angry. I turned the wheel to the right and was getting ready to step on the gas when the bike on the right moved up blocking me in. I turned my wheel to the left, but the bike on the left did the same.

"Oh no!" I cried.

"What?!" Shante screamed. She was clutching the dashboard with a death grip

"It's Kaleb!"

"What?!" Keturah and Shante turned to look out the back window just as Kaleb, dressed in an all-black three-piece suit stepped out of his truck. He fastened the button on his jacket and slowly approached my side of the truck. I quickly locked the doors. Shante gave me a "really?" look.

He came to a stop next to my door and motioned for me to let down the window. I did, but only halfway. He leaned down looking into the car, he had that deadly smile on his handsome face as he took in everybody. When his eyes landed on Eve, who amazingly was still asleep, his look softened just a bit.

"Damn, he fine as hell," Shante whispered. I turned to look at her and returned her "really?" look.

"Hey, sweetheart," he finally spoke. "Did you forget we had an appointment today at two down at city hall? Good thing the judge is a good friend of mine and is willing to see us at three. But we need to hurry, so I'm going to need you to follow me, okay?" I shook my head.

"Not okay, I'm not marrying you." I stared straight ahead, too chicken to look him in the eye. He chuckled.

"Sure, you are, you don't have a choice."

"I have a choice, 'cause I ain't going!"

"Oh yea? You ain't going?"

Now see, it was something in his tone that should have made me pause and think about the next words that came out of my mouth. But I didn't, and well, what happened next would be something I don't think I would ever forget.

"Naw, I ain't going!" That deadly grin on his face caused the hairs to rise on the back of my neck.

"Look at me, baby." He demanded quietly.

And I promise, it was as if my head had a will of its own because it turned to look at him. Shante was right, he was extremely hand-some. "You feel brave, huh?" He asked the question as if he felt sorry for me.

"You feel brave 'cause I said that I won't hurt you?" He chuckled shaking his head a bit as if he had never seen anything sadder. I was waiting to see if he was going to go back on his word and hurt me. I can't say that I would be surprised.

"Oh, don't look like that. I'm a man of my word. You always think the worst of me." If you didn't know that Kaleb was a maniac, you would think the placating look on his face meant that he was getting ready to forgive and forget.

However, I was there when he killed oh boy with the big wrenches. Yea, he wore the same look!

"I will never hurt you." He spoke low and almost lovingly. "You're the mother of my child, I'm not a savage. But them," He pointed to Shante and Keturah.

"Us, what did we do?!" They both yelled at the same time.

"Don't worry, y'all, I locked the doors," I told them hitting the button to let up the window. With that devious smile still on his face, he reached into his pocket and came out with a keypad that looked a lot like the one that was on my keychain.

Oh crap!

"Pull off, Monica!" Shante yelled.

He hit the button and the locks opened. Before I could lock it back the passenger door and the back door where Keturah sat was snatched open. Quickly Tiny snatched a screaming Shante out, putting his big hand over her mouth. Easily he lifted her off her feet and carried her back to the Cadillac truck that was off to the side of the Land Rover. At the same time, Keturah was being yanked out by G. She beat at him with her bag.

"Let me go, thug!" He made quick work of dragging her out the car. She looked back at me.

"What have you done to us?" She asked before he covered her mouth and scooped her up in his arms.

I began to hyperventilate. *Oh No! Oh No!* This was all my fault. I let the window back down.

"Please, Kaleb, don't do this, I'm sorry. I didn't mean to miss our appointment!" Tears were coming out of my eyes. I felt so bad. I was selfish. I had used my friends as a distraction and had gotten them kidnapped. Kaleb was right, I was selfish!

"Shh, don't cry, Mon, just follow me to city hall, it will all be over soon. And your friends will be right as rain."

"Kaleb, let them go and I will go with you." He chuckled.

"That option has passed, we tried that the first time. Now we're going to try it this way. You go down to city hall and behave, we get married and your friends walk away healthy and whole. You do anything other than what I just said, and I make your little friends go on a little vacation." I was crying now. He leaned back down and brought his big hand up to wipe away my tears.

"Come on, Monica, you knew who you were dealing with. Now I'm going to ask that you be a good girl and follow me." I nodded my head. What else could I do?

Casually, as if he had not just rocked my world, Kaleb walked back to his truck. A few seconds later he rode past me, and I followed him. I thought about calling the police, but I quickly thought better of that.

There was no doubt in my mind that if Kaleb ended up in jail, my friends were dead. Two of the mystery riders rode on both sides of my car and the third at my rear. With Kaleb in the front of me and the bikes on the side and the third behind me, I was good and cornered.

When we pulled up to the city hall, Kaleb opened my door and then went to the back and took Eve out the car seat. He took my hand and led us into the building. My heart was pounding out of control. We passed so many police officers and I wanted to signal to one of them that I was in distress, but I had been selfish enough, I had to think of Keturah and Shante.

Kaleb introduced me to the judge and the three motorcyclists that would be the witnesses to our marriage, but I was numb. I smiled on cue and nodded. Shook hands, but if you asked me what everybody names were, I couldn't tell you. I just wanted this to be over so my friends, who probably hated me right now could be safe. As the judge married us, Kaleb stood next to me with Eve in his arms. She looked around at everything with wide eyes, probably wondering what was going on.

"Do you have rings?" The judge asked Kaleb, who sat Eve in a chair that was next to us. One of the bike riders carried a brown box to him. I frowned, that was too big to be a ring. He held the box as Kaleb opened it. My mouth fell open as he came out with a beautiful gold arm bracelet. The diamonds in the bracelet sparkled in the office light. I held up my hand, I couldn't help it, I was enthralled. Carefully he slid it over my hand and up my arm. It entwined like a golden vine up my arm.

It was amazing. On the tip of the delicate leaves were little diamonds. I held up my arm looking closer at the beautiful script that had been weaved into the leaves.

It read, *Kaleb's Monica.*

Surprised I looked back up at him, completely taken aback by the beauty of the bracelet. But he wasn't finished. He picked up my other hand and began to slide my hundred percent, genuine imitation gold bangles off my wrist. When he was done he held them up looking for a place to put them before dropping them into the wastebasket.

"Hey!" I screeched.

I mean, I know I got them from the beauty supply store, but they were mine. He chuckled before going to the box and lifting another golden bracelet out, this one for my wrist. It was even more amazing. The beauty of it took my breath. I held the bracelet up to get a better look at it. This one had ballet shoes artfully etched into it. The shoes danced on a fine script that also read, *Kaleb's Monica.*

He reached into the box and lifted out another bracelet, that one he put on my other wrist. It was identical to the other one except this one read, *Monica's Kaleb*.

Oh my goodness! I had never seen anything more beautiful than these three bracelets. But then he went back to the box and lifted out one more, this one smaller. He squatted down in front of Eve, who had watched him put the bracelets on me. And before he could reach for her little arm, she held it up putting it right in his face.

Everybody chuckled at that. Eve was a mess. I smiled proudly, Yah knows that's my child.

I don't know, watching him put that bracelet on her made me feel warm inside. Right then I got the notion that no man would ever treat Eve like her father. What man would have done what he just did?

When he was finished he scooped her up in his arm kissing her fat cheek before coming back to stand next to me, taking my hand in his strong one.

If the judge found it strange that Kaleb put three bracelets on me instead of a ring, he didn't say anything, he just picked up with the ceremony and ended with "You may kiss the bride," before I could take in the fact that I was now married.

Kaleb reached around my waist with his free arm and pulled me to him. When his lips touched mine, everything else in the room just seemed to fade away. I moaned when he deepened the kiss. Hungrily he took my mouth and I was lost.

"Damn, baby, you always taste so good." He whispered to me before he was taking my mouth again.

However, the sound of Eve making kissing sounds was like a splash of ice-cold water. And it must have been that for him too, because his head jerked back at the same time mine did. We both looked at Eve, who had her little lips meshed together, making loud kissing sounds.

"Okay, remind me not to do that in front of her again." He said looking at Eve with a horrified look on his face.

"I now pronounce you man and wife." The judge said. The three motorcyclists began to clap behind us.

Kaleb held out his hand to shake the judge's. "I really appreciate this, man." He told him.

"No problem, I'm glad to see you settling down, you deserve a break." Kaleb chuckled shaking his head.

"Marriage does not mean a break, my good man."

As we left out the building I contemplated his words. What did the judge mean by he deserved a break? Last night he seemed tired, yet he was up and out of the house before the sun rose. But before I could ponder more on it, he was opening the passenger door of his Land Rover for me. The cream Land Rover and the motorcyclists were gone. Kaleb put Eve in a car seat that he must have already had in here because it was a different one than what was in the cream truck. I watched him as he strapped her in, he almost looked like a real daddy.

"Did you let my friends go?" I asked as soon as he slid into the driver seat. He nodded.

"I did." I sat back and put on my seatbelt.

"We only have to stay married for a little while, right?" He didn't say anything as he pulled out into the busy downtown traffic.

I looked back at Eve, who was touching her bracelet. It was so beautiful. When I turned around I couldn't help but look at mine. I wanted to ask him about them. How did he choose such beauty? I had been expecting a plain golden band, not these fine creations of golden art. I ran my finger over the bracelet that said, *Monica's Kaleb.*

"You like them?" He asked so low that I almost didn't hear him. I started to lie and say that I didn't, but even I could not deny such beauty.

"I do, they are very beautiful. Why did you choose bracelets over a wedding ring?" He gave a dry chuckle. Suddenly he sounded tired, that same tiredness I saw in him last night.

"It is what the men in our culture do." Wow! Okay... Was not expecting that to come out of his mouth.

"What do you mean our culture?" He turned his head to look at me.

"You've been around Shelomoh and his wife all this time and you haven't taken the time to learn who you are?" Ouch! I couldn't help but feel slightly insulted. He asked the question as if I was some kind of dummy.

I put my elbow on the armrest of my seat and leaned my head on my palm, staring up at him.

"I'll have you know that for the last few years, I haven't had time to do much but work and go to school. After graduation, work and work. Not to mention taking care of Eve." Yea I said it with a lot of stank in my voice. But one thing I wasn't going to put up with was him insinuating that I have been wasting my time, 'cause I ain't the type, playa!

"Why you working two jobs anyway?" It was my turn to chuckle with no humor.

"You know there was a time I didn't have to work so much, back when my brother was alive. But some asshole had him murdered and well, now all the responsibility of taking care of Nana, the boarding house and Eve has fallen on my shoulders."

Nah! I dare him to say something after that. He looked over at me again. He was not happy with my words, but I didn't care, not one bit.

"Sit back and listen to the music!" He grumbled before he reached over and turned up the music.

That's what I thought!

After a while, I saw that we weren't heading towards the boarding house.

"Where we going?" I asked sitting up, looking around as he turned down the street heading towards Mama Rita's.

"I'm hungry," was all he said. Obviously, he was still sulking over our conversation earlier. We pulled up to the door. A young man in a red coat quickly came to open the door for me. Kaleb got out and took Eve out the car.

"Good evening, Mr. Jacobs!" the young man said overeager to please Kaleb.

"Evening, Jeff. How's everything?" A smile spread across Jeff's face from ear to ear, so thrilled he was that Kaleb was asking about him.

"Good, everything is good! And thank you so much for your recommendation. My little man starts next week, and they put him in the gifted program." Kaleb stopped and clapped Jeff on the back.

"Oh, good deal! How did it go with the scholarship?" Jeff beamed.

"Full scholarship!" The man was barely holding onto his excitement. Kaleb smiled for real, the first time I saw him do it all day. He was truly proud of Jeff and his son, who he had apparently helped get into a really good school. I turned away to look at the beautiful fountain to hide my surprise. Never would have pegged Kaleb for the type.

When he was done talking he put his hand on my lower back as we walked through the doors that were being held open by a pretty hostess. I could tell by the way her eyes were raking over Kaleb that she either knew him personally or that she wanted to get to know him personally.

"Good evening, Mr. Jacobs, your party is already here. Mama Rita have you guys in the banquet hall."

"Thank you, Ronda." He guided me through the busy restaurant.

Mama Rita had a really nice place. There were pictures on the wall with her and all the black celebrities that have come here while they were in town. The reservation list was always full. People still came to wait at the bar just in case somebody canceled. Everybody here seemed to know Kaleb very well. Several people got up from their tables to shake hands with him. No wonder, he was a black celebrity in his own right.

We walked to a pair of golden doors and there was a man standing in a red and black uniform that opened the door for us when we got there.

"Congratulations!" My hand flew to my chest as I had a slight stroke.

"Dear Yah!" I cried out looking up at Kaleb.

He smiled down at me. "Surprise!"

Oh, my goodness! With tears in my eyes, I looked around. Everybody was here. Stormy and Shelomoh stood by the fireplace, there was a big happy smile on Stormy's face. She waved at me. Still in shock I waved back. Shante and Keturah stood with Rasheed. My girls had a smile on their faces as they clapped their hands. What the world? All this time I had been panicking, imagining the worst, and they were here sipping on champagne.

Tiny, G and the three motorcycle riders came and shook Kaleb's hand.

"Congratulations, Boss!" they said to him before lifting my hand and kissing the back of it.

"Congratulations, My lady!"

"Thank you," I whispered.

Oh, my goodness...I was about to freak out. Y'all, this felt like the real thing. I looked up at Kaleb and was surprised to see a genuine smile on his face. I looked around stunned at all the people I had never seen before. A beautiful brown skinned older woman that was wearing a gorgeous blue suit was heading our way with a warm smile on her face.

Oh wow! It was Mama Rita! I was getting ready to have a meltdown. I had never seen her before in person, just on the commercials.

Oh man! I was getting ready to act like a straight groupie.

"Look, Kaleb, oh my goodness, it's Mama Rita! She smiling at us! Oh, she getting ready to speak to us!" I was pulling on his jacket talking out the side of my mouth, while still smiling at the approaching legend.

"Kaleb, she is stunning!" She said coming to a stop in front of me picking up my hand.

Man, I was cheesing from ear to ear.

"I just want to say, it is such an honor to meet you. You have always been one of my role models. You and Stormy," I gestured toward Stormy who was coming towards us. "I tell my daughter every day that she can defeat the odds stacked against her. Just look at you."

Mama Rita blushed. I beamed up at Kaleb. I made Mama Rita blush! I wanted to yell that out loud, but I didn't want to make myself look any worse than I was already looking. I still clutched the woman's hand and if I shook it any harder I'm pretty sure I was going to break it.

"Is this Eve?" She asked holding her hand out in front of Kaleb. Eve looked at me to see if it was alright. I smiled at her and nodded. She opened her arms and let Mama Rita hold her.

Oh my goodness! Mama Rita was holding my child.

"She is so beautiful. Hey, baby, I'm Mama Rita." She cooed to Eve, who was taking everything in with wide eyes.

Mama Rita grabbed my hand again and gave it a warm squeeze.

"Will you walk with me, so that I can introduce you to some family and friends before Kaleb start sucking up all your time?" She asked. And for a moment all I could do was just stand there and stare dumbfounded.

"Oh, yes ma'am, I'll be honored." I looked up at Kaleb as he put his hand on my lower back and guided me across the floor.

"Mama Rita is holding Eve; can you believe that!" I whispered up at him. He looked down at me and chuckled.

"That's a good thing, seeing as to how that is her granddaughter." I came to a complete stop.

"Mama Rita is your mother?"

Chapter 6
BROTHER'S KEEPER

MONICA

"Why are the two of you standing there grinning like this is a happy occasion?" I snapped at Keturah and Shante who stood by the bar before I leaned over and asked the bartender for a bottle of water. I had finally been able to break away from Kaleb's mom, who had dragged Eve and me around to introduce us to all of their friends and relatives.

The whole time Kaleb was angry with her because it was supposed to have been a small dinner with a few friends. But Mama Rita said she never did anything small and had managed to get most of their family and friends to attend tonight although it was on such short notice.

Kaleb had to rescue Eve from her because even after I had managed to break away to talk to Stormy and Shelomoh, she still carried poor Eve around so that folks could pinch on her cheeks and gush over her. Kaleb had taken the poor child out of his mother's arms and Eve had almost instantly gone to sleep on his shoulder. He now stood by the window holding the slumbering baby as he talked with Shelomoh. I couldn't believe they knew each other. How in the world had that happened?

"We thought you were happy, hell, you was doing all that

smiling with his mama. Coming up in here blinging. So much ice made me cold." Shante said gesturing towards my bracelets.

"What?!" I looked at her as if she had gone dumb on me. "Maybe I'm mistaken, but didn't y'all just get kidnapped?" Keturah waved her hand.

"Yea, but the fellas was real cool. After they put us in the car they let us know that we weren't their prisoners and was free to go. They said they would drop us off where ever we liked." She chuckled. "They even asked if we would prefer to have dinner at Mama Rita's with you the guys to celebrate your nuptials." Shante interrupted her.

"And I was like brother, you ain't even got to ask! I'll take a free Mama Rita's steak any day!" She did a little dance on her stool as she sipped on her fruity cocktail. I stared at the both of them with my mouth open.

"Wait a minute, let me get this straight. You heffas lives wasn't in danger?" They shook their heads. Keturah wore a sympathetic look, but that damn Shante wore a smirk that made me want to slap her.

"Son of a—" I turned to look at Kaleb, so mad and frustrated I could have cried. The bastard had the nerve to wink at me from where he still stood talking to Shelomoh.

"You got to admit though, he is fine," Shante whispered leaning in close to me.

Hmm! She spoke the truth. Nobody wore black like this man or a suit for that matter. He had taken his tie off when we got into the truck coming from the courthouse, so now he stood with a couple of buttons undone on his shirt, exposing his strong neck and Adam's apple that moved up and down as he talked to Shelomoh.

"I can give a damn how fine he is! The bastard tricked me!"

"Gurl, you tripping...He could trick me any day if he gon' deck me out with them kind of jewels." Shante laughed. Keturah sucked on her teeth and rolled her eyes at her.

"What's wrong with you? Monica ain't no gold digger like your trifling self."

"Why I got to be a gold digger just 'cause I can appreciate a man that can take care of me? I keep telling you everybody dream ain't to marry some African tree climber and live happily ever after in the bush eating bush berries."

"That's a shame you talk about your own people like that." Keturah snapped putting her hand on her hip.

"And I keep telling you them damn African's ain't my people! Just 'cause they black don't make us kin."

Keturah rolled her eyes again at Shante and then turned away from her to fully face me.

"You know, if you don't want to be married to him you can always get your marriage annulled." I frowned at her.

"How can I do that if I already have a child by him?"

"I don't think it matters. You just have to make sure you don't consummate your marriage."

"What the hell does consummate your marriage mean?" Shante asked Keturah, who exhaled in a long drawn out breath.

"It means to have sex with him."

"Wait!" Shante held up her hand. "So you think she can live with that fine a$$ brotha over there and not consummate her marriage?" She held up air quotes.

"Yes I do, she's a strong independent black woman and she don't need a man to make her happy." Shante and I stared at her blinking.

Ummmm....

"What am I, a lesbian?" I couldn't help but ask. Shante held her head back and laughed as loud as ever.

"Gurl please..." she said to Keturah. "You can go somewhere with that feminist I think I'd rather be with a woman mess. I got a hundred dollars say she consummate her marriage if not tonight definitely within the next couple of weeks." Now it was Keturah and I that stood blinking at Shante.

Ummm...

"What am I, a hoochie?" Both of them were tripping. I ain't no feminist, I would love to be able to depend on my man, but I ain't no hoochie either. Kaleb said we only had to stay married for two years. I had enough control over myself to remain untouched till then. Shew!

"Naw, baby." Shante's voice cut into my thoughts as if she heard them.

"Being a hoochie ain't got nothing to do with it. However, what you are is married to a six foot plus, strongly muscled, dripping fine, alpha male that has been looking at you all night like you are one of Mama Rita's steaks and he a hungry man that ain't ate in months." She looked at me out the side of her eyes pursing her lips in a way that told me she was getting ready to say something scandalous.

"Or shall I say two years....If you know what I mean!" She did a little roll with her body that was so Shante like. But she had a good point.

Oh, my goodness!

My gaze went back to Kaleb. And sure enough, he was watching me. The look in his eyes was hungry, there was no doubt about it. His gaze slowly went from my mouth to my neck and lower, and then he licked his lips. I had been so caught up in everything that has been going on today that I hadn't even paid attention to how he has been watching me all night. Even when we were in the court-house vowing to live as man and wife, he had that predatory look in his eye.

"And darling, when he gets a hold of what has put that..." She paused for just a minute. "Look in his eye, he ain't gon' let it go until it has been good and thoroughly loved." She spoke these words softly as if she was the voice in my head narrating my thoughts.

"And ummm, yea, my girl strong, but even Mother Theresa ain't got the kind of strength to resist a man like that, especially if it's been two long years since he's tasted the honey. So like I said, I give it two weeks tops."

"You think you know Monica so well, but you don't. I'll take that bet. When my girl put her mind to something, she follows through. If she say she want out of this marriage that has been so ruthlessly forced on her, then that's what she's going to make happen. A hundred dollars she stay firm and not give in to her oppressor." With a frown on her face, Shante shook her head at Keturah.

"Oppressor? He ain't her oppressor! He her man. And you got it...if after two weeks miss Monica here, that you claim you know, have not let the boss man over there dip his hand in the cookie jar, then I'll give you a hundred dollars. But if she has, you pay me and shut the hell up about Africa."

And as they shook hands making a bet on my life, my eyes as if they had a will of their own strayed back across the room to Kaleb. He nodded at something Shelomoh said before he turned to look at me. And it was as if he could read my mind because the grin that came on his face said loud and clear that he wasn't going to play fair. And that he most definitely had a taste for honey.

"Ladies, can I steal Monica away for a few minutes?"

Stormy's voice came from over my shoulder. For a brief moment, I closed my eyes. Dang it! I didn't need this right now, but I knew there was no way I was getting out of here without having a one on one with Storm. She was like a big sister to me. For as long as I could remember she's been there for me. She had helped raise me. But I had no idea what I was supposed to say to her. I was tired of lying. Lying had gotten me in so much trouble.

And yet, I still had to answer to Nana in the morning. I turned on the ball of my left foot.

"Damn! She must be nervous, she dancing." I heard Shante whisper to Keturah behind me.

"Hey, Storm!" I said with a big bright smile on my face that I did not feel. She returned my smile and hers was just as forced.

"Hey Mon, can I talk to you for a minute?" I nodded. "I'll be back y'all." I threw over my shoulder as I followed Stormy to her table across the room. I eased down in the chair next to hers. Oh Man! Oh Man! Here we go. I inhaled.

"Look at you," she began and for a moment, I thought that maybe she won't chew me out too bad.

"You're a married woman." I exhaled and forced another smile on my face.

"Yep, I am." I picked up a fork and began to lightly tap it on the table.

"To Eve's dad."

"Yep, to Eve's dad." The tapping got faster.

"So…" She took the fork out of my hand and placed it on the table, drawing my gaze back to her.

"How did that happen? I thought you told me he was gone and was never coming back. What are you doing, Mon?"

What am I doing?

What am I doing?

I don't know what I'm doing! I have gotten myself into trouble and I don't know how to get myself out!

I felt the tears coming to my eyes. And I had no power to stop them

"Storm, I messed up so bad!" I whispered to her, my voice quivered with my tears.

"No, not here…This is your wedding day. Everybody is watching you. Here," she said putting a napkin in my hand. "Dry your eyes, put a smile on your face and follow me."

It took everything I had in me, but I managed to put a smile on my face as I wiped away my tears. I prayed that for all those that were watching I looked like a happy bride overcome by joy. I continue to smile as I crossed the floor following Storm out the banquet hall. I smiled at the wait staff that was very curious about me as I made my way through the dining room. And then finally I smiled at Jeff the valet parker as he held the front door open for us. We sat on a bench on the other side of the fountain.

"Okay." She took my hands in hers. "What did you do?"

I stared down at our joined hands and told her everything, not leaving out one detail. When I was done she was looking at me with a very disapproving look on her face.

"I don't have to tell you, you could have gotten yourself killed." I nodded.

"Monica, I just don't understand the way your mind works. You got to learn how to stop and think things through. You can't just go off your first thought." All these things she was telling me she had told me before many times.

I held my head down. "I don't know what's wrong with me," I mumbled. She gently lifted my head with her hand.

"You're fearless and that scares the heck out of me." I grinned.

"But I'm afraid right now," I whispered. And I was. I was married to a mob boss.

"What am I going to do now?" I asked Stormy. She exhaled giving my hands a little squeeze.

"What do you want to do?"

"I want to be free. I don't want to be married. I lost so much of my young adult days already taking care of Eve and Nana. And now I'm married. I'm beginning to feel like I'm suffocating." She tilted her head to the side and lifted her mouth in a grin that didn't reach her eyes.

"Oh little sista, believe it or not, I know exactly how you feel. Solomon pushed his way in my life when I was very young and I was afraid. I didn't trust him. More than anything I wanted to be free of him, but look at us now. He's my best friend. I don't know what my life would be like without him. I can't even imagine it." She reached up and pushed one of my locs that had fallen in my face behind my ear.

"Sometimes the thing we least expect to be a blessing turn out to be a gift from Yah." I shook my head.

"Kaleb ain't Shelomoh! He a drug dealer, Stormy! He don't work for his money! He kill his people for his money! He killed my brother! He ain't no blessing!" And then the tears that I had been holding back erupted.

"Shh, sweetheart," Stormy said before she wrapped her arms around me and hugged me close. I cried in her arms like I had done so many times when I was a little girl. And gently she rubbed my hair. She didn't rush me, she let me cry until I was all cried out.

"How do you feel?" she asked taking the napkin out my hand and drying my eyes with it.

"Better," I told her and it was slightly true. Actually, I felt exhausted, but that cry had been stuck in my throat ever since my friends got pulled out the car earlier.

"So, what are you going to do now?" she asked quietly, a slight smile on her face.

"He says after two years I'm free. I guess he's going to make arrangements for Eve. You know, help me out with her." Stormy nodded.

"Mon, my husband is a pretty good judge of character. And he likes Kaleb." I looked up at her.

"Yea, what's up with that? How did that happen? Why did that happen?" Stormy chuckled.

"Yah guides him to people. And he says Yah guided him to Kaleb." I shook my head.

"I don't know why! He's not a good person!"

"Well, it's like a very wise man once told me, our ways are not like Yah's. Our mind is not like his mind. He sees things that we can't, we're only human. I don't know why the Father led my husband to Kaleb, but if he did, it's for a reason. So let that be of comfort to you." I know Stormy was just trying to help, but her ear wasn't to the streets. She didn't know the things I knew about Kaleb.

I smiled at her. "You right, I'll try to look at it that way." She patted my hand.

"Good," she said seeming more cheerful. "Shelomoh said Kaleb was coming by the house for the Shabbat. Are you coming with him?" I started to shake my head, but then her face began to fall and a frown started to take the place of the warm smile she just wore. I exhaled. Stormy was such a nice, warm-hearted person, one hated to let her down. I nodded.

"Yea, Eve and I will be there."

"Yay!" She said clapping her hands coming to her feet.

"Let's go back in."

"You go ahead, I'm going to sit here for just a couple of more minutes then I'll be in." She looked around.

"Are you sure?" I smiled. Stormy the mama hen.

"Yea, I'm sure. Go ahead, I'll be there shortly, just want to enjoy this breeze a little while longer." She nodded, but I could see she didn't want to leave without me.

"Go on," I told her. And reluctantly she walked inside. When she was gone I let my shoulders drop and rested my back against the fountain. It's amazing how everybody thought I was so fearless. I wasn't, I was scared senseless most of the time. Scared for my Nana's health. Scared that I wasn't giving Eve all the things she needed to be a well-rounded human being. Scared that I won't be able to keep up the boarding house.

"Hey, sister-in-law," Rasheed said before sprawling out on the bench next to me.

"Ahh!" I screeched because he wasn't gentle about it.

"Oh, my fault. Did I bump into you?" I could tell by the humor I heard in his voice that he knew damn well he bumped into me. And he wasn't the least bit sorry.

"Yea, you did." I snapped. "What do you want?" It wasn't any need for us to even begin to pretend we liked each other.

"Damn! Can't I talk to my sister-in-law that just showed up out of nowhere with my brother's baby without having a motive?" I rolled my eyes as I slid as far away from him as I could. I didn't like touching him at all.

"Everybody has a motive," I told him, wishing he would just get up and leave.

"Yea, everybody do. So..." He turned to face me on the bench. "What's yours?" I frowned.

"Excuse me?" A grin appeared on his face. I would've said handsome face, but every time he looks at me, it's always filled with hate. So to me, his face was ugly.

"Come on, sis. You just show up with my brother's bastard child, forcing him to marry you." What the world was with these people and bastard children. Hell, half the people in the ghetto were bastards. I was a bastard. I had never even met my father.

"I don't know what you're talking about. I didn't force him to marry me. It was quite the opposite." He reached for one of my locs, but I slapped his hand away from me.

"I heard a little rumor." He spoke slowly as if he was telling me a secret. "I heard you was responsible for my brother getting locked up. Is that true?" Something in his tone told me that at this moment my life was in danger.

"Again, I don't know what you're talking about." He smiled.

"If I find out that it was you who was responsible for putting my brother in a f*^*ing cage!" He growled. "He gon' be a single daddy."

"Yea, I'll be right back, I'm just going to check on Monica." Kaleb's voice came from somewhere on the other side of the fountain.

"Shh!" Rasheed said putting his finger to his lips.

"We over here, bro!" he called out to Kaleb.

Kaleb

My irritation level grew when I rounded the corner and saw my wife sitting with my knuckle-headed brother. I clenched my fists together trying to calm my anger. It was bad enough my mother didn't understand a small dinner to celebrate my marriage. No, in true fashion, she had to go overboard as usual. She invited family and friends I haven't seen since I was a kid. And now something that should have taken only a couple hours had dragged on for the better part of the night.

The only thing I wanted to do was take my wife home, lay her out on the bed and taste what I was now starved for. For two and a half years I have thought of nothing more than that sweetness that I sampled the night I went to jail. What is the irony of hungering for someone that I should have put to rest?

"What's going on?" I asked as I took in the distressed look on Monica's beautiful face. Her shoulders were tense and she was clutching the bench so hard her knuckles had turned white.

"Come here, baby." I held out my hand for her.

There was something in me that was extremely possessive of her. I had never felt this way about a woman. She hopped up off the bench or more like pointed her right foot forward and did a little leap off the bench. That was something else I dug about her. She danced when she moved. Sometimes when someone called her name and she turned around, she went up on her toes and did a little pirouette. Most of the time when she stands, she would have one foot planted and the other toe facing down. My little ballerina.

When she came to me, she took my hand with both of her hands and squeezed it tight. I frowned, that kind of affection from her wasn't normal, something was wrong with her. My eyes flew to my brother as I pulled her closer wrapping my arm around her. She didn't fight this action, in fact, she tucked herself up under my arm.

What the hell?! She was shaking.

"What's the matter, baby? Did Rasheed say something to you?" I asked. My irritation was building swiftly into anger. If he said something or did something to upset her, I was going to hurt him! Bad!

"What you say to her?" I said from between clenched teeth. The stupid look on his face made me want to lay hands on him. She put her little hand on my chest, trying to calm me. Another thing she did that I loved, because it did in fact calm me.

"Nothing, man! How you gon' get married with an anger problem?" Rasheed asked. I bit down on my teeth. I had nagged him into going to school. He took one semester that included a psychology class. Ever since then, he has diagnosed me with an anger problem.

"Rasheed, don't play with me, I ain't in the mood. I will scrape the concrete with you a$$! What you say to her?!" I spat.

"Kaleb, I'm just tired. I want to go home." She spoke softly looking up at me.

"Yea Kaleb, she just tired. She want to go home."

"Shut up!" I pointed at him. Then I looked down at her, trying to see what she was hiding from me. My brother had said something to upset her. There was no doubt about it. But what?

"Tell me what he said, sweetheart." I touched her soft cheek because I needed to touch her. I needed to touch more of her, so bad that I feared when I did, my hunger will cause the savage to come out of me.

"He didn't say anything, it's just been a long night." She even tried to smile to reassure me, but I wasn't buying it. I smiled back at her.

"Okay, go ahead in and start getting Eve ready. We'll leave in a minute." She nodded her head and practically ran back into the building. I waited till she was through the doors before I snatched Rasheed a$$ up off the bench.

"Hey, man!" He yelled as his feet came off the ground.

"What you say to her?" I growled in his face. He grabbed at my hands.

"Nothing, I just welcomed her to the family!" I shook him.

"Stop lying!"

"I ain't lying!" I threw him back on the bench. I was too tired to deal with him right now.

"Let me find out!" I pointed at him.

He straightened his shirt out. "Man, forget her. What about the Cubans? Dominic ain't trying to do no business with me until he hear from you. But you know that already! You been acting funny as hell since you got out! I been trying to get up with you, but you act like you ain't got time for a nigga." I exhaled.

"I had a little hottie set up for you for after you got out and you faked me. Been trying to get up with you to hang out with you a bit and all of sudden you too busy to even holla at your boy." He began to pace in front of me. I felt like crap because I *had* been avoiding him.

Things had changed with me. Truthfully, I didn't even understand fully what was happening. But I always felt change when it had come in my life. Like when my real father died, and King, who at the time had been my dad's lieutenant had reached in to hug my grieving mother, telling her that he would always be there for her. Or that night Monica danced on my patio. However, when I first saw Shelomoh sitting on the other side of the glass partition waiting to speak with me, I had felt my world shift. I knew that after that day, I would never be the same.

"I mean, what's up? I ain't yo' mans no mo'? You ain't got my back no mo'?" I rubbed the back of my neck, I was so tired. I haven't slept for more than a couple of hours a night for the last three years.

I loved my brother. I raised him like he was my own, but he had become a burden to me. He was determined to continue in his father's legacy. At first, it didn't bother me. He did his thing I did mine, but he was getting reckless and sloppy in his dealings. The Cubans had wanted to kill him. I had to go and talk to Dominic myself to assure him that I would keep Rasheed in line.

But even that had begun to wear me down. I told him that if he was determined to move weight like his punk daddy, then he had better keep it away from any of my establishments. But he hadn't and it was because if him that I ended up with two years. I used my fingers to try and rub away some of the tension behind my eyes.

I reminded myself for the thousandth time that if something happened to him it would kill our mother. She depended on me to keep Rasheed alive, to keep him from ending up like his daddy. So whether I liked it or not, I was my brother's keeper.

"Look," I exhaled. "You know I always got your back. Never doubt that."

"You ain't acting like it though. Brah, I'm so sorry about the stash, had I known the feds was getting ready to raid your warehouse, you already know it wouldn't have been there. And you got my word, as soon as I find out who snitched, they dead! I promise you that!"

"I've already taken care of that. You don't need to worry about it." The last thing I needed was for him to find out that it was Monica who got the ball rolling in that direction. He frowned at me.

"What you mean don't worry about that? You my brother, I may not be your main mans no mo', but you still mine. You got my loyalty forever. Somebody set you up and got you thrown into a cage like an animal. And that person gon' pay. That person gon' pay for what they did to you!" See, this is what pissed me off. Just like his punk a$$ daddy, he always placed the blame for his mess ups on somebody else.

"What they did?" I asked taking a step toward him as I felt my anger rising. Wisely he backed up a few. "Nigga, it was you who put dope in my parts warehouse!" I pointed my finger at his head. But what I really wanted to do was knock him in it.

"I told you to keep that sh*t away from my place! You put it in there anyway! You did that! Nobody else! You the reason I got locked up!" I drew myself up straight. No, that wasn't true. Here I was doing what I'd just accused him of doing. I shook my head.

"You know what? I take that back. *I'm* the reason I got locked up. I should have shut down your operation a long time ago!" The muscle ticked in his jaw. He was speechless because how could he deny facts? He looked off to the side and spat on the ground, before taking his ball cap off and running his hand down his immaculately waved hair. Something he did when guilty ever since he was a small boy.

When his gaze came back to mine his guilt had passed, no doubt he had already placed the blame for his action on someone else.

"I went by your apartment yesterday and waited for you to come home. Mama made you some food. I called Tiny, but he told me you was staying in a damn boarding house. What's up with you? What happened while you was locked up? You ain't the same!"

He spat on the ground again and shoved his hands in his pockets.

"And now all of sudden you got a wife and a kid? Come on, man! How you even know that's yo' baby?" The look in my eye caused him to take a step back. He threw up his hands.

"I'm just saying, you know how these tricks—" He didn't get the chance to finish. I snatched him up off his feet again throwing him against the wall. With one hand I held him there by the collar, with the other I pointed in his face. I was only going to tell him this once, and he and I were never going to have this conversation again.

"Monica ain't no trick! She ain't no b*^ch! She ain't no ho'! She the mother of my child! And you gon' respect her!" He snatched away from me with a frown on his face that reminded me of when he was little and use to throw tantrums.

"When the hell was you gon' fill me in on all these changes!" He yelled. "The Cubans waiting to hear from you! You ain't even reached out to them for me!"

He was good and into his fit. But that was my little brother for you. When the world got tough he ran to his big brah to smooth things out for him, but I had changed. I had a family now. I had found out who I was and most importantly, I may have found what has been calling me for years.

"Look, I ain't supporting you with the Cubans no more. It's time for you to let that go." He looked at me as if I had just spoke a curse on him.

"Let that go?! What you mean let that go?"

"Just what I said. We need to lay that part of the family business to rest."

"Then what am I supposed to do?" I exhaled because I knew what was coming next. This has been an ongoing argument between the two of us ever since my stepfather died.

"Dad—" He began, but I cut him off.

"He ain't my father!" I corrected. My brother chose to turn a blind eye to the way his father treated me. But it wasn't a day that went past that old Jerome King didn't remind me that I was a bastard and not entitled to his empire. That legacy he left to Rasheed.

"Dad," He continued anyway. "Left you the legit side of the business. He left me the dope side. Now you want to take that from me!"

"First of all, *Dad* didn't leave me nothing. I worked that side of the business. I built it to what it is today. Without his help, he ain't do sh*t but take credit for it!"

"And I built the other side of the business to what it is today!" he said hitting his chest with his fist. I bit down on my teeth. He was pissing me off.

"Then what you need me for?" My voice was raised because I was getting really close to hurting my little brother. "If you built that side of the business, then why you always running back to me?" Instantly I regretted my words. Although it was true that King treated me like crap, Rasheed and I were always very close. He was mine, I raised him. Yah knows his father was never there.

"Oh! So we finally got to the root of the matter. You tired of me, I'm a burden to you! And now that you got a new wife and baby, you don't mess with me no more. Right?" I rubbed my hand over my head.

"You know that ain't what I mean. It's just time for you to do something different. Get out of the dope game. I ain't calling Dominic and telling him I got your back if anything happens, 'cause I don't. I shouldn't have supported that sh*t in the first place. I just did it 'cause you felt like that was your legacy. But that's a sh*t legacy! It ain't nothing to be proud of! And your daddy was a piece of sh*t for passing that on to you."

"My daddy was a piece of sh*t for the way he treated you. If he was alive I would kill him because of it! But he wasn't wrong for teaching me how to survive on these streets."

I opened my arms. "Rasheed, I'm surviving just fine, why not follow after me? Why you got to follow after that nigga?"

"'Cause it's all I know. Everybody didn't go to the fancy schools like you. Remember that? My sh*t daddy sent you to the best schools."

"'Cause he wanted to get rid of me, get me out his house. So yeah, he shipped me away to school."

"And while you was there, brother, I was out here on these streets. And now you say you gon' take away the only thing I know." I reached out to him and grabbed him by the neck bringing him in and wrapping one of my arms around him in a hug.

It broke my heart what his father did to him. Every day I worked to undo the damage.

"We gon' get through this together. I'm gon' always make sure you eat, brah. And I'm gon' make sure you get paid." He looked up at me.

"What about the girl?" I frowned at him.

"What girl? My wife?" He nodded.

"How you gon' look after me and ma with her in your life?"

"Just like always. Having a wife won't change nothing. I'm gon' always take care of you and Ma."

He took my arm from around his shoulder. "Yeah, I bet." He said softly under his breath before turning to go back into the restaurant. I stood for a minute and watched him go. I was all Rasheed ever really knew as a father figure. I had looked out for him ever since our mother had come home from the hospital with him when I was nine. Even when his father had shipped me off to school, Rasheed and I spoke on the phone several times a day. And when I came home on the weekends, we were inseparable.

Naturally, he feared now that I had a family of my own that he and I would lose what we have. But I would just have to show him and Ma that I can still take care of them and their needs, and take care of my wife and child at the same time.

Chapter 7
LADY IN THE YELLOW DRESS

MONICA

Okay, I'll admit it, I was taking the coward's road out right now. However, I wasn't ashamed, not one bit. I needed to do whatever I could to stay out of Kaleb's arms. That was a dangerous place for me to be. Right now as we are speaking, I am hiding in my room behind a locked door. I know that seems a little childish, but the man had skills. The way he touched me just made me turn to butter in his hands. And I refuse to prove Shante right, I would not fall for the man that had my brother murdered!

Earlier after we left Mama Rita's, we had driven home in silence. I had so many things to ponder about, one of which was Rasheed. He hated me, there was no other word that could be used. He hated my guts. He thought that I had gotten pregnant by his brother on purpose just to trap him. Ha! Please, if only he knew. I would be willing to do anything to get his bully of a brother out of my life.

I knew girls like that, they thought that getting pregnant by a man would miraculously make him love them. That was just tomfoolery in my opinion. If a man didn't love me for me, then I loved myself enough to walk away. There were too many fish in the sea to settle for a piranha. I peeked at Kaleb out the side of my eye.

This was no piranha, this was a damn shark. Before he knew about Eve he had gotten it in his mind that I was going to play the role of his whore for two years.

After he found out about Eve, he said the game had changed, and I guess it had because now I was his wife, so technically, he had used the child to trap me. For the life of me, I can't understand why. A man like him can get any girl he wants. Seriously, he was that fine. So why had he gotten it in his mind to trap me?

Damn, what part of the game was that?

Whatever the reason was, it wasn't going to work for me. Keturah said that I could get the marriage annulled, but I think it was too late for that. There had to be another way out of this situation though. But until I figured out what that was, I know for sure that I had to do whatever I could to avoid sleeping with him again. That would only complicate things even more than they already are.

I figured that the best way to avoid that foolproof was to never be alone with him. Something happens to my willpower when it's just he and I in a room and when he looks at me with those wanting eyes of his. I am not made of steel. I am a flesh and blood woman and there was only so much I could handle. So, I decided to take the coward's way out.

Kaleb carried a sleeping Eve upstairs and laid her in her crib. She was out, I changed her diaper and put on her PJ's and she didn't budge. I could hear Kaleb next door in his room moving around. When I was done with Eve, I all but ran to my room shutting the door and locking it behind me.

Grinning as I leaned my head against it. Yes, I made it. I would just wait him out. When he stopped moving I would go and take my shower.

Yea, this could work.

I walked to my dresser and very carefully took off my bracelets and laid them on it before slipping out of my clothes and hanging them up in my closet. Putting on my robe I picked up my *Plumbing for Dummies* book and settled in to wait for Kaleb to fall asleep. And judging by the sounds coming from his room, I probably was going to be waiting a while. His phone rang a few times and sounded as if he was in a meeting or something. I couldn't hear him clearly but I'm pretty sure he was talking auto parts and shipments. I could also hear him typing on his laptop.

Goodness, it was eleven o'clock at night and the man was still working.

However, after about an hour everything had gotten quiet. I think he was asleep.

"Perfect!"

I cracked my door and eased out into the hall before tiptoeing down the hall past his room. Right when I passed Eve's room the floorboard creaked. I came to a stop, closing my eyes waiting to see if I heard any movement from him or Eve, Yah knows the last thing I wanted to do was wake the baby. It would be a long night if that happened.

When after a moment I heard nothing from either room, I continued down the hall. The second-floor bathroom was around the corner with the four bedrooms that needed some serious repairs, my old room being one of them. It was my favorite room in the house because it had a big round window with the perfect few of the top of the trees out front. When I was a little girl, I used to sit in my window seat and pretend I was in the jungle.

Smiling at those old memories I turned the corner and came up short because the bathroom light was on and the door was closed. Before I could turn and hightail it back to my room the door opened and Kaleb, wet from the shower in only a pair of basketball shorts stepped out. My eyes nearly bugged out my head looking at him hardly dressed.

Goodness gracious! I put my hand on my chest. I had forgotten just how ripped he was, more so since the last time I saw his chest, no doubt from his time in prison. I tried to turn away, I did, but his body was a sculpted work of art that seemed to attract my gaze.

"Thought you was going to be too chicken to come out your room." He said in a dangerously low, sexy bedroom voice that started working on my resistance instantly. I took a step back and then another.

"Had I known you wasn't asleep I would have never come out at all." I have no idea why I just told him the truth. His eyes slowly raked over my body, taking in my short robe that left most of my thighs and all my legs exposed. Although I had it tied I clutched it between my breasts so that none of me showed. However, when his eyes landed on them he bit down on his lower lip as if he could already taste me.

Goodness, I was coming undone. When his gaze finally rose to my face, his hunger was clear. It caused something inside of me to twitch. I gasped.

"So, you were hiding from me?" He shook his head as he slowly walked towards me. "I thought you were a brave girl. Monica the fearless." I took another step back and then another and another.

Abort! Abort!

I raised my head. "I am brave, but I'm also smart and some battles are better fought at a distance." I went to turn and run, but he moved so fast that I didn't get far in my turn before his arm wrapped around my waist and he was pulling me to him.

Oh wow! The heat coming from his muscled body was too much. I put my hands flat against his chest and tried to push out his arms.

"Kaleb, let me go!" I whispered trying not to panic. I didn't know who I was more afraid of, him or me.

"Shhh, baby! It's our wedding night!" He pleaded pulling me closer.

I shook my head. "I can't do this, I can't sleep with you!" Although I was no longer pushing at his chest, my hands as if they had a will of their own was still resting against his massive pecks.

"Why not? You're my wife! I'm your husband, it's what we're supposed to do." He whispered.

"I'm not ready!" He frowned down at me.

"Mon, we have a child together. We've already done it!" He said this as if he was speaking to a special needs child. I nodded my head.

"I'm aware of that, but it's been a long time. And I was drugged that night. Did you know that?" The frown disappeared from his face.

"You were?" Although he didn't let me go, he took a step back so that his body was not pressed up against mine anymore.

"Yea, I was!" Oh, thank you, Yah. His aggressive energy was dying down. Goodness! Aggressive Kaleb was a challenge to deal with.

"I thought you were just tipsy or something." I shook my head.

"Nope, somebody had slipped me a mickey."

"Who?" Something about the way he said that reminded me of the poor man that had punched me.

"I—I don't remember." I lied. He narrowed his eyes at me. Why is it, y'all that it felt like this man could see straight through to my soul? It was like he could peer deep down inside me where nobody else could.

"So, you don't even know if you like my touch?" he grumbled.

Hmmm... *I like your touch very much*. But you don't need to know that.

I shook my head putting on my sad vulnerable face. "I don't think I like your touch. I don't even remember that night. I'm afraid. So, can you please just give me some time? I have never been with another man and I feel like a virgin." He chuckled pulling me closer so that our bodies were pressed up against each other.

"The second part of that pretty speech I believe. But you're lying about the first part." Gently he palmed my cheek before rubbing his rough thumb scandalously over my lips.

"I think you like my touch, I think, you want my touch, and you're just too chicken to admit it." His head slowly lowered towards mine and his deep midnight gaze seemed to hold me in a trance. This is what I told y'all about, my will was going down fast. Damn, this man was a sexual magician.

"But like I told you before, I am a patient man. When I make love to you again, it will be because you asked me to." he assured quietly. I almost laughed in his face.

Yea right, he'll be waiting until hell freezes over!

I couldn't help the smirk that broke through. "Brother, the day I ask that of my enemy will be the day I put on a chicken costume and moonwalk down the street." A smirk appeared on his face and my spidey senses started to rise.

"Bet, you got a deal. When you ask me to make love to you and you will, I am going to lay you down and love your body in a way that you will never have to wonder if it was the drugs that made you respond to my touch the way you did that night. And then the next morning, you're going to put on a chicken costume and stand outside my shop with a sign promoting King and Son's Restorations."

Oh, hell yea, a challenge. Eww, boy I loved challenges!

"And what do I get if you lose, and I don't break character and beg my enemy for sex?" He chuckled.

"What do you want?" Hmmm...This could not have happened more flawlessly. I raised an eyebrow looking him square in his eyes because I didn't want him to mistake me in any way.

"I want a divorce." At first, he didn't respond, his mind was like a calculator. I was dealing with a shrewd businessman here.

"If by some phenomenon you don't beg me to take you, I'll give you your divorce." He rubbed his thumb across my bottom lip again as if begging for entrance and I had to force myself not to open my mouth.

"But when..." He chuckled again. "I mean *if* I make love to you, you're mine! No more talk of divorce."

See...do y'all see what he did there? I told you, a shrewd businessman indeed. But he didn't know me at all. I lived for challenges like this.

"*If*...we make love and I do mean if... it will be because I have foolishly fallen in love with you and at that point, will probably not want a divorce. But you see, I can never love the man that killed my only brother, so you've already lost." The muscle began to tick in his cheek. He was angry, just like he was every time I brought up my brother, but I didn't care. He was a murderer and I wasn't going to ever let him forget it.

He gently stroked my cheek as he studied my face. He was standing so close I could smell the Dove soap he had just used in the shower.

"Okay, my little dancer, you got it. Let's seal the deal with a kiss." I bit my lip. *Oh man! Oh man!* He couldn't do anything to me, right? He said he wouldn't make love to me unless I asked. And I wasn't going to do that, which meant I was safe. He chuckled.

"Do you know that your every thought shows on your face? Right now, you think you're safe because no matter what I do you will never beg for my touch. Poor little Monica, you have no idea what you've just gotten yourself into." He pulled me closer and lowered his head taking my mouth in one swift movement. I was so startled that my lips parted in a gasp and his mouth took full advantage as it began to ravenously rob me of my senses.

Oh...My...Goodness!

He took my hair in his fist forcing my head to stay at an angle so that his lips could have their way with mine. The only thing I could do was hold on to his big shoulders as he plundered my mouth. This man's kiss was so erotic it made me clutch my thighs together. I moaned getting swept away in his storm. Images of that night he made love to me with the same fever floated through my mind and a fire that I had been so afraid of was lit in my belly.

This fire made me want to throw caution to the wind. It didn't care about my pride, it didn't care that he was my enemy. It wanted what it wanted. And what it wanted right now was for Kaleb to love me like he had that night, thoroughly and without mercy.

"You always taste so sweet!" He whispered as his hungry mouth lowered to my neck just below my ear.

"When I was locked up, I dreamed of taking you over and over again!" His ravenous growl was causing me to need...Mmm, I needed.

I brought my hands up to the back of his neck pulling him closer. His hard body felt so good pressed up against my soft one. He lifted me off my feet and I wrapped my legs around his waist and moaned when I felt his need for me.

"I want you so bad... why baby? Why are you forcing me to wait?" The whole time he whispered his lusty words against my neck while open mouth kissing my skin, he rotated his hips driving me wild. He took my mouth again, plunging his tongue between my lips in the same rhythm as his hips. The fire that he had lit earlier was now a burning inferno. I needed a release or else I was sure to explode.

His mouth was back on my neck sucking strongly. My moans were getting louder. I wrapped my arms tighter around his neck. I was getting ready to...

He pulled his head back and looked down into my eyes that were now just as hungry as his. I wanted to yell at him not to stop, but then he put his finger against my mouth hushing me. I saw it then...just underneath his lusty gaze. A smirk. His mouth slowly lifted in a smirk.

"I'll help you out this time and give you a courtesy pass." His intense dark gaze bore down into my very soul. "But this is your only one. The next time, you're mine."

My mouth fell open as he stepped back so that my legs could slide down his body. And then casually as if he did not just leave this fire ablaze in me, turned and walked away.

"You bastard!" I said to his back as he headed towards his room.

"Yep, I've been called that my whole life!" He called over his shoulder.

I stood there for a minute, long after he'd gone in his room and shut his door. What the hell just happened? There were two emotions yelling inside of me, that of being unfulfilled and then that of embarrassment. I had almost come this close to begging him to release the pressure that he had built up in me.

Wow! That was really low down of him. He didn't have to do me like that. So you know what this meant, right?

Mmmhhmmm....

This meant war!

So, he wanted to play the game of teasing, did he? Tomorrow I was going to show him how it was done. I'll call it Operation Now You Have Me, Now You Don't.

"Mama!" Eve yelled before she jumped on my head.

"Ouch! Eve!" my muffled cry came from my pillow as her knees landed in my back. Dang, it felt like I just closed my eyes. I tossed all night long because that fire that he had started in me kept urging me to throw my pride to the side and get up and cross the hall and beg Kaleb to make love to me.

And when I did finally manage to get to sleep, it was only to dream about him making love to me in the back of one of his classic cars straight up Titanic style. I turned over and caught Eve just as she was making another dive on top of me.

"Got you!" I said to her before I started tickling her. She squalled at the top of her lungs.

"Shhh! Child, you gon' wake up your da—"

I brought my hand up to my lips. Oh! Wow...I can't believe I was about to say that. I mean, I know that Kaleb is her dad, but saying things like you're going to wake your dad, or, go to daddy just made it seem as if I was in an agreement, you know? Which reminded me. Today I was on a mission. Operation Now You Have Me, Now You Don't. He thought he was so clever, making me all hot and bothered while he walked away looking like a hero.

I threw the covers back and got out the bed. Two can play that game and I assure you, a man can't tease better than a woman. We invented that game. I went to my closet opening it. Today's mission was going to call for something special. I think The Lady in the Yellow Dress will do just fine.

"Yeah!"

The thing about the yellow dress is it was a conundrum. It buttoned up in the front and had a really cute belt that tied in a bow around my waist. But what made it a conundrum was the split that went up the right side of it that played peek-a-boo with my leg as I walked. This dress was modest unless I wanted it not to be.

Okay, maybe I was being petty, but my pride had taken a blow last night. So at certain points today, my yellow dress was going to prove to be very immodest. I needed to reverse the energy, you know what I mean? I needed for the ball to be back in my court. The way he left last night made me look like the desperate one. Naw, we couldn't have that.

I wanted to have him begging for me. So that I can be like, 'Sorry for you!' And then walk away laughing.

Yeah, that was the plan!

Still in my PJ's I made my way downstairs to start Nana and Eve's breakfast. I didn't know if Mr. Man was still here, but if he was, I guess I was starting his breakfast too. Yah knows Nana would have it no other way. I shook my head carrying Eve into the kitchen. Surprisingly Nana was already at the table drinking her coffee. I frowned.

"Who made you coffee?" Nana didn't do much standing these days. She walked from her room to the living room and from the living room to the fridge to take out whatever lunch I prepared for her and Eve to toss in the microwave. But outside of that, she did very little standing.

"Kaleb did on his way out to work, while he explained to me why he gave you a car." I paused in sitting Eve down in her high chair as my eyes flew to Nana.

"He did?" Oh wow! What the world did he tell her?

"He sure did, and it was like I said yesterday. It's a good thing I didn't listen to you and kick him out."

"Umm, yeah," I eased Eve down in her seat. "So what did he say?"

"Well, he said he saw that you took the bus back and forward to work and he thought the least he could do is to let us use one since he had access to so many cars." She chuckled.

"Heck, he even asked if I need one! I said, Oh no, child. I ain't drove in years." Sighing she sipped the last of her coffee.

"But it was nice of him to ask." I nodded.

"Yes, it was." I couldn't keep the relief out of my voice.

Wow! I had almost just had a heart attack. I didn't even want to imagine what the conversation would be like as I explained what I had done the night I got pregnant to my Nana. After my brother died she had turned into a nervous wreck. Her health really deteriorated then. Having to tell her that I was pregnant with Eve had been hard. Having to tell her that I had lost my scholarship to Julliard had been torture.

And the bad thing about it was that she placed a smile on her face and bravely told me screw Juilliard if they couldn't understand that life happened. She said she would rather have Eve any day. I know she said that because I had been so depressed at the time. I had told Nana that I had been curious about sex and had let my boyfriend at the time break my virginity.

And when he found out I was pregnant he had skipped town. She had said screw him if he wasn't man enough to raise his child. She said together she and I would get it done. As I prepared their breakfast I listened to her read to Eve. She hadn't lied. She had always been there for us and has been ever since my mother died. I loved her so much, y'all. I would do anything to stop her from feeling pain, no matter what.

My goal from the moment I told her about Eve had been to make her proud of me again. I needed to bring joy back into her life. Praying that the more I did that, the better her health would get. So I had picked up teaching her dance class at the center. I had convinced her not to worry about anything here at the boarding house, my two jobs would cover everything, even though they didn't come close to handling even a half of what needed to be done.

But that's okay. Since I was not working right now, tomorrow, I was going to start on the repairs that I had been reading up on how to take care of.

"You not taking my girl with you today, are you?" She asked from behind me. "With you always busy, Eve is all I got to keep me company." I shook my head.

"No, Nana, I'm not taking her with me."

"Good!" I could hear the relief in her voice.

Poor Nana, the kids had become a big part of her life. But ever since her legs had been upsetting her she hasn't been able to travel to the center. So now Eve was her only link to what her life used to be. This was actually perfect. For me to pull Operation Now You Have Me Now You Don't off, I was not going to need Eve underfoot.

"I'll be back in time to make dinner." She nodded.

"We'll be here."

After I finished making breakfast I started on lunch while they ate, making extra for Kaleb. I took my time today with his lunch, giving him double of what I made before and making sure it was very pretty. This was all a part of my diabolical plan. Instead of putting his lunch in a plastic bag like I had done last time...I put it in a basket, arranging everything perfectly, then I went upstairs to get dressed.

When I was finished I stood in the mirror admiring my work, turning around so that I could see the whole picture.

"I look good!"

And I did too. This yellow dress went so well with my bracelets. The top of the dress was made like a peasant blouse. So if I moved my arm a certain way the dress would fall off my shoulder very seductively. I smiled. *I'm ready!*

After prying a screaming Eve's arms from around my leg and promising her that I would be right back, I made my way to the shop. Making a mental note to stop by the grocery store and pick up something nice for dinner. I hated walking away from my daughter when she cried for me to take her with me. It just really made me feel like a bad mother.

Miss Thang at the desk had a whole new attitude today. As soon as I walked through the door of the shop she was all smiles.

"Good morning, Mrs. Jacobs." She called my way in a fake cheery voice. I turned to look behind me, wondering who in the world she was talking to. There was nobody behind me. I put my hand on my chest.

"You talking to me?" I asked as I approached the desk.

"Yes ma'am, Mrs. Jacobs." I frowned.

"No, dear, my last name is—"

Oh, wait a minute! My last name is Jacobs. I signed Monica Jacobs on my marriage certificate last night. She blinked up at me waiting for me to continue my sentence. I smiled at her instead. No wonder the attitude adjustment. I was the *wife* now and could probably get her fired.

Hmm... This nasty heffa was so phony. Even now, she was waiting for me to say Jacobs is not my name so her messy tail could be messy.

"Where is Mr. Jacobs?" I asked instead.

"He's in the garage, so if you go through those doors you'll find him around back." I nodded.

"And what is your name, pumpkin?" That fake smile on her face was getting ready to make it crack.

"Keisha."

"Keisha, what a pretty name. Can you run and get me some tea, dear, with a slice of lemon and honey, no sugar...? Thank you.' I didn't wait for an answer, I just headed toward the doors that led to the garage. I smiled because I could feel her hateful gaze boring a hole in my back. Oh Ms. Keisha, you and I are going to have a lot of fun.

The garage was noisy; 2Pac was playing over the loudspeaker, but you could barely hear the music due to the sound the power tools were making. And somebody was banging the hell out of something. It reeked of gasoline and oil in this part of the building. There were several stalls with classic cars at different points of restoration. I was careful where I walked, I didn't want to step in oil and ruin my red flats.

A little man slid from under the first car as I passed and looked up at me. His eyes grew wide as he took me in. He jumped to his feet.

"Wow! Pretty lady, how can I help you?" His eyes greedily raked up my body.

"I'm looking for Kaleb," I told him smiling at the silly look on his face.

"He's down at the end." He pointed with dirty fingers, his eyes still taking me in. I chuckled as I headed the way he pointed. As I passed the stalls, more of the men that did the real work around here while his highness sat in his nice comfy office in fancy suits, checked me out. I even heard one of them whistle at me.

Good!

Lady in the Yellow Dress was having the effect I had hoped for. The pounding was coming from the end stall. Someone in a dirty jumper was under the hood pounding away at something. I looked around for Kaleb, but I didn't see him.

"Excuse me!" I called to the man under the hood. He didn't hear me because he kept pounding.

"Excuse me!" I called louder. The pounding stopped and my mouth dropped as Kaleb stood from underneath the hood.

Good googly moogly!

My word!

If I thought the man looked good in a suit, it had nothing on the way he looked standing here in a dirty grease stained full body jumper that he wore only on his legs. The top part hung around his hips. He wore a dirty white tank top that lay beautifully over his muscled chest.

It was something about him covered in the evidence of his hard work that made him pure uncut temptation to me. The crazy thing about it was that I had been so caught up in finding out that Kaleb not only ran the business but also worked on the cars that I had not noticed the effect the Lady in the Yellow Dress was having on him.

He rose from under the hood, his eyes going from the top of my head slowly down my body to my red flats. He licked his bottom lip the way he did sometimes when he looked at me. And although I had just had at least five men check me out, none of them looked at me the way that he did. It was as if he saw more than my outer appearance as if he could see my inner self as well.

"Damn, shorty!" He put his dirty hand on his chest. "You look good as hell!" I grinned.

Perfect!

Chapter 8

OPERATION NOW YOU HAVE ME, NOW YOU DON'T

MONICA

"You work on the cars too?" I asked completely shocked at this new revelation. He looked at me for a moment before he shook his head slightly and chuckled bringing his water bottle back to his mouth.

"Of course he does, beautiful, he's the best mechanic in Chicago." The little man from the first car said plopping down on a stool that was sitting next to the car Kaleb was working on. He posed real GQ style while he let me know with his eyes that he was very interested in me.

"And umm, who are you, pretty lady?"

"My wife!" Kaleb growled from on the other side of me. One second the little man was sitting on the stool and the next he was hopping right up off of it.

"Okey-dokey!" was all he said before walking back toward the front of the garage to the car he was working on without even slightly glancing my way.

I raised the basket I carried.

"I brought lunch!" I made this announcement with a big bright smile on my face. He leaned back against the car and looked at me through lowered lids. The way he looked at me let me know his thoughts had become licentious.

"Did you now?"

I nodded, that bright smile plastered on my face, although my nerves were beginning to get the best of me. The way he mumbled those words reminded me of a fact I seemed to keep forgetting, Kaleb was a grown man with more experience that I could even begin to imagine. There was a good chance that what I was attempting could very well backfire on me. The seducer becoming the seduced.

His eyes slowly raked over my body before he did that thing he did with his tongue and bottom lip.

"Good timing, baby, I am pretty hungry." He spoke these words low and it seemed as if they vibrated through the base of my stomach. Oh goodness, I was losing ground before I even got started. I squared my shoulders.

Damn that!

So what if he was older than me and more experienced? Obviously, it was something about me he liked, which meant I had the upper hand. Now all I had to do was remember that and take back my control.

"Great, let's go eat." I turned to lead the way back into his office. He hadn't moved from the car he leaned against. When I got halfway across the garage I turned to look back at him over my shoulder. His eyes were glued to my hips. I turned slightly to face him, moving my leg in a way that caused the dressed to fall open exposing my thigh to him.

"You coming?"

The grin he got on his face could be described as nothing less than that of a predator. Slowly he nodded.

"Yeah, I am!" Then he stood up straight and followed me into his office.

"Let me wash up, I'll be right back." He said shutting the door behind us.

I took the time while he was in there to set everything up. Instead of putting the food on his desk I spread everything out on the table that sat in front of the brown leather couch that was off to the side of the room.

~

Kaleb

My wife was a source of constant entertainment. You just never knew what she was going to do next. It's one of the things I loved about her. For as long as I could remember my life had been full of responsibility for others. Before King took over my father's operation, my dad had lined up his six most loyal men, one of which had been King.

"You see them, son? They are your family. You always take care of your family." He had told me at the tender age of eight, just a few days before he was murdered.

"No matter what, take care of those who are loyal to you." As I stood there that night with my father, who had begun to train me up to take his place once he was gone, I knew that a change was coming. I could feel it like I felt my clothes on my body like I felt the mist that had clung to the air. A few days later someone had murdered my dad as he stepped out his car.

King took over my father's operation under the guise of finding his killer. A few months later he was married to my mother. And it wasn't long till he placed the blame of my dad's death on the other five men that stood with him in front of me and my dad that misty night and had them murdered.

Shortly after that, he had me been shipped off to boarding school. I didn't doubt for a minute that if he didn't think my death would destroy my mother, who that bastard had the nerve to genuinely love he would have had me killed as well.

Who knew that him shipping me off to school would turn out to be the best thing that could have ever happened to me? It was there I learned something about the world. It was there I learned that my people had been set up to fail. The ghetto was a self-destructing trap and it angered me. It challenged me. I could not change who I was and how I was raised. The streets were just as much a part of me as my education, so I learned all that I could.

My passion has always been cars, it is something about bringing an old car back to life that fulfills me. However, it was business I studied at MU. During my second year, I convinced King to open the restoration shop, selling him on the idea of taking his dirty money and cleaning it, the whole time remembering what my father said about family and loyalty.

You see those men that King murdered all had families and they were now my responsibility. My step-father had very little to do with the running of the business. The first thing I did was to make sure all my father's men's offspring were working. Then I used the shop as collateral and opened Mama Rita's for my mother.

And when King was murdered I took back over the family business and was able to do much more for my family. Now, most of my father's and King's men and their offspring now worked for me. I know my little empire wasn't much, but I supplied as many jobs as I could for the hood. It hadn't been easy cleaning dirty money. And with Rasheed determined to stay in the dope game just made it that much more difficult.

I rubbed the towel over my face looking at my reflection in the mirror. Stepping up to this challenge had taken its toll on me. I must admit to having some selfish reasons for tying Monica to me. She was the one thing I had *selfishly* done for me. She was everything I never had, fun and laughter, life and adventure. I have laughed more in the short time I have known her than I have done in my whole entire life. The way her mind worked was just an oddity. I have never met anybody like her.

And dear Yah, she was amazingly beautiful. Jaw dropping

gorgeous and she wasn't even aware how much so. I loved the fact that she didn't wear a lot makeup, just that shiny stuff on her lips that made me want to take her mouth every time I saw her. Her beautiful curly locs were long and surprisingly very soft. And they always smelled good, like fruit. She always smelled good. My hunger for this woman was past what was healthy.

But no matter how much I wanted to take her, I needed to curb my lust. I didn't just want to own her body, I wanted to own her mind as well. Maybe I was the monster she accused me of being because I wanted to control her completely. And I didn't care what anybody thought about it, she was mine, completely mine. She just didn't know it yet. Her body was easy. She had about as much control over her lust as I had over mine. Her mind was the challenge.

And I really enjoyed a good challenge. There was nothing in my life that had not been one. So why should my wife's mind be any different? She has got it in said mind to seduce me. I chuckled as I pulled the dirty tank over my head and put on a fresh one.

Goodness! What will this woman think of next? Don't get me wrong, that little yellow demo she had on is definitely causing everything within me that hungered for her to wake up with a vengeance. When she let it slide off her shoulder it took all my strength not to pull her to the nearest nook and taste her. She is so damn sexy.

Yeah, I'll play along for a little while. I've got to admit to being very curious to see how far she was willing to take her little game of seduction. The thought of it excited me so much so that I had to wait another few minutes to leave my bathroom.

Damn!

Monica

When he finally came out of his bathroom I had to bite my lip to keep from making a surprised sound at how good he looked. I had never seen him in jeans. They rode low on his waist showing off his perfectly muscled torso. He had changed into a clean tank but still wore his work boots. Wow! This man was so damn fine.

I sat with my legs crossed working this dress. The split left my whole leg and thigh showing. His gaze raked over my leg causing me to fill warm all over. As he walked towards the couch I couldn't help but notice his manly swagger. He sat down on the couch right next to me, so close his right side rubbed up against my left. He exhaled reclining back resting his head on the back of the sofa.

"You tired?" I asked turning my body so that I was slightly facing him giving him a better view of my exposed leg. I bit my lip when his heated gaze fell on it before he brought his big hand down to rest on my thigh very possessively.

"I am," he responded and his deep voice caused butterflies to dance inside of my stomach. Oh boy! His voice coupled with his big strong body that was at rest next to me and his warm hand palming my thigh as if he had all the right in the world to do so was causing me to feel a little nervous.

You're in control here, darling. You can do this! He's just a man, easily seducible. You just have to remain in control while making him believe you're losing control. Easy peasy!

I reached for a Tupperware bowl of fruit I cut up for him. "Maybe you shouldn't work so hard."

He chuckled. "If I don't work hard how can I take care of my family?" I opened the bowl.

"This coming from the man that criticized me for working two jobs to take care of my family."

He stared at me for a minute before he spoke, his deep midnight gaze causing me to feel uncomfortable. I didn't like the fact that it always felt as if he saw through my masquerade.

"Now I work hard so that you don't have to. I've been doing it my whole life, it's all I know."

"I understand that, but even *you* need rest sometimes." He looked at me through lowered lids. He was so at ease it looked as if each blink would be the one that sends him off to dreamland.

"I don't know about rest, but I do need food." He spoke quietly.

Oh yea! What was I doing? If this man who was my enemy wanted to work himself to death what the hell did I care?! I looked down at the bowl of fruit and picked out a piece of juicy melon that I had cut in perfect bite-size portions. I had a seduction to administer.

I held a piece of fruit to his lips.

One of his eyebrows rose. "You're going to feed me?"

I pouted. "Your hands are so dirty. I wouldn't want you to get any germs on your food." I ignored the fact that he had just gone into his bathroom and washed all the oil and dirt off of himself. I could smell the soap he had used.

"You first!" He whispered.

Oookay...

He wanted to see me eat the fruit. I could do that, I think. I forced myself not to rush in my nervousness and took my time and very slowly put the fruit in my mouth and as I chewed a little of the juice escaped from between my lips. Reaching up I went to catch it with my finger, but he took my hand stopping me.

My breath stalled out somewhere between my belly and my throat when he sat up and used his mouth to gently suck away the juice from my lips. The muscles in my stomach contracted in a painfully aware way. Then as casually as if he had just flicked away a piece of dust on my shoulder he relaxed back against the couch, watching me like a hungry lion did a gazelle. Nervously I licked my lips.

This was not going according to plan. Who was the seducer here? *That's alright, you had a little setback, you can do this, go back to the original plan.*

I picked up another piece and held it to his mouth. "Your turn." With my eyes, I dared him to eat from my hands.

It was then I learned something about Kaleb, like me, he couldn't resist a dare. Gently his big hand wrapped around my wrist.

"That is very considerate of you, baby." He said before he brought my hand that held the piece of melon to his mouth. He took the fruit from my fingers with his lips and slowly chewed it up as he smiled at me, still holding my wrist.

"That was very good, sweetheart, uh oh! It looks as if you have a little juice left on your fingers. Here, let me get that for you." He brought my fingers back to his mouth and proceeded to lick the juice off my fingers. As if under his spell I leaned in closer, watching him scandalously lick the juice off my fingers. I almost moaned as I was forced to cross my legs tighter. When he was done he let my wrist go.

Okay, I needed another plan. I handed him the bowl of fruit. It may not be wise to try and feed him again.

"Monica!" he admonished. "That's not how you feed someone fruit. Here, let me show you how it's done." He sat up and moved closer to me completely crowding my space as he leaned his big body over me.

All the alarm bells were going off in my head because I could feel myself weakening. I sat back on the couch, now good and nervous.

He took a piece of fruit out the bowl that was too big for my mouth and held it to my lips.

"That's too big, Kaleb!" I cried as he gently began to push the fruit against my mouth.

"Oh come on, be a big girl and open wide." I frowned at him.

"Come on!" He was rubbing the fruit against my lips causing its juice to stain my lips. I opened my mouth, but the melon was too big and half of it hung out my mouth. I saw his eyes flash hungrily as he lowered his head kissing me. When he sat back he was chewing on half the fruit.

Oh dang!

He continued to feed me this way until all the fruit was gone. Then he was kissing me for real, his aggressive mouth attacking mine. The way this man kissed could be considered a drug because it held you paralyzed as it had its way with you. When he broke his mouth away from mine my lips were deliciously sore and swollen. My dress had fallen so low off my shoulder that the top half of it rested just above my breast.

Gently he used his finger to trace my shoulder.

"Your skin is like honey," he spoke softly weaving me further into the trance he was masterfully putting me under.

"Can I taste you?" his question was quiet, just a whisper against my skin. Although everything within me was telling me to say no, with jerky movements I nodded my head. I thought he was going to kiss my shoulder, but his finger continued to swipe down my arm to my elbow taking my dress with it.

My heart was beating so hard I thought that maybe it will beat right out my chest. For a moment he just looked at my flesh that he had just exposed. I brought my hand up to cover myself. He stopped me looking up into my eyes.

"Why are you trying to hide yourself from me?" he whispered I looked down not able to take the intensity of his gaze any longer.

"You're making me nervous," I muttered.

"Why?"

"Because I don't look like what you see on TV," I told him. And it was true. My body was not like anything that is shown on TV or the magazines.

"No, it's not. It's so much more. I think it's the most beautiful body I ever seen." I looked up at him then and the truth of his words was there in his eyes. I inhaled as his head slowly lowered. A moan tore from my throat when he began to use his mouth to show me just how much he desired my body. His big hand made its way up my thigh.

I leaned back against the couch lost. I can't tell you how much time passed, only that it passed. The things he was doing to me had caused me to forget all about my mission. The only thing that mattered now was this fire that he had blazing inside of me, this fire that he relentlessly stroked until I felt physical pain. I needed, I needed...

He brought his head up and looked at his watch before looking back down at me.

"Sorry baby, my lunch break is over." He kissed me on my sore lips and then jumped up off the couch from where he had been holding himself up above me. I sat up on my elbow watching him, my mind was muddled. He opened the basket and took out all three of the turkey sandwiches I had made for him before unwrapping one of them and taking a huge bite out of it.

Then he turned to look down at me, still sprawled on his couch half dressed as he chewed.

"Damn girl, you sexy as hell?" he said as his eyes raked over my body.

He took another bite out the sandwich dang near finishing it off after only two bites, his eyes looking at my flesh that was still exposed to him. I could see the hunger there, so why wasn't he taking me? He turned away shaking his head.

"Damn shame," I heard him say as he left out his office.

What the world had just happened? My mind was so muddled as my body, still on fire with desire came to the realization that once again it was going to go unfulfilled. I looked down at myself. Somehow, I ended up laid out fully on the couch. I hadn't even been aware of it. The top of my dress had been lowered to my waist and the bottom of it was practically opened to my waist. The man had used my body like his damn playground.

"Damn!" I sat up on the couch fixing my clothes. The bastard had done it again.

With all the dignity I could muster, I cleaned up the basket from his lunch and left. For a while I just sat in my truck going over what had happened, trying to figure out where I had gone wrong and it came to me. My vanity had been my downfall. You see, I had vainly thought I could tangle with a shark. I thought I could sashay my way in there and tempt the creature and not get bitten.

But hadn't I known that it was dangerous to be alone with him? In my vanity, I thought that I could handle it. That had been foolish. The man was a master at manipulating a woman's body to respond exactly how he wanted it to.

I turned the key to start the truck. That's alright. I may have lost this battle but the war still rages on. Already I was formulating a different approach in my head. Operation Now You Have Me, Now You Don't was not dead yet!

I stopped by the grocery store on the way home. Tonight I would make Eve's favorite, fried chicken and mac and cheese. Maybe add her less favorite, spinach. But there really was no vegetable she cared to eat.

While I was shopping Kaleb texted me asking me what time was dinner. I started to tell him to screw him and that I wasn't feeding him, but that would just make me look like a sore loser. So I told him dinner will be done at seven and he assured me he would be there.

Before I started cooking I jumped in the shower, deciding to take mine early so that we would not have a repeat of last night. When I got out I put on a pair of my in-the-house shorts, the ones that was so short and so tight that I wouldn't dare wear them outside, but would be perfect for a little revenge. At this point, even a small victory would make me feel good.

To go with my shorts, I put on one of my tank tops, not worrying about a bra. Then I piled my locs high on my head and went downstairs to begin cooking.

Nana and Eve sat in the kitchen and talked to me while I did.

"You know, child, now that we have a male tenant, do you think it is wise for you to walk around like that?" Nana asked as she and Eve snacked on some blueberries. I shrugged, turning up the radio when my song came on and began dancing around the kitchen to the music.

"What's the matter, Nana, you don't want him to see all this junk in my trunk." I began to do a little dance with my hips. Nana put her hand over Eve's eyes as she shook her head.

"That's what wrong with this generation now. Ain't got no sense." I laughed as I began to shake my hips harder and dance around her. I leaned down and took her shoulders in my hands and kissed her hard on her cheek. She squalled with laughter.

"Get on away from me, you crazy child!" She yelled swatting at me. I dodged her swat and kissed her hard on the other cheek! She squalled again and Eve cracked up with laughter.

"Oh, come on, Nana, don't be no prude!" I cooed. Her laughter died down. She cleared her throat and slyly pointed to something behind me.

Eve said something that sounded like Dada and reached up towards the door. The hairs rose on the back of my neck as I turned to face whoever it was that had Nana's and Eve's attention.

Kaleb stood in the door with a grin on his face as his eyes lowered to my hips. In one of his hands, he held a huge bouquet of flowers.

"Please, don't let me interrupt." He walked into the kitchen and I saw in his other hand he had a couple of brown bags. The whole time his eyes greedily took in my outfit. I smiled to myself and turned back to the stove giving him a full view of my hips. Now I know this could be considered scandalous behavior, but hey, this is my husband after all, at least for the time being.

Eve continued to reach for him from where she sat in her high chair, her little face lit with excitement.

"Hey, Nana," I heard him say. Before he leaned in and kissed her on the cheek I had just kissed. Then he handed her the flowers.

"Oh Kaleb, they are gorgeous," she cried. "You've got to excuse what you witnessed when you came into the kitchen. Sometimes my granddaughter gets in these goofy moods and there is really no stopping her." He chuckled.

"I see," his deep voice was like a caress on the back of my neck. I inhaled and took the last batch of chicken out the grease. Eve yelled something at him, stretching up as far as her little arms would go reaching for him. He lifted her out of her high chair and into his arms chuckling.

"Hey, sweetheart." He gave her a loud kiss on her cheek and she squalled like Nana had done earlier. Still holding her in his arms he sat in the chair across from Nana. I heard him exhale.

"You had an exhausting day at work?" Nana asked him.

"It was a little hectic. had a stubborn bolt that had rusted on really good to an engine mount and didn't want to come off, no matter what I did. Had an unexpected inspection. My fender shipment didn't come in. They sent the wrong side panels for an 82' Mustang that should have been finished last week and I'm pretty sure somebody tried to break into my parts warehouse last night. But you know, there was a very pleasant point of my day." Nana leaned on her hand as she listened to him.

"Oh yea? And what was that, shugga?"

"Surprisingly, I had a really amazing lunch. Very mouthwatering!" I blushed as I seasoned the spinach. I couldn't believe he had just told my Nana that.

"Oh well, now that is wonderful. After all you had to go through today, you deserved to have that mouthwatering lunch." I began to choke.

"You alright, child?" Nana asked looking over at me as I drank down a glass of water trying to get myself together. I shot Kaleb an angry look and he returned a mischievous smile before turning to look back at Nana.

"You know what, Nana? I think you are right. I am going to set aside time each day to have a lunch like the one I had today."

"Good for you!" She reached over the table and patted his hand. I narrowed my eyes at him as I walked towards Nana.

"Here, let me put those in water for you," I said taking the flowers from her. Eve was busy trying to look in the little brown bag her father teasingly held in front of her.

"Deeme!" she cried trying to open his hands. He chuckled as he continued to tease her. She squealed trying to pull his thumb all the way back. Finally, he moved his hand and let her delve into the bag. She came out with a fluffy pink teddy bear. The joy that registered on her face was priceless. She hugged the soft bear crushing it in her arms.

Chuckling he kissed her cheek again. "How did you know I had a gift for you?"

"Child, Eve can spot out a present a mile away. Thank you so much, Kaleb, you are a real sweetheart." Nana told him. I put the plates on the table. Okay, so everybody got a present but me. Of course that's fine. I didn't care, I didn't really expect him to give me a gift anyway.

"Time to eat," I told Eve before lifting her out of his arms and instead of walking around the table to put her in her high chair, I stretched my body out across the table right in front of Kaleb and slid her in. I was practically in his lap.

Then in no rush to move, I pushed the bear down in her chair next to her, because there would be no taking it from her. Still, in no rush to move, I slid her plate in front of her and using my fork, began to cut her meat, making sure my butt and hips jiggled just right as I cut through that 'tough' meat.

My Nana eyed me over her glasses before she slowly shook her head astonished.

"Goodness gracious!" she said under her breath as she watched me all but lay in the man's lap. He sat back in his chair and with a wolfish grin on his face, didn't even pretend to look anywhere else.

Still shaking her head, Nana picked up her knife and fork and began to cut her meat. "Right when I think I've seen it all with this child, when I think there is nothing more she could do that would surprise me, she goes and proves me wrong." She muttered.

I stood up straight making sure to arch my back so that my breasts were right in his face. "Oh, I'm so sorry about that. How rude of me to practically lay in your lap like that." I told him.

His eyes had not risen past my chest. He licked his bottom lip the way he did whenever he was aroused.

"That's okay, no harm, no foul!" He spoke low and I could tell that my little stunt had gotten to him.

And I felt amazing. The rest of dinner was a breeze. In fact it was very pleasant. Kaleb kept complimenting me on the meal. This man was serious about his food. He ate nearly three plates. When dinner was done he even offered to help me clean up the kitchen, but Nana would have none of that.

"Oh, sweetie thanks for offering, but we got it. Won't you head upstairs and take a hot shower and just relax. A man that work as hard as yourself need to be able to come home to peace and that's what you're going to find here. We're going to take care of everything else." I looked at her over the plates I was carrying to the sink. Really now? Is that what *we're* going to do? My Nana is a trip.

Anyway, I cleaned the kitchen up with no problem and got Nana settled into bed.

"Wasn't it nice of that young man to bring us home gifts?" she asked as I tucked the covers in around her. Eve was already asleep in the bed next to her.

"Sure was." She looked at her flowers that now sat on the nightstand next to her bed.

"He's a good boy." My hand paused in fluffing her pillows.

"Nana, just because a man buys you pretty flowers don't make him good." She shook her head.

"No, it doesn't. But a man that steps up to the plate and does what needs to be done no matter how hostile the environment..."

She paused in her speech eyeing me. My mouth opened insulted. "Is not just a good man... He's a *damn* good man! And instead of being so mean to him, you should try and be nice to him. He's single, you're single...why not be together? And did you hear Eve call him daddy?" Oh, my goodness! Subject change quickly! I kissed her cheek.

"You see love in everything. I'm telling you, you read too many romance novels."

After I made sure Eve and her new pink bear were tucked in next to Nana I kissed her little fat cheek. I then bade Nana good night. Before I went upstairs I made sure the front and back doors were locked and turned the lights off.

As I was walking up the stairs two strong hands reached out and snatched me up the last few stairs picking me up clean off my feet. I screamed as my back was gently pressed against the wall and a big strong body pressed into my front, but my scream was muffled because a hand covered my mouth. I blinked my eyes trying to adjust them to the dark.

Kaleb

Although I couldn't see him I smelled him. I knew his scent anywhere, Dove soap and citrus spice. He was bare-chested. The heat coming from his big strong body bled into me. I wrapped my legs around his waist.

"Kaleb, you scared the heck out of me!" I yelled into his palm. He chuckled.

"Did you think you was going to be able to walk around in those itty-bitty shorts challenging my manhood all night and nothing was going to happen to you?" He whispered in my ear as he pressed his body up against mine.

I closed my eyes as the unfulfilled pleasure I felt earlier woke up as if it had never been asleep. He took his hand from my mouth and his lips slammed down on mine.

I gasped from the force of his hunger and his mouth took clean advantage, invading mine in a way that left me wanting and in need. His hand fisted in my hair holding my head still for his ravishment. I broke my lips away from his as I desperately drew air in my lungs. His hungry mouth went to my neck.

"I have a present for you." He whispered.

"Really?!" I couldn't keep the excitement out of my voice. So he hadn't forgotten about me. If I was honest with myself, I kind of had feelings about that.

"Did you think I would bring Eve something and Nana something and not bring you anything?"

"I thought maybe you didn't care," I whispered. He chuckled.

"Your gift is in my room, are you going to come and get it?"

I couldn't help but feel like Little Red Riding Hood being tempted by the wolf. Going into his bedroom was dangerous, but how could I not when he had a gift for me. I nodded my head and he let my feet slide to the floor before he took my hand and led me into his room. I blinked as my eyes got used to the lights. The hall had been really dark. He walked me over to the old dresser and turned me to face the mirror. Then he lifted a box he had on the dresser and opened it.

Coming to stand behind me he took a necklace out the box putting the empty container back on the dresser. Then he put a delicate gold necklace around my neck. Hanging from it were two ballerina shoes encased in diamonds. This piece would go perfectly with my bracelets. I sucked in my breath taken aback by the beauty of it as I leaned close to get a better look.

"It's beautiful," I cried. He stood behind me bigger than life. His hands rested on the dresser on both sides of me. He leaned in and buried his face in my hair smelling it. This is something he had done a couple of times now.

"Is it beautiful enough for a volunteer kiss?" he whispered close to my ear. I turned in the circle of his arm, staring up at him. He wanted *me* to kiss him. Sure, we had kissed before, but it had always been him kissing me. I chewed on my bottom lip. If I kissed him, then that would mean I am in some way happy with him. I mean, I was happy with his gift, but a kiss from me would be me admitting it.

"Just one kiss," I said holding up one finger. His unfathomable midnight gaze read me. It was like he knew my thoughts. Slowly he nodded his head.

"Just one kiss!"

I inhaled feeling more nervous than I've felt all day. This would be the first time I volunteered to kiss him. On legs that shook I stood on my toes and wrapped my arms around his strong neck. We both knew and understood the significance of this moment. Gently I touched his lips with mine. I waited for that force that was him to turn on and dominate the kiss, but he didn't. He let me lead.

I took his mouth again and again in soft swipes, moaning when the kiss deepened. It was so different from the way we kissed before, I couldn't tell which way I enjoyed more. He put his hands on my waist and lifted me so that I was sitting on the dresser in front of him, I wrapped my legs around his waist. Right then his phone began to ring and vibrate on the dresser next to me. I broke the kiss off looking down at it.

He reached for my face turning it back towards his and took my mouth again, but this time he led so it was more aggressive. I wrapped my arms around his neck pulling him closer. But then his phone began to ring and vibrate again. I broke the kiss looking down at it.

"Damn!" He growled snatching it up, looking to see who was calling.

"Ma, why you calling so late?" He answered the phone, his irritation apparent in his tone. The frown increased on his face.

"Wait! What?!...Slow down and tell me again." He listened for a moment his body growing very tense. I rubbed my hands across his chest trying to comfort him. I could hear Mama Rita saying something in a very frantic tone.

"Where is he?" Kaleb growled. Seconds later he hung up. He let my feet slide to the floor.

"Get dressed!" He told me. "I need to go beat my little brother's a**!"

Chapter 9
A GLANCE INTO HIS WORLD

MONICA

"My mother is an enabler, Rasheed throws these fits that he knows will rattle her and thus rattle me. She calls me for help, then when I get there begs me not to hurt him." Kaleb told me as we drove down Lake Shore Drive heading to the Gold Coast area.

"He still lives at home with her? How old is he?" He nodded.

"He's twenty, and yea still at home with his mommy. He's a big a$$ kid. I told my mother to kick him out a long time ago, but she won't, too afraid he'll get out there on his own and perish."

I shook my head as I leaned back against the leather headrest. On the outside looking in, you would never know Rasheed was like that. He was the big man on the block, and although young, most people feared him. Rumor has it he supplied dope for most of the sets in K-town. And the fact that Kaleb was his big brother only sealed his throne in gold.

I turned my head and looked up at him. "You're not like, going over here to put him across your knee and spank his bottom, are you?" He turned to look at me with a shocked look on his face.

"'Cause that would really freak me out. I probably would never be able to get the image out my head." He stared at me then back at the road and then back at me until he realized I was joking. I blinked at him innocently and he barked with laughter.

"Damn shorty, the stuff you say out your mouth." He shook his head chuckling. "Naw, I ain't going spank his bottom, but I might break his jaw. It all depends on what I find when I get there."

There was a two-story masterpiece called a home. If it wasn't a mansion, it had to be a mini-mansion. It being located on this side of town testified to its glory. We rode through a gate and down a long tree-lined driveway. Kaleb brought his truck to a stop in the back of Rasheed's burgundy BMW.

I would recognize that car anywhere. Whenever it rode down my block the girls perked up and craned their necks in hopes that he'd stop and ask them if they wanted to go for a ride. Just the other day I had heard a couple of the teen girls in my dance class discuss seeing him drive past the school earlier that day. In my neighborhood folks treated him like he was some kind of god, a god with a burgundy BMW with Spinner rims.

Also parked out front was the black Cadillac truck that I will also recognize anywhere because it was the one that had been the getaway car during my kidnapping. As soon as we stepped out the car, Mama Rita rushed out the house wringing her hands. She was dressed in a nightgown with a matching robe. There were unshed tears in her pretty eyes.

"Why did you go and call Tiny to come over here and deal with Rasheed? Your brother is mad as hell!" Her voice quivered.

Kaleb smiled at her as he walked around her heading towards the house. She followed close on his heels her hands were wrapped around his arm as if she was subconsciously trying to pull him back.

"What should I have done mother, allow him to tear up your house more than what he had already done?" His voice was calm as if he was speaking to her about the weather.

"Don't hurt him, he just going through some things, he just need to cool down a bit. And he didn't do much damage, just tore up the living room a bit." Something crashed in the house and Kaleb removed his mother's hands from where they were around his arm and hurried into the house. We were right behind him.

"Let me go, Tiny, I swear to God, you dead if you don't get your damn hands off me!" Tiny had Rasheed pinned up against the wall. The crash sound we heard was a painting falling that used to be there.

"You don't go nowhere 'til your brother say you do!" Tiny growled.

This pissed Rasheed off more because he began to buck his body and swing at the giant, but his arms were just too short to box with Tiny. His punches had no effect.

"Hey, baby brother, what's going on here?" Kaleb asked looking around the trashed living room as he walked in.

There were three other guys in the room with Rasheed and Tiny. G I knew, but the other two I did not. Judging by the way they were dressed, my guess was they were here with Rasheed because like Rasheed, they dressed like dope boys, expensive gym shoes, expensive jeans, gold chains, and watches. The one that was sitting on the beanie chair next to the PlayStation had a diamond Jesus piece hanging from his neck.

"Kaleb, man, get your boy 'for I put a bullet in his head!"

Kaleb chuckled. "Let him go, Tiny."

As if it was just another request Tiny let go of Rasheed allowing the smaller man's feet to once again touch the floor. With angry jerks, Rasheed straightened up his clothes.

"What's up with that? How the hell you gon' call your goons to come in my house and tell me where I can and can't go!" he snapped.

"What's up with this?" Kaleb said opening his arms indicating the mess Rasheed had made in his temper tantrum. There was broken glass on the carpet. It looked as if he had snatched pictures of the wall and threw them to the floor. There was a bookshelf toppled over. A hole in the wall that looked as if it had gotten there with the help of the young man's Jordan covered foot. It really was a shame because the house was really nice.

"First of all, this your *mama* house." Kaleb held up his hand quieting Rasheed when he was going to speak and interrupt him. "Second, you've been a busy boy, going behind my back trying to make deals. What happened? It didn't go the way you expected it to go? Is that why you having a fit?" Rasheed made eye contact with his boy with the Jesus piece. Kaleb laughed.

"What, you didn't think I was going to find out about that?" Rasheed opened his mouth to say something else, but Kaleb raised his hand quieting him again. Instead, he addressed Rasheed's boys.

"This had to be your idea, Marcus, 'cause my little brother wouldn't just outright disobey me." The guy with the Jesus piece shook his head empathically.

"Naw K, it wasn't me. Look" He held up his hands before he came to his feet. "I just take orders, I don't give em! I'm getting on out of here, 'cause I ain't trying to get in the middle of this family drama!" His other friend must have agreed because he stood too.

"Man, sit yo a**es down!" Kaleb snapped. And the men took a seat instantly.

"Kaleb!" Rasheed began but once again he held up his hand cutting him off. Causally he walked to the side table and began to take off his watch.

"Ma, won't you take Monica in the kitchen and make her a cup of tea." He said without looking up from what he was doing.

"Kaleb," Mama Rita pleaded going to stand by him. "Please baby, don't hurt your brother. Whatever he did he didn't mean it!" Kaleb looked up at her then. And for the first time since we got here, the anger was there on his face.

"How do you know that, ma?" he snapped. She jumped from the force of his voice.

"Wow! Such a splendid example you are, big brother. What? You the only one allowed to lose your temper?" Rasheed muttered.

"Nigga, look at ma house! Hell yeah, she piss me off constantly sticking up for your trifling a**! But I ain't never gon' disrespect her or damage her stuff!"

"Oh right, I forgot. You the good son. The one that can't do no wrong. What was I thinking?"

The muscle began to tick in Kaleb's cheek. "Shut up, Rasheed!" His younger brother threw open his hands and gave a sarcastic laugh.

"I'm sorry, bro, I'm sorry I continue to be your burden. If only I can die like my father then you can really be free. Free to live with your new lovely wife." Kaleb moved to go towards Rasheed but Mama Rita caught his arm.

"He only acting out like this to get your attention! Don't you see that, baby?" She pleaded with her eyes.

"No!" he snapped, snatching his arm from her. "He's got to grow up! I can't just drop everything to cater to him all the time. How much is enough?!"

"Ain't you heard, mama? He don't have time for us no more. He got himself a brand-new wife and a little girl. There ain't no room in his busy schedule for us."

"Shut up, Rasheed!" Mama Rita cried before she looked back up at Kaleb.

"I know you tired, but just talk to him. See why he acting out." Kaleb looked down into his mother's pleading eyes and I could see the battle that was raging in his head. This was a heavy burden. Rasheed reminded me so much of Man-Man. This was the same kind of stuff he took us through, but there was no Kaleb to rein him in. When he snapped Nana and I just gave him his space until he calmed down.

Kaleb exhaled before he turned to look at Rasheed's two friends, who looked as if they were on death row.

"Beat it!" He told them and they didn't waste even a minute saying goodbye. They just high-tailed it out of here.

"Tiny, G, I'm good for the night. I'll holla at y'all in the morning." Both men nodded before they too left out the front door. Rasheed sat down angrily on the couch.

"I don't know why you forcing him to talk to me. Obviously, he don't want to be here. And you keep calling him on me, so obviously you don't want me to be here either."

"Baby, don't say that!" Mama Rita cried. Kaleb rolled his eyes. "Mama love you so much."

"Ma, take Monica in the kitchen and fix her a cup of tea or something." Kaleb interrupted.

And now I saw what he meant. Rasheed said things like what he just said and Mama Rita goes overboard to assure him that he's loved. And yeah, being a huge enabler. Kaleb was so mad the pulse was throbbing in his forehead. The last time I saw that look on his face was when he was riding away in the back of a police car.

"Kaleb, wait, just—" she began. But this only seemed to anger him more.

"Now!" He yelled. Mama Rita jumped. Rasheed laughed turning to look at me.

"You bet' not ever get on his bad side 'cause he got a temper—" he never got those words out because Kaleb grabbed him and snatched him clean off the couch. Rasheed swung at him but missed. The next instant his body was flying over Kaleb's shoulder being slammed on the ground. Hard! I flinched and Mama Rita screamed running to him trying to pry his hands from his little brother's throat.

"Kaleb, take your hands off him!" She screamed.

"Look ma, look how your perfect son doing me!" Rasheed hissed through his crushed throat.

"Shut up!" Kaleb growled down at him picking his body up and slamming it back down on the ground.

"Kaleb, please! Kaleb, please let him go!" Tears were now

running down her beautiful face. He looked up at his mother his frown growing fiercer before he stood letting go of his brother's throat. Okay, this was getting crazy.

"I sure would like a cup a tea!" I told Mama Rita, it was probably good if she got out the middle of the brother's issues. She was not helping the matter any. She slightly nodded at me before looking back at Kaleb.

"Please don't hurt him!" Her tears still flowed down her cheek. Kaleb didn't say anything, he just stared down at Rasheed with a murderous look on his face. Mama Rita looked back at Rasheed and put her finger to her lip, subconsciously telling him to stay quiet so that he won't upset his big brother anymore.

I sat down in one of the chairs at the kitchen table and watched as Mama Rita with shaking hands lit a cigarette and took three pulls off before she put it down in an ashtray and put on the teapot to boil. When she was done she brought her cigarette back to her lips wrapping her other hand around her waist.

For a minute, we both just sat and listened to the brothers argue in the living room. Rasheed was loading on the guilt, accusing his brother of not liking him because he didn't like his father. As I listened I learned something else about Kaleb. He had called his mother an enabler for always giving in to Rasheed's guilt trips, but he was falling prey to them as well.

The more Rasheed apologized for being the bad seed and coming from the wrong tree, the more Kaleb assured him that he loved him and that was not the reason why he brought an end to his side of the business, whatever that meant.

"This is all my fault." Mama Rita finally spoke.

We had been sitting here so long quietly listening to what was happening in the other room that I had almost forgotten she was there. But looking at her staring off into the distance lost in her thoughts, I wondered if she was speaking to me or just thinking out loud.

"Don't be so hard on yourself. Me and my brother fought all the time. It's what siblings do." She didn't respond to what I said so lost was she in her own misery. And the words Rasheed was saying now didn't help. He was accusing Kaleb of being their mother's favorite.

"She always saying stuff like my oldest son this and my oldest son that! Kaleb has accomplished so much! And anytime she doesn't know something, it's let me call Kaleb, he'll figure it out!" I could not hear Kaleb's responses anymore.

"I drove a wedge between them." Mama Rita continued. "I had put the burden of raising Rasheed on Kaleb and they never got a chance to form a brotherly relationship, because Kaleb was too busy being Rasheed's father."

She wiped tears from her eyes and put out her cigarette. I remained quiet because it seemed as if she just needed to talk, so I encouraged her to continue with my eyes.

She chuckled without humor. "Rasheed thinks Kaleb has an anger problem, but he doesn't." She shook her head. "I know my children, he's just tired and he been tired a long time." Her voice quivered as she spoke. She took another cigarette out of her case and lit it.

"He's carried the weight of the world on his shoulders since he was a small boy and it's all my fault." Finally, she looked up, blinking at me through her tears.

"He chose you because he needs peace. He need it so desperately that he stole your freedom to get it." My eyes widened in surprise. She chuckled dryly.

"I told you I know my children. I keep a close watch on both. Kaleb has never been selfish. He has lived his whole life giving to others, except when it came down to you. You were the one thing he was selfish about." She took another pull from the cigarette. When she spoke again smoke escaped from her lips.

"I ain't no fool, young lady, I know you wasn't happy about being married to my son. But can you please do me a favor? One mother to another?" I nodded my head.

"I know I may be selfish in asking this, but now I'm desperate! If he can't find happiness with nobody else but you, can you please make him happy?" She put the cigarette out, not looking for an answer.

"I'm sorry I'm not in any condition to be a good host, but I just need to be alone right now. The next time you come, I promise to do better." She came over and kissed me on my forehead.

"Kiss my little Eve for me." She said softly and without looking back she made her way out of the kitchen and up the stairs.

Kaleb

I was afraid to write my brother off as a lost cause. I know that as soon as I did he would be dead shortly after, but he was draining me. He felt like a cancer that I could not get rid of. I loved him, I raised him. I don't want to see him die. But I could not continue playing this game that he seemed made to play.

"How you gon' just shut down my operation? Just like you I supply jobs for the hood. What all my niggas gon' do when they can't feed they family?"

"They can come to my office and I'll find work for them." Rasheed waved that away using his whole body with a look of disgust on his face.

"Everybody ain't made for no nine to five bullsh*t!"

I looked down shaking my head. Trying to hold on to my temper. My little brother was stupid. It wasn't another word that could sum it up.

"They trying to feed they family or not?" I asked. He came to a stop in his pacing, his face transforming as if he had just figured something out.

"Okay, now it make sense!"

"What?" I couldn't help the frown that came to my face. I already knew his answer was getting ready to irritate me.

"You shutting me down." He clapped his hand together. "You ain't straight unless I'm up under your shadow. What? The fifteen percent I was giving you wasn't enough? Damn, I'll make it twenty. Just don't shut me down."

See what I'm saying?

"Nigga, I don't want yo 'money. It ain't no percent that's gon' be good enough for me to be your support." I walked to stand in his face so he understood me fully. "I'm done with the dope game and so are you! Period!" He looked up at me barely holding on to his rage.

"What happened to you in jail? You changed."

I chuckled. "Change is good if you changing for the better. Maybe you should try it." He nodded his head and his eyes flashed wildly.

"You know what, big brother? I think you right!" He reached down and picked up his car keys off the table.

"Tell ma I'm moving out!" He called over his shoulder as he walked towards the door.

"Wait!" I yelled. He came to a stop without looking back.

"What you finna do?"

He turned. "I'm getting ready to prove to you and Ma that I ain't like my daddy. And I don't need to leech off another man to get paid." He turned and slammed out the front door.

"Wow!" I rubbed my hands down my face as that feeling of change settled in on me. I was at a crossroad. If I ran after him like I always did, it will never stop. If I let him go... Damn, I was almost afraid to think about what that could mean.

Monica

When I heard the front door close I came out of the kitchen. Kaleb was standing there rubbing his hand down his face in a way that he did when he was frustrated.

"Wow!" I repeated after him. "Your family is dysfunctional." He looked back at me surprised that I had come up behind him without hearing me.

"I'm a dancer," I told him. He nodded his head chuckling.

"Yeah, you are. You ready to go?" I nodded.

As we drove back down Lakeshore Drive I couldn't help but feel like I needed to do something to lighten the mood. He was so lost in his thoughts he had not even turned on any music. I turned in my seat to face him.

"Let's go to the beach!"

He frowned at me. "Tonight?"

I nodded barely able to keep my excitement off my face.

"The beaches are all closed."

I shook my head. "I know a way in."

He thought about it for a minute. "Naw, Monica we shouldn't go to the beach at night."

My excitement died. I turned back to face front smacking my lips as I did.

"Dang, I forgot that quick," I put an extra dose of disappointment in my voice.

He glanced over at me and chuckled. "What did you forget?"

"I forgot that you were old and didn't have a spontaneous bone in your body. And you know what makes it really bad? I'm married to your old not fun self!"

Okay, I knew I was laying it on thick and judging by his laughter, he saw right through what I was attempting to do. But because like myself, he couldn't resist the challenge and caved.

"What exit should I take?"

I clapped my hands together thrilled and told him how to get to the Lakeshore Drive condos. It is true all the entrances to the beach were closed, but in front of the Lakeshore condos was a bridge that led to one of the many Chicago beaches.

It was a beautiful night. The moon was huge in the sky and it cast its peaceful glow over the lake. As far as the eye could see Lake Michigan stretched out in front of us in all her regal splendor. A gentle breeze blew lifting my locs that had escaped from my bun from where they rested against my back. I turned to look at Kaleb, who was now sitting in the sand with his elbows resting against his raised knees. He was looking out across the expanse of the lake lost in his thoughts.

"Hey!" I told him squatting down next to him. "Let's go swimming."

He chuckled shaking his head. "Naw, shorty, I'm good."

"Come on, don't be no old frump frump!"

He shook his head looking at me with that look of his that told me his frame of mind had taken a carnal turn.

"You go." He lifted one of his eyebrows in challenge.

"You think I won't?"

He shook his head. "You won't."

"Ha!" I stood and kicked off my shoe before carefully taking off my bracelets and laying them next to my shoes, then I reached up and took the band out of my locs so they fell around my body. He watched me the whole time, his tongue came out and licked his bottom lip.

I smiled down at him before I took off towards the water, letting out a screech when the cold waves washed over my feet. The rush I experienced was like nothing I felt in a while. With my adrenaline pumping high I ran all the way in submerging myself underneath. It felt amazing. I stood and dipped under again before lying flat on my back floating, looking up at the moon that stared down at me.

This was peace, it was moments like these that you wanted to hold on to so that you can remember when the storm came. I thought about what Mama Rita asked me to do. Her pain was real and I felt sorry for her, but her son was my enemy. She wanted me to make him happy. Could I do that for her? If maybe just for the night. Yea, I could. Mama Rita was a hero of mine. It was the least I can do.

There was a little child's pail floating not too far from me in the water. I filled it up and stood slowly walking out the water with the pail behind my back. My clothes clung to my body. Kaleb's eyes raked over me. He was so caught up into looking at my shirt clinging to my breasts that he didn't notice I held something behind my back.

He had taken off his boots and socks so his feet could enjoy the sand. Perfect! When I stood just in front of him I smiled down at him. It was then he realized I was up to something but it was too late. I doused him with the water. His mouth opened in surprise. He held up his hands.

"Sucka!" I yelled laughing at him as he got to his feet water dripping from his face and shirt. He took off his watch and put it on the sand next to my jewelry and our shoes. And it was then I saw the intent in his eyes. I turned to run, but I didn't make it far before I felt his strong arms wrap around me. A squeal ripped from my throat when he scooped me up off my feet and ran with me towards the water.

"Kaleb, wait!" I screeched, but it was too late. He walked in knee deep and tossed me into the water. Then he turned and walked back towards the shore. Oh hell no, I don't think so, buddy. I ran behind him and jumped on his back, the water from my body wetting him up the rest of the way. He yelled out when my cold body touched his back.

Right then I bucked back causing us both to crash into the water, after that it was on and popping. He stood and then dove in taking out my legs. I put him in a headlock and tried to take him under, but he was too strong and ended up lifting me and dunking me under again. But I didn't let go of his neck and he went under with me.

I got such a thrill wrestling with him in the water. I can't remember the last time I had so much fun. And judging by how much he got into our play, laughing and trying to take me under the water, I would say that he too was having an enjoyable time. It's hard to believe this is the man that so many men feared. I remembered the look on Rasheed's friends' faces. They thought they were goners. And yet, here was the same man playing in the water with me as if we were two kids.

Seconds later he proved my thoughts true. I was clinging to the front of him. With my legs wrapped around his waist and my arms wrapped around his neck tightly, waiting for him to try and dunk me under because I was going to take him with me. But he didn't, instead, he settled down in the water looking at me with a grin on his face, then slowly the grin disappeared.

"I can't believe I let you bait me into this water." He said quietly.

I bit my bottom lip so that my grin wasn't too cheesy. I was really proud of myself. I had baited the mob boss into frolicking in the water.

"Did you have fun?" I asked, just wanting to hear him say the words.

He chuckled. "Yeah, I did!"

I did a little jig in his arms now super proud of myself. He laughed at me shaking his head. Right then a light flashed at us. With both looked back towards the shore.

"Dang it!" I muttered because standing there by our stuff flashing a light at us was a police officer. Kaleb turned to look back at me. I half grinned, half frowned.

"Oops!" was all I could say.

As we walked out the water Kaleb looked down shaking his head. I even heard him chuckle. He was probably beating himself up for listening to me. Hey, at least the cop was black, maybe he will show us mercy.

"Were you two aware that the beach is closed?" the officer

asked. Oh goodness! He sounded mean. Dang it, we were going to jail.

"Umm, yes sir. "Kaleb said bending down to pick up his watch and my jewelry which he handed to me.

"And yet you still decided to come for a swim?" Kaleb looked down and chuckled. I smiled because he was still having fun. He opened his mouth to say something to the officer but he cut Kaleb off.

"Wait a minute! Don't you own King's Restoration?"

Kaleb turned to look at me on the sly and winked before he turned back to the officer. I put my hand over my mouth to stop my laughter. Who knew he was capable of being this silly.

"Yes sir, have you got some work done with us?" He asked with a grin on his face. At this point, he was barely holding on to his laughter. The officer's whole face lit up.

"Man, I've been on the waiting list for about six months. I call every week to see if you got a spot open for me!"

Kaleb chuckled. "You know what? Something just opened up for Monday morning!" The last of his words came out as a laugh

The officer clapped his hands together. "Yessss!"

And then he must have remembered he was on duty because he straightened up erasing the grin from his face.

"You to go ahead back to your car and next time no swimming after eight." Kaleb nodded grabbing my hand.

"Thank you, sir!"

"And I'll see you Monday." The officer called to our backs. Kaleb laughed before holding up his index finger.

"Monday!" he called without turning around.

When we were out of earshot, I burst. I could not hold back my laughter anymore. Still chuckling Kaleb walked around the car to the trunk. He pointed at me.

"You... are a trouble maker!" I put my hand on my chest, opening my mouth in feigned shock.

"Me!"

"Yeah, you!" he laughed as he popped the trunk. I went to open the passenger side.

"Naw, shorty, you can't get in my car wet."

He paused giving me a sorry look before he pulled out a packet of tank tops, using his teeth to open them. Then he pulled out a new pack of boxers opening them the same way. Next, he pulled out a pair of jeans before reaching up and undoing his wet jeans. He slid them and his boxers down his leg. I was so glad his t-shirt was big or else I would be here blushing like crazy. He slid on a pair of clean boxers and the pair of dry jeans, then he reached up and snatched his wet t-shirt over his head before sliding the tank top over his head.

"Umm, what am I supposed to change in?"

He shrugged. "I don't know. I always keep a change of clothes in my car."

I folded my arms. "How is that going to help me?"

Once he slid his feet back in his boots he picked up his wet clothes and tossed them in the trunk. Before he came around his car to my side and leaned against it staring at me. He still wore a grin on his face only it was now accompanied by that thing he did with his tongue and his bottom lip.

"I don't know how that's going to help you, but you got to figure something out. If you get in like that you going to mess up my seats." He blinked up at me like he was really concerned.

"Well...do you have something in there for me to wear?"

The wolfish grin on his face grew. "I might!"

I fingered the diamond ballerina slippers on my necklace, I had to bite my bottom lip again because my grin was too cheesy.

"Can I have it?" I shivered for good measure. He went back to his trunk opening it. He took one of the tank tops out the bag and a pair of boxers, tossing them to me before he closed his trunk.

"That's all I have."

I put my hand on my hip. "You expect me to ride all the way home in your underwear?"

He leaned back against the car facing me, that devious grin on his face.

"This can't be the same girl talking who just convinced me to swim in Lake Michigan at eleven o'clock at night."

Oh okay, I see where he was getting at. If he thinks I was scared he had another thing coming.

"Okay!" I told him reaching in to grab his arm pulling him up from the car. "I need your big body to block for me."

Although it was dark and there wasn't anybody else in sight. I wasn't taking any chances. He came to stand on the other side of me, trapping me between his body and the car, but he was facing the wrong way. I folded my arms looking up at him.

"Turn around!" He chuckled shaking his head as he put his hands on the car on both sides of me, trapping me in the circle of his powerful arms. He leaned in close invading my space. Gently he rubbed his lips and nose just underneath my ear, giving me a feather-light kiss. A shiver went through my body and I gasped from the unexpected feel of pleasure.

"Naw, shorty, I can't do that. I told you, I'm not going to let you hide your body from me." The feather-light touches of his lips turned into a gentle hungry mouth kiss on my neck. My heartbeat accelerated along with the awakening of my unfulfilled lust.

"You're mine, you gon' have to get use to that fact as well as me looking at your body because there ain't no sight in this world more beautiful to me."

I closed my eyes as a little moan escaped my lips. The way he was kissing on my neck was causing me to remember what took place earlier in his office. He raised his head looking down at me and I think I was going to drown in his intense dark gaze.

"Be a big girl and show daddy what he starving to see."

His whispered words were more potent than his kiss. I bit my lip extremely nervous, but I couldn't help the exciting power I felt at the hunger I saw in his eyes. I couldn't help but wonder how his look would change if I took off my clothes in front of him. I grabbed my wet shirt, my gaze never looking away from his and slowly lifted it over my head.

His ravenous eyes lowered to my breasts that could be seen clearly through my wet bra and that sense of empowerment grew inside of me. He licked his bottom lip.

"So damn beautiful," he whispered. I stood for just a second allowing him to look at me, but then I lost my nerve and quickly put the tank over my head. The rest went very fast. I stepped out of my wet jeans and then into his dry boxers, then I smiled up at him.

"Done!" My voice was super cheery because I was super nervous.

He was in no hurry. He took his time looking at me. Because his t-shirt was really big and I had on a wet bra that caused it to cling to me a bit, it was quite scandalous. The boxers were big but not to the point of falling off of me. I may not have much up top, but I did have butt and hips.

"Can you open the door? You making me nervous." My voice shook slightly.

I don't know why I just admitted that to him, but he was. It was so dark out here and he was so big. He oozed power, it was almost overwhelming. He chuckled reaching past me for the door handle, but the way he did it caused his arm to rub up against my chest. I tried to back up but there was nowhere for me to go, his body was blocking me. I was good and trapped in his arm.

"Aren't you going to give me a kiss for giving you a pair of my underwear?" he mumbled. I laughed. Oh my goodness! He was a mess. He grinned down at me raising his eyebrow to let me know he was serious.

"You would take advantage of me this way?" I whispered.

He nodded. "I would."

There was no shame in his tone, his hungry gaze had lowered to my lips. Nervously I licked them as I looked off into the darkness before turning back to look at him.

"Fine—" I barely got out before his lips were on mine. His

aggressive mouth seemed to steal my will away. I moaned as he deepened the kiss pinning my body up between him and the truck. At some point, my feet left the ground as he lifted me so that he could have better access to my mouth. The sound of a police horn interrupted us. We looked up and the officer that had told us to leave the beach flashed his lights at us telling us to move on.

Kaleb opened the door for me, still using his big body to shield mine from the officer. I slid in and exhaled when he shut the door closing me into the darkness of the car. He waved at the officer as he picked my clothes up off the ground. As he stopped by the trunk to toss mine in with his, the officer rode past yelling, "See you Monday," out his window.

When we got home I hurried to get to the shower first. Once out I dressed in a pair of old gym shorts and a t-shirt, then because I wasn't quite sleepy yet, I went downstairs and laid on the couch. It had been a while since I enjoyed a good movie. Normally by the time I got home from work, I would be too tired to do anything outside of showering.

I turned on the TV and was thrilled to see The Color Purple playing as a late-night movie on channel nine. This was my favorite movie. About fifteen minutes later Kaleb plopped on the couch and had the audacity to half lay on me, resting his head in my lap. The way that I laid with my leg up over the back of the couch kind of made the way he lay his head very indecent.

"Umm, what are you doing?" I asked, not sure of what to do.

Should I push him off of me or just chill? The lines were starting to get blurred on the way I should be acting toward this man that was my enemy. I got to admit him laying on me kind of felt nice.

"Watching a movie." He muttered sounding as if he was already half asleep.

I looked down my body at him. He was dressed in a pair of black jogging pants but nothing else so his big muscled back literally lay between my legs. His strong arm draped over my thigh. And his eyes were halfway closed.

"You like The Color Purple?" I asked quietly, gently putting my hand on his head. Slowly I began to rub it.

"Hell no!" He muttered.

I chuckled as for the first time in my life I rubbed a grown man's head. He must have liked it too because moments later, he was out. I thought about Mama Rita saying how tired he was. It was true, he went to sleep almost instantly. I don't know how much of the movie I watched after that, but it wasn't long till I too succumbed to the beckoning of my eyelids as well.

Chapter 10
DISCOVERING HIM

MONICA

"Child, sit down and eat!" my Nana said as I put Kaleb's plate in front of him. This will be the first time he actually had breakfast here. Today was Saturday and he had taken off work so that we could go to Stormy and Shelomoh's house for the Sabbath Day. I was kind of looking forward to this because I was really curious about his and Shelomoh's relationship. How in the world had a guy like Shelomoh, who I had looked at as a superhero since I was a little girl get involved with a gansta from the hood?

"Nana, I'm okay. You know I don't like eating in the morning." I picked up Eve's toast and smeared a little jelly on it.

"Breakfast is the-"

"Most important meal of the day!" I finished for her. "You tell me that every morning."

"And yet you still manage to skip it every morning!"

Kaleb's phone rang. "Yeah," he said in the receiver as he forked a load of eggs in his mouth. I turned to the sink getting ready to start the dishes.

"Monica," his deep agitated voice came from behind me. I turned to look back at him confused as to why he was talking to me and whoever it was on the phone at the same time.

"Get you a plate, eat!" was all he said before he continued explaining to the person on the phone why he wasn't coming into the shop on their busiest day of the week. I opened my mouth to tell him that he couldn't tell me what to do, but before I could say anything, he shot me with a look that made my hand fly to the nearest empty plate and pick it up.

"Now, eat!" he snapped and brought his big finger down on the table in front of my empty chair. And even the thunk of it screamed *don't mess with me right now 'cause I ain't in the mood*. I didn't know if he was irritated with me or the person he was talking to on the phone. But either way, an agitated Kaleb is an intimidating thing. And I ain't no fool, I've made it this far by learning how to pick my battles.

I didn't want to look but I could feel my Nana's gaze drilling a hole in the side of my face. Hesitantly, I peeked at her...she had a little satisfied smirk on her face as she all of a sudden got busy cutting her turkey bacon with her knife.

I exhaled loudly and ignorantly before turning to the stove and piling food up on my plate. He may have intimidated me into eating, but I didn't have to like it.

"Nobody even cuts bacon with a knife, so you can stop pretending." I hissed at my Nana, irritated with the look she had on her face. She had the nerve to pick up her coffee cup and take a sip, looking at me with her raised eyebrows straight up Kermit the Frog style. I rolled my eyes at her and mean mugged Kaleb, but he was paying us no never mind. The frown had intensified on his face.

"I pay you to handle these situations. Damn, y'all can't do sh-" he caught himself looking up at Nana.

"Nothing, without me there. Just leave the damn Malibu, I'll have to come in tomorrow and handle it. And Tony, make sure you don't call me again today!" He hung up the phone and placed it angrily on the table.

"I must of have been crazy to think that I would be able to be out of the shop on a Saturday. This the main reason I almost told

Solomon that I couldn't come through today." As he spoke, he piled his eggs and bacon up between his toast and took a massive bite, chewing angrily with his powerful jaws.

"Well, the devil wouldn't be no good at his job if he didn't do the best he could to stop you from keeping the Sabbath day Holy." What? I paused in taking a bite out of my toast and looked at Nana surprised.

"What you know about the Sabbath day?"

She chuckled. "You think you the only one Stormy and Shelomoh been preaching to? But unlike your highness, I stopped for a minute and listened." I frowned as I chewed. What did she mean, unlike me? I listened, I mean sure, I got busy and it kind of got pushed to the back burner. But what black person born here in this country would not want to know where they came from?

I have been meaning to look further into some of the things Stormy had told me, like how the slaves that were brought here to America and the Caribbean were from a tribe called Igbo. And how the Igbo people was hated by the African tribes surrounding them because it was well-known that they were a different people with different customs, which was also the reason those tribes helped the Muslims and Europeans capture and take the Igbo into slavery.

When she told me that, I remembered that Keturah and I had gone to the slave exhibit at the DuSable Museum and had read a real flyer that had been preserved since 1804 and sure enough, it read Igbo Men, Women and Children for sale, proving what Stormy said to be true. But because I was always at work, the research that I had planned on doing got pushed to the back burner.

Note to self: Find out about the Igbo and their customs. If that was the tribe we came from, then of course I wanted to learn all I can about them. Growing up in school, we learned about many different nations of people and their culture and I often wondered why we were the only group of people whose history started with slavery. When I was a little girl, I thought that the first black person born had been born a slave, then I learned that we were from Africa, but there were so many different groups and tribes of people in Africa, I always wondered which tribe we belonged to.

And now that I had been forced by a bully to stop working, I might as well take advantage and find out all I could about the tribe our people came from.

Eve climbed down out of her high-chair and up into her father's lap. Goodness! She had taken to doing that more often. Nana's gaze was extra speculative as she looked at the two. I cleared my throat drawing her attention.

"So, you believe what Stormy and Shelomoh say about us being cursed?" She shrugged.

"It makes sense to me. I have always wondered why we seem to end up at the bottom of the barrel, no matter how high we think we've climbed. Hell, you got people born in third world countries that say to themselves, "It could be worse, we could have been born a nigga." She shook her head.

"In my day, we couldn't wait to run the race. We just wanted a fair chance. But what would end up happening is, we were told to stand at the starting line, then somebody would come along and tie our shoes laces together. And when we'd reach down and try to untie them, so we didn't trip and fall we were hunted down and murdered 'cause that was considered poor sportsmanship coming from a nigga. So, we'd line on up and get ready to run the race anyway, knowing that it wasn't fair while looking to the side at our white running mates."

"Of course, they'd have on brand spanking new running shoes that were not tied together like ours. They could stretch their legs out and run fast and free. And if you fell, you better not say it was because your shoe laces were tied together, 'cause then, they'd point their fingers at you and yell that you were just too lazy and too slow and just flat out too dumb to run the race." All though they didn't fall, tears came to her eyes as she spoke. She stared off into the distance, lost in her past.

"I'd look around at these people and they would intentionally avoid looking down at my tied shoes laces. And no matter how hard I tried to show them, they would say, 'Stop whining, nigga, you just want a handout. You don't want to run the race fair and square like the rest of us.'" One of the tears escaped her eyes. I had heard her stories of struggle my whole life. Even Madam Queen had told me how amazing of a dancer my grandmother had been. And how many times she was passed up simply because she was black.

"We always have to be smarter, stronger, wiser...just to get to that starting line." Kaleb, who had been silent as he listened to her muttered. His earlier irritation had disappeared to be replaced by a look of reserve.

"When Shelomoh first told me our people was cursed, something resonated in me. I too often wondered how in the world black people were being allowed to be treated this way. It seems that it was some hidden force out there holding us down. But the way in which it is done is so subtle. It's so calculated that it is outright brilliant." He moved his knife away from Eve's reaching fingers before he continued.

"Not much has changed sense your day, Nana, except for the fact that most of our youth don't even bother trying to run the race that will require them to win against all odds. Instead, most of them choose to run other races, races where there is only a proverbial finish line, fed to us through music videos and "Black reality TV". But it's a trap and there are no winners. They're made to believe that they're lazy and stupid." He shook his head getting lost in his own thoughts.

"I know these guys, they're not lazy and they are far from stupid, so why can't they rise?"

"Close your mouth, child." Nana said putting her finger under my chin. I snapped my mouth shut without looking away from Kaleb.

What the Hell?!!!

I had never heard him speak this way. Oh, my goodness, I think he had just turned me on. I picked up the newspaper he had been reading while I made breakfast and fanned myself. What the world? What kind of Mob boss thought this way? He had been surprising me more and more each day.

The other evening while we were eating dinner, Tiny brought a man by that was down on his luck. He came to Kaleb in tears begging him to help him get out of the ditch he had unwisely dug for him and his family.

Kaleb listened patiently as the man explained how he wanted to get out of the dope game, but he had a wife and four kids and he could not afford to work at McDonald's and still take care of his family. But he didn't want to go to jail because his children needed him.

"What can you do?" Kaleb asked once the man was finished pouring his heart out to him. Instantly, he pepped up at Kaleb's words.

"Well, I've got some training in carpentry. I'm not bad with a nail and hammer." Kaleb nodded and made one phone call, getting the man an interview the next day with somebody he knew that built houses. I had been surprised by his generosity. Never once did he degrade him or make him feel like he was less than a man. However, he did give what most people would consider something of a threat.

"I'm putting my name on the line for you. Don't tarnish my image," was all he said.

But the man was all smiles as he nodded his head assuring him that he will make him proud. Now, I'm not a nosy person, observant at most—and one of the things I have observed is that Kaleb's phone rang nonstop. He literally has to turn it off when he sits down at the table to eat, but most of the calls are people looking for work. And I have never heard him turn anyone down, he finds them something. If not working for him, then working for what he calls a *good friend* of his.

He's like the Godfather of the freaking hood. I was beginning to think that everything I originally thought about him was wrong and that maybe he had not ordered the hit on my brother after all. Amazingly, I had never even asked the man if he had done it or not, I just accused him of the crime.

Oh, my goodness!

What if he hadn't done it? What if I had set him up for nothing and he was in fact innocent? I then treated him like complete trash upon his release. My hand flew to my mouth. Oh, dear Yah! I never even considered the fact that he could have been innocent.

"Why are you looking at me like that?" He asked, pulling my plate that I had not touched in the last ten minutes in front of him where he began to polish off my leftovers.

Oh goodness. I was getting ready to freak out!

"What's wrong, child?!" Nana asked reaching for my hand. I stood from the table pushing my chair in.

"Nothing," I mumbled before turning to the sink and submerging my hands in the dish water. As I washed the dishes, my mind raced. Could it be possible he and I could have a real relationship? There was no denying the fact that he was dripping fine and had a banging body. And his mind! The way his mind worked was beginning to have more of an effect on me than his body.

Okay, confession time.

Ever since I was a young girl, maybe twelve or thirteen, I have had a thing for Malcom X. Wheew! A smart thug or what most people would call a thug. I call them warriors, have always been something I found very attractive. Malcom embodied all of that for me and those glasses. Mmm mm mm, let's just say that listening to Kaleb speak a minute ago had roused up some feelings.

It was more to him then what I thought. And for the first time, I was considering giving our marriage a try. The only thing that was standing in our way was rather or not he was behind Man Man's death. I am going to ask him tonight after we get back from Stormy and Shelomoh's house.

As soon as we arrived at their house, Stormy took Eve out of my arms. Eve squealed as she began to kiss under her fat cheeks. Stormy and Shelomoh had only one son and joked about being denied a daughter. So, whenever Eve was around, Storm spoiled her ridiculously.

"Hey Shalom, Ach," Shelomoh said as he clasped hands with Kaleb before he took the pan of lasagna I had made from him.

"Shalom Ach, thanks for inviting us over."

"Man, it ain't no problem we're glad y'all came by."

"Nana said to make sure you send her a plate because she knows you got down in that kitchen." I told Storm and she laughed.

"You know I did and of course, I will make sure Ima has a plate. Y'all come on in and have a seat." Stormy and Shelomoh's house was nice. It was big like my Nana's, but that is where all the similarities ended. Where the boarding house was run down and in serious need of repair, Shelomoh and Stormy's house could be featured in the Ghetto version of *Look at That House*.

I used to love coming over here to babysit their sons, Benyamin and Yahudah. They had all the cable channels and kept a fridge full of food. And yeah, Storm did her thang in the kitchen. She cooked like one of the grandmamas that always had a good pot stewing on the stove. Well, most of the grandmamas. When my Nana should have been learning how to cook, she was dancing. So that pretty much left me to learn how to cook or us starving.

And guess where I had come to learn. You got it, Stormy's house.

"Monica!" Yahudah yelled as he barreled down the stairs and wrapped his little five-year-old arms around my waist.

"Hey man! I missed you so much!" I kissed his little cheeks and pinched them. He was so handsome, he looked like a miniature version of his father. And he's smart like him too.

I sat on one of the love seats and was secretly thrilled when Kaleb sat next to me. I know that sounds goofy, but now that there was a chance that he had not killed my brother and that he and I could actually be together. I was experiencing all of those little corny relationship firsts with a new heart.

Like, this was the first time we visited a friend's house and sat right up underneath each other like couples do. Yay!

Stormy brought a tray of sandwiches out. Shelomoh, who was just sitting in what Stormy and I called Shelomoh's old man chair saw her and jumped back to his feet.

"Here, baby let me get that for you! You know Saff said you can't be lifting heavy stuff in you condition." My hand froze from where I was taking Eve's sipping cup out of the diaper bag.

"Your condition?" Eve who was sitting on her dad's lap waiting for her cup whined to let me know to get my hand moving. I handed her the cup, but I never took my eyes off of Storm. She smiled at me and put her hand on her stomach.

"Oh, my goodness! Are you pregnant?"

"Kayn!"

I screamed and jumped up from the couch running to wrap my arms around her. She and I both did a little happy dance.

"How far along are you?" I asked putting my hand on her still flat stomach.

"Only about three months."

"That is great!" I hugged Shelomoh. "I'm proud of you, man! I thought you was too old to still have kids?" He narrowed his eyes at me and with a smirk on my face, I blinked innocently at him.

"I got your too old," he threw back at me before he reached up and ruthlessly ruffled my hair.

I screeched! "Shelomoh! Dang it, you messed up my hair!" And he did too. When I turned back to look at Kaleb, he was trying not to laugh while indicating that my bun that I had spent dang on near all morning putting up, was now hanging off to the left.

"Shut up!" I huffed as I sat back down next to him. That caused him to chuckle more.

We had a really nice time. And believe it or not, I learned some more thing about my husband that left me speechless. My first surprise had been before we even came in the house. When we got out of his truck and he went to the trunk to take out the pan of lasagna. He also pulled out a bookbag that actually looked used.

"Is that yours?" I had asked as we walked up the stairs. He looked down at me as if my question was strange.

"Umm, yea! Why do you ask?" I shrugged.

"It ain't every day you see a mob boss with a book bag. I mean we know you're street smart, but book smart?" I scrunched up my face a bit and shook my head. He came to a stop looking down at me as if I had just insulted him. I held my head back and laughed as I continued up the stairs without him.

Now my second surprise came when he and Shelomoh got to talking scriptures and he actually opened his book bag and pulled out a Bible and a notepad...and get this, both had been well used.

"You have a Bible?" I asked sitting a bottle of water on the coaster next to him. He picked up the bottle and opened it, the whole time, he was giving me a look as if I was once again asking him a strange question.

"Yea, why you ask?" He said after he drank like half the bottle down in one gulp. I shrugged my shoulders.

"I don't know, it ain't every day you see a Mob boss carrying around a Bible." That made Shelemoh, who was sitting on the other side of the table with his Bible and notebook open chuckle. Now I'd like to say that was the last time my husband completely floored me, but it wasn't.

After the sun had gone down and Shelomoh and Kaleb had put up their Bibles, Stormy and I had come into the living room in the middle of them arguing over whose alma mater was the best.

"Close your mouth, dear!" Stormy said putting her finger under my chin. As I snapped my mouth closed, I looked at her, completely taken aback by the deju vu moment. But I couldn't focus on that, hearing him speak of his fellow alumni left me floored once again.

"You're a college graduate?" I asked as I sat down next to him on the couch. Shelomoh just shook his head chuckling to himself.

Later that night, I lay in my bed. In my hand was one of the bracelets he had given me on our wedding day. Gently, I traced his name with my finger as I played all the things I had learned about him today over again in my head. He actually had a Bible, one that he reads. He had a notepad with questions he had written down to ask Shelomoh.

"I was reading in Numbers chapter 25 verse 16," he had said. "And it said that Balaam had showed the Moabites how to weaken the Children of Israel by causing them to act treacherously against Yah. And then in Revelations chapter 2, verse 14, it said that there are some among you who hold to the teaching of Balaam, who taught Balak to entice the Israelites to sin, so that they ate food sacrificed to idols and committed sexual immorality. What does that mean?" Shelomoh looked surprised at first.

"Wow, Ach! You eating up these scripts, that there is an upperclassman question." Kaleb chuckled, nodding his head as if to modestly say that's because he was an upperclassman.

"One of our biggest enemys is the tribe of Edom. "

Kaleb frowned. "You mean *was*?"

Shelomoh shook his head. "Naw, Ach...I mean, *is*."

"How is that possible?"

"The blood remembers." Kaleb nodded his head understanding him. I was amazed because I was lost. I had no idea what they were talking about. Who is Edom? And how were they our enemy today? Goodness, I felt left out and I didn't like the feeling.

"Baalam was a great wizard, so great that he knew and understood where the true power lies. He was never fooled. But like Ha Shatan himself, he felt slighted and chose to seek vengeance against Yah's chosen. In that day, they could not stop our people. Word had spread over the whole earth about us. We were feared everywhere we went and nobody could figure out why we were so powerful. It was Baalam who showed our enemy how to weaken us. And it's the very things that's still implemented today to keep us separated from Yah." Kaleb nodded his head taking in the information that Shelomoh was giving him, understanding what to me, sounded like a riddle.

I looked up at Stormy and she jerked her head in a way to tell me to meet her in the kitchen. I excused myself from the intense study session, but I doubt if they even noticed, so focused were they on each other.

"What is that all about?" I asked her as soon as I walked through the door. "Who the hell did I marry?"

"Shhh!" She grabbed my shoulders, looking me directly in the eye.

"Okay, I have to tell you something, but you have to promise me you're not going to freak out." I inhaled. I could tell by her gaze that she was getting ready to rock my world, but I braced myself and nodded.

"You are the wife of a very special man."

I shook my head at Stormy. "You know I'm surprised at you. I would expect the girls in my dance class to be impressed with drug kingpins, but you Storm—?" I just shook my head again.

She shook my shoulders. "Girl, forget that, being a kingpin is nothing! Shelomoh told m, that Yah had chosen Kaleb to be one of his warriors." I blinked at her. She said that like I was supposed to understand what the heck that meant.

"Stormy, can you simplify that just a bit?!" I didn't mean to snap at her. But I was being introduced to a side of Kaleb that I had no idea existed. I mean, I knew he was a mob boss, but he actually had a brain in that head of his, a very impressive one at that. The intensity in which he and Shelomoh were studying was blowing my mind away. I had never seen anybody study scripture like that. They sat facing each other, their heads only feet apart. It was like Shelomoh was a crash course and Kaleb was a sponge, no, a vacuum sucking it up.

"He has been chosen to fight in a very special battle!" I started to get a weird feeling.

"Battle? What kind of battle?" She looked at me for a while before she spoke again.

"I'm speaking of the Exodus." I opened my mouth to ask her what the Exodus was, but she shook her head cutting me off.

"Some things are not as simple as to tell someone. I can't tell you what the Exodus is because you won't understand." She pointed towards the living room.

"But your man knows and he understands more than you can imagine. So, if I were you, I would stop being stubborn and learn all that I could from him. Because we are running out of time." I was speechless. How could she say that about me? I was not stubborn. She didn't know Kaleb, not like I did.

Really, Monica? After all the surprises you got today, you can say that? Really?

"Soon he's going to take him to meet Lyon!"

"Lyon?" I asked wondering if I had heard her wrong. She nodded.

"Lyon, little sista..."

Okay, I eased down into a chair at the kitchen table. She sat down across from me with a worried look on her face.

"Wha—what does that mean?" I was so confused. Lyon was a legend. He was the man everybody lied and said they knew. I had seen him only once. He had come to the center to see Shelomoh and I had stood there like a groupie, staring at him in shock. He had walked past me and chuckled at the spectacle I was making of myself.

"Shelomoh is taking Kaleb to be trained by Lyon." Stormy said breaking through my memory. My mouth dropped open. That was huge!

"Are you kidding me, Kaleb? Why, ho—how?" I couldn't even get my thoughts out clearly. She shrugged.

"It's Yah's will." I put my hand to my mouth as the fullness of what this meant settled in on me. Lyon was not only a legend, he was also a folklore. There were rumors going around that he was not human. Some people say he is an avenging angel that had chosen to live on earth and not just any place on earth, but the ghetto. And the government had been trying to kill him, but every time they get close, something bad happens to them. It's said he's protected by Yah himself.

I don't know how much of that is true, but I do know that nobody gets close to him unless he invites them. Word around town is that he is the best MMA fighter in the world and fighters from all over wanted to get into the Lyon's Den to train with him, famous men, men that were already title holders. But again, only the ones that he invites are allowed and most of the time are not the famous men. Most of the time it's men that nobody has ever heard of.

Now, that was what the outside world knew about him. Because I was so close to Stormy and Shelomoh, I had managed to get a glimpse of the inside workings of the Lyon's Den. Although technically, I had never been there. Still, I had overheard Stormy and Shelomoh talking many times about some things that goes on there. When I was a little girl, I overheard them talking about some damage he had done to some cars with just his fist while he was chasing after his wife, who at the time had been trying to leave him.

Shelomoh said his father, who had also been named Shelomoh and had been an attorney as well, had a tough time trying to get the city off their back about the incident. They ended up paying the city a lot of money to make them go away.

I don't know if Lyon is really an avenging angel, but I do know there is something different about him. He's not an ordinary man. And there is something different about his son Dawid too. And not to mention Gideon, the black man that spoke Spanish and his dangerously handsome white-haired son. Heck, there was something different about that whole Lyon's Den crew. And now Shelomoh was taking Kaleb over there. So, did that mean there was something different about Kaleb?

Once again, I had the strong feeling that everything I thought I knew about my husband was wrong. And as if to prove that point, we heard the furniture being moved. We went back into the living room just in time to see Shelomoh hand Kaleb a sword. I think this is when my biggest shock of the evening came in because he began to work that sword like damn Bruce Lee. Shocked I looked at Stormy who gave me the I told you so smirk.

Goodness, it had all been a bit much. And as I lay here in my bed, I couldn't help but feel left out. Kaleb's destiny was to be a warrior for Yah and fight in the Exodus. What the world did that mean? Stormy said somethings could not be explained, only learned. She also said that Kaleb could teach me. I wanted to know.

With my mind made up, I got up out of my bed and placed my bracelet back on my dresser. Quietly, I walked to my door that I didn't bother to close and saw that Kaleb's light was still on in his bedroom. He had not closed his door either. Suddenly I felt nervous. Kingpin Kaleb had been intimidating. Warrior of Yah Kaleb almost felt untouchable.

I tiptoed across the hall and peeked my head in his door.

Oh Yah!

I nearly drooled on myself. He was lying shirtless in his bed, with only a pair of basketball shorts on reading his scriptures. Lying next to him on the bed was his notepad. And get this, on his face was a pair of glasses. Glasses, y'all!

He looked up at me and smiled and I nearly turned into a puddle of pudding right where I stood.

"Hey, you," he said as he finished writing something.

"Hey." I stepped into the room. I didn't know what to say, so I opened my mouth and proved how big of a dork I was.

"I didn't know you wore glasses." I could have kicked myself.

Smooth, Monica!

He took them off placing them on the bed before he put his powerful arms behind his head causing he chest and stomach to flex beautifully.

"Only for reading." His deep relaxed voice was playing havoc on my girly parts.

I nodded as I looked around his room that I knew like the back of my hand as if it was my first time being here. Then my eyes fell on his book bag that was also on the bed and his laptop that sat next to it, then back up to the old flower painting on the wall.

"You want to sit down?"

I grinned really big at him, relieved he had put me out of my misery.

"Sure, if you insist." He chuckled as I climbed up on his bed and sat with my legs folded at the foot of it facing him. There were so many things I wanted to ask him, but I didn't know where to begin.

"So, whatcha reading?" I gestured towards his Bible.

"I'm reading about Yah's Sabbath days. I feel kind of bad that I had second thoughts about going to work today."

"Oh yeah, what did you find out?" He paused for just a moment looking off towards the side.

"I think from this moment on, the shop will be closed on Saturdays."

"Really? I thought you said it was your busiest day." He nodded.

"It is, but the fact is it's a sin to work on the Sabbath day."

"But you didn't work."

"Yea, but I still made money, 'cause others worked for me. That counts." I nodded picking up his Bible opening it.

"It says that in here?"

"Yep."

"Hmmm..." he chuckled.

"What does that mean?" He asked sitting up a bit. I traced where he had jotted things down in his Bible with my finger. I thought about what Stormy said about how some things could not be told, they had to be learned.

"I think that I feel left out." I admitted to him.

"Why is that?" His deep voice was now calming and soothing.

I swallowed. "Because, I don't have a Bible." He chuckled and reached into his bag.

"I got one for you." He tossed a yellow skinned bible to me. It was brand new. I opened it and sure enough he had written my name in it. I looked up at him surprised.

"Why didn't you tell me?" He shrugged.

"I figured I'd wait until you asked me for it."

"But what if I never asked?"

"I was never worried about that. I knew you were going to ask." I couldn't help the grin that spread on my face. The fact that he believed that about me made me feel like a million bucks and then a thought came to me, there was only one thing left standing between him and me and I couldn't go any further until I knew.

"Kaleb?"

"Yea."

"Can I ask you a question." He smiled.

"Sure."

"Did you call the hit on my brother?" The smile left his face as his eyes searched mine.

"I—" he looked away before his eyes came back to mine.

"No... no, I didn't."

Chapter 11
MONICA

A s I sat on the studio's floor stretching out my stiff muscles, I smiled at Eve, who sat across from me trying to duplicate my movements. This was my me-time. Wednesday was the day I could do what I loved.

Dancing!

I taught three classes every Wednesday because school was out for the summer. My day began with my older girls at ten o'clock, then my middle school girls at one, and finally, my tiny tots at three. One by one, my older girls came in dropping their bags to the side and joining Eve and me in our stretch. During this time, we didn't speak to each other. Stretching time was a time of meditation, a time to reflect on our week and think about our goals for the near future while preparing our bodies for the dance.

I smiled a little while I thought about my week. I smiled because my thoughts were full of my husband, my handsome, strong, smart, capable husband. I imagined that I would never say that and it gives me a little thrill.

Yes, my husband!

Oh! He was amazing!

And innocent!

Over the last few days, I've been trying to overcompensate for the fact that I had wrongly accused him of the death of my brother. But how does one compensate for getting an innocent man sent to prison? I had been pondering over that question since Saturday night and the truth was, I didn't know. But I wasn't the kind of person that gave up. If it's the last thing I do, I was determined to make up for it, even if it didn't make up for it completely, I was going to at the very least, show him that he didn't make a bad choice in his pick of a wife.

Every day, I took him breakfast and lunch to the shop. I made sure dinner was waiting for him when he got home. I had even taken to cleaning his room for him, washing his clothes, the whole nine yards. I was feeling so bad that first night he had told me he was innocent that I cried.

"What's the matter, baby?" He asked pulling me into his arms from where I sat at the foot of his bed bawling like a baby.

"I got you sent to jail for nothing! I'm a horrible person!" I wailed. He shook his head trying to hold back a smile.

"No, baby, you not a horrible person. Believe it or not, that time I served saved my life!" I wiped at my tears looking at him.

"What do you mean?"

He slowly shook his head looking off into the distance. "If not for that, I would have never met Solomon. I would have never stopped long enough to look at myself and know that I needed to change. I never would have heard the voice of Yah. There are some people in the world that Yah has to slow down in order to speak to. I was one of those."

He caressed my bottom lip with his thumb. "You looking at me like I'm innocent. I'm not. I've done a lot of dirt in my time. And one thing I have found to be true, it never fails, you reap what you sow every time."

His whispered words were meant to make me feel better about what I did and I felt a little better, but not much. So, ever since then, I've been trying to do all that I could to show him how sorry I am.

And he is still so awesome. Every night we read scripture together and talked about our people and the crisis they face. He is everything I could have ever wanted in a man and more. I mean yeah, he's a brute and really bossy, but on the other hand, he's smart and incisive. He told me how he took his father's drug empire that had taken from the people for years and flipped it so that it now gave back to the people.

I had judged him so wrong. He did not sell drugs. All this time I had thought he was this big-time drug kingpin and he wasn't. He was just a black businessman doing well for himself. And of course, I felt horrible about that. How many times have I spouted about the injustice of our successful brothers being judged as drug dealers or gangbangers by other races only to turn and do it myself with Kaleb?

And I blame myself. I knew better than anybody how dangerous it was to listen to gossip. Gossip was almost always wrong. I can't even begin to tell you how humbling this has been for me. I stood and began to do my standing stretches, my girls followed suit.

Tonight, I had something very special planned for my spectacular man. I was more than ready to consummate our marriage. Seeing him walk around the house at night with just a pair of basketball shorts on or a pair of jogging pants...

Goodness gracious... it has taken its toll on me.

I can't stand it!

I want him so bad I'm ready to get on my knees and beg for him. Let me tell you. Had I never lain with him and did not know what that brother was capable of, I would be fine. I would not be feening like this because I wouldn't know what I was missing.

But I *did* know what I was missing and I wanted it again! I had the perfect little piece of lingerie, but I still had my dignity, so I had a plan. Tonight after dinner, after I cleaning up everything and getting Eve and Nana squared away downstairs, I was going to implement 'Operation Marriage Consummation Plot.'

You see, I will take my time preparing myself for him. Then I will put on my robe and tonight when I go into his room for our little late-night chat, I will put on a little show for my king, a show that I would love to see him walk away from.

"Alright, ladies, as you know Madame Queen's end of the summer talent show is coming up. Stormy says the tickets have already sold out, so we're going to have a full house. If anyone has ideas on our theme this year, I'm open for suggestions. I was thinking Madame Butterfly."

Rhonda, my star pupil raised her hand.

"Whatcha got?" I asked her. Her eyes brightened as she spoke.

"We read Westside story last year." I nodded my head. She attends the same high school I graduated from and we read Westside story sophomore year as well.

"And I was thinking we can do a rendition of that, especially since we on the Westside of Chicago." I frowned trying to see her connection.

Rhonda was a good dancer. The girl had so much potential I had already started preparing her to get into Julliard, but she was struggling in her books. I think most of it was her lack of paying attention. When I sat with her and tutored her, no problem, but as soon as I left the room, her mind would instantly start to wander.

"Umm...I don't see the connection," I told her trying to sound encouraging rather than demeaning. I didn't demean my kids, ever! Tee-Tee, another very good dancer and fellow classmate of Rhonda's laughed.

"That's 'cause while the rest of us were reading Westside story, Rhonda was texting Paul boy, caking, telling him how much she missed him since last period. That girl don't got no clue what the book is about!" The other girls began to laugh.

"Shut up, Tee-Tee, you just jealous 'cause I got a man and your ugly butt gots none!" I held up my hand stopping this before it got out of hand. These Westside girls were strung tight, got to nip any of their spats in the bud when they first spark. If not, I could end up having to throw myself in the middle of a battle royal.

"Alright! Alright, ladies! Westside story is a very good idea. Any more suggestions?" Most of their hands flew up.

"Oh damn, he fine!" I heard one of the girls say about thirty minutes into our rehearsal. I turned around to admonish her for her potty mouth but came up short at the sight of Kaleb walking into the door. He was so big it looked like he had to duck to come in the room. Eve screeched something that sounded a lot like da-da before bolting across the floor to him.

Smiling big, he reached down and scooped her up in his arms.

"Hey, baby!" He told her kissing her loudly under her chubby cheeks. Madame Queen slid shamelessly past him.

"Ummm, Sweet Tart!" She said to me without looking away from Kaleb. And I do mean she was looking at him all kinds of inappropriate.

"I found this here—" her eyes slowly raked up his body. "Gentlemen roaming the halls. Said he was looking for you. Tell me, Sweet Tart, do you know this man?" The last of her question was a purr. Poor Kaleb didn't know rather to be horrified or flattered by Madame's blatant flirtatiousness. He rubbed his hand down his head chuckling to himself.

"Why yes, I do know that man. That wonderful man that you are enjoying so much with your eyes *is my husband*." She whipped around in a cloud of red and purple silk looking at me with a startled gaze.

"Husband?!" She looked back at Kaleb. "Oh, Sweet Tart, excellent job, my girl! Excellent job..." She held out her hand for Kaleb to kiss, but he shook it instead, choosing to pretend he thought that's what she wanted.

"Nice to meet you, Hubby. Do you have a name?" She purred. He chuckled.

"My name is Kaleb, ma'am."

"Oh Kaleb, please don't call me ma'am, you naughty boy." She patted his chest to admonish him, but then her hand seemed to have gotten stuck on his peck.

"WOW! Aren't you quite strong?" He gently removed her hand from his chest while shooting me a look that said, 'Help Me'! But I just shook my head enjoying the scene he made trying to escape Madame's clingy hands.

"So how did the two of you meet?" She asked reaching up towards his neck. He dodged her hand by looking at something Eve did not point at.

"What's that you want to show daddy? Oh look, mirrors!" He carried Eve toward the back of the class, but if he thought that was going to put Madame off the hunt, he had another thing coming. Two things she prided herself in being able to sniff out were money and good man flesh, her words. She moved to follow him, but I took pity on him.

"Ummm, Madame did you need something?" I called from across the room. She halted in her chase of Kaleb, turning back to face me with layers of red and purple silk floating around her. I do believe the blouse she wore had silken wings stitched in the back of it.

"Oh, yes Sweet Tart, I came to tell you this year I want you to do a dance solo as well." I frowned.

"I don't think so, Madame, the show is for the kids." She drew herself up as if I had just slapped her.

"You dare to tell me how to direct my own show?"

"Oh no! I would never try to tell you how to direct your show! However-" She clapped her hands together cutting me off mid-sentence. A big smile replaced the insulted look she had just worn.

"Good, then you'll do it! This year I want to close the show with your performance!" She waved her hand in front of her as if she could see it all coming together before her eyes. "I need something soul-stirring." Her gaze landed back on Kaleb.

"Maybe you can do something honoring your spectacular

husband and if my nose is correct..." Her eyes scanned his watch, his designer jeans down to the leather boots on his feet. She lifted her face and made a showing of sniffing the air, then she lifted her hand and gently drew the scent of his cologne towards her.

"Is that Clive Christian #1 you're wearing, dear?" Kaleb looked surprised.

"Why, yes, it is!"

"Hmm, I thought so, future financial backer to many more wonderful productions to come." She purred so scandalously I believe Kaleb blushed before he got really busy pointing at something out the window.

"Look, Eve, there is a car. Can you say car?"

Madame inhaled closing her eyes as she took in his cologne one more time, then she popped them back open turning to me.

"Yes, I think that shall do just fine! You and Stormy let me know that all my hard work wasn't for naught. You both have made me so proud." And then with all the grace and air of a duchess, she glided towards the door, but before she left, she turned and looked at Kaleb one more time.

"I'll see you later, handsome!" She blew him a kiss before continuing through the door leaving a trail of Channel #5 behind her. Kaleb shuddered as I approached him.

"Thanks a lot for rescuing me from that man-eater!" he grumbled wrapping his other arm around my waist and pulling me to him before burying his head in my neck. I chuckled because his beard tickled.

"Aww! Come on, a big strong man like yourself ain't afraid of a little harmless old woman, is he?" The look of unbelief that crossed his face caused the girls to laugh behind me, reminding me that I was teaching a class.

"Please, you didn't see what I saw in her eyes. If y'all wasn't here, she would have tried to take my innocence!" His statement caused the girls to laugh harder.

"What are you doing here?" I asked playfully hitting his chest like Madame had done and letting my hand linger on it. He shrugged.

"I was in the neighborhood so I decided to stop by and take my two favorite girls out to lunch in Hyde Park."

"Ohhh! That's sounds interesting, I've never been to that side of town."

"Stick with me, kid and I'll show you how to do a lot of things you never did before," he whispered indecently in my ear.

"I'd like for him to show me how to do some things I never did before!" I heard one of my little fast students say. I took a step back away from him clearing my throat, going back into teacher mode.

"I have two hours before my next class, so lunch will be great. But first I have to finish up here, don't know if you want to stay and watch." I frowned my nose up, surely he wouldn't be interested in sitting and watching me teach dance to a bunch of girls.

"Are you kidding me? I finally get to see if you can really dance. For all I know, you been selling wolf tickets and really got two left feet." The look of challenge he sent my way made me laugh.

"I can dance and I don't need to prove it to you. However, if you sit quietly, you may learn a thing or two." I sashayed away from him.

"Okay, ladies, let's take it from the top."

It was a little unnerving feeling his eyes on me as I danced. And you know, of course, I had to do it really good because he was watching. Today, I had chosen to wear one of my black leotards and black tights. I wore my Nana's little black heels like I always did. When I went down into a bend, I made sure I put an extra arch in my back. With each dip and turn, I put just enough hip in it to keep his eyes drawn to my curves. And when I went up on my toes, I made sure to do it with all the grace of a hundred swans. All in all, I think I gave him quite a show.

"Monica, I would like to challenge someone to a dance off!" Rhonda called out to the hoots and hollers of her fellow classmates.

This was nothing new. I believed healthy competition was good.

So, I encouraged the girls to challenge each other in dance-offs. This was a good way to not only let off some of the frustrations they face with day-to-day-life, but to also keep them striving to be the best.

However, it was rarely Rhonda challenging anybody, she was my best student. Normally, it was one of the other girls wanting to challenge her. I was curious to see who she felt the need to compete with. I smiled as I went to stand next to Eve and Kaleb.

"You're in for a treat, the girls are going to have a dance battle." I looked back at Rhonda.

"Okay, Ms. Rhonda, choose your opponent and y'all do your thing!" She put her hand on her hip and her mischievous little grin settled on me.

"I challenge you, Monica." My mouth dropped. *No this little heffa-*

"Girl, stop playing, choose somebody else." I waved away her silliness. She shook her head.

"What? You scared? Don't want your husband to know you second best?" The expression on the other girls' faces was a mix between shock and excitement. They had never seen me dance against anyone. I laughed shaking my finger at her.

"I know what you trying to do. You ain't slick!"

"Gone, shorty, don't let this lil' girl show you up like that?!' Kaleb said nudging my arm with his. I turned to look up at him.

"Please, don't encourage her madness." He grinned at me.

"I don't know, I think she might be right. You do look a little scared." Oh okay! I turned to face Miss Thang.

"Choose your battle!"

Her face brightened. "Destiny's Child, *'Lose My Breath*!'"

"Get the fan!" I told her.

"The Fan?" Kaleb asked.

Patty, one of my newer students laughed. "Yea, anytime we do a Beyoncé challenge, you got to have the fan!" Two of the girls ran out of the room and came back pushing the big fan that Stormy got for the gym when our AC system temporarily went down last year.

"Oh, this gon' be good!" I heard Kaleb say as he squatted next to Eve getting comfortable. I can see he was all excited to see this.

Rhonda should know better than to challenge me. I had to bring it because the girl was good. And there ain't no way she finna show me up in front of my man.

"What's the rules?" I asked her as I stood facing her. She was so excited, there were sparkles in her eyes. It seems as if my little pupil has been waiting to challenge her teacher for quite some time.

"Follow the leader. I go first!"

"You sure you can keep up with me, baby doll?" I muttered as the excitement of this challenge began to settle in on me. She nodded her head with much attitude.

"Oh, I can keep up! Let's do it!" I nodded towards Tee-Tee and she queued the music. At the same time, Patty hit the big fan that filled our small studio with wind. It blew my locs around my shoulders and face in true Beyoncé fashion.

Rhonda began moving, carefully I watched her committing her steps to memory. Another reason why I encouraged the girls to do the challenge is because if any of them truly wanted to pursue dancing, they were going to have to be able to learn a routine on the fly. Meaning, they had to watch the routine done and then be able to duplicate it like now.

However, this was not a big challenge for me. I had seen Rhonda do this routine many times. And although it was true she shut down the other girls in her class with this routine, she was not going to be successful today for the same reason I had often warned her about.

She had studied Beyoncé moves in the video and was duplicating them perfectly. She looked just like Beyoncé doing the dance. I will defeat her today because I was going to show her Monica doing this dance. She finished her routine with flare, before signaling that it was my turn to duplicate her.

I went through the routine flawlessly, but I did it like Monica. Mid-way through my rendition of her dance, Rhonda put her hand on her face embarrassed. I toned it down a bit. I didn't ever want my kids to feel discouraged. Signaling for them to kill the music, I gestured for the other girls to come in close.

"Tell me why you're looking like that?" I asked Rhonda.

"'Cause, I knew I shouldn't have challenged you!"

"Can you tell me what I did differently from you?"

"You added your own flair to it without changing the routine." I looked around at the girls.

"That is what it is going to take to be noticed out there in this highly competitive industry if you get called for an audition. In some cases, there can be hundreds more auditioning for the same spot. What's going to make you stand out is taking the routine you are given and adding your own flicker to it." I looked around at each of them as I demonstrated a move that was one of Rhonda's favorites.

"How many of you have watched Rhonda slay someone with this?" I went up on my toe and did a spin throwing my leg out and then swiftly bringing it back in. All the girl nodded agreeing that it was one of Rhonda's best moves.

"Now watch me do the same move, but just add a little Monica to it." I went up on my toe going into the spin, but instead of keeping a straight back, I put an arch in mine and let the top half of my body sway into my extended leg. When I brought it back in, I swayed slightly the other way.

"Do you see what I'm saying? In that instant, that little small adjustment can be what draws the eye to you. I challenge you this week to find your voice in dance. Let the movement of your body be your signature." They applauded and I smiled loving the determination I saw in their eyes.

"Alright, ladies, I'll see you next week." Rhonda came over to hug me.

"You know, I didn't really think I could beat you. I just wanted your new husband to see just how good you are."

"And how do you think I did?" She grinned.

"If we wasn't in the room, Eve would probably have a brother on the way!" I opened my mouth shocked as she laughed and ran out of the room to catch up with her friends.

"Wow! You are really good!" Kaleb said as he walked over to where I now stood drinking water. I smiled at him.

"Told you!"

"Not too humble, but you're a great dancer." I laughed.

"Thanks!" Still holding Eve in his arms, he stared at me as I slid in my skirt. He had something on his mind.

"What's up, what you thinking about so deeply?"

"I was just wondering why you held yourself back while you were dancing. It looked like you wanted to break out, but you didn't."

Wow! That was very observing of him. I'm amazed that he saw that. Yea! I did want to break out. The only time I ever got to dance these days was when I came to rehearsal with girls. And I didn't like throwing my ability in their faces. I wanted class time to be about them. For some of them, it was the only time they had where they mattered most.

"Well," I told him. "I don't want my girls to feel discouraged. I want them to feel like their dreams are attainable." I shrugged.

"I just want them to know that there is life outside of this ghetto. So, I try to be an encouraging teacher rather than a showboat. They need somebody to put them first sometime." He listened and nodded his head slightly.

"But what about you? You love dancing! How often do you get to just let go and do that?" I laughed at that. With Eve, my Nana and my two jobs, forget about it.

"I thought about turning my old bedroom into a dance studio so that I could have someplace to let go. But I've just been too busy with everything else." I exhaled. I had so many plans, but obviously, they weren't meant to be.

"So, what you're saying is what I saw here today is not the tip of what you are capable of doing?" Leave it to him to use my vanity to make me feel better.

"Psk! Brother, you have no idea what I am capable of." I know that was not helping my case for being humble, but it was true. If I could let go and just be me, I'd dance rings around just about anybody and I ain't being vain, I'm just being honest. He looked thoughtful again.

"The sexiest dance I think I ever seen performed was the samba. Can you samba?" *Was he kidding me?* It was one of the first forms I studied.

"Can Eve draw liquid from her sippy cup?" He chuckled taking my hand with his free one.

"Come on, I know the perfect place to have lunch. And I promise, you won't have to hold yourself back with this crowd."

He took us to Hyde Park to a Brazilian restaurant or what I think was a restaurant. I say this because the outside of the building looked like most of the other stores in this area. There were what looked like apartments on top and the restaurant on the first level. However, when we walked in, it was clear to see that it was much more to this building than what I initially thought.

Yes, it was true, there were a few people sitting at the tables eating, but the place looked more like a juice bar. The main action was happening in what looked like a square courtyard in the middle of the building. A big glass window revealed a large group of men and women in the courtyard doing capoeira.

"Yo! Kaleb!" A male voice boomed from outside in the courtyard before a young dark handsome man jogged through the door to greet him.

"You come to work out with us?" He asked as he and Kaleb clasped hands.

"Naw, not today, Carlos. I'm just watching, maybe have a little lunch." The man was super-excited about that.

"Oh yeah! Wait till I tell my papa you here! Come on out, your table in the courtyard is free." As we followed him, I looked around amazed at their production. They took capoeira serious here. Surrounding the group of fighters, who practiced their art was a small group of men who played instruments.

From what I knew of capoeira, they were the timekeepers or more like the pacesetters. The fighters fought to whatever speed the musicians set and thanks to Keturah dragging me around to the events that happened in the Pan-African circuit, I was able to recognize a few of the instruments, the *pandeiros,* which kind of look like tambourines, the *atabaque,* which is a wooden drum, and the *reco-reco,* which makes a very unique sound.

We took a seat and Carlos brought us out two glasses of sangria and brought Eve a cup of juice that I poured into her sippy cup. With all the activity going on, she was in baby heaven. She wanted out of her seat.

"It's okay, she can walk around!" Kaleb said when I caught her trying to escape for the third time.

"Are you sure? They're not like going to get mad at her for getting in the way, are they?" He chuckled.

"You see all these kids? Trust me, she'll be alright." Carlos came back to the table with his father, who was thrilled to see Kaleb. They embraced like they were family, then his father insisted on making us a special Brazilian dish. Carlos sat with us and talked while he did it.

"I was telling my wife about your sister and how she was Samba Queen three years in a row at Carnival in Brazil." I damn near choked on my water. *That sneaky bastard didn't say anything about a Samba Queen.*

"Who, Angela?" Carlos chuckled. "She wants to take the crown again this year. She loves dancing!" I narrowed my eyes at Kaleb. The look he had on his face let me know he was up to no good.

"You know, my wife does too. She says she knows the samba like the back of her hand." Oh, I was going to kill him. Carlos's face lit up before he jumped to his feet. He walked into the group speaking in rapid Portuguese. I turned to look back at Kaleb, who wore a smug look on his face.

"What's happening?' I asked him.

"Well, you said you wanted to dance and that you just need a little motivation." His grin turned into a full-blown smile.

"Now you're going to get your chance. Nothing these Brazilians like better than proving no one can samba like them." I pointed my finger at him.

"You feeling real good about yourself, ain't you?" He nodded his head, the stupid grin still on his face.

"You think I was just talking out the side of my neck earlier, huh?" He shrugged.

"I don't know, you say you the best. Now is your chance to prove it!" I grinned taking another sip of my sangria. This man obviously didn't know who he was dealing with, but after today, he will know my name. They all will.

"You two come join our circle," Carlos called from across the courtyard. As soon as we approached, a beautiful girl dressed in the traditional capoeira garb walked towards us with a warm smile on her face.

"Hey, Kaleb!" She said going up on her toes to hug him. Then she looked at me and her smile was contagious.

"Hey, I'm Angie, I heard you samba, girl! Let's dance, mama!" And as if on cue, the musicians began to play. Eve wrapped her little arm around my leg as she watched Angie begin to move her waist. Oh yea, the girl was good. Really good! One of the other fighters danced with her in the center of the circle. She did quick work at shutting him down before another man came and tagged him out.

"I don't know, baby, you might hurt yourself if you try to compete with those hips!" Kaleb whispered in my ear. My mouth fell open as I looked up to catch him, in fact, watching Ms. Angie's hips and the girl was swinging them. Oh, hell no! I drank the last of my sangria before I headed towards the circle to tag Ms. Angie out.

Kaleb grabbed my arm and gently pulled me back to him. "Wait! She barefoot. You're going to dance in them heels?" I smiled up at him.

"Poor baby, heels are what separate the hobbyist from the professionals. Watch and learn!"

Oh, y'all I can't remember the last time I had so much fun. And Kaleb was right, I could let go and dance. And dance I did. My samba didn't look like Angie's, because my samba was Monica's. Angie and I had the same roots, but different struggles and that difference was reflected in our style.

Partner after partner I shut them down because you better believe I know how to move my hips. And after the tenth man was tagged out, Kaleb came and wrapped his arm around me pulling me out the circle.

"Okay! Enough! I'm jealous as hell! Damn, girl, seeing you move your hips like that got me losing focus!" he whispered in my ear. I threw back my head and laughed.

"What was that you said earlier about me breaking a hip?" He grinned down at me looking so damn sexy.

"Naw, you breaking my heart dancing with all these men, showing them my good thang. We better get out of here 'for I snatch the lining out of one of these brothers, 'cause I promise to do just that if another one of them reach for you." I scooped Eve up in my arms. It was time for me to get back to class anyway.

"Hey, Kaleb, where you taking Monica!" Carlos called.

"Away from you!"

Everybody laughed because Carlos had danced with me a couple of times. I hugged Angie as Kaleb hugged their dad promising them we'll be back.

"You good girl!" she told me. "You'll have to come to Brazil with me for Carnival. They wouldn't be able to stop us." I laughed and bid everybody goodbye thanking them for the coolest lunch break in the history of lunch breaks.

Kaleb dropped us off in front of the center. I assured him that I didn't need him to carry a sleeping Eve in. A few of my middle school girls called out to me as they went inside the building. I waved at them and told them I'd be in shortly.

"I'll be home a little late tonight, but I should make it in before dinner is ready."

I told him that was cool and kissed him goodbye. I even stood and watched his truck ride down the street. I exhaled. I think I was falling in love with my husband.

When I turned around to head into the building, I came up short at the sight of Rasheed sitting on the steps. Slowly I approached him. He was obviously here to see me.

"Aww! Y'all look like a happy family!"

"We are!" I snapped not liking the tone of his voice. "What are you doing here? Your brother just left." He grinned at me.

"Naw, I ain't come to see my brother. I came to see you."

"Well, I don't want to see you!" With Eve in my arms, I went to walk past him, but he stood blocking my way.

"So, I was doing a little investigating and I found out some interesting information."

"I don't care!" I told him trying to walk around him, but again, he stepped in my way.

"Oh, come on, sista-in-law, surely you got five minutes to spare. We are family after all!" I looked up at him, letting all my anger and distrust for him show in my face.

"Rasheed, just say what you have to say and leave me be!" I spoke those words through my pressed together lips. He laughed and it grated on my nerves because it sounded like a bird.

"It'll be quick 'cause I simply got one question for you?" I rolled my eyes.

"What?" He nodded, smiling at me again reminding me of the damn Joker.

"That's exactly what I'd like to know. What kind of woman lay up with the man that killed her own brother?" My gaze flew up to his.

"What did you say?"

"You heard me! Poor Man-Man probably rolling around in his grave knowing his sista up here f****** the nigga that put a bullet in his head."

My legs got weak and Eve suddenly felt really heavy in my arms. I sat down on the stone step behind me. *No! He was lying! He wasn't telling the truth!*

Slowly I shook my head at him. "You not telling the truth!" I whispered. He threw back his head and laughed.

"Why I got to lie to you? I ain't the one f****** you! I ain't got nothing to lose!"

"Bu—but he said—"

"What? What he say? Knowing Kaleb, he probably pretended he didn't even know who you were talking about. And you just sucked it up, believing him!" He shook his head before his eyes came back down to me.

"You a disgrace to your brother's memory!" He spat on the ground at my feet and then walked away.

Chapter 12
YOU CAN'T HANDLE THE TRUTH

MONICA

I threw the Tupperware bowl with Kaleb's breakfast on his desk. He sat back looking up from the papers he was filling out. He held up his hands as the bowl skidded across his desk pushing the papers to the floor.

"What the hell is your problem?!"

"*You* my problem!" I told him before I turned and walked towards the door. He jumped up from the desk and rushed to me, grabbing my arm and turning me around. I snatched my arm from him.

"Don't touch me, liar!" I spat.

Angrily the muscle ticked in his cheek as he glared down at me. You see, I was ready to fight. Last night, I had stayed in my bedroom after telling him and Nana that I had a headache so that I could think over some things. I didn't want to believe Rasheed, but some things just weren't adding up.

Like the fact that every time I mentioned my brother's name, Kaleb pretended like he didn't know who he was. But if Rasheed knew who he was, then Kaleb's a$$ knew who he was.

"What are you talking about?!" He growled. I pointed my finger in his face.

"You know what I'm talking about. You lying about Man-Man, you know who he is and you know what happened to him. Why don't you be a man and just tell me?" I could tell he knew more by the way he was looking down at me. It was like he was having a battle in his head. His nostrils flared angrily before he turned around and snatched his car keys off his desk.

He was so mad when he turned back and walk towards me that I took a step back because it looked as if he was going to run me over, but he didn't. However, he did grab my arm and not too gently.

"Let's go! You want the truth?! I'll give you the truth!" I didn't try to take my arm from him, because he was so mad right now, I really didn't want to rock the boat. As we walked past Kesha, the receptionist, at first her face registered shock before barely contained glee. I mean-mugged the witch and she had the nerve to smirk at me.

He half-dragged me to the truck and after opening the door, damn near shoved me in. I went on and got in although I felt like walking away after being treated so rudely by him, but I couldn't walk away. It seemed that finally, I was going to get the truth about what happened to my brother.

We drove out of the loop back to the westside. He brought his truck to a stop in front of a house in K-town. He was still mad, he didn't speak to me the whole way. When he got out of the truck he slammed the door. I sat in the truck and watched him angrily come around to my side, he snatched the door open.

"Get out!" was all he said. I frowned at him as I got out. He slammed the door and turned around walking towards the house. He took the stairs two at a time and rang the doorbell. I looked around confused as I followed him up the stairs, not understanding what this place had to do with my brother.

Just a short distance away, someone had placed a bunch of teddy bears and flowers by a tree. It was a memorial. Someone must have gotten killed right there. And because they were teddy bears, it most had been a child. Probably a drive-by.

I shook my head. That was happening more and more these days. These streets had no respect for the young or the old. It was just ridiculous. A woman that looked to be a few years older than me answered the door. When she saw Kaleb, she smiled although the smile didn't reach her eyes.

"Hey, K!" She said opening the screen door. When he walked in she hugged him.

"What's up, Mika, how you feeling?" She exhaled as she turned and walked into the dark house. Kaleb held the door for me and after I walked in, he pushed it up, casting the house in complete darkness. She sat down on the couch.

"I know that I should tell you I'm doing good, but then I'c be lying." Kaleb walked to the window and opened the curtains slightly letting a little bit of sunlight in. She put her hand over her eyes.

"Come on, K! That's too bright!" He chuckled.

"Little sunlight ain't gon' hurt nobody." For the first time, she looked up and saw me standing there. She smiled, but again it didn't reach her eyes.

"Hey."

"Hey," I returned.

"Monica, this is Tamika, but we all call her Mika. Mika, this is my wife, Monica." She smiled for real this time.

"Oh my God! I had heard that you got married. Congratulations, man, it's about time. Ro said you use to clown him about having to go home to his wife. Now you got a wife!" Kaleb held his head down shaking it chuckling.

"Yea, well! Can't be a bachelor forever!"

"I know that's right! If Ro was here, he'd get a real kick out of that." She looked up at me. "Please have a seat. You guys want anything to drink." She exhaled sounding tired. The little joyful inflection she had in her voice when teasing Kaleb about getting married was gone.

"I haven't been to the grocery store in a while, but I may have some soda in there or something." I sat on the couch off to the side of the one she was sitting on. Kaleb still stood by the window. There something wrong with him. He seemed tense, no longer angry, just tense, as if he was afraid to step farther into the house.

I started getting a bad feeling. Mika was pretty, but she looked weary as if she was depressed or sad.

"Why haven't you been to the grocery store, you need money?" Kaleb asked. She chuckled dryly.

"Naw, K, you done enough. Because of you, I don't even have to work no more, which is blessing 'cause I don't really want to be around people, you know?" As she spoke, she stared off into the back half of her house that was completely dark.

"Maybe you should get out more!" He suggested softly. She nodded.

"Yea, Mama be nagging me about it. She say it's been over two years and it's time for me to try and help myself heal. She says I should go to counseling." She shrugged.

"Counseling may help, I could go with you if you want!" Again, Kaleb's response was quiet. I couldn't take it anymore, I had to know what was going on and what this had to do with Man-Man. I prayed I didn't sound insensitive.

"Umm, if you don't mind me asking, what happened?" I took Kaleb's lead and asked my question softly. She looked up at me and smiled sadly. Tears came to her eyes.

"No, I don't mind. Nobody else will talk to me about it. It's like they never existed."

"Who?" She looked back toward that dark hallway.

"Ro, Po and Nay!" She smiled as she said those names.

"I was in the kitchen cooking and Ro, my husband, had just bought the twins these cute little matching bikes. Po's was blue with little green streaks and Nay's was pink with little yellow streaks. And of course, as he walked through that door with them, they jumped all over him..." She turned to look at the door as if she could see him walking in. The tears began to fall from her beautiful eyes.

"Daddy, come show us how to ride! Po said...he was so much like his father..." she smiled through her tears. "He told him, let daddy rest a bit. Your uncle Kaleb worked me like a slave." Kaleb chuckled, but there was no humor in the sound he made.

"But what did five-year-olds care about they daddy being tired? So, he went on and took 'em out there...right out front. And they was so happy!" Her voice cracked as her tears really began to flow. The air got really thick in the room and for the first time, I noticed my breathing was labored. Suddenly, I was afraid. I shook my head.

"No, you don't have to continue," I whispered, but I think it came out more of a plea. She nodded with a determined look on her face.

"No, I want to...I need to!" She looked at me. "They existed dammit!" she screamed. I nodded telling her to continue, even though the lump in my throat felt like a fist.

"I stood in my kitchen window watching them. I could remember thanking God for a good man. My Ro...He worked hard for us...He came home every night...I wasn't having none of them problems my friends was having with they men..." she shook her head.

"Ro was good and he loved me and his kids—" her voice cracked again. She wiped at her tears.

"It was time to flip my chicken in the grease... I walked away from the window and I heard it...like ten shots...Bam...Bam..Bam bam bam... I screamed out 'cause they were so loud. And my heart..." She put her hand on her chest.

"A sharp pain went through my heart. I ran out the front door and I saw Ro...he was hunched over the twins, like he threw hisself over them. I saw the blood on his back and I knew he was gone... but he—" she began to breathe heavily. No, it was me...my breathing became too loud. I began to shake from the inside. I wanted to tell her to stop! I wanted to put my hands over my ears because I didn't want to hear any more.

Kaleb stood in the corner with his fists balled, his nostrils flared, he was having a hard time.

"He had thrown his body over our babies and I thought that they were alive...but I could see their legs...I could see both of their legs!" She stared off into the darkness reliving that moment.

"And they wasn't-"She broke off putting her shaking hand in front her mouth, maybe to stop herself from screaming. She looked up at Kaleb.

"They wasn't moving, K! They wasn't moving!" Her voice quivered so badly her words were barely audible. Although they didn't fall, there were tears in Kaleb's eyes. She looked back at me.

"I was scared to move him...I was scared of what I was going to see! I heard somebody yelling to move him off the babies. And I stood there staring down at my man...looking at the holes in his back and couldn't move...I couldn't move!" She held her shaking hands up.

"Doug ran over and he..." Her breathing became labored.

"That's enough, Mika..." Kaleb growled...but she continued talking as if her life depended on it.

"He rolled his body off our babies and they both had holes—" Instead of saying it, she patted her forehead with her shaking hand.

"He had shot both of my babies in the head..."

I put my hand on my chest as sharp pain shot through it. I knew who the he was and I couldn't breathe...

No! Man-Man! No!

I tried to desperately draw in air, but I couldn't breathe... The house was too dark, it was too stuffy. I felt like I was suffocating. I had to get out! I stood and ran to the door... I needed to be away...I couldn't—I just couldn't...

I ran down the stairs and my steps halted when I saw the memorial. That's where it happened. That's where Man-Man shot and killed Mika's family. I clutched my stomach! I was going to be sick! I was going to be sick!

Desperately, I turned away from the scene, not able to look at those little teddy bears anymore and ran to the back of the house into the alley. I barely made it to the side of the garbage before I began to vomit. I felt Kaleb's strong arm come around my waist holding me up. He moved my locs so that I didn't get vomit on them. I vomited everything out of my stomach and once empty, I continued to dry heave.

It was painful. I wanted to die! My brother!

"Oh! Yah! Help me!" I cried out. I wanted to die! I needed help! Kaleb moved me away from the vomit and placed me on the ground, I balled up within myself wanting to die! I couldn't get the image of Ro outside teaching his five-year-old twins how to ride their new bikes out of my head! Kaleb took off his shirt and wiped my mouth with it before he sat on the ground next to me lifting me in his arms.

"Shhh, baby! I'm sorry! I'm sorry, I shouldn't have brought you here!" He whispered to me over and over again as he rocked me in his arms. I clung to him. I couldn't stop crying! I couldn't get the image of Ro throwing himself in front of his kids to stop them from being shot out of my head.

"Dear Heavenly Father," I heard Kaleb begin to pray softly in my ear. "We need you now, Father. We need strength!" His words were soothing as he continued to pray, my air passages opened and I could breathe easier. I prayed with him. I prayed for forgiveness. I prayed for Ro, Po, and Nay. I prayed for Mika, I prayed for Man-Man. The more we prayed, the better I felt. And something happened to me in that alley. I felt something change me.

Although it was Kaleb holding me in his arms, I felt another's arms wrap around me. And I knew it...I knew right then that our Savior was holding me and keeping me from falling in the dark hole that had suddenly opened underneath me. I had reached the turning point in my life in that alley and all I could do was thank

Yah! Thank him for not giving up on me! Thank him for not forgetting me! Thank him for giving me one more chance! Thank him for touching me in that alley!

I don't know how long we sat there, but at one point Mika came out and put a blanket around us. I reached out and grabbed her hand and my tears started anew. She came down to her knees next to me and the only thing I could do was wrap my arms around her and apologize over and over again. And for a while, Kaleb held us both. Her body shook with her tears.

"I'm going to help you!" I promised her. I felt that it was my duty. No, my mission! It was like Yah was telling me that now that I had been given another chance, I needed to perform this one unselfish act and help Mika.

Eventually, Kaleb helped us both back into the house. If Mika found it strange that I grieved so for her family, she didn't say anything. I wasn't brave enough to tell her who I was. I didn't know what she would do if she found out. And I wanted to help her, I didn't want her to push me away. So, I didn't tell her.

When we were leaving, I hugged her for a long time. She thanked us for visiting and talking with her. We road back to the shop in silence. He pulled up next to my truck and killed the engine. For a minute, we just sat in silence.

I wondered if I hated Man-Man for what he had done. I didn't. He was my brother. There were too many good memories for me to just wash him away. He used to help me practice my dance moves and there were times he would have me and Na-Na laughing so hard as he tried to duplicate them.

I remembered the night of our mother's funeral. He and I had laid out on the ground in the back yard and stared up at the stars. He held my hand in his and he told me not to be afraid and that everything was going to be okay because he would always look out for me.

I looked over at Kaleb, who sat staring straight ahead, lost in his thoughts.

"Who was Ro to you?" I asked quietly. He didn't answer right away.

"He was my best friend. Po and Nay were my godchildren.' He eventually said. Tears came to my eyes again and I silently wiped them away.

"How did you know it was Man-Man who had done it?" He exhaled.

"There were a bunch of witnesses. Mika said when she first ran out of the house, he was still standing there pointing the gun at Ro and the kids. He looked up and saw her and that's when he ran."

"I understand why you had to make that call." He turned to look at me then, his eyes searching mine to see if I told the truth. I nodded.

"I do, I understand. And I'm not mad at you. I just thank Yah that you called a hit on him rather than do it yourself. You know?" He stared at me for a moment before he slowly nodded his head.

"It's like you said, everybody reaps what they sow." I reached for the door, but before I got out, I picked up his hand from where it rested against the armrest and gently kissed his knuckles.

"I'll see you when you get home," I told him.

When I got home, I held Eve for hours. She didn't whine or try to shimmy out my arms like she normally does when held too long, she just rested her head against my chest and let me hold her.

I picked up the Bible that Kaleb had bought me and opened it to the beginning, ready to begin my journey, ready to answer the call. The feeling of being held in Kaleb's arms and then those of our Savior was overwhelming and it was a feeling that I never wanted to let go of. Eve eventually nodded off. Nana surprised me by bringing her Bible into the living room and quietly reading with me.

She didn't ask me what was wrong with me and I thanked Yah for that. I could not ever tell Na-Na what her grandson had done. Eventually, we moved on into the kitchen so that I could start cooking dinner. After reading my scriptures all afternoon, I felt good. I felt cleansed.

"Why you smiling out that window, child?" Na-Na soft question came from behind me from where I stood washing the dishes at the sink.

"I feel.." I began searching for the right word. "Changed."

"That's a good feeling, ain't it?" I nodded.

"Yes, ma'am."

"Today when I walked in the living room and I saw you reading your Bible, it did my heart good. I've been praying for you." I turned around and looked at her.

"Well then, Yah answered your prayer, 'cause he touched me in here today!" I put my hand on my chest and my vision blurred with tears. My Na-Na opened her arms for me and I ran to her. I thought I had cried out all my tears, but I hadn't.

As I cried, she stroked my hair like she used to do when I was younger.

"It ain't nothing wrong with crying, baby." She whispered. I looked up at her.

"I don't deserve Yah's love, I've been so wicked!" I told her. She shushed me.

"Honey, only Yah know who deserve his love and who don't. And it's natural for you to feel this guilt. That's what the Bible say gon' happen when we come back to him. It say we gon' remember our wickedness and mourn." She gently pushed my locs back from my face looking down at me with love.

"I am so proud of you, sweetheart. It won't be easy, 'cause it ain't nothing the devil hate more than a soul choosing Yah. But you be brave and you be the strong girl I know you to be and walk bodily with the Most High. In all things, give thanks and don't be afraid to call on Yah for strength." I would later learn that her words had been gems.

That night after the house had grown quiet, I took me a long hot bubble bath. What a difference a day could make. This morning when I woke up, I never would have imagined this would be the day my life changed. Yah had come to me in my time of need and he had used my husband to do it. I don't doubt that it was Kaleb's prayer that brought on the change.

It was during his prayer that I felt the presence of Yahoshua. I know it was him. I felt it in every cell of my body. Now I understood what Kaleb meant when he told me about the day he had met Shelomoh. He said he knew that his life would never be the same.

I couldn't even begin to explain to someone what happened to me. It is something that one must experience. I thought back to Stormy's words the other day when we were in her kitchen.

"Somethings are not as simple as to just tell someone." No truer words had ever been uttered.

By the time I got out of the bath, I had made up my mind about another situation. It was time for me to kill my pride. It was a big part of my old self. And I didn't want it anymore. It felt dirty to me. I went into my room and took my time and oiled my body with mango butter, then I went to my closet and pulled out the little red negligee that I had bought the other day for this occasion.

I took down my loc that had been piled on top of my hair from the bath and after putting on a little lip gloss, I dabbed a few spots of perfume behind my ears and on my wrists. I was a little nervous. Kaleb also had an emotional day. Because of my pride, I forced him and Mika to relive a very painful experience.

Maybe he will turn me away. Maybe he would take one look at my outfit and I will appear desperate to him. I shook that away. Maybe he will do all those things, but I'll never know unless I try. I squared my shoulders and crossed the hall to his door.

Gently I knocked on it.

"Come in!" his deep voice came from the other side. I closed my eyes for just a moment as it washed over me and after taking a deep breath, I opened the door.

He was lying in the bed looking yummy, shirtless with just a pair of grey gym shorts on. He had on his glasses, reading his scriptures. His eyes came up to me, then back down, but flew up to me again. Slowly he took off his glasses as his gaze raked over my body. I stood there waiting for it—

Finally, after he took me in completely, his eyes fell back on my breasts that were barely contained in the thin lace. I smiled as he did that little thing that he does with his bottom lip when he's aroused. That was the sign I was waiting for. As I walked towards his bed, he closed his Bible and sat it on the nightstand as well as his reading glasses.

I crawled across his bed really Eartha Kitt-like, making sure that each time one of my arms came forward, he got a little peek of my tender breasts. He licked his lip again. I didn't stop crawling until my mouth was only inches away from his. Instantly he dipped his head to take my lips. I moved my head back out of his reach.

He frowned.

"Dammit, Monica, don't tell me you came in here to tease me!" Grinning I shook my head.

"I came in here to ask you a question." His frowned deepened.

"Ask me a question?" he said that as if the thought disgusted him. "Dressed like that?"

I nodded. "Emmm Hmmm!"

He exhaled lying back against the pillow. The disappointed look in his eyes made me want to laugh, but I held it together keeping a straight face.

"What's your question?" He muttered. I licked my lips feeling so nervous.

"Will you make love to me, Kaleb...Please?!"

Chapter 13

OPERATION SEXY CHICKEN

MONICA

I felt the bed dip sometime before sunrise. Although still half asleep, my body was protesting the loss of his heat. When I didn't hear him leave the room, I cracked my eyes just a little to see what he was doing. And I was surprised to see him go down on his knees facing the east window.

Oh y'all, something settled inside of me watching that powerful man submit himself to the Most High. If I was a painter, I would stop at nothing to capture the image, if I was a writer, I would use the most phenomenal words in the English language to describe this feeling so that all who read my work would know and under-stand the significance of such a moment.

He was such an extraordinary man in every way, I don't know what I had done to deserve him. I grinned thinking about last night. Just like the first time he and I made love, I had to beg him to let me rest. I don't know if it was normal, but he had a way of loving me completely, leaving my body feeling utterly depleted. The man seemed to have an insatiable appetite. Before my heart could regulate from our previous joining, he would be kissing me and whis-pering those dirty suggestions in my ear.

I would tell him I couldn't and that I was tired, but I might as well have been preaching the importance of patience to Eve because it went in one of his ears and out of the other. It was like my objections were a personal challenge for him and he took immense pleasure in proving me wrong.

Moments later, he would have made me forget all about my reservations and anything else. Later, after he had finally tired himself out, he apologized, confirming my beliefs. He had not been with another woman since he and I had conceived Eve.

I watched him silently pray until my eyes grew heavy again. When next I opened them, he was leaving out of the room dressed for his morning run. Where he got the energy I would never know, I didn't plan on getting out of this bed till noon. After what that man had done to me last night, my body needed to recuperate.

His morning runs spoke volumes about him. This neighborhood was dangerous, I wouldn't walk my pet gorilla around it. And yet he had no fear. He ran every morning except on the Shabbat.

I must have fallen asleep again because when next I woke, he was kissing me telling me that he was leaving for work. Right then, Eve burst into the room in true Eve fashion and charged us both. She jumped into his arms and he pretended to fly back on the bed.

"Ahhh!" he yelled pretending to be injured, causing Eve to squeal in laughter at the top of her lungs.

Oh well, there goes my plan to sleep till noon. I sat up in the covers and gave them both a stern look.

"It is too earlier to be making all that noise!" I hissed in my angry teacher tone.

Both Kaleb and Eve looked up at me from where they had just been tussling on the bed. Both blinked looking so much alike. I nodded my head at them as if to say, *damn right, they better keep it down* before I laid back down and pulled the covers over my head.

Moments later, it was me who was squealing because Kaleb had come around the bed and picked me up covers and all and tossed me up in the air to bounce on the bed before he grabbed me and did it again.

"Kaleb!" I screeched trying to fight my way out of the cover. But by the time he stopped and I was able to unwind myself from all of the layers, the coward was gone. I looked down at Eve, who stood on the side of the bed all eyes and smiles.

"That's not funny!"

She erupted in a slew of laughter and baby talk. I scooped her up and tossed her slightly in the air so that she could bounce on the bed like I had.

"Nah, how did you like that?"

She was laughing so hard she couldn't speak, she just held up her arms for me to do it again.

Eventually, we made our way out of Kaleb's room after straightening it up a bit and got dressed for the day. I made Eve and Nana's breakfast, then I left out to run a few errands. My first stop was to the Coffee House and then Mika's.

She cracked the door open peeping around the side, much like she had done yesterday. I held up the two mocha-lattes with extra whipped cream and chocolate sauce I bought smiling brightly.

"I've got lattes that's heavy on the fat!" She stared at me for a moment and I could see that she wanted to send me away, but then her eyes fell on the lattes and as if on cue, a glob of chocolate and whipped cream dripped onto the cup holder.

"Wow! That does look good," she finally grumbled opening the door for me to come in. Like yesterday, the house was completely dark. I put the drinks on the table and went to the curtains and opened them just a bit like Kaleb had done.

Mika grabbed one of the lattes and then settled back on the couch. She still had on the clothes she had worn yesterday and her hair was all over her head as if she had just gotten up.

"I'm sorry! Did I wake you?" I asked grabbing my latte sitting on the couch with her. She chuckled without any humor.

"Naw, girl, I been up since five." She spoke like someone who really didn't want to speak at all, but was doing it because they were being pressured to.

"Oh, okay." I didn't know what else to say at that point.

I'd admit to not thinking this plan all the way through. I bought lattes because these fattening drinks always make me feel better when I'm depressed, but I hadn't thought about what to do after that, like what should I say to her.

What can you say to a mother that has lost her husband and her children?

I had no idea. So, we just sat in silence and drank our lattes. And I know she enjoyed it cause when she got down to the bottom where all the whipped cream and chocolate was, she popped the top, ignored the straw, turned the cup up and drained it of its settled goodies.

"Thanks for the coffee, Mon, it was good," she mumbled when she was finished.

I smiled, pleased that she enjoyed it. When the silence got too thick and uncomfortable, I blurted out the first thing that came to my mind.

"I've got to wear a chicken outfit today!"

Dear Yah, I can't believe I just said that! Great job, Monica! A chicken outfit? Really?!

Surprisingly, she turned to look at me with a grin on her face.

"What? Why?" I exhaled, so relieved that she didn't kick me out her house for being a verbal clutz that I had to send up a silent thank you.

"I lost a bet to Kaleb." This seemed to get her attention because she actually turned a bit to face me on the couch.

"What was the bet?"

I settled in and told her about the bet and she laughed so hard that I went on to tell her about the rest of his and my adventures. By the time I was finished, she was wiping tears from her eyes from laughing so hard.

"You went to his apartment building and told them folks he had Ebola? Girl, you is crazy! That's what Kaleb butt get. When me and Ro first got married, Kaleb acted out so bad. He accused me of taking his boy away and all kind of madness. Ro said Kaleb had the nerve to tell him he had the getaway car ready if he changed his mind." She looked at me before smacking the couch.

"He told him this at our wedding, girl!" We both erupted in laughter.

"Wow! Wait till I talk to him. During our wedding, I wish he did offer me a getaway car. I sure would have taken it!" My statement caused her to erupt with laughter again.

"I don't feel sorry for him, "she said when her laughter died down.

"I pray you give him the works 'cause he deserve it!"

"Well, I can promise you one thing, from this point on, he'll never be able to say his life was boring!"

She and I chatted and laughed a bit more before I told her I had to go. We hugged and she thanked me for coming by, saying that we had to do this again. I smiled to myself, she just didn't know how often we were going to do this. Poor Mika probably thought that I was the type of person to let her sit here in her dark house while the rest of the world rotated. Bless her heart!

You see, I learned something about her today. She needed folks to stop tiptoeing around her. Had I been a weak person, I would have taken the go away look she wore when she first opened the door and ran.

But I'm not weak and I dug in and forced her to let me in. And by the time I left, she had turned on the living room light, her kitchen light, and her bedroom light from where she had taken me in there and shown me the wedding gift Kaleb had gotten her and Ro.

She had been so animated and had laughed until tears came from her eyes. Yeah, she would be seeing a lot more of me alright because I was not the kind of person that gave up. And I wasn't giving up on Mika.

When I walked into the center, I came up short at the sight of Stormy, who sat by one of the windows looking out at the world with a look almost as bleak as Mika's. There were only a couple of kids here this early, the only classes today were Madame Queen's drama classes, but they didn't start till later. So the few kids that were here were probably here for a meal.

"Hey, big sista!" I called to her as I approached. She turned and smiled up at me, but her smile didn't reach her eyes.

"Hey, sweetheart," she turned and look back out the window. I sat on the bench next to her.

"What's the matter?"

She inhaled while shaking her head slightly. "Shelomoh and I lost two people that are real close to us yesterday." I put my hand to my chest.

"Dear Yah! How did they die?" Her startled gaze flew to me.

"They didn't die!"

I blinked at her confused as I went back over her words in my head. She did just tell me that she and Shelomoh lost two people that were close to them.

"I'm confused. If they didn't die, how did y'all lose them?" She chuckled dryly.

"That's just it, we lost them. They're gone and nobody knows were."

I frowned. "Were they kidnapped?" She shook her head.

"Did they run away?" Again she shook her head.

"Okay, now I'm good and confused."

"Well, that's cause I can't explain what even I don't understand." I nodded.

"Fair enough. Are you going to be alright?" She exhaled looking back out the window.

"Yeah, I'm going to be fine. It's those boys' parents that I hurt for. They're going through a lot right now." I stood and hugged her.

"We'll keep them in our prayers." She looked up at me surprised. I smiled down at her.

"That's right, I said it! Your little sista is praying now!" She smiled then and this time, it did reach her eyes.

"Aww Mon! HalleluYah!! You have no idea how glad I am to hear that."

"You were right, some things, one just have to learn for themselves." I picked up her hand and gave it a reassuring squeeze.

"I'll tell you all about it a little later. I need to find Madame Queen." Her gaze sobered and she held on to my hand stopping me.

"Why, has she started harassing Kaleb for money?" I chuckled shaking my head.

"No, not yet, but I'm sure she is already working on her game pitch."

"It's something wrong with her, Mon, she is driving me nuts! She claims she has to have sand flown in from Egypt for one of her sketches and no other sand will do!" The desperate look on her face caused me to erupt with laughter.

"Poor Storm, I don't envy your position." I kissed her on the cheek and headed on down the hall toward The Madame's wing. I found her sitting at her make-up table applying mascara.

"Hey, Sweet Tart!" she cooed as I approached.

"Hey, Madame."

"And why have you come to visit me so early in the day?"

I sat on one of the desks that was not covered in costumes and props.

"Well...I need a favor."

"Mmmhmm, I figured as much." She began to brush rouge on her cheeks. "Are you going to tell me what you want or are you going to make me guess?"

I chuckled. "I need you to make me look like a chicken."

The brush stilled on her cheek. "Oh! Sweet Tart, that mind of yours." She put down her brush and turned on her little stool to face me.

"Now, when you say chicken, do you mean sniveling coward or poultry?"

"Poultry."

"First, tell me why," she pleaded. "And don't leave anything out. You know I live vicariously through you!"

I laughed and for the second time that day told how I lost the bet. When I was done, Madame jumped up as if motivated.

"I have the perfect costume!"

An hour and a half later, I stood in front of the mirror.

"Umm, Madame, I said a chicken. I look like I'm on my way down the Victoria's Secret runway when they premiered their Angel line!"

You see, I was leery when she handed me the sequin halter bra top and told me to put it on. But then, she wrapped a piece of yellow cloth around my waist and hips, something like a tight miniskirt but not quite. I thought to myself, this is going down-hill fast.

And as if to prove my point, she put another sheer piece of cloth over the yellow tight skirt and began to build me a tail of yellow feathers. I waited for her to add more clothing, but she never did.

It took her thirty minutes to design the headpiece that was typical Madame Queen, over-the-top extravagant. And I guess because there were red feathers in it, we could say it was a chicken comb maybe...possibly. It had started out as a simple red headband, now it sat about two feet high on my head, a crown of red feathers, gold wires, and rhinestones.

Maybe when I was done with it, I will give it to Angie. She could probably use it as part of her costume for Carnival. When Madame was satisfied with the costume, she pulled up a stool and began to apply my make-up. The end result was something that was way too glamorous for what I needed to do.

"Madame, I can't stand outside of Kaleb's shop dressed like this! I'll cause a traffic pile up and be arrested for disrupting the peace." She stood back admiring her work with a huge grin on her face.

"That's the point Sweet Tart. You don't really want to stand out in this heat holding a stupid sign, do you?" She waved away that idea.

"Keep this shawl on till you get him alone." She wrapped a long shawl around my shoulders, leaving just my feather tail sticking out.

"Once you get him alone, slowly unwrap yourself and tell him you came to fulfill your end of the bargain. Now, if he's the man I believe he is. You'll never make it out the door."

Oh yeaaahhh! The grin that spread across my face was that of awe and amazement. Madame was brilliant.

"Yeesss, Madame. We can call it Operation Sexy Chicken!" I was super-excited now. I couldn't wait to see his face, but there was only one problem.

"But how am I going to drive in the car with this crown on?"

She playfully smacked my hand. "Silly girl, just slide it off like this." She slid the headband off and handed me the elaborate headpiece.

"Wow! That is easy. Okay, thank you so much! I'll tell you how it goes!" I turned to hurry out of the room, but she stopped me.

"Wait, Sweet Tart! Don't forget your sign!" She held up the big piece of cardboard. It read, *Stop by King and Son's Restoration and See What Makes the Chickens Cluck!*"

I shook my head as I walked back to get the sign. Madame Queen was a mad scientist, there was no doubt about it. But what made this so frightening was how willing of a test subject I always seemed to be.

Kaleb

"We got a problem, K!" I looked up from my computer as Tiny came through my office door. I could tell by the look on his face that I was not going to like what he had to say.

"Rasheed?" I asked, already knowing the topic. Tiny nodded as he took a seat in one of the chairs in front of my desk. That feeling I get when my world is about to shift settled over me. I sat back in my seat.

"How bad is it?" Tiny shook his head.

"Boss, I swear I hate bringing you news like this. You doing so good in making yourself better. Hell, you even motivating me to change some things in my life." I grinned at the big man.

"Damn, Tiny, you must got real bad news 'cause you in this piece talking like Dr. Phil! Come on, brother, tell me what I need to know about Rasheed." I looked down at his hands for a second before taking a deep breath.

"What? He went on and made a deal with the Cubans, huh? How far is he in Dominic's pocket?" I asked to get the big man talking. The fact that Tiny was hesitating like this was not a good sign.

"He in Dominic's pocket real good. Somehow, he convinced him you was still onboard." I nodded, I figured he was going to go and do something dumb like that.

"Why didn't Dominic call me?"

Tiny shrugged. "I don't know, but things done got ugly."

"How so?"

"I guess Rasheed had in his mind that the only way he can take the power from you was to expand his area of operation. All week, he and his crew been riding down on niggas putting pistols to they head, telling them that they had to shop with him. And in order to keep up with supply and demand, he had to grab more than his normal ten from the Cubans."

"How much?" My question was quiet, I knew he was getting ready to tip me over. Rasheed was barely paying for the ten keys of dope he got from Dominic. Twice I had to pay for the nigga.

"Fifty keys."

"Son of a—" I stood from my chair and began to pace as I tried to wrap my mind around what this meant while trying to control my rising temper.

"That stupid mutha—" I slammed my fist down on my desk needing to destroy something. There was no way he was going to be able to cover such an amount. There was no way! Even if he took over every set from here to Oak Park, he still couldn't get off that much dope in time enough to pay Dominic when he was ready. Which meant... I felt myself slipping back into my old man. This wasn't good.

"K, that ain't the worst part!" Tiny continued in a hesitant voice. "His boy Marcus got popped yesterday in a moving truck. And guess what them boys found in the back of that truck."

I inhaled. "The Cuban's dope," I muttered through clenched teeth. Tiny nodded.

"And your lil brother running around desperate trying to find a way to get that money 'for word get back to Dominic about the bust."

I looked away from Tiny as I fought to stay cool, but I felt like finding my brother and putting him out of his misery. How many times have I told his stupid ass to stop transporting dope in moving trucks? That's the number one vehicle cops looked for. See, this was one of the main problems with these young dope boys, they felt like they were the smartest cats on the block. And they didn't have to listen to the OG's because somehow, the OG's made it to where they at by being stupid.

"You know he gon' try everything he can but, when none of that stuff works, he gon' come to you to clean this up for him." Tiny continued. "You want me to contact Dominic?"

I shook my head. "Hell no! I told him I'm done coming to his rescue. This one he gon' have to figure out on his own." He nodded.

"Should I put extra boys on watch just in case them Cubans try to run up on us." Tiny's statement was harmless. But it was enough to tip me over. Just like that, all the leeway I had made in this truth and my walk with the Most High was lost. This situation did not call for Kaleb Warrior of Yah. This situation called for Kaleb the Goon. Because there was no way this was ending without blood being shed. And to keep my family safe, I will wipe all them niggas off the face of the earth!

"Dominic ain't stupid! He don't want to go to war with me! But I ain't taking no chances with my wife and child's life. I want somebody watching that boarding house at all times! If anything look suspicious and I mean *anything*, I want to know about it instantly. Put somebody on Monica. If she not with me, they are to never let her out their sight."

"Send some more men over to the restaurant and just tell my mother I hired them as security because they needed work." He stood.

"You know eventually this will lead to—" I lifted my hand cutting him off.

"War! Yeah, I know. But picture me in my crib hiding from a nigga! Whoever think they britches big enough to go to war with me they can bring it. As a matter of fact, I ain't sitting waiting for a nigga—" A knock on the door interrupted me.

"Come in!" I called expecting Rasheed. I sent up one last prayer because I was getting ready to crush this fool. At this point, my anger was almost blinding. However, all the building pressure oozed out of my head when Monica walked in wearing some kind of bedazzled costume. The impact of her beauty and my anger being brought to a screeching halt rendered me speechless for a moment.

"Wow, you look amazing, Mrs. Monica!" Tiny muttered as he turned to look at her. I didn't like the way he was looking at her. My anger began to silently simmer again. I was going to kill my friend.

She flashed him with her beautiful smile. "Now Tiny, what did I tell you about all that Mrs. stuff? Just Monica!" She shook her finger at him admonishing him as if she was a school teacher and him her student.

I sat and silently watched as the three-hundred-plus pounds of muscle that was Tiny actually blushed under her admonishment. She patted his arm.

"It's alright, Tiny, I'll charge it to your head and not your heart." She cooed up at him.

"Why thank you, Monica. I sure do appreciate it!" This woman had turned my killer into soft butter.

"Hey Tiny, go ahead and take care of what we discussed. I'll catch up with you later." He nodded before turning to look back at Monica.

"You have a good day, Monica." He went to tip his hat, except he didn't have one on, so he just rubbed his bald head, playing it off.

She flashed him with one of those smiles that rendered most men useless, further wrapping him around her little finger.

"See you later, Tiny." He walked toward the door but turned to look at me over her shoulder, giving me the thumbs-up with a goofy grin on his face. I did not return his smile. In fact, I felt my mood slipping into very dangerous territory. Seeing this, the smile left his face. He paused in shutting the door.

"You okay, boss?" He asked.

"I'll talk to you later, Tiny, be ready." He nodded before closing the door. My eyes came back to my wife, who had managed to bring the hopeless romantic out of a goon.

I couldn't blame Tiny though. Hadn't she done the same to me? Didn't she have me living in a damn boarding house just to be close to her? She was beautiful, amazingly so. Any man with eyes could see that. Poor Tiny didn't know what hit him. She had walked through my door dressed like one of the royal Hebrew queens of old...

I sat back in my chair. "That smile of yours will be the death of some unfortunate fool, wife."

Monica

My smile disappeared as I took him in. His quiet threat resonated in the room. He was angry. Very!

"What's the matter with you?"

He threw up his hands. "Just one of them days I guess."

Okay, he was throwing out mixed signals, but I don't think he was angry with me. I smiled, even more excited to reveal my surprise.

"Well, I have good news. I've come to fulfill my half of the bargain."

He frowned. "What bargain?"

I placed the sign facing away from him on the couch. And slowly began to unravel the shawl.

"Remember you said you would make me beg and I laughed and said that if you did, I would dress up like a chicken and stand outside your shop holding up a sign." As I took off the shawl, his eyes slowly raked over my body.

Grinning, I picked up the sign to show him. As he read it his frown grew.

Okay, not the response I expected. I lowered the sign placing it back on the couch. When I looked back up, he was wearing that deadly grin, the same one he wore before he hit that guy with those two big wrenches, the same one he'd worn before his men snatched my girls out of my car.

And I ain't gon' lie, it was making me very uncomfortable. Slowly he stood, never taking his eyes off of me. This was not my Kaleb, this was mob boss Kaleb I was talking to. Something had made him slip back into his former self.

"Oh yeah?! You gon' stand outside my shop dressed like that?" His question sounded calm, but he always sounded like that before he did something completely wild. He chuckled without humor as he slowly walked around his desk.

"What, Monica?" He asked holding up his hands as he began to walk towards me.

"You think 'cause I read the Bible and I'm trying to be a better man that won't kill a nigga?!" He balled his fist up and slammed it into his open palm and I nearly jumped out of my heels.

I held up my hands, speaking calmly to him. I don't know what pissed him off like this, but he was trying to take it out on me.

"Kaleb, it was just a joke! You wasn't supposed to get upset."

"Oh really? You tell me how I suppose to feel when my wife's beauty attract every nigga within twenty city blocks?"

I began to slowly step back, something was wrong him and it didn't have anything to do with my outfit, but the way he was walking towards me was a little threatening.

"Kaleb, what happened? Why are you so upset?" I asked my question softly, pleading with him with my eyes to talk to me. His gaze slowly raked down my body again and I saw when his lust started to go to war with his anger because he did that thing with his bottom lip. And I think there may be something wrong with me because I was extremely turned on by it.

My back came up against the door and he continued to walk towards me until he was standing in front of me. I put my hands on the doorknob; this position caused my body to thrust out a bit as if it was an offering to him.

He put his hand on the door by my head as he gazed down into my eyes and I saw it then, the battle that was going on within him. Something bad had happened. I reached up and gently palmed his cheek.

"What happened, baby?" I whispered. For a moment, he closed his eyes as he took in my comfort. When he opened them, the anger was completely gone, replaced by his lust. He slammed his lips against mine. At first, I was taken aback by the fierceness of his kiss, but then he gentled it just a bit and that was all it took for my mouth to soften for him.

He moaned when he felt my surrender. "Thank you, baby, I need you so bad!" he whispered. He put one arm around my waist and lifted me against the door. I wrapped my arms his neck and my legs around his waist and held on for dear life as he deepened the kiss.

His hard body rubbing up against my softness, which was still sensitive from the last time he made love to me was enough to cause the fire to build as if it had never been extinguished. I reached up and snatched the crown off my head, causing red feathers to rain down around us.

He turned with me in his arms, causing me to laugh out at the sudden movement as he carried me to his desk. He swept his arm across it, clearing a space for my body. The way he looked down at me made me feel like the most desirable woman in the world. He reached up and snatched his t-shirt over his head before ripping my skirt from around my waist, causing more feathers to take to the air.

I think I will never forget that day. My husband had thoroughly made love to my body in the midst of those feathers. Needless to say, Madame had been right. Operation Sexy Chicken had been a smashing success!

Chapter 14
MEET THE CREW

MONICA

W hatever it was that was going on with Kaleb caused him to make love to me in a way that almost consumed me. First, there on his desk and then again in his shower. I was very aware that he was taking his anger and frustration out in the act of making love.

And...

Hmmm...

Maybe there was something seriously wrong with me, but it was the hottest most erotic thing I have ever experienced. Okay, technically, my experience isn't all that extensive and I really don't have anything to compare it to since Kaleb is the only man I've ever been with.

But I know down to the deepest part of my being that what happened in this office today was earth-shattering. As we dried off after the shower, I couldn't help but study him in wonder. His mind had gone back to whatever he and Tiny were talking about before I came into the office. The frown was back on his face.

My eyes traveled down his body as his strong muscles flexed as he slid his legs into his pants. He took a t-shirt down out of his closet, but before he could put it over his head someone knocked on his office door.

"I'll get it, keep getting dressed," he told me before he walked out of the office bare-chested with his shirt in hand, pulling the door up behind him.

Instantly, I thought about all those feathers that were everywhere in there and prayed he didn't open the door all the way up for whoever it was so that they could not see into the office.

However, the male voice I heard at the door caused me to cringe.

It was Shelomoh!

"Dang it!" Quickly I slid into the rest of my clothes glad I had brought my jean skirt and sweatshirt, something easy to put on. When I was dressed, I took one last look at myself in the mirror praying I didn't look like I had just done what we'd just done.

"Oh crap!" There was a huge hickey on my neck.

Well, there goes my trying to play it off like I was just in the area and decided to use his shower. I put my hands on my face blushing big time. I had no idea how I was going to be able to look the man I had come to view as a big brother in the face.

But then a memory surfaced.

I didn't have anything to be ashamed of. In fact, several memories surfaced of Shelomoh being very improper with Stormy on several occasions. A time that really comes to mind is when Stormy had first come back to the center. At the time I had to have been like nine or ten. She and Shelomoh had taken on the task of organizing the equipment room that was inside the gym.

Nana had told me to take some jump ropes down to them and oh my goodness, what I had caught them doing had made me yell out. For years after that Shelomoh had tried to use some kind of Jedi mind trick and convince me that I had dreamed the whole thing.

Chuckling at the memory I put lip gloss on my lips before I

eased the door open and slipped out the bathroom. Just in time to see them embracing in a brotherly hug.

"Hey shalom, ach!" Kaleb muttered, but I could tell he was not really happy to see Shelomoh, but not for the same reasons I'm wasn't happy to see him at this moment.

"Shalom lil brotha, how are you?" He looked at Kaleb seeing more than either of us could imagine. Kaleb reached up and rubbed his hand down his face, his tension and stress apparent.

"Man, I'm alright I guess. Just got to make some moves, may need to put some things on hold."

"Let's talk about it, ach!"

Kaleb didn't really move back and invite Shelomoh in as much as Shelomoh kind of just stepped around him and on into the office. A smile came on his handsome face when he saw me pulling the bathroom door up behind me.

"Hey, troublemaker, how is it going?" I gave him a nervous smile because the office looked like exactly what happened in it happened.

"I'm good, Shelomoh, ummm..."

"Wow! What happened here, did somebody beat up a chicken?" Shelomoh asked chuckling as he looked around the office. I started choking.

Oh my goodness! My freaked out gaze flew to Kaleb, who just chuckled a bit before shaking his head slightly as he walked to his desk. However, by the time he sat down in his chair the smile had disappeared from his face. He exhaled.

"Look ach, I know why you're here, man, and the situation is out of my hands. I got to handle this business."

Shelomoh leaned down to dust the feathers out of the seat across from Kaleb's. As he did it he looked at me.

"This has your name all over it," he muttered before easing down in the seat.

I ignored him and on the low key started sweeping feather together with my feet. But I didn't even know why I bothered, the feathers were not the only telltale sign of what Kaleb and I had just done.

The stuff on his desk was still pushed to the side leaving an empty spot in the middle that anybody with good sense could guess why.

Oh my goodness!

I knew my face was beet red. I was so embarrassed that it took me a minute to see that neither Shelomoh nor Kaleb was paying attention to the desk. These two were involved in a silent battle of wills.

"I understand that something has come up. That's life. But unfortunately, we can't choose when Yah calls. There is no availability sheet to fill out. These things happen when it's time."

Kaleb rubbed his hand through his beard.

"Solomon, I—" He shook his head. "Man, I'm sorry. What has come up is going to need my undivided attention."

"You've been invited to the Lyon's Den. He wants to meet with you today." I could tell Kaleb was irritated with this news. He frowned at Shelomoh.

"Don't you think that's a bit convenient for him to want to meet me *now*? I've been waiting for that invite since I got out. Why now?" Shelomoh chuckled without humor, for the first time looking his age. Suddenly he looked tired.

"Little brother, there is nothing convenient about this situation for either of you. Lyon and Gideon both just lost their sons, the strength of their loins. I can't even begin to describe the pain they're going through right now."

"I'm sorry to hear that, but that seems to me to be more of a reason to postpone this meeting. That way, they can handle things on their end and I can handle things on mine." Shelomoh shook his head.

"That's not how this thing works. Lyon closed the gym down today to meet with you because Yah said it's time. And when Yah says its time, little brother, you drop everything to answer his call.

You are just a man, you know not what is in store, but be brave and step up to the plate."

Kaleb rubbed his hands down his face good and frustrated. He was so torn. I could see the battle he was fighting within himself. What the world had happened? What was he going through?

"Can I come too?" I asked walking around Kaleb's desk to stand next to him. I reached down and took his hand in mine. I don't know what he was going through, but there was a strong feeling in me that he needed to do this. It felt like it was a matter of life and death.

Shelomoh smiled up at me and I could see that he was proud of me.

"Sure, Troublemaker, you can come too." I turned to look down at Kaleb. He was looking up at me and the conflict he was going through was there in his eyes.

I pulled his hand to my lips and kissed his rough, scarred knuckles.

"Come on, baby. You can do this. Everything happens for a reason. At least find out why." He frowned up at me as he thought about it, but then he nodded.

"Yeah, alright."

Kaleb

I paused after stepping into the gym. The air felt different in here. Shelomoh turned to watch me. I frowned, wondering if I was tripping.

"What's the matter, ach?" he asked. I shook my head.

"Nothing, I just-." I couldn't even think of the words to describe what I just felt when I crossed that threshold, so I just shook my head again. "Nothing."

With a slight grin on his face, he looked at me a moment longer before he nodded slightly and turned to walk farther into the gym. I took Monica's hand pulling her closer to me. The air was different in this place and until I knew why I wanted her close just in case I had to get us out of here quickly. I relied heavily on my instincts and my instincts were telling me we had stepped into something unlike anything I was used to.

I thought about everything I had ever heard of about this place that was tucked deep in the heart of the ghetto. There wasn't a fighter in Chicago or the near area that hadn't tried to get into the Lyon's Den and I was no exception. So, you can imagine my surprise when Shelomoh first told me that he knew the owner and could get me in.

At first, I was looking forward to it, but now I couldn't focus on much of anything outside of the men I was going to have to lay to rest. And although it pained my heart past words, I couldn't shake the feeling that my baby brother was going to be one of them. Yah knows I don't want to make that call, but if it came down to making a choice between him and my wife and child...

I shook my head. I didn't want to think about that; I had to find a way to fix this without it coming to that, which meant that I really didn't have time for this. I needed to lay hands on Rasheed and see just how much damage he has done and then decide how best to deal with the Cubans.

"Shalom, achim!" Shelomoh's voice boomed out to the handful of men that were in the spacious gym.

I had never met Lyon in person, but I knew him instantly. He sat off to the side wiping some weights down with a lightly oiled rag. When Shelomoh called out, he stood and headed toward us, his shrewd eyes taking me in and sizing me up to determine what kind of man I was.

On the way here, Shelomoh had told me that I was coming to the gym at a perfect time because not only would I be training with Lyon, but also with someone named Gideon, who's going to be in town for a while. He said both achim were having a tough time because their sons had gone missing and nobody knew where.

I asked him why Lyon and Gideon were taking the time they could be using to look for them to train me and his answer was chilling.

"Their lives are not their own. They understand something you have only begun to know. And it's that they are simply vessels for The Ancient of Days to do with as he will. And so are their sons. Sure, they're hurt. They miss them. It's tough to comfort their grieving wives, but the journey their boys are embarking on is a journey they have prepared them well for. And now, Lyon and Gideon have to continue with their work, which is to continue to train the achim who Yah send their way *when* he sends them their way."

"Each of the warriors they train has their own journeys to take, just like their sons Dawid and Monroe."

I understood his words, but he didn't understand that I'd already had a journey, one that if I ignored, could cause my family to be hurt, one that escalated out of control because I had decided to leave the game as if I could just walk away. In theory, it would be great to become a better man, but the truth was, that was not my destiny.

I belonged to these streets and once they had you, they didn't know how to let you go. Had I not been distracted by the things Shelomoh was teaching me, it would not have gotten so out of hand. I would have kept a better watch on Rasheed and continued to protect him from himself. Although Yah knows it's an exhausting job and one that I am tired of.

Still, I had to tell these brothers that although I was honored that they had chosen me to fight with them, I needed to decline because quite frankly, I had other matters to attend.

Monica

Okay, Monica, don't groupie out and embarrass your husband!

That was great advice, but the closer Lyon got to us, the less likely I felt as if I could listen. Oh my goodness! I could not even begin to describe the might of this man. I saw something move from the corner of my eye and I let out a little squeak as I squeezed Kaleb's hand while moving as close to him as I could possibly get.

That lion! Dear Yah, it was huge! And it was looking at me.

"Relax, Mon, King don't eat troublemakers," Shelomoh said chuckling.

I looked over at King with a measure of doubt. This lion was famous in the hood, mainly because nobody could understand why he was allowed to be here since it was technically illegal to own him here on the west side of Chicago. Rumor had it that the police were too afraid to say anything to Lyon about it, so they just pretended they didn't know he had a pet lion.

Maybe I would one day work up my courage enough to ask him how he goes about keeping him as a pet or maybe I wouldn't.

My Nana would say, *"Now Monica, that's just too nosy. It ain't none of your business what kind of pet them folks got over there!"*

When finally we reached Lyon, he held his hand out to Kaleb.

"Shalom ach!" His deep voice filled the room. There was something in his tone that reminded me of Mika's like he really didn't want to talk, but he did it because he had to.

"Hey shalom," Kaleb responded as they embraced in a brotherly hug. It ended up being a three-way hug because I was practically glued to Kaleb's side, my leery gaze still on Mr. King, who at that moment came to rest on his hind legs next to his master before he opened his huge mouth in a wide yawn.

"Lyon, this is Kaleb, the young brother I've been telling you about. This kid is gifted from the Most High. He's Fast! Just need a little tuning that's all." Lyon nodded.

"Okay, we'll check him out."

"And the little troublemaker glued to his side is his isha, Monica. Monica, Lyon." Lyon chuckled although his grin didn't reach his eyes.

"I think I remember her. Little thing this high," he held his hand to his waist, "Little locs sticking straight up everywhere."

Oh my goodness, he remembered me! I was cheesing so hard my cheeks hurt.

"You remembered me!" I said on a sigh.

Kaleb turned to look down at me and frowned. I looked up at him, I was so thrilled that even his frown couldn't dim my mood.

"He remembered me!" I told him. Both Shelomoh and Lyon chuckled. Kaleb just shook his head.

"Hey, come on in, make yourselves comfortable. BeniYah!" he called to a guy that was about my age, maybe a little older who was lifting weights over to the side.

"Go downstairs and get Gideon for me." The youth took off at a jog toward the back of the gym.

"GinaYah!" Lyon called back towards the same direction.

"Yeah, daddy!" A pretty young girl that looked to be about fourteen or fifteen came from a room that looked as if it was a kitchen.

"Where is your sister?" he asked when she came to a stop next to him. She put her hand in King's mane and scratched his head. The big cat must really enjoy her touch because he began to purr so loud it vibrated through the floor.

"She won't get out the bed!" Lyon exhaled. "Mama won't either."

For just a moment, she looked at her dad with angry eyes. He wrapped his arm around her and pulled her close.

"Yeah, I know...Listen, do daddy a favor and take Monica in the kitchen and make her a snack." It was so weird seeing this big fierce man in father mode.

"Go with Gina, troublemaker," Shelomoh said.

I went to follow her, but Kaleb still held on to my hand. My gaze lifted to his face. He studied Lyon and his daughter then he looked around the gym sizing it up. I put my hand on his arm.

"I'll be okay, baby," I whispered. He looked down at me, the muscle ticked in his cheek before he nodded.

"Don't go too far, we won't be here long." I smiled up at him encouragingly.

"Take all the time you need." I didn't wait for his response, I just turned and followed GinaYah.

~

Kaleb

The man named Gideon had joined us. He, Lyon, Shelomoh, and I now sat in a few fold-up chairs watching BeniYah spar with another man. Every now and again, Lyon or Gideon called out something that they were doing wrong and complimenting them on something they did right.

It was really a shame my life had taken the turn it did and I needed to go back into doing gangsta sh*t because I really felt that I could learn a lot from these two men, but it was no need of me prolonging my stay. I had things I needed to handle.

"Look, I appreciate you guys agreeing to train me, but something came up and I got to take care of it." Lyon and Gideon turned to look at me, their stares feeling as if they saw more than what I was presenting.

"What came up?" Gideon asked. His bluntness took me off guard.

"Something," I told him because it wasn't any of his business.

"What?" Lyon asked.

They both turned to face me fully and it was intimidating as hell. I turned my head to look at Shelomoh, who sat reclined in the fold-up chair with his legs stretched out in front of him, ankles crossed. He folded his arms across his chest and looked away from me towards his ankles chuckling a bit as if to tell me I was on my own.

I turned to look back at the two goons who I was more than positive were trying to punk me. I sat up a bit squaring my shoulders. Although I know it may be futile, I will try and take these niggas if I got to.

"Why you want to know?" Hell, if they want to play the blunt game I was an expert.

Lyon held up his hands. "Calm down, son, it's just a question."

"Yea, well, I don't really know you cats to be telling you all my business." Gideon grunted. Lyon nodded his head.

"Fair enough, I ask 'cause no matter what it is, I can pretty much guarantee it's a distraction."

"Distraction from what?"

"From your path, young man," Gideon finally spoke. "You were called for a very important purpose. And there are forces out there that will stop at nothing to see you fail."

I rubbed my hand over my head trying to alleviate the pressure that was building up in my brain. At the same time, that feeling like my life was shifting again washed over me.

"I know it seems like there is no other way to go, but it is. Smoke and mirrors these things are, little brotha," Lyon said quietly, his words irritated me a bit, I frowned.

"Smoke and mirrors, but you don't know what's going on. How can you call what I'm going through smoke and mirrors?"

"'Cause you ain't unique. You ain't going through nothing that each one of us sitting here ain't went through," he continued.

"What I'm telling you is there are higher powers at work here, powers that if you allow, will play you like a pawn. Your spiritual eyes are brand new. If you give us a little time, we'll teach you how to use them so that you too can see through the facade and know that my words are true."

Gideon leaned forward putting his elbows on his knees.

"And after that, if you still need to damage something," he sat back holding up his arms, "You my ach, I'll roll with you. All we ask is that you give us some time to show you how to see through the smoke and mirrors to the real world underneath."

"I thought you were training me how to fight better."

All three of the men chuckled without humor. Gideon sat back in his chair folding his arms in back of his head.

"It's all a part of the training, kid."

I thought about their words. They said that higher powers were at work. Could it be a coincidence my brother decided to completely show his a$$ when I came into this truth? Could it be a coincidence Shelomoh showed up at my office as soon as I decided that this truth wasn't for me? Could Yah be fighting for me? And if so, why?

Monica's words to me before we left my office came back to me.

"Come on, baby. You can do this. Everything happens for a reason. At least find out why."

I looked at Lyon and Gideon.

"Yeah, okay...what do I have to do next?" Shelomoh, who still sat with his arms folded across his chest looking down at his crossed ankles began to chuckle again.

"Bruh, I sho' hope what it looked like happened in your office today happened. 'Cause the cookie jar is going bye-bye!"

Chapter 15
DID SOMEBODY CALL A PLUMBER?

KALEB

"I know you this child's father."

The big gulp of juice I had just drunk came spewing from between my lips. Eve erupted in laughter from where she sat in her high-chair eating her breakfast.

"Wow," I mumbled as I grabbed the roll of paper towel to clean up the mess that I made.

"I am so sorry about that! Here, let me get this cleaned up. I swallowed my juice wrong." With desperate eyes, I looked back toward the kitchen door for Monica.

"Don't try to look for your little professional liar. This is you and Nana talking now," the shrewd old woman said from where she calmly sat stirring her coffee across the table from me as if she did not just rock my world.

Eve picked up her sippy cup and took a swig of her juice before spitting it out of her mouth like she had just seen me do. But instead of it projecting like she'd hoped, it ended up just dripping down her chin. I chuckled because it was really funny.

"Don't do that, sweetheart," I told her, putting way too much attention into cleaning her up. I ain't gon' lie; I was at a loss for how to respond. Nana had waited till Monica left the room and sucker punched me.

"Come on, Kaleb, talk to me. You can do it, baby."

Oh man! Damn! Monica!

I was at a loss. I didn't know what to do. Eve began to whine because she was waiting for me to stop wiping her mouth so that she could spit her juice out again.

I cleared my throat. "Umm, I don't think I know what you mean."

"Sure, you do. My grandchildren have always thought me to be too slow to keep up with their mischief, but I took you for a smart man. Surely you know it's futile to try and pull the wool over my eyes. This here child looks just like you. And if you and Monica think I don't know what's been going on between the two of you in my home, you're delusional. As delusional as you think I am." She held up her hand.

"When is the wedding? 'Cause I don't support no fornicating!'"

My shoulders slumped. Oh wow! I can't believe this lot had fallen on me. Monica believed that if Nana found out what had happened between us it will make her already failing health worse.

Just this morning she had a coughing fit that brought tears to Monica's eyes as she'd tried to convince her grandmother to go to the hospital for the hundredth time. If I said something and it made the situation worse Monica will be pissed.

Damn it!

"Nana..." my words faltered. Right then Eve spits her juice out again. Relieved for the little reprieve I went to wipe it, but the older woman stopped me.

"Young man, if you don't start talking this instant, I know something!" I chuckled. Nana thought she was so tough.

"Okay... If I tell you, you have to promise not to tell Monica."

"My lips are sealed." She brought her fingers to her lips pretending to zip them and throw away the key.

I exhaled. Damn! I had way too much on my plate to add this to it. My brother has been blowing my phone up all morning, which meant he had reached the breaking point and things have gotten serious between him and the Cubans. This was something I really needed to be looking into, but I wasn't because I'd let men who called themselves my brothers talk me into training to be some kind of end of days warrior.

Please Yah, don't let my words cause any harm to Monica's beloved grandmother.

"Yes, I am Eve's father." She hit the table with her hand.

"I knew it! I knew it when you first came through that door I may not have Madame Queen's eye, but I can tell a man that come from wealth. Came up in here talking 'bout you need a place to stay! Only one thing make a man live in squalor when he don't have to."

"Oh yeah? And what's that?"

"Monica!"

I barked with laughter. Oh man! She'd hit it on the nail! She laughed with me for a little while before she erupted in another fit of coughing, I stood to try and get her some water or something, but she gestured for me to sit back down.

Easing down I watched her with a wary gaze. "Are you alright?"

Nodding she struggled to clear her throat. "I'm alright! Now..." she said when her fit had passed.

"When is the wedding?" This she asked clear as day.

I hesitated, not sure how she would take the news that the wedding had already happened. Would she get angry that she wasn't there to see it? I rubbed my hand over my head, searching my brain on how best to tell her. I didn't want to lie to her.

"I see it in your eyes, I know you love her! And I understand that marriage is the last thing you young men want to talk about, but... I ain't got long. And I need to know that when I'm gone my babies are going to be taken care of." She reached out and took Eve's hand into hers.

"When you walked through that door, I knew Yah had answered

my prayer... you got here just in time. I feel like I can rest easy if I know that Monica is your wife."

"I married Monica the day after I moved in." My words were quiet. For a moment her mouth opened in surprise before a huge smile spread on her face.

"Oh! HalleluYah, child! HalleluYah!" She clapped her hands together.

"That sho' is a blessing—"

Monica, looking good as hell in only the way that she could, walked through the kitchen door interrupting her.

"What's a blessing?" she asked, her grandmother's sudden end of words drawing her attention.

~

Monica

"Hold it right there, young lady!" Nana said instead of answering my question, "What do you think you're doing with those tools?"

I woke up this morning on a mission. I had put the repairs I needed to make around the boarding house off for as long as I could. The upstairs plumbing was the *squeaky wheel* and it was time for me to go ahead and get in it.

After I prepared breakfast for my little family I snuck out the kitchen before Kaleb noticed I wasn't eating. Because Nana had complained to him so often about me skipping breakfast, he had taken it upon himself to rectify it.

But not this morning!

Ha!

I went upstairs to change into my brand new repair woman's clothes. It's like Madame Queen always said, dress for the job. So, you know, I had to go shopping. There was some serious work ahead of me, which meant I had to have the fly gear. I found Eve and I a matching pair of jean overalls that had these cute little flowers stitched on them.

We even got the matching utility belts which were perfect to hold all my tools and Eve's plastic set. After I was dressed, I bundled my locs up on top of my head and wrapped a head wrap around them Erykah Badu style, then grabbed my *'Plumber's For Dummies'* book and headed downstairs.

According to the book, the first thing I needed to do was turn off the water at the main valve, which they said was generally located in the basement or out on the street. I was on my way to check the basement first when I interrupted my Nana's and Kaleb's conversation that she so cleverly switched subjects when I inquired about.

Note to self: Ask Kaleb about that later.

"Why grandmother, whatever does one do with tools? I'm getting ready to tackle some of the repairs around here!" Her eyes widened and a look of utter horror crossed her face.

"What—no!" She looked across the table to my husband.

"Kaleb!"

He grinned as he took in her distress. Trying not to laugh, he cleared his throat.

"Mon, I already got a guy coming out to take a look at it... so—"

"Don't even try it!" I screeched cutting him off pointing at the two of them as I walked toward the table.

"You don't think I see what the two of you are up to? You dare to sit here and try to insult my intelligence?" I narrowed my eyes at them.

Kaleb shook his head. "I don't know what you're talking about. The knocking in the shower has been really bad for the last couple of days, so I asked Nana if she wouldn't mind if I called someone in to take a look at it and she said that she didn't." The lying little weasel put his hand on his chest as if he was sincere.

"It's the least I could do for all that the two of you have done for me." He had the nerve to blink innocently up at me after unloading all that crap.

I put my hand on my hip. If he thinks for a minute he can outfox a master fox, he had another thing coming. Two could play at this.

"Oh no! That won't be necessary, K. You've done more than enough for us. You already pay more than your fair share of the rent. And you were so kind to let me *borrow* that truck so that I can easily navigate town. Not to mention covering the cost of food—"

"Well, it's the least I can do since you agreed to cook for me!" he interrupted, still trying to hang with the pro. Nana nodded her head in agreement as she sat in her chair silently rooting Kaleb on. I had something in store for the both of them because I will not be swayed. I smiled down at Kaleb.

"Cooking for you is the least I can do, seeing as to how you convinced Nana here to let you cover all the utility bills. I won't mention the fact that you didn't have to convince too hard before somebody readily accepted!" I cut my eyes at Nana, she sucked in her breath.

"Excuse me, little girl! What are you trying to say?" Ignoring her question, I continued with my point.

"Hell, it's because of you, *Mr.* that I don't have to flip burgers anymore. And as your landlord, it is my duty to provide the best living experience. You said those pipes are banging, well after this week, they won't be banging anymore. All I ask is that you don't get in my way and allow me to do my job!"

Chuckling Kaleb threw up his hands. When Nana saw that she shook her head at him.

"Don't give up!" she whispered.

"And you!" I snapped pointing at her. She sat back staring at my finger as if she was going to be reaching for her switch soon. I didn't care! Her intimidation factor had dimmed in my older age. Eight years ago, I would have been frightened.

"Don't think I don't know what you're doing?" I told her.

She huffed, "I don't know what you're talking about!"

"You know as well as anybody that I have been looking forward to this project. I have read so much study material I feel like a pro!" She looked at my book over her glasses.

"Plumbing for Dummies!" she said dryly, "Is that the study material that has you feeling

like a pro?" Kaleb Chuckled. I flashed my eyes at him. He stopped laughing holding up his hands again.

"I'm not in it!" he muttered.

"Well zip it! No cheerleading from the sideline!"

He nodded. "You got it!"

I held up my book. "This book was written for dummies. Can you then imagine what happens when someone with my intellect reads it? Must I remind you that I was my class valedictorian? You know why, Nana?"

She ignored me as she brought her coffee cup to her lips.

"Don't worry, you don't have to answer, I'll tell you anyway! It's because I was the smartest student of my graduating class. One does not gain that title unless they possess the capacity for abstract thought!" I pointed to myself.

"That's what you're dealing with, brilliance! Now, if the both of you naysayers will excuse me, I have some pipes to repair!" Then I proceeded to leave the kitchen with an exit that would have made the Madame proud.

By Tuesday I was in desperate trouble. I don't know how, but I ended up with a gaping hole in the shower wall and a leak that I could not stop. Well, I don't quite know if *leak* was the right word to use. It was more like a small gush.

I read in the book that a little plumbers putty would work for a small leak. So, I went out and got some. Figuring a lot of putty would work for a big leak. It had to work. I had run out of ideas on what to do. And after watching like a hundred YouTube videos, I was no closer to the answer.

This is when good ole' grade 'A' ingenuity came in. And I've always been grade A. I had found the miracle cure to plumbing in this putty. It was some wonderful stuff. Not only did it seal up that gush, it also helped hold together some more pipes I couldn't seem to get to stay connected before.

Hell, I went out and got another pail of the stuff and used it to put the wall back together. When I was done, I stood looking at my work.

"*Not bad, Mon?*" It wasn't the prettiest patching job in the world, but it would do for now. When I'm done with all the piping in the house, I will come back and replace the siding on the tub. I saw the exact one I wanted in Home Depot today.

Looking at my watch, I grinned because I still had time to prepare dinner. Dang, that girl is vicious. Mama, wife, repair woman, and talented cook. I was going to love smearing my victory in Kaleb and Nana's faces after this.

The instructions on the putty said to let it dry for a couple of hours before using the shower. So, I took my clothes and used my nana's shower downstairs. It should be dry by the time Kaleb came in from work, which will be perfect.

For the last few days, he had to use the shower downstairs that nobody ever uses, can't wait to be able to tell him he can go back to using the shower he was used to. And guess what, brother... no banging! Who did that? Monica did it... that's right! Tomorrow I will get started on the downstairs plumbing.

As I was making dinner he came in looking extremely tired. Poor baby, ever since he had started training at the Lyon's Den, he came in every night looking like something the cat dragged in out of the alley. He was convinced Lyon and Gideon were trying to kill him.

Last night I had to rub his shoulders and back. He was in so much pain he could barely lift his arms. And he had been so tired that he'd gone to sleep in the middle of the message.

"How was work?" I asked as he took a seat in the chair across from nana, who sat at the table helping Eve color her letters.

He exhaled as he leaned back in the chair. Eve climbed down from her high chair and jumped in his lap. She actually brought her knees down in his stomach causing him to jerk up because she'd knocked the wind out of him.

"I should take you to the gym with me. You're a little warrior in the making!" he said as he caught her in his arms before kissing her under her fat cheeks, causing her to giggle. I looked at Nana to see how she was taking Kaleb's interaction with Eve. She didn't seem to notice. No doubt she probably just thought it was natural for them to have developed this relationship since Kaleb had been living here for a while now.

And I mean come on, who wouldn't fall in love with Eve after being around her for a little while?

"Work was fine," he told me when he had finished tickling Eve, who now laid her head against his big chest.

"It was the gym that nearly killed me. Them dudes are not human."

Nana chuckled. "That is exactly what I thought when I first laid eyes on that Lyon. Goodness!" Something in her tone caused me to look over at her.

"What you mean, goodness?" Emm, emm, Nana was up in here being fast.

"Child, I ain't blind."

I slid my pan of fish in the oven. I had waited long enough to get my gloating session on.

"Now that I have the both of you here, I have an announcement to make." They both gave me their attention.

"Three days ago, the two of you doubted I would be able to accomplish my goal of changing out a few old pipes and replacing them with new ones... correct?" Neither of them answered, but you know, I didn't expect them to because that's what playa haters do.

"No need to answer. I'd just like to let the both of you know that the upstairs plumbing is complete, and I will be starting on the downstairs tomorrow. Kaleb, feel free to shower anytime you like." A grin spread across his face.

"Oh yeah! So, I can go shower really quick before dinner."

I gestured toward the door. "Be my guest. It'll be the best shower you've ever taken." He stood putting Eve back in her high chair.

"Well, alright. I will take you up on that offer. I'll be back in ten."

"Ummm, excuse me?" I said stopping him before he left out the door. He turned to look at me.

"What's up?"

"Isn't there something you'll like to say to me?" I looked at Nana. "And you?"

They looked at each other and chuckled. "Come on guys, don't be sore losers. You two doubted I could do it, and I did it. I'm sure you could put both of your big brains together and come up with something to say to me right now."

Nana mumbled something. I put my hand to my ear. "What was that? I didn't hear it, you know with you mumbling and all."

"I said!" she yelled, "Good job, I shouldn't have doubted you." Then she rolled her eyes. I huffed.

"Well, I know the sting of embarrassment hurts a little, but I'm sure you could have done better than that." I held up my hand toward her. "You know what, don't worry about it, I'm sure your partner in crime can do better." I turned to look at Kaleb, who stood there studying me with a tired grin on his face.

"Good job on fixing the plumbing, Mon, I really do appreciate it!" I nodded.

"No problem... but let this be a lesson. It's never wise to doubt me, *son!*" This caused him to hold back his head and laugh out loud as he walked on out the kitchen.

I was just beginning to set the table when something strange happened. At first, I thought I was imagining it until Nana stopped and looked up.

"You hear that too?" I asked her. She nodded. There was a high-pitched noise that at first started out really faint but was growing louder by the second. Then a loud rumble that felt like it shook the floor. Then banging... that was so loud Eve started to cry.

I turned to pick her up out her high-chair just as a loud pop filled the air followed by Kaleb yelling the f-word. Then there were several more pops before water started shooting up out of the sink soaking us.

"Oh my goodness!" I screamed handing Eve to Nana as I raced to the sink to try and turn off the water. It was shooting up so fast and hard that I couldn't even get my hand by it.

"Get a bowl!" Nana yelled. And like a fool I grabbed a bowl to try and stop it. Neither of us was thinking straight. Eve was yelling... water was spraying, soaking everything and I was freaking out. Kaleb shot past us in only a towel running down to the basement.

A few seconds later the water stopped. I stood there in shock dripping wet, staring at Nana, who held Eve in her arms rocking her. When Kaleb came back upstairs, he just stood there in the door frame staring at me with only a towel wrapped around his waist, his ripped abs and muscled chest on full display.

"My, my, my!" Nana muttered when her eyes landed on him. I put my hand over my mouth as I stared at him. He was steaming mad. And I'm pretty sure it had something to do with the nice size lump he now sported on the side of his forehead.

"Is everybody alright?" he growled without taking his angry glare from me.

"Yes, we're alright! Good thing you were here!" my Nana purred.

"Nana!" I scolded, gladly looking away from Kaleb's heated gaze.

"What, child? I told you I'm not blind!" she mumbled.

"Monica, don't you have something to say to me?" Kaleb snapped.

Reluctantly my gaze went back to him, but it just ended up landing on that huge knot that had probably gotten there when that loud pop happened right before he yelled out the f-word.

If I was a better woman, I would admit that maybe... just

maybe, I had misused the plumber's putty and that I might have bitten off more than I could chew. It's also a slight probability that I had no idea what I was doing. But because I was a sore loser and had talked entirely too much stuff early to turn back now, I decided to try and reverse some of the shade he was throwing my way.

"Yeah, I do have something to say," I muttered.

He grunted, folding his massive arms causing his chest muscles to do all kinds of sinful things that were probably making poor Nana feel like she was menopausing again.

"Good, speak up so that we can hear you clearly!" he angrily returned my words to me from earlier. I cleared my throat before I put my hand on my hip. Nana started shaking her head knowing me too well.

"Why the hell did you carry yo' big butt up there and mess up all my hard work—" I didn't even finish my sentence before he charged me. And honey... I ain't never been nobody's fool. You would have thought I ran track and field with how fast I made it through the living room and out that front door.

Okay, so the plumbing thing didn't work out. Hell, I can't be good at everything. Naw, let me stop tripping. I had managed to do some serious damage. I feel so bad. Kaleb got a crew in there and they worked around the clock to restore our water.

After that, he got another crew in that began to make the other repairs that the boarding house needed. Because I had messed up and messed up really bad, he had no troubles out of me. He told me he didn't even want to hear my opinion. And well... hell, what could I say to that but okay?

Nana told me she overheard him talking to the plumbers and that they were telling him how outdated the pipes were. She said he had told them to run new pipes throughout the whole house. Now I don't know how much that cost, but I know it's a lot.

The boarding house was huge; eight bedrooms, four bathrooms, two downstairs and two upstairs. There was a bathroom in the master bedroom that I never used because we had to shut the plumbing down way back when I was a little girl. So now I just used it for storage. However, it was now being renovated with the rest of the house. This had to be costing him a fortune.

He'd even taken Nana's old car to his shop. I'd found this information out one day after I had come from the Center. Now that we were rehearsing for Madame's end of the year show, we met three times a week instead of once.

Anyway, I had come in and plopped down on the couch tired; the ever-present sound of drilling and pounding of the contractors greeting me as I entered. Nana was sitting in her chair as happy as a kid in a candy store.

"What are you so happy about?"

"Kaleb is fixing up Bessie for me!" Bessie is the name she had given her Monte Carlo that she had purchased new off the showroom floor in 1976.

"He said it's a good car and had a lot of potential. I told him that I didn't drive anymore, so he told me he's going to take me for a ride in it!" She clapped her hands together.

"Isn't that wonderful?" I stared at her as if she had lost her mind. I didn't even know who this woman was. My nana hated asking folks for stuff and she really hated being a burden on people. Kaleb was completely renovating the boarding house, doing way more stuff than I would have approved of. But since I had promised both him and Nana I would stay out of it, I hadn't said anything about it.

But this!

This was just too much.

"How much are you going to allow this man to do for you?" She didn't even blink an eye before answering my question.

"All that he wants because I know he's really doing it for you and Eve."

Okay! Not what I was expecting her to say. What the world did she mean she knew he was doing it for me and Eve? Oh, my goodness! Did she know I lied to her? I studied her, trying not to show how rattled her statement just made me.

"What does that mean?" I asked because I was just too tired to try and guess. Sometimes it felt like my nana played head games with me.

"It means, when I go, I will be at peace knowing you and Eve have a solid roof over your head and not one that leaks." Her words angered me.

"Why do you say stuff like that?"

"Stuff like what, Monica?"

"When I go, I go in peace!"

She laughed. "You do know that one day I'm going to die, right?"

I put my hand over my ears, trying to block out her words. I didn't ever want to think about that. Nana and Eve were all I had left of my blood family. The thought of losing either was incomprehensible.

"You're not going anywhere! And you should stop saying stuff like that because words have power. I need you here with me! I cannot make it without you." It took everything within me not to yell those words at her, but she was breaking my heart and my emotions were unstable.

"You will be just fine when it's my time to go. I've lived my life, child. You have to live yours—"

I jumped up off the couch cutting her off. "Don't get comfortable with that idea. I won't be just fine if you die! I will go crazy because I ain't got no sense! So, you see, I need you here with me because it's you that keep me sane!" I turned and took the stairs up to my room two at a time.

I don't know why, but my grandmother's words made me feel like weeping. I needed a distraction. It was time to call Keturah and Shante.

Chapter 16
DESPERATION

MONICA

The summer flew by or maybe it just seemed that way because I was blissfully happy. Kaleb, Nana, Eve and I had settled into a little pattern. We had become the family that I didn't know I needed; a family with a strong black man at the head.

True to his word, he began to close the shop before sundown Friday and on Saturdays because of the Sabbath. He told Nana and I that we had to stop cooking and cleaning on that day as well. So Stormy taught me how to prepare my household the day before, so that we could just rest on the Sabbath and study scripture.

I got started early Friday mornings cleaning the house or doing the best I could with all of the construction that was still going on. Then I would prepare food for Friday night and Saturday. I had to prepare a lot because Kaleb's appetite is lethal.

I began to look forward to the Sabbath because it was the one day we were all just able to relax. Most times we didn't even change out of our pajamas. Kaleb shared with Nana and I what he was learning from the brothers at the Lyon's Den. His warrior training was just as much scriptural study as it was physical labor.

His growth has been amazing. It's like he's becoming a new man. One night, he came in really late after everyone had gone to bed. Well, everyone except me. It was the first time since he'd lived here that he was a no-call, no-show for dinner and I was worried. I had texted and called him several times—no answer. Something was wrong! I felt it in the pit of my belly.

I heard him when he came through the door and quietly came up the stairs. Kaleb had his contractor remodel the master bedroom first. So now he and I both slept in here while they remodeled the other rooms on this floor. We had gotten all new furniture because he said mine was too girly for him. He had insisted on getting a king size bed, saying that he needed room to make the things that he made happen between the sheets.

Shaking my head... men!

Anyway, as I was laying in our huge bed facing the wall, I heard him come in rather than see him. But I knew right off something was wrong because he went straight to the bathroom. A minute later, the shower came on. I slipped out of bed and went to the door knocking gently, no answer.

"Kaleb!" I called... nothing

I opened the door slightly and peeked around it to see him sitting on the side of the tub. He was staring down at the floor, lost in his head and covered in blood. There was blood on his hands and splatters of it on his face and clothes.

"Oh, my goodness! Baby, what happened to you?" I cried running toward him, searching him with shaking hands. I was freaking out because I didn't know if the blood was his or someone else's. And instead of him responding to me, he just wrapped his strong arms around my waist pulling me close, burying his face in my stomach.

"Kaleb, what happened? You're shaking!" I wrapped my arms around him trying to comfort him the best way I could. Eventually, I helped him get undressed. He did have some cuts and bruises, but the majority of the blood wasn't his.

I had to get in the shower with him to help him wash. I don't know where his mind was, but it was far away from the here and now. Whatever had happened to him at the Lyon's Den must have blown his mind.

After the shower, we laid down in the bed and he literally pulled me close, burying his face in my chest, seeking comfort. I held him because he needed me to. I had never seen him like this. What in the world could have happened to cause an ex mob boss to ball up like a small boy that had been traumatized?

When I asked him about it the next day, his only response was... "Until last night, my step-father was the biggest monster I knew."

Ummm... vague much? I pondered on that for days after. I even tried to get him to

expound on it, but he wouldn't.

"Baby, some things ain't meant for you to know."

What?

Heck naw! That wasn't gon' work for me. I went to Stormy about it.

She chuckled shaking her head. "Oh! You will learn soon enough. And like the rest of us, once you see it, you're going to wish you never had. Don't rush it. Let Yah grow you in your time."

What?

So, yeah! Apparently, it wasn't time for me to know or see whatever had stunned my husband the way it did that night. But whatever happened changed him. He was not the same man. It was like his eyes had been opened to a brandnew reality and his old reality just seemed minute in comparison.

One Sabbath, his brother came by. Kaleb, Nana and I were in the living room listening to a brother on YouTube that Lyon had told him about. He was teaching about the importance of fasting. I'll tell you why Kaleb needed to watch this in a minute, but first, let me finish telling you about what happened with his brother.

WE WERE SITTING THERE, me still in my pajamas, Kaleb in a pair of sweatpants and his tank, Nana in one of her multi-colored muumuus, and Eve was asleep in her bed. The house was quiet because Kaleb didn't let the contractors work on the Sabbath either.

However, his phone was blowing up with calls and texts. The calls he didn't answer, but the text he did, but he wasn't happy about it.

Shortly after somebody knocked on the door, Kaleb looked really angry before he got up and answered it.

"What?!" was all he said. Nana and I both frowned at how rude he had answered the door.

"What, you mean what?" When I heard who it was I exhaled looking over at Nana. I knew for a fact that Kaleb had intentionally not let Rasheed come here because he was too ignorant. And he didn't want Nana to know that he had a brother like that.

"Nigga, what?!" His voice rose slightly. He was mad and getting madder by the minute. The muscles in his arms and shoulders bunched like he was going to hit Rasheed.

"Man, I've been trying to get in contact with you. I know you didn't want me to show up here, but what else am I supposed to do when you won't even answer my calls?" Kaleb exhaled before turning to look back at us.

"Give me a minute, ladies," he said before going out the door shutting it behind him.

Only instead of stepping around his brother, he pushed him back out the way.

"What do you think that's about?" Nana asked. I shrugged. "I don't know, that's his little brother."

"Oh!" she said nodding like that explained everything.

Anyway, he was in no better mood when he came in off the porch from talking to his brother. Something was going on with Rasheed. I think he was in trouble. But of course, that was another

280

topic Kaleb would not discuss with me. So, I took his advice and didn't worry about it.

Okay, so let me tell you why Lyon was having Kaleb watch videos on the importance of fasting, poor baby. Apparently, Lyon put him on some kind of sex ban that's driving him crazy. If not for me standing strong and just outright refusing him, he wouldn't make it. Every night, he tried to talk me into breaking his fast.

"Come on, baby!" he'd say sliding in the bed next to me. "It ain't like Lyon gon' know. Here, let's just do it real quick. Come on, girl, I'm feening!"

"Emm, emm... 'cause see? Stormy told me you were going to say that. And Lyon may not know, but this fast you on don't have nothing to do with him. This fast is between you and Yah. Are you saying he ain't going to know?"

He would stare at me for a while looking really salty before turning his back toward me.

"I'm going to sleep! And no, I can't hold you. I suffer, you suffer!" At that point, I could

no longer hold on to my laughter.

"Aww, K, don't be like that!" I purred leaning against his shoulder, but he would only shrug me off.

"No, you don't even care that I'm dying!"

I fell back in the bed laughing. You wouldn't even think to hear those words coming from a man like him.

"It's almost over. Lyon said that you should be done with that part of your training by

Madame Queen's end of the summer show." He sat up and looked down at me.

"Baby, that's like three weeks away. I'm not going to make it!' I smiled up at him

rubbing my hand across his beautiful chest.

"You're going to make it, because you're strong, you're focused and capable. Yah didn't choose wrong when he chose you. You can do this, baby." He smiled down at me before kissing my lips.

"Yeah, I can do this."

Now, with all that being said, on the flip side, just between me and you, I wasn't that strong. I mean, don't get me wrong, I wanted to see my king become all that he was meant to be, but a girl has needs too. So, I went to Stormy.

"You shouldn't just look at this as his fast. It's a fast for the both of you. Like him, you should be taking this time to get closer to the Heavenly Father. You two are co-heirs for that spot in the kingdom, which means you must pull your own weight and establish your own relationship with Yah. Sure, your husband can teach you and guide you, but you still have to do the work."

"Learn how to pray. It doesn't matter what for. You need strength to get through the fast, pray for it! You need Yah to help guide you through your studies. Pray for it! He answers prayers. He's listening, just talk to him." And so I did.

I began to join Kaleb in his morning prayers and we prayed together again at night. My scripture reading was going good as well. I had made it to the book of II Kings. I was beginning to feel like I was developing a personal relationship with Abba Yah and it felt good.

Everything was going perfect. I'd even managed to get Mika out of her house by inviting her to join Shante, Keturah and myself at Mama Rita's for lunch. I figured she could use a little distraction and there were no better distractors than Keturah and Shante.

"All I'm saying is, if those Africans were my people, why they sell us into slavery in the first place?" Shante asked Keturah.

Just like I knew they were going to do, they had started in on each other. I had already warned Mika about them.

"They're like oil and water, and it's no better entertainment for miles around."

Surprisingly Mika was all for it.

"Yeah, I could go for watching a little cattiness!"

"Child, a little? You better get ready to laugh 'cause these two don't do nothing little." "Oh my goodness! It sounds as if you actually picked up a book and read." Keturah responded to her before she took a sip of her fruity cocktail.

"Oh, 'cause I'm ghetto, I got to be illiterate?" Shante asked putting her hand on her hip. Keturah grunted.

"You know what? You're a racist!" Shante threw at her. Keturah nearly choked on her

drink.

"Racist! Great, I complimented you too soon. This poor ghetto soul doesn't even know

what the word 'racist' mean. Bless her heart. Words with more than three letters ain't her strong

suit." Mika brought her napkin to her mouth to cover her laugh.

"I know exactly what it means! You're racist against ghetto people." Keturah opened her

mouth insulted.

"How am I going to be racist against my own people?"

"That's just it! We ain't your people! Your people over there eating monkey meat and

berries!" Mika had to turn away after that one. I shook my head. That was funny.

"Shante, you ain't right for that!" I told her.

"What? It's a difference and I don't know why Keturah can't see it. My people like chicken." She held up a piece of chicken from her plate.

"Your people like monkey meat!" As she said that, she did an imitation of a monkey, causing Mika to lose it laughing.

We were laughing so hard at our table we attracted Mama Rita, who came and joined us for a little while. This was my third time having lunch with her this week. She hadn't opened up to me about what was going on with her sons, but whatever it was had her worried.

"Where is my baby?" She asked pulling out an empty chair and joining us. The last few times she and I had met, I had brought Eve with me. She wanted Eve to get comfortable with her so that she could spend the night over her house sometimes.

"My nana wanted to spend some time with her today." Mama Rita cut her eyes at me over the table.

"You tell your Nana, that's my grandbaby too!" she pouted with a smile on her face. I nodded. But I had no idea how I was going to tell Nana that. Look y'all, don't judge me too harshly. I would have been told her who Kaleb was if she hadn't been so sick of late.

She's not stupid. She knows something's going on between us. She just doesn't know about our history. And I figured I could just let it play out naturally until she starts feeling better, then I will tell her everything.

Well, almost everything. I wasn't ever going to tell her about what I did that night Kaleb went to jail or that he had called a hit on Man-Man. That news would kill her for sure. When she was feeling better, I was just going to let her know that Kaleb was Eve's father and that he'd done the right thing and married me as soon as he found out.

But first, I had to get her feeling better. I decided to go and talk to Stormy's friend, Saffiyah. I know Nana was going to be upset about it, but I was desperate. The things Saffiyah could do with herbs and plants were nothing short of amazing. I knew she could make something that could help Nana with her coughing that seemed to be getting worse. The other day, she tried to hide it from me, but she'd coughed up blood. I saw the tissues in her wastebasket I cleaned her room.

I begged her to let me take her to the doctor, but she'd stubbornly refused. And of course, I went on to torture myself by asking Google about her symptoms. Every medical website I looked at said the same thing. She needed to see a doctor.

When I asked Storm about Saffiyah, she said now would be a good time to talk to her because she and her husband Gideon would be leaving to go back to the Dominican Republic soon and there was no telling when they would be coming back. She said that she would take me by their house, which wasn't too far from the Lyon's Den tomorrow.

After we got through with eating, Mama Rita went and packed some food for Kaleb's lunch. As we said our goodbyes, I promised her that I would bring Eve over to her house Sunday so that she could spend some time with her and then we headed out and dropped Mika off first.

She thanked me for getting her out the house, telling me she had an amazing time. When it was just Keturah, Shante and I in the truck, I thanked them for just being them.

"That's alright, we gon' start charging you for how you use us!" Keturah grumbled. "Straight up, I can use the money too, 'cause them damn Chinese done went up on the hair again!" And you already know that got Keturah started again.

Eventually, I got those crazy girls out of my car, dropped Kaleb's lunch off to him, but I

didn't have time to chat with him because I was running late for my dance class.

"Wow, where you rushing off to so fast?" he asked wrapping his arms around my waist bringing me to a stop. I turned in his arms lifting my hand gently rubbing my fingers through his beard. Did I tell y'all how handsome my man was?

"I'm sorry I can't stay longer, I'm late for class." He frowned. "But you just got here, you not even gon' have lunch with me?"

"I already had lunch with your mother, Mika, Keturah and Shante." At first, he looked surprised.

"Wow! You got Mika out the house?" Chuckling, I nodded my head.

"I sure did. All I had to do was offer to treat her to one of your mother's steaks. I keep telling you... there is nobody in the hood who would turn down a Mama Rita's steak." It was his turn to chuckle. Then he leaned down and gently kissed my lips.

"What was that for?"

"That was for a very special woman?"

285

"Really?" His words made me feel like spun sugar on the inside.

"Yep! I'm the luckiest man in the world..." He paused. "Damn luck! I'm *blessed!*"

Man, I was cheesing so hard by this point, my cheeks hurt. Standing on my toes, I

returned his kiss.

"What was that for?" he asked.

"It's *me* who's been blessed. I can't imagine my life without you."

"It's amazing how Yah works, isn't it?" he whispered and I nearly drowned in his gaze.

"Yes, it is?"

As I drove away from the shop, I thought about the words I'd just told him. Where would

I be without him? All this time, I'd thought he'd ruined my life, when he actually saved it.

Stormy had been right. Our minds were not like Yah's. We can only see one dimension while the Heavenly Father sees through all dimensions. The very thing I had thought to be a curse, was a blessing. And the very thing I thought would be a blessing, would have turned out to be a curse.

I had been so lost in my view on life. For as long as I could remember, my goal had been to go to Julliard and become a famous dancer. But had I done that, I would have missed out on four major blessings, Yah, Yahusha, Kaleb, and Eve.

I couldn't imagine my life without them, they...

The sound of loud oncoming honking drew my attention. I looked up just in time to see the headlights of a white truck coming fast before it slammed into the side of my truck. I cried out as pain exploded in my head, while trying to turn the steering wheel so that I didn't hit someone else. Eventually, my truck came to a stop, but the only thing I could do was brace myself for the impact of another car.

When it didn't happen, I looked around trying to focus. Something warm dripped in my eye. I wiped at it with hands that shook before staring down at my fingers confused. They were covered in blood.

Was I bleeding?

My thoughts were muddled as I tried to figure out what happened, but before I could get heads or tails of the situation, the driver side door was snatched open.

"You coming with me, b****!" I heard before somebody reached in and took off my seat belt. I recognized that voice.

"Rasheed?" I whispered barely able to speak because I was fighting to stay conscious. There was another man with him, but they both had on masks.

"Rasheed, what are you doing?"

"Shut up!" he growled before he punched me—hard. I didn't have to fight anymore, after that, everything went black.

Chapter 17
TAKEN

MONICA

W hen I came to, I was almost lulled back to sleep by the gentle rocking of my bed. It took me a minute to realize that something wasn't right. Why the heck was my bed rocking? I sat up but clutched my head from the pain that shot through it.

"Ahh!" I cried out. My head felt like I got hit with a hammer. Then I remembered the car crash. Someone ran into the passenger side of my truck and I must have struck my head on the window.

Was I in the hospital?

Looking around the dark room, I tried to let my eyes adjust. I could make out shapes of things but couldn't see clearly because it was pitch black. There was a loud sound of a motor and I could hear people walking above my head.

This was definitely not a hospital! The acrid smell of cigarette smoke and diesel fuel stung my nose. I wrapped my arms around waist as I struggled to comprehend what was happening. I didn't have to wonder much longer because right then, a door opened from what looked like the ceiling, causing a bright light to shine in.

I cupped my hand over my eyes, the sudden brightness causing my already pounding head to become unbearable. It was then I saw the stairs underneath the door before a pair of Jordans appeared on the first step. A sinking feeling came over me as I watched the jean covered legs come into view. By the time the t-shirt clad torso with the big gold chain materialized, I knew who it was. Rasheed continued down the steps with a huge smile on his face. He flipped on the light.

"Oh good, you're awake!" he said as he came farther into the area. I drew myself up, backing up until my back hit the wall. But he didn't come near me, instead, he pulled out one of the chairs from the table that sat in the center of the room and straddled it.

As I looked around I realized that I was in the belly of a boat. It wasn't a real big area. It was about the size of a small studio apartment. There was a little stove, sink and fridge against the far wall. In the center of the room was the table Rasheed sat at. There were two doors to the side that probably led to a closet or bathroom.

My gaze fell back on Rasheed and the way he looked at me caused chills to race up my spine.

"Where am I?" I spat wanting to get up and claw his eyes out.

He chuckled. "On your way to Cuba."

"Cuba!" I cried out not expecting him to say that. I thought I was somewhere on Lake

Michigan. Oh no!

"Why?"

"To pay off your husband's debt."

"What debt?"

He leaned back in his chair laughing at my fear. "Shorty, you asking the wrong question. What you should be asking is what am I going to do to you if you don't do what I tell you to."

Anger shot through me. He had taken me away from my husband and child. My nana! To hell with him! What's the worst he could do, kill me?

"Damn you! You can go straight to hell!" I folded my arms frowning at him so he could see how serious I was. I hated Rasheed! I know that was strong language and a horrible way to feel about my husband's brother, but I hated him with everything I had in me.

He reached in his pocket and took out his phone. "How did I know you were going to say something like that? Which is why I went on and made arrangements for your grandmother and that little bastard. If I make this call, they're going to know what hot metal feels like when it pierces their skulls!"

Oh my goodness!

I stared at him for a while trying to determine whether he spoke the truth. I know he hated me, but Eve was his niece. Surely he wouldn't hurt her! The smirk on his face said differently and for the first time since waking up in this strange place, I began to feel panic.

Think, Monica, don't lose your cool!

"You're lying!" I told him. He chuckled.

"Your family was the first thing I went after. You see, if my brother hadn't been so busy over there playing house with yo' aS$, he would have seen that everything he and I have built together is tumbling down." He lifted his hat and ran his hand down the top of his wavy head.

"Now, I'm trying to be nice and just get rid of you, but if you force my hand, I will get rid of that little bastard and that old a$$ woman too!" He reached for his phone.

"Wait!" I cried. If it was just me, I would tell him to go screw himself. But Eve and Nana, I couldn't take that chance with their lives.

"What do you want?" He sat back with a satisfied grin on his face.

"Good girl, you've made the right choice. Now look, I ain't no complete dick. If all go according to my plan, you won't have to die."

"What plan? You speaking in circles, I can't understand you!" I hissed, letting all the hate

I felt for him bleed into my voice.

"Oh, my bad, let me simplify it for you. Kaleb and I owe a man a lot of money. This is a big bad man that's going to kill somebody if he don't get paid. You, my sweet Monica, are going to be gifted to him to pay off our debt on your back." My being instantly rebelled against going anywhere near another man in that way, I could not believe my ears.

"You're going to sell me into slavery?"

He grinned. "Yep!"

"But what if he don't want me instead of his money?" He stood from the chair and walked toward one of the doors.

"I thought about that, which is why I did a little shopping." He reached in for a bag he had hanging on the rack.

"Once you put on this little number, he gon' be all over you." He handed me the bag, but I didn't take it.

"Come on, big sista, let's not play these games." His free hand went toward his phone. I snatched the bag from him. With the grin still on his face, he sat down on the bed next to me, but before his body could touch the little mattress, I was up and off of it.

He smiled at me as he stretched out on it, putting his arm behind his head.

"Damn baby, you agile, ain't you? No wonder my brother was over there sprung out on you." He pointed toward the little bathroom with his other hand.

"Go in there and freshen up. Use the make-up and stuff in the bag. If when you come out and I don't want to f*** you, I'm making that call, no questions!" Tears came to my eyes as I shook my head.

"Rasheed, don't do this, it's got to be another way." My words must have angered him because his face contorted in rage before he jumped up off the bed.

"There *was* another way, but yo' p**sy whipped a$$ husband wasn't trying to hear me! Now, his wife gon' pay what he should have! Half of everything he got is mine! But he chose to stunt on me like it ain't! So now, he gon' pay whether he want to or not! He gon' have to live with the fact that because he made the wrong choice, another nigga gon' be dipping between his wife pretty thighs, tasting that sweetness he thought was only his!"

My tears were now running down my cheeks. "But can't you see this ain't right? I'm his wife!"

"No! What ain't right is you coming along f****** up my brother's head! You got him walking around reading bibles and s***! My brother was a damn legend before you brought yo' a$$ in his life! Now go in that damn bathroom and change 'fore I make the call and destroy yo' world." He reached for his phone, but I didn't wait around to see him use it.

After locking myself in the matchbox bathroom, I fell to my knees and wept feeling so helpless. How had it come to this? Rasheed was deranged. He hated me because his brother loved me. Dear Yah!

Dear Yah?

Stormy's words came to me. Learn how to pray to Abba Yah. He does answer prayers and he's listening.

"Dear Father!" I cried out loud. "Please don't leave your servant forsaken! Help me, Father! Please!"

"Hurry up! We ain't got time for all that bulls***!" Rasheed yelled from outside the door.

I stood and looked at myself in the mirror, cringing at the sight I made. There was dried

blood in my hair. I reached up and felt the knot just inside my hairline. The wound had scabbed over, but it was still very sensitive to the touch. There was also a bruise on the side of my face from where he had punched me.

With hands that shook, I took out all the make-up and things he had in the bag. I used the washcloth to clean away the dried blood. It took everything I had in me to apply make-up on my face to cover the bruises when it was the last thing in the world I felt like doing.

When I was done and my face looked pretty again, I pulled the dress out of the bag and had to force myself not to cry and ruin the make-up that I had so painfully applied. It was a red maxi-dress, but it would cover nothing. The top of it was just straps that I had to tie around my breast. However, my stomach and back would be left out on full display.

The skirt had several big splits in it that ran from my waist to the floor that left both of my legs exposed. There was a pair of red heels with straps that would tie up my leg to match. When I was dressed, I stood staring at myself in the little mirror disgusted with the view. Just like the last time I wore something I was ashamed of, I left my hair to fall around my face and shoulders.

How ironic it is that we've come full circle and once again, I found myself dressed in a way to play the whore for another mob boss.

"Kaleb!" I whispered, needing him so badly. I wondered if he even knew I was missing. Would he try and find me? Would it be too late?

"Come on, Mon, you've had enough time!" Rasheed yelled.

Kaleb

I frowned down at my phone thinking about ignoring it as I was eating my lunch, but when I saw the number I dropped my fork and picked it up.

"Yeah!"

"Boss! Sh*t, I don't know what happened!" James, one of the men I put on guarding Monica yelled through the phone accompanied by the sound of tires screeching. Quickly I pulled open the drawer taking out my Ruger putting it in the holster I wore on my lower back.

"They grabbed her!"

"Who?" I yelled sprinting across the shop to my truck. My phone beeped! I looked down at the number and felt myself move into the first metamorphosis. It was Landis, the man I had on the boarding house.

I clicked over and heard shots. In the background, I could hear Eve crying.

"Landis!" I yelled in the phone as ice settled into my veins. Somebody was getting ready to die! There was another shot before the sound of tussling.

"Landis, hold on! I'm on my way!" I got in my truck and stepped on the gas before

clicking back over to James.

"Who was it?" I yelled trying to hold onto my temper, I needed to be able to think

clearly.

"It looked like your little brother, I couldn't tell for sure because they wore masks! I'm

heading in the direction I think they went, but it was an ambush. They hit her car and grabbed her in all the confusion! Boss I'm--"

"Damn it, James!" I hissed cutting him off, in no mood to hear his excuses. "If something happens to my wife, I am going to rip you apart!" I hung up the phone and dialed Tiny.

"Boss?"

"Rasheed grabbed Monica!" I growled, so angry I could barely speak coherent words.

"I need you to go to the warehouse and gather the supplies. Bring out everything. Prepare for war! Tell G to meet me at my place, them nigga's got Eve!"

I hung up the phone and dialed one more number; it was my last conscious act before my rage settled in, taking over my limbs.

"Achi, they at my house; they got my family! Ach, I'm getting ready to lose myself; all I see is red!" After that, I let the phone slide from my ear as coldness settled over me.

I had become the reaper and will be satisfied with nothing less than destroying everything and everyone that lay one hand on what was mine. When I pulled up to the boarding house, I barely put the truck in park before I was out of it sprinting across the yard. My brain had become a computing predator, taking in everything around me as I went, feeding me information as needed.

There were several cars here that didn't belong. The tussle had begun on the porch; three bullet holes, two in the door and one through the window, all shot from within out. I burst through the front door and came up short at the sight that greeted me.

Nana sat in her chair with Eve in her lap. As soon as my baby saw me, she reached for me. Lying dead at Nana's feet was Landis, next to him, an unknown, dead. Against the wall was another unknown, dead. An unknown young man between the age of twenty and twenty-six stood over Nana with a gun to her head, his hand was shaking, he was afraid.

"Hold on, K! Take another step and I will put a bullet in this b**** head!" His voice shook, testifying further of his fear. I heard silent footsteps above my head; unknown, weighing a buck fifty or a buck fifty-five creeping my way. I held my hands up.

"Calm down, shorty!" I told him.

"Come on out with that heat!" he said nodding toward my waistband; unknown approaching me from behind.

"You alright, Nana?" I asked as I eased my gun out of my back holster. She nodded her head.

"I'm alright, baby!"

"Yo, get his gun!" unknown number one said to unknown number two that had finally made it to stand behind me. He snatched the gun from my hand, his hand shaking; unknown number two, also afraid.

For just a split second, a beam of red light flashed against unknown number one's temple.

"It alright, fellas!" I said calmly and easily, lifting my hands as if I was going to put them behind my head. I made eye contact with Nana and for just a moment, I put my hands over my ears. She frowned but duplicated my movements, bringing her hands up over Eve's ear.

Seconds later, a single shot filled the air before unknown number one's brain splattered on the wall. I was moving before the bullet hit his temple, turning on unknown number two, grabbing the hand with the gun in it, crushing it. He opened his mouth to yell out, but before a sound could be uttered, he caught my fist.

Over and over again I pounded his face, feeling his bones breaking underneath my

blows, but for the life of me, I couldn't stop. My wife, my child, my house!

"Ach!"

"Ach!" Shelomoh's voice penetrated the red haze that settled over my gaze. I looked up blinking surprised to see him, Daniyah, Gideon and Gideon's pet all looking down at me. Nana held Eve's head to her chest, covering her eyes as she too stared at me with her mouth agape.

Fist still raised, I looked down at the grotesque face underneath me that no longer resembled a human. I jumped to my feet and pulled my daughter out of Nana's arms, hugging her close.

"Boss?" G said coming through the door. "We have to go. Jaquan just gave your brother

a lift on one of his planes to Miami. He said he didn't know the girl they carried was your wife?" "Monica!" Nana cried.

"Tell him to call his pilot and turn the plane around!" G shoulders slumped as he shook

his head.

"The pilot said Rasheed pulled a gun on him, told him if he turned the plane around he would kill him."

"Miami sounds like my stomping ground. I can get us there fast!" Gideon, who stood just

inside the door supplied.

Shelomoh nodded. "You and Daniyah go with him. I'll stay here and help Adam clean up this mess." He put his hand on my shoulder.

"Ach, I will protect your daughter like she's my own!" I nodded before I hugged her

close. As I handed her back to Nana, I kissed the older woman's head.

"I'm so sorry for this!" I told her, my words were barely over a whisper. She shook her head, there were tears in her eyes.

"Just bring Monica back to me!"

Gideon arranged for his chopper to meet us at my warehouse. By the time we got there, Tiny had all the artillery and the men waiting. I walked over to my computer bringing up Monica's tracker that I'd had designed into her necklace.

Gideon joined me as we looked at the map. I could hear Daniyah, who was the one responsible for taking out unknown number one talking with Tiny about some of the weapons.

"He's heading to Havana!" I told him pointing at Monica's tracker on the map. "Why Havana?"

"He owes a drug lord there named Dominick a lot of money." Gideon whistled before a

grin spread on his face.

"Aww, isn't that precious? Little Dominick still playing at big boy games!" I looked at

him surprised.

"You know him?" Gideon shrugged.

"Our paths may have crossed a time or two. Listen, bring your boy Tiny and leave everybody else. I'm going to have some of my men from the Armory meet us there."

I nodded. Those islands were Gideon's stomping ground. I trusted that he knew how to

navigate them.

~

Monica

When I emerged from the belly of the boat, several Hispanic men with guns stared at me. I wrapped my arms around myself feeling exposed. One of the men licked his tongue out and did something very lewd toward me. I looked away from them and to the shoreline as the boat docked.

If I wasn't on my way to be gifted to a strange man as his whore, I would have thought the island was beautiful, even though the tropical air was hot and muggy. Every now and again a gentle breeze blew, lifting my hair off my shoulders.

For a moment I closed my eyes envying the free wind. When I opened them, a Hispanic man was reaching for me to help me off the boat. The sun had just began to set and it looked as if the pier that may have been busy during the day, was slowing down.

I wanted to cry out for help, but the people on the island seemed afraid of the men with the guns. They held their heads down as they hurried past them. One thing was for sure, we were not in America anymore.

Rasheed had brought a few of his guys with him, but they were outnumbered. And for this first time, I noticed that they all had a nervous energy about them, including Rasheed. It was almost as if they were as afraid as I was. The Hispanic men laughed and joked with them, but at no point did they lower their guns. This was not a friendly visit.

We were greeted by a short stubby man in a shiny suit. He wore a smile on his face, but he was not a friendly man. He was a killer. I knew it like I knew I was in a whole lot of trouble. Suddenly, the threat had shifted past Rasheed who had no power here.

"Rasheed, how are you, brother? The Boss has been waiting to hear from you. Come, he's at his club, I will take you to see him."

We were all led to several trucks that met us at the dock. As we rode, I stared at Rasheed, who was so nervous he had developed a case of restless leg syndrome. His shifty gaze kept watch of each man in the truck with us and their weapons.

Oh, dear Yah! I was in the middle of some mess! Rasheed looked like a little boy way out of his element.

"You better do the best you can to please Dominick or he's going to give you to all his men. You won't survive the encounter," he whispered to me as we followed the short man in the shiny suit into a very seedy looking club.

"You come with me!" another man said grabbing my arm. I turned to look back at Rasheed for help, but he didn't look my way. He just continued into the club. My heart was pounding so hard I could hear it over the Latin music that filled the building.

I tried to snatch my arm away from the brute, but it only caused him to dig his fingers painfully in my flesh as he nearly dragged me up some stairs and down a long hall. He came to a door with a Spanish word written on it.

I had passed my Spanish class with flying colors, but I had no idea what the word said and had no time to examine it because he opened the door and shoved me in.

"You stay here till it's time!" Then he shut the door. I turned around to see one other girl in the room. She was young and beautiful and judging by the tears in her eyes, very afraid. As I headed her way, I looked around to what appeared to be a dressing room, although it was fairly empty.

"What's your name?" I asked coming to my knees in front of her. She wiped the tears from one of her eyes with her hand.

"Alita!" I had to strain to hear her. "Where are we?"

"Hell!" she muttered in a very thick accent. Her words didn't bring me any comfort. "What are you doing here in hell?" She sat up and dried her eyes with her sleeve.

"My papa was late on his payments to Don Dominick, so he took me for sex till papa comes up with the money." Now that I was able to get a better look at her, I could see that she was only a child.

"How old are you?" "Fourteen!"

My hope that I would be able to reason with this Dominick fella, sizzled and died. There was no reasoning with a man that forced a child to have sex with him. Tears came back to her eyes and before I knew it, I pulled her in my arms, hugging her close. And I could tell she was afraid because she clung to me, needing the comfort that only an older woman could give.

As I held her, I prayed to Yah again, but this time I prayed for us both. We needed a miracle. Sometime later, Rasheed walked through the door that was opened by another Cuban man with a gun. The closer he got to me, the clearer the desperate look in his eyes became.

"Come on, you have to dance for Dominick!" He grabbed my arm, but I snatched it away from him.

"Are you crazy? I'm not dancing for him!" A grin came to his face, although it was without humor.

"If you don't dance for him, we both die; and not just us, your family and mine. He will exterminate our very existence." He was not making demands now, he was pleading with me to save our lives. As I stood I had to pry Alita's arms from around my waist.

"Don't go, Miss!" she cried.

"Shh! Sweetheart, everything is going to be alright!" I told her, although I doubted my own words. As I followed Rasheed and the man with the gun out the room and down the hall, he confirmed my earlier thoughts.

"My meeting with Dominick didn't go as well as I thought it would. He said that if you are not all that I claimed you to be, he would put a bullet in both of our heads instantly."

The guard pushed me out on a little dinky stage that had a dirty red curtain covering it. Rasheed gave me one last look before the guard led him away. In that look, he told me to dance like I had never danced before.

The music changed on the loudspeaker and a very erotic tune began to play. I had to turn off my fear and turn on my professional. My life depended on it. And as the curtain rose, I did just that.

Chapter 18

HAVANA NIGHTS

KALEB

As soon as the chopper touched down in Havana, we were met by several of Gideon's men, who had traveled here from the Dominican Republic as well as Colonel Santiago, Havana's chief of police. Apparently, the islands were hypersensitive to Gideon and his men's movements.

Colonel Santiago was the nervous type. He wore a suit that was wrinkled and at least two sizes too big, which was a huge fit for his short, pudgy body. The stiff smile on his face spoke volumes. He was either afraid of us or of the big black wolf that shadowed Gideon's every step. His eyes kept shifting back and forth between us and it.

"Señor Gideon, to what do we owe this great honor of your visit? And look, you've brought your pet!" He fell into step with the four of us as we carried our duffle bags to the two Joint Light Tactical Vehicles that awaited us. Gideon chuckled.

"Vacation!"

The Colonel wiped his sweaty brow with his handkerchief before putting it back in his vest pocket.

"You know I would never get in your business, señor, but I have to ask, what's in the bags you're carrying?"

Gideon held up the duffel that was in his hand. "This?" Nervously the police chief nodded.

"Oh, this is nothing, mi amigo. Just my swimming trunks and a little light reading to enjoy while I sit back and work on my tan."

Hell, if I wasn't worried sick about my wife, that would be funny. Tiny fell into step next to me and together we studied Gideon's men, who were dressed like us in tactical gear. These were the Goons of the tropical islands. No wonder the chief of police was sweating buckets.

"Shalom, ach!" one of the men said who wore only a bullet-proof vest with several dents in it for a shirt. "Man, I'm so sorry to hear about Monroe," he continued.

A shadow came over Gideon's face. He shook his head slightly. "I miss my boy something fierce!" he muttered. The man nodded.

"He's in our prayers, ach!" Gideon stared off into the distance for a moment before he seemed to get a hold of himself.

"Lee, let me introduce you to a real good ach, Kaleb." He put his hand on my shoulder. "Kaleb, this is my oldest friend, Lee!" I shook hands with the man.

"Shalom, ach!"

"Shalom," he responded.

The nervous colonel took all this in. He stood practically wringing his hands as he waited for Gideon to give him his attention. Tiny and I loaded our bags in the trunk. You see, I didn't care what his problem was, I wasn't leaving this island without Monica. If I had to tear it down with my bare hands, so be it.

The colonel can work with me or he can be destroyed like everybody else who stands against me. I slid in the passenger seat of the first vehicle. Tiny got in behind me. Lee got in the backseat next to him. Daniyah and the rest of the men got in the second truck.

Gideon was now saying something to the fat man in rapid Spanish as he held the back door open so that his pet could jump in before placing his bag next to him. Then he slid behind the wheel. The colonel put his hands on the door, stalling him from closing it.

"Okay, just do me a favor and keep it to a minimum. The last time you were here I nearly drowned in paperwork." Gideon slammed the door before putting the truck in gear.

I was praying for strength not to reach past him and choke the hell out of the little man. Every second wasted was a second my wife could be going through Yah knows what at the hands of Yah knows who. But when I find out who, may Yah have mercy because I'm not.

"I don't know what you're talking about. I'm just here to enjoy the Habana nights!"

Gideon growled before he stepped on the gas, nearly dragging the man with him.

"Yeah, that's what I'm afraid of!" he yelled after us.

Monica

Dancing has always been a way for me to lose myself within myself. It was easy for me to tune out all those that watched and dance as if my life depended on it. I opened my limbs giving them free rein to coil and glide across the stage. In my mind, I pirouetted through the streets on a Havana night.

I became the petal of a rose as it drifted with the breeze along the earth. I became the wings of a swan as it did its regal dance of flight. I became the end of a painter's brush as it caressed the empty canvas with its colorful touch. Where I abide no man could come. It was just me and grace intertwined in a dance as old as time.

At some point, the music came to an end and I was forced to open my eyes. The small group of men before me sat staring with their mouths agape.

Rasheed blinked coming out of his revere first. "Damn!" he

muttered from where he sat next to the one they called Dominick, who could be the poster boy for a Latin drug lord; from his fleur-de-lis patterned silk shirt, to the gold chains, rings, and the watch he wore around his wrist.

His long, curly black hair was slicked back on his head to hide the fact that he was balding on top. It looked as if at one time he took care of his body but had slowed down in his older age. The little pouch in his stomach testified to that.

He had a sharp gaze that missed nothing. And it was that gaze that now raked over my body leaving me feeling cold on the inside. He lifted his ring studded hands and began to clap, looking to his left and then his right, giving the signal that his men should clap also.

"Si! Si, señorita!" He clapped Rasheed on the back.

"You are offering me a woman worth more than you owe." The smile that appeared on Rasheed's face was one of great relief. He looked up at his boys, who stood to the side surrounded by several of Dominick's men, looking as nervous as I felt.

They didn't share in his relief. I guess I didn't blame them. Dominick was not a stable individual. He had an air of trickery about him.

"Nothing but the best for you. When I saw her walking down the street, I knew she needed to become a part of your famous collection!" Rasheed told him, speaking with more confidence now that he knew Dominick was pleased with his gift.

"You saw her walking down the street, you say?" Rasheed nodded.

"Yep, I grabbed her as soon as I saw her!" Dominick lifted his hands.

"Come, bring..." He looked at Rasheed. "Hennessy? Isn't that what all you black boys drink? Hennessy." The nervous veil fell back over Rasheed.

"Naw man, I'm good." Dominick hit his shoulder again.

"Naw, man, I insist!" He did a bad interpretation of a hood

accent, causing his men to laugh. Rasheed's two friends wore stiff smiles on their faces that did not reach their eyes as they were forced to tolerate this man's blatant racism. Something had shifted in the air.

I still stood there in the center of the stage breathing heavily from my routine because nobody told me to move. This is going to sound crazy, but I was beginning to feel sorry for Rasheed and his friends.

"Let us toast to the men who have brought war to my shores!" Dominick's voice rang out.

Suddenly, the two guards that stood on both sides of Rasheed's friends pulled out a gun and shot them both in the head. I brought my hands to my mouth stifling a scream as I watched their bodies fall to the ground.

"What the f***!" Rasheed yelled jumping up from his chair. The big Hispanic man that stood behind him grabbed him by the shoulders and slammed him back in it hard!

"Where you going, homey? We got to pour out some liquor for the niggas that ain't here!" Dominick said continuing to speak in his fake hood accent. He laughed with his men before his eyes got really serious.

"You don't think I know that this is your brother's wife?" he spat.

"I make it my business to learn all there is to know about my enemy. I know about his wife! I know about his child! And I know that you're a little jealous brat that did everything within your power to take away his happiness!" He lifted his glass in the air before his lecherous gaze came back to me.

"Well... I accept!" His words caused my skin to crawl. I wrapped my arms around my stomach. I think I was going to be sick.

Right then one of his men rushed in and said something in his ear.

"What?!" he growled coming to his feet. "He's here?" The man nodded speaking in rapid

Spanish and whatever he said got everybody moving swiftly!

"Bring her!" Dominick said gesturing toward me. Moments later, I was lifted off my feet from behind. I began to struggle.

Who was here? Kaleb?

Dear Yah, was Kaleb here?

"Help!" I yelled before he covered my mouth with his smelly hand.

"What about me?" Rasheed asked. In all the bedlam, nobody did or said anything to him. Dominick halted at the door his men were bustling him out of, turning back to look at him.

"You have gifted me with your brother's wife. Consider your debt paid. She's worth that and more!" A wicked grin came to his face.

"You're free to go! However, I don't know how far you'll get. Kaleb just touched down in Havana." Rasheed eyes rounded in fear. Dominick held his head back and laughed as he continued out. The last thing I saw before I was carried out the door behind him was the back of Rasheed's head as he disappeared out the exit door on the other side of the room.

The male guard carried me to the limo Dominick had just disappeared in and practically threw me in it. The car took off instantly. As soon as I landed on the seat, I was roughly snatched up by Dominick and into his lap.

"Get your hands off me!" I yelled as I began to struggle with him. He was very strong and judging by the smile on his face, he was enjoying this.

"Oh, come on, señorita. Let me make you forget about your husband!" He grabbed my breasts so hard it brought tears to my eyes. I yelled out bucking in his arms. The next thing I knew, he and I both were flying off the seat.

Somebody had rammed the back of the limo. The next few minutes seemed to fly by in a blur. Dominick scrambled back up on the seat, yelling for his driver to go faster as he put on his seatbelt. I pulled myself up just in time to see what looked like an army tank cut hard to the right. My heart dropped! They were leaving me!

"Wait, don't leave me!" I yelled. Just then the limo turned sharply to the left sending me slamming hard into the door.

I turned around and put on my seatbelt, then I closed my eyes and prayed for Yah to bring them back. I didn't understand why they left me. When I opened them, Dominick was smiling at me from across the seat looking like the devil.

"When this is over, and your husband is dead. I'm going to take immense pleasure in

sampling what he gave his life for!"

"You're crazy. It's *you* that's going to die!" I cried as the car made another sharp turn. I take that back. I'm pretty sure the driver of the limo was going to kill us all. I couldn't help but sigh in relief when after another five minutes the car rolled through the opening gates of what had to be Dominick's palace before coming to a stop in front of a huge statue.

I gazed up at it through the window and would have laughed if I wasn't so frightened. It was a statue of Dominick sitting on top of a huge warhorse. And it just looked ridiculous. Whoever designed it tried to make him look like some kind of general instead of a racist drug lord.

"Let me go!" I yelled as he dragged me out of the car pulling me into his house.

"Nobody gets past the gate!" he told his men, who were all running with their guns to

take up their positions.

"Come on, my little ballerina, you can dance for me while your husband and his *homies*

get shot up." He laughed at his own bigotry.

Kaleb

We parked the trucks a few blocks into Edgar's, Dominick's rival turf. When he found out Gideon was here for his arch-enemy, he became more than willing to assist in any way we needed. Achi Daniyah slipped out the second truck with his sniper rifle attached to his back and disappeared into the night.

Now we waited, although it was killing me inside. When I saw them carry Monica out of that club kicking and screaming, I damn near lost my mind. Gideon had to reach over the seat and physically restrain me from jumping out of the truck, a task he would not have accomplished if he didn't have the strength of Samson.

He killed the engine and hit a button on the dashboard that brought up a monitor. On the monitor was a split-screen. Mouse, Lyon's hacker showed on one half of the screen. He was typing away on his laptop from what looked like his couch. And Felix, Gideon's hacker showed on the other half of the screen. He sat behind his computer in what he so fondly called the Tech Lab at the Armory.

"Alright, what ya'll have for us?" Gideon asked settling back in his seat.

"Good job on alerting Dominick to your arrival. He did exactly what I wanted him to do, which is to gather all his soldiers that was nicely spread out before into one place. They are all behind his walls to keep his royal highness safe; thus, making our job easier." Mouse said as his fingers flew over the keys.

"I'm sending heat coordinates to each of your phones," he continued. However, Felix made an annoyed sound, clearly unhappy with that plan.

"Ach... really? You're still going through with the little red dots? Didn't you learn anything from nearly getting everybody killed the other day when your little red dots picked up more than human heat? The damn dots picked up everything from roaches to birds!"!

"Felix! Ach! Your selective amnesia is kicking in again. Must I remind you that had you cut the lights in the time we discussed, my heat sensors would not have gotten tangled?" He held up his hands.

"You had one job!"

"Bruh, they heat sensors! Not light sensors!"

I exhaled, tuning them out as I prayed for patience. Before today, I had found the dynamics of Lyon and Gideon's relationship quite fascinating as well as entertaining. Somehow, the two had managed to become best friends without really caring all that much for each other. And that pretty much equated to them arguing all the time.

Shelomoh told me they used to physically fight each other years ago. And because their strengths were equal, they destroyed more stuff than they could pay for. So, these days, they scaled back from throwing blows to engaging in verbal battles. They argued over everything, from how to throw a proper punch to how to spread mayo on bread.

And somehow, their working relationship has trickled down to their men as well. They had identical teams that worked well together, but like Lyon and Gideon, they argued all the time. Until this moment, I had been amused by it. Now, I was ready to put my fist through the monitor.

"Achim," Gideon said interrupting the both of them. "You two don't feel the violent energy coming from this young brother next to me. If we don't hurry this up, I might have to physically restrain him again, something I do not enjoy!"

Mouse cleared his throat. "As I was saying before I was so rudely interrupted!"

Felix grunted but amazingly did not rise to the bait.

"Look at your phones." My phone dinged in my pocket. I pulled it out and was not surprised to see that Mouse had complete control of it. The floorplan of Dominick's mansion appeared on the screen. Inside and surrounding the house was about fifty red dots.

"Each of those dots is a live body. Do you see the blue dot?" One of the dots amongst the sea of red turned blue.

"That's Lady Kaleb, so be mindful of how you use your toys around that dot. Daniyah, can you hear me?" he asked.

"Loud and clear, ach!" Daniyah's voice also came from the speaker.

"Okay, boys, if we do this in the order I say, we'll be home in an hour. DaniYah, let me know when you're in position."

"10-4!"

"I've been looking for the best way to enter the place. Outside of the front gate, there is no other way in. It's damn near as secure as the Armory," Felix supplied. Gideon grunted.

"I doubt that!" he muttered.

"So how are we going to get in?" I asked, losing patience.

Both Gideon and Mouse told me to be calm at the same time. Mouse said it over the loudspeaker and Gideon with a hand gesture, I grinded down on my teeth. Easy for them to say, I wonder how calm they would be if it was one of *their* wives in there with that maniac.

Right when I was about to say to hell with it and find my own way in, Daniyah's voice came over the speaker.

"I'm in position!"

"Alright, bruh, you know how this go. The red dots are your targets." One at a time, the red dots turned green, indicating death. I could hear the whisper from Daniyah's rifle as he began to lay 'em down.

"Gideon, when I say, drive toward that gate at full speed; it's the only way in. Congratulations, my brother, we gon' have to do this one the way you do it best, slicing with the hammer."

"Yeah!" Gideon muttered before he revved the engine.

∾

Monica

I slid from in between Dominick's clinging hands, pushing him away as I smiled up at him.

"I have a special dance. Do you want to see it?" I purred, praying my voice didn't crack and give me away. I needed to buy some time. He was all hands and I couldn't stand him touching me.

With a huge grin on his face, he nodded, sitting down on the plush couch facing me. I did my best impression of Jessica Rabbit and sashayed to the bar across the room, putting as much distance between us as I could. Taking my time, I climbed up on top of it like I had seen Tyra Banks do in the movie, Coyote Ugly.

Two of his guards stood with guns in hand by the entrance smiling at me. I had to ignore them or I was going to lose my nerve.

"Oh yeah, sexy lady!" Dominick growled rubbing his hand over his private area. I threw up a little bit in my mouth, I kid you not! It took everything within me to continue with my act when what I really felt like doing was balling up in a fetal position and crying.

I put my hand on my hip and winked at him. "Well, if I'm going to dance, I'm going to need music, silly!" He raised his hands and clapped them together. I nearly jumped out of my heels when *Kelis-Milkshake* began to play from somewhere out of the state-of-the-art ceiling.

My mask slipped. "Are you serious?"

With that rascal grin on his face, he nodded as he began bobbing to the beat. "Si, hot mama!"

I rolled my eyes as I began moving half heartily to the music. You couldn't make this up.

I felt like I was stuck in a horrible twisted dream. What was up with this guy? Either he had a lot of confidence in his security team or he was a fool that was easily distracted because he seemed to have forgotten my husband was here to kill him.

"If you're wondering why I don't seem to be in the least worried about your husband, it's simple. My house is a fortress. There is only one way in, and if he comes that way, he's already dead!" He grinned at me as he lifted his drink to his mouth, still bopping to the beat.

"I'm a big fish, señorita, you don't become a big fish unless you rule the—" Whatever he was about to say got drowned out by the sound of a loud boom! A great wind swept through the room filled with glass and debris. The whole front of the house had just been blown to pieces. I put my hands over my ears as loud rapid gunfire filled the room as his guards began to shoot toward that direction.

Several more of Dominick's men ran inside, but something rolled in front of them. They looked down realizing what it was too late. It exploded, sending their body parts flying all over, an ear landed on the bar at my feet.

I fell to my knees fighting not to throw up but ended up screaming because my hand touched it. Dominick jumped up from the floor he had dived to during the explosion running toward me, his last few remaining men supplied cover fire for him. But it seemed as if they were dropping one at a time. He snatched me off the bar by my hair. I cried out struggling to remain on my feet.

One of his guards said something to him in Spanish and he took off running toward the back of the house still pulling me by my hair. Another loud explosion rocked the house and some of the ceiling began to fall around us.

While looking back toward the gunfight that was happening in the other room, Dominick opened the back door. Suddenly, Kaleb dropped from the roof, landing softly in front of us. I had never seen him look so deadly. Time seemed to slow down. Dominick had not yet seen him because he was too busy looking at the immediate threat behind us. He turned around just as Kaleb raised his gun, pointing it directly at his head.

"Impossible!" was all he was able to get out before a single shot filled the kitchen.

His body had not hit the floor completely before I was stepping on him, jumping into Kaleb's arms. I think the sudden impact of my body against his had taken him off guard because he had to take several steps back. I cradled his face and just started kissing him all over it. I was so happy to see him.

"You alright?" he asked holding me in his strong arms.

"No!" I told him continuing to cover his face with kisses. He squeezed me tighter. Behind us, the gunfight continued, but none of that mattered at this moment. It was just him and me.

"I was so scared, shorty! I ain't never been that scared in my life!" he whispered.

"Me too! I didn't think you was gon' find me!" He cupped my face staring into my eyes.

"I told you! I'll always find you, no matter what!" When his lips took mine, a flood gate of emotion washed through me. I wrapped my arms around his neck as he deepened the kiss. I missed him so much. I needed him so badly. He groaned as I pressed my scantily clad body against his, just wanting to feel all of him.

"Bae, you can't kiss me this way!" He groaned when I broke away from his lips to kiss his neck. I don't know what was wrong with me. I forgot all about his fast. At this moment, I just needed him.

"Well, damn!" A dry voice came from behind us. "No, ach, don't worry about us. We were just in a minor shootout!"

I turned around to see Gideon, Tiny, and a few other men I had never met standing behind us with grins on their tired faces. Kaleb chuckled.

"My fault, I don't know what came over me," Kaleb replied. Gideon grunted.

"Yeah, I know what came over you." He tossed my husband a coat. After draping it over my shoulders, Kaleb let my feet slide to the ground.

"Let's get out of here!"

On the way back through what was left of the house, I looked around surprised at the damage these few men had done. I couldn't help but wonder what kind of destruction would happen if all the achim came together to fight against an enemy.

I shivered. Dear Yah, nothing would be left standing in their wake.

On the way back to Gideon's chopper, I told them we needed to stop and help the little girl who was still locked in that room at Dominick's club. When we got there, I showed Kaleb and Gideon what room she was in. Gideon hit the door lightly with his hand and my mouth dropped when the lock shattered.

I turned to look at Kaleb, who just chuckled shaking his head at me. Allita cried out when she saw the two big men that stepped into the room. I slid between them and relief washed over her face, so much so tears came to her eyes.

"You can go home now!" I told her.

"Really?" She didn't believe me. Probably because she was intimidated by Kaleb and

Gideon whose presence dominated the room.

I gently touched Kaleb's arm. "This is my husband. He came to rescue me and you."

That was all she needed to hear. Jumping to her feet she ran to me and wrapped her arms around me.

"Gracias, señora! I will never forget you!" she whispered before timidly going around Kaleb and Gideon and disappearing out the door.

As we walked out of the building, panic shot through me. The achim were standing in front of the door, guns raised. Surrounding them were several vehicles. Standing outside of those vehicles were men with guns pointed at them. Kaleb pulled me behind him as Gideon stepped around his men.

A door to one of the cars opened and a well-dressed man stepped out. Right off, I could tell he was like Dominick—a drug lord! But where Dominick had been almost clownishly dressed, this man's suit was tailor-made.

"We have a problem, Edgar?" Gideon grumbled. The man smiled shaking his head as he held up his hands.

"No, bro, I don't have no problem with you. I've come bearing gifts." His English was barely understandable.

"Then tell your boys to lower their weapons, they're beginning to make us feel as if our lives are in danger. And well... then we'll be forced to protect ourselves."

Edgar gestured for his men to lower their weapons. Only then did the achim relax, but just slightly.

"To thank you for ridding the world of that piece of trash, I brought you a gift." Gideon chuckled.

"Don't thank me too soon. I may be coming for you next."

"No, bro, not me. Like you, I'm a law-abiding citizen." His statement not only caused his men to chuckle. It caused the achim to chuckle as well, loosening some of the tension that was in the air.

"Jose, give them their gift." Jose was nearly as big as Tiny. Rotating his shoulders, he walked to the trunk of his car and opened it. He reached in and pulled Rasheed out, throwing him on the ground.

I felt Kaleb's muscle get tensed all over.

"Let me catch you slipping, nigga, you dead!" Rasheed yelled toward the giant as he jumped up off the ground. Without saying another word, Edgar and his men got back in their cars and drove off.

Rasheed whipped around to face his brother.

"K, bruh! I'm so glad to see you!" Gideon looked back at Kaleb.

"We'll meet you at the chopper, ach!" he muttered before he and the other achim got in one of the trucks and drove away. Tiny and the man with the bulletproof vest stayed behind with us before they got into the truck leaving only Kaleb, Rasheed, and myself standing on the dark deserted street.

Kaleb

I didn't hear or see anything past the man pulling Rasheed out the trunk of that car. I stood there waiting for the strength it would take not to kill my brother. But the only thing I could see was Monica's banged up truck that had been hit on the side where Eve's car seat was.

Had my daughter been in that seat, she would have not survived the impact. Rage pumped through my veins and filled my vision. My breaths became shallow as my body and mind prepared itself to make the toughest kill it will ever have to make.

"K, I'm sorry, man!" Rasheed said taking an unwise step toward me. "I don't know what's wrong with me. My pops f***** me up!" He shook his head. "But you right! I'm done with this sh*t!"

I shook my head. "Naw, it don't matter no mo,' little brotha!" I saw when the change came over him. Before, I would have thought it was just him taking a stand, but because my spiritual eyes had been opened, I saw when the demon settled on Rasheed.

He inhaled, expanding his chest in the way that the damned did when they first took over a body, then a grin settled on his face. "What... you gon' kill me now? Kaleb the judge!" he yelled into the night, still very much sounding like Rasheed.

"You know what, your honor? I think it's time for your hypocritical a$$ to stand on trial!" he continued. "Won't you tell your lovely wife about what really happened to her brother!"

Sh*t!

When he saw that he had hit a mark, his eyes rounded in a surprised look.

"Uh oh! Bet you didn't think *that* was going to come up! But what better time to be judged than when you are standing there feeling like somehow you're right?" He spat each word in anger, the entity that now controlled him filled with hate and rage to match my own. I didn't feel sorry for my little brother, who had become a host to such a foul being. I just wanted to put them both out of their misery.

"Turn to your wife and tell her how it was *you* who put the gun to her brother's head and pulled the trigger." He no longer sounded human. He sounded like the filthy serpent he was.

"Tell her how he begged you not to shoot him." He looked up toward the sky holding up his hands. "Tell her how you emptied your clip in 'em!" he yelled before he erupted in laughter.

I snapped. Before I even knew I was moving, I had his neck in my hands. He grabbed at my arms, but his strength was nothing against my rage. My whole body shook with it as I choked the life out of him.

He stared up at me through tear-filled eyes. "You don't get to live happily ever after, bruh!" he somehow managed to get out of his mouth before he breathed his last breath.

Chapter 19
TRAGEDY

MONICA

I stood there looking at Kaleb, waiting for him to deny his brother's words. The coward couldn't even look me in my face. This whole time it *had been him* who had murdered my brother. It had been *him* who had pulled the trigger.

"Say something!" I yelled at him while his back was turned toward me. My voice cracked from the tears that were rushing their way up to the surface.

"Say something!" I screamed at the top of my lungs. But he just stood there staring down at the body of his brother with his fists balled up at his sides. I know he was probably going through some form of shock because it must've just registered to him that he had slain his little brother. And I was trying to tell myself to be understanding about it, but I felt betrayed in a major way.

I felt lied to. I felt like he didn't respect me enough to tell me the truth. We are all victims of this tragedy, but he tried to have his cake and eat it too. It's tragic that my brother killed his best friend and children. It's tragic that Kaleb then killed my brother. What is *not alright,* is for him to lie to me because he decided he wanted the little sister of the man he killed. At last, that's the last tragedy. He does not get to have me. It's not alright!

I opened my mouth to yell at him again, but right then, Tiny jumped out of the car drawing both of our attention. He held his phone to his ear.

"Kaleb, we have to go. They just rushed Monica's grandmother to the hospital."

Dear Yah—*no*! For a moment my mind fractured as my world tilted. The only thing I could do was reach out. Kaleb was there before I even realized he was supporting me. He helped me get in the car and as soon as the door closed, he was on his phone.

The man who wore the bulletproof vest as a shirt floored the gas, causing the tires to screech. As we drove past Rasheed's body, Kaleb's gaze went to him. The muscle ticked furiously in his cheek, and he moved his legs restlessly as if it took everything in him to leave him there. At the same time, he listened to G with listless eyes. He began to rub his hand over his head in a way I had only seen him do when he was physically and emotionally tired. It looked as if he was getting ready to break down.

"What's he saying?" I asked him, trying to get him to say something. He just listened and that concerned me. He moved as if he was trying to hold onto his rage or grief. I prayed it was because he'd just left his brother dead in the street and not because G was telling him anything bad about Nana.

"Is she alright?" I clutched at the front of his shirt trying to get his attention, desperate for any information he could give. His gaze came to me and that muscle in his cheek started ticking out of control. Whatever G was telling him, it wasn't good.

"Tell me!" I yelled at him. He hung up the phone and for a moment, it looked as if he was going to try and not tell me.

"Tell me, *coward*!" I yelled and I slapped him with everything I had in me. He was having a hard time, but I didn't care. Frustratingly, he ran his hand across his face. I raised my hand to hit him again, but he caught it.

"She had a heart attack!" His voice cracked, and there were tears in his eyes. Pain!

I stared at him confused. Did he just say I was having a heart attack, or that my Nana had a heart attack? Surely it's me because my heart hurt. It felt like I had just got hit in my stomach with a bat.

I blinked.

Slowly, I turned my head to face the front. The man with the bulletproof vest on was driving very fast and recklessly, but it didn't matter to me.

I blinked.

I could not escape into the haze that seemed to settle over me. I needed answers. I looked back at Kaleb. He watched me with concerned eyes.

"Is she alright?" I whispered. A look of compressed pain settled on his face. I had never seen him this way. Maybe it was me who was dying.

"Tell me," I said just as quietly. He shook his head. "She didn't make it, baby!"

Rage!

"You're lying!" I yelled at him at the top of my lungs before I hit him again. I wanted to kill him!

"You are such a liar!" I continued to swing. He caught my arms and pulled me close, but I broke away from him.

"No! Don't touch me! You're a liar! I don't believe you! You're such a *liar*! Take me to the hospital!" He was lying, just like he'd lied about Man-Man. That's what he was—a liar. And now he tried to lie and tell me that my Nana was dead. There was no way that was true. There was no way Yah would do that to me... *no way*!

I didn't speak to anyone when we got to the helicopter. I just got in and waited impatiently for them to pull off. The whole ride there I didn't say anything because the only thing I could do was call Yah's name over and over again in my head.

I was slipping and falling into a place that was scary. It was dark, it was lonely, and it was calling me. Calling on Yah's name was the only thing keeping that place from sucking me in.

There was no way my Nana was dead! No way!

The chopper landed on the roof of the hospital. As soon as we walked into the emergency room, I saw Shelomoh hugging a weeping Stormy. In her arms was Eve, who was also crying.

My knees gave out, but before I could hit the ground, Kaleb caught me, lifting me up.

"I won't let you fall, baby! I promise! Lean on me! I know you don't want it, but my strength is yours!" He whispered in my ear as he lifted me in his arms. He carried me the rest of the way to Stormy and Shelomoh, but I pushed out of his arms.

Oh, dear Yah! My Nana was dead! Stormy wouldn't lie. My world shifted. It was too much! I was on overload and I could not relate to my environment. Stormy reached for me, but I had to see with my own eyes. Eve held out her arms for me, she was afraid. I took her in my arms and held her close, trying to give her what I had left.

"Where is she?" I cried... Stormy took my hand and led me into a small room and lying there in the bed was Nana. I could tell she was gone by the slack in her mouth.

"No! Yah wouldn't do this to me!" I said to Stormy clutching at her hands, needing support because I was falling. Shelomoh took a screaming Eve out my arms while Kaleb lifted me up in his again.

"He wouldn't do this to me!" I told him. "Ain't I his servant?" I asked him. There were tears coming from his eyes.

"Yes, baby, you are!" His words were barely audible.

"Why he do this then?" I asked him, I needed him to tell me something. I was confused. I was lost! Why would Yah take her from me? With hands that shook, I reached for my Nana's and my soul cried out when I felt how cold they were.

These couldn't be my Nana's hands. These couldn't be the same hands that mended my tutus or fixed my ballet shoes. I looked down at the hands through blurry vision. They looked like the same hands. They looked like the same hands that rubbed my head when I cried. I lifted her hand and put it on my head, but it just fell off.

"No! Nana!" I wailed. "Please, Nana! Don't go! Come back! Please! Please! Please! Nana! Please!" My tears were now flowing freely. I laid my head on her chest and held her tightly, determined to hold onto her for as long as I could. I tried to remember the last time we hugged or the last time I told her that I loved her.

Kaleb

She kept pushing me away. She didn't want me to touch her. That was unbearable pain. But hearing her mourn like this and not being able to comfort her was ripping out my heart. She wept from the pit of her being, and it was tearing me apart. This was all my fault.

I can't lose her!

I can't lose Monica!

I searched my brain trying to think of a way to fix this. Father Yah, I can't lose her! Please, Father, help me because I couldn't think my way through this. Every time I tried, my thoughts centered back on my brother.

Rasheed...

Rasheed was dead! Tonight, I killed my brother—my baby brother!

How do I begin to deal with that? I looked down at Monica's back from where she laid her head on Nana's chest, and I felt like the most selfish human being on the planet, because I needed her right now, more than I ever needed anybody in my life. I needed her to open her arms for me. I needed her to rub my head the way she sometimes did and tell me how strong she thought I was, and how capable she believed me to be.

Whenever she did that, it made me feel powerful. It made me feel as if I could overcome any obstacle. She was my other half. For the first time in my life, I didn't feel alone. I needed her to let me comfort her and she comfort me. I rubbed my hands over my head.

Tonight, I killed Rasheed. And now I was getting ready to lose my wife—my peace. How do I even begin to deal with that? I needed to fix this! But for the life of me, I didn't know how. For the first time, I didn't know how to fix something, and I couldn't relate.

"Nana!" she wailed.

I had to bury my hands underneath my arms to keep from grabbing her and comforting her. She needed to say bye to her grandmother, but I was not made to see her suffer this way and just stand idly by. I felt like a complete waste of space.

As if Shelomoh could sense the turmoil I was in, he handed me Eve. She wrapped her little arms around my neck so tightly; I closed my eyes taking comfort in that, assuring myself that all I did was for her. It was all for her. And Yah knows that if I had to do it all over again, I

would in a heartbeat. She is mine just like her mother is. And it's my job to protect them from

everything and everyone; including my brother.

I wrapped my arms around her and buried my face in her little shoulder. Dear Yah, I killed my brother... painful tears came from my eyes. I killed Rasheed and just left his body lying there in the street. Tiny put his big paw on my shoulder and pulled me close.

"It's alright, boss! You did what you had to do! Rasheed died a long time ago! He had been taken over by the spirit that ruled him. Remember, he almost killed your wife today, and if Eve had been in that car, she wouldn't have made it!" His words were true. But what was I going to tell my mother? She would not understand. I didn't know how to fix this!

Shelomoh and Stormy helped me get Monica to my truck that G had driven up to the hospital. She still wouldn't accept my touch. She assured them that she didn't need them to come back to the house with us. We drove back in silence, both of us lost in our thoughts. I looked through my rearview mirror at my daughter who was asleep in her car seat. She was depending on me to fix what was broken, but her daddy didn't know how.

Gideon assured me that he and his men would make sure Rasheed's and his friends' bodies got back to the States. I still needed to go to my mom's and break the news to her. However, it was a good chance she already knew, because she had not stopped calling my phone since we landed on the roof of the hospital. I had to put the ringer on vibrate just so I could deal with the present situation at hand.

It's the only thing I was able to do, just try and deal with the present situation at hand. I had messed everything up. This was all my fault and my mind was too exhausted to think through it. When we pulled up to the boarding house, I put the car in park and reached up to turn the key off, but Monica touched my hand stopping me.

I bit down on my teeth. Here it is! I knew this was coming! I told myself to respect her wishes, it was the least I could do for ruining her life. But my heart accelerated, sending panic signals to my brain.

I could not lose Monica!

"Don't turn the key off." She said in a quiet voice. I took my hand away from the key and turned to look at her. She sat staring straight ahead. There was a look of resolve on her face.

"You don't need to be alon—" I began, but she spoke cutting me off and ending my world.

"I want a divorce."

Those four words. I rubbed my hands over my face and head as I fought to hold onto my sanity, but I was losing the battle.

I had the might to force her to stay with me! I had the power to force her, but what will that help? It will only make things worse. I knew I had to walk away. But everything in me raged at the idea. She got out of the car.

I opened my door and jumped out getting ready to stop her, but instead, I clutched the frame of the door for dear life and watched as she took Eve out her car seat. My face balled up in rage as my insides screamed at me, calling me a weak bastard for allowing her to walk away.

I couldn't say anything, because if I opened my mouth, threatening words were going to come out. I closed my eyes as she walked away from me without looking back.

I can't—I wanted to kill somebody! I balled up my fists and got back in my car slamming the door. I wanted to kill! I needed to release. I lashed out at the nearest thing to me, which was the steering wheel. It felt amazing! I proceeded to pound the sh*t out of the wheel, needing the release.

And when I was done, although it was the most painful thing I ever had to do, I put the car in drive and drove away from my heart. The next few hours although painful, paled in comparison. When I pulled up to my mother's house, she stormed out it in her robe. Her face was contorted in her grief and rage.

"How could you?!" she yelled. By this point, I felt numb. I had killed my brother and lost my family. It was only right that this was to happen.

"He was your brother!" she yelled as she pounded on my chest. I didn't try to stop her. I knew she needed this outlet, just like I had pounded on the steering wheel a minute ago. When she was done, she let me hold and comfort her.

She even tried to comfort *me*, but there was no comfort for me. I would have to make it through this, just like I had to make it through my painful life—alone. I sat with her until she fell asleep. Still feeling numb, I let myself out of her house and drove to my penthouse.

I hadn't been here in so long it felt strange. It didn't feel like home anymore. Home had become the boarding house that was filled with Eve and Monica's laughter. It was filled with Nana's wisecracks and news reporting. Every day when I came in from work, she had a new end-time event to share with me.

"Kaleb, do you know the police had to shoot a man for eating another man's face?!" She'd shake her head. "Child, we living in the last days..." I'd settle back on the couch as Eve crawled all over me because she was excited that I was home. Monica would be in the kitchen finishing up dinner, causing the house to be filled with its mouthwatering smell.

"Yeah, Nana, you might be right," I would always tell her as I settled back, relaxing on the couch.

"I *know* I'm right. Dem folks say the sun doing some strange stuff. You mark my words, one of them flares gon' hit us. You wait and see." By this time, Monica would have handed me a beer. I'd crack it open and take a deep long swig, the perfect ending to a long day.

"Yep, you might be right." I'd tell her.

"Good afternoon, Mr. Jacob," The doorman said as he held the door open for me. I was too exhausted to speak, I just nodded.

How did I get back to this? I was back to this cold and sterile greeting. A far cry from the greeting I had grown used to. As I rode up the elevator, I reflected on the fact that losing my place had been just another lie I had told Monica. I laughed with no humor. How can I lose a place in a building that I owned?

Well... there you have it, folks. That's how I ended up back into this cold, lonely place.

Lies! Our relationship had been built on many lies.

After showering, I opted out of lying in bed. There was no way I could get any sleep without the feel of my wife's warm body next to mine and I needed rest. My brain needed to be rejuvenated so that I could figure a way through all the mess I've created.

Instead, I settled back in the chair in my living room. It had an amazing view of the lake, A view I would trade in a heartbeat for those old walls that Nana had decorated with velveteen paintings. My body slipped into sleep out of pure exhaustion. Rasheed's last words haunted my dream.

"You don't get to live happily ever after, bruh!" In my dream, I experienced the pain of killing him all over again. When I was startled

awake some hours later, my heart was filled with pain when my lonely apartment came into focus. However, the one good thing about waking up to my present-day reality was that the gears in my brain had rested enough to begin working again.

The first thing I did was pick up the phone to call Monica. I wasn't surprised that she didn't answer, so I sent her a text.

> Hey baby! I know you're hurt and you need to grieve the loss of Nana. I can't begin to explain to you how your pain is ripping me apart. If I could, I would take it away from you and carry it all on my shoulders, but I can't. What you shared with Nana is yours alone. But what I can do, I will. Don't worry about funeral arrangements, I will take care of everything, you just take all the time you need to grieve. I will give you space. You don't have to worry about me. But what I cannot give you is a divorce. If you don't want to see me for the next few days or months or years, so be it. But I can't give you a divorce, because without you, there is no me. I love you! And if you need me to take Eve sometime so that you can be alone, I can come to pick her up whenever you want and drop her off whenever you want. You just let me know. And whatever you do... please remember that you are my heartbeat and I can't make it without you. I love you!

She texted right back...

You can get Eve from Stormy and bring her
back to Stormy. I don't want to see you!

I settled back in my chair. That was a beginning. That I could deal with. It was the divorce thing I could not. I did not linger long; I had two funerals to arrange. Over the next week, I threw myself into getting everything in order. It was not easy. My mother fluctuated in her feelings toward me. Some days she wanted to hold me close and others, she didn't want to see me. All the people that mattered knew the truth about what happened that night in Havana.

However, word on the street was that Rasheed and his friends went there to settle some beef they had with the Cubans and got killed in the process. But his crew felt better about his death because word on the street was that Dominic also gotten killed in the process. Without having any real facts, they showed up to the funeral with their heads held high wearing t-shirts with Rasheed's picture on it, because to them, he was a hero and would go down in the street hall of fame as one of the best to play the game.

I stood next to my mother and shook my head when they started chanting his name. But when I saw that it only upset her more, I looked at Tiny giving him the cue to break it up. My men silently left from where they were standing against the wall and in a matter of seconds, brought silence to the misguided youths. And as tough as that situation was to get through, Nana's funeral was worse.

Monica was not handling it well. When it got to the portion of the funeral where friends and family said their last goodbyes to the deceased, she laid her head on Nana's chest and refused to move. Her wails filled the funeral home breaking my heart. I had respected her wishes and gave her space. So, I stood in the back of the room with my men holding Eve so that she didn't have to see me. However, I could not stand here and do nothing when her sounds of pain flooded my system like that.

I walked to the front of the room and handed Eve to Stormy, who stood there rubbing Monica's back trying to comfort her. Then I scooped my wife up in my arms and carried her out of the room. Thank Yah she didn't fight me. She just laid her head on my shoulder and let me hold her while she wept. The toughest part was having her once again push away from me when that wave of pain had passed.

∼

Monica

After Nana's funeral, I didn't want to see anybody but Stormy. She was truly my soul sister. She understood exactly what I was going through. I'll never forget the day she took me out for ice cream after her grandmother, who had also taken care of her most her life had died. That day, she explained to me how she had to go away to school and try to build a new life. At the time, I didn't understand why she had to leave, but she said she had to because although her grandmother was gone, she still needed to live life.

"Little Miss Rhonda has taken over your dance class. She told me to tell you not to worry; she will have the girls ready for the show tomorrow," Stormy said as she walked through my house opening curtains. I lay on the couch under my covers. Eve was perched on my legs. She had a box of animal crackers and the remote control in her hand. I chuckled without any humor because she had her little finger on the volume button and was turning it up so that she could hear her Sesame Street over Stormy. Goodness, she was a trip.

"But I assured them that their teacher will be there to show some support because she knows how hard they worked and would not leave them to do the show alone," I grunted. I wasn't going back.

"Thank you, ma'am," she said taking the remote out of Eve's hand, who had turned the volume up very loud, completely drowning out her voice. Eve opened her mouth to whine but Stormy gave her a look and she thought better of it.

"Now, what was I saying before I was so rudely interrupted," she continued giving Eve the side-eye as she turned the volume back down to a reasonable level and set the remote on the table away from her little fingers. She had brought a bag of groceries and was heading into the kitchen to put them up.

"You are going to be ready for the show, right?" Her face brightened. "And guess what." She placed the bag on the floor by the kitchen door and came back into the living room sitting in Nana's chair. That kind of bothered me a bit but I didn't say anything. I kind of just wished she would take Eve's bag that I had packed and sitting by the door and leave. She was dropping her off at Kaleb's shop for me.

"Madame Queen is going to dedicate the whole show to Ima Naomi, isn't that great?" I

smiled, but it didn't reach my eyes.

"Yeah, that is. Tell her thank you for me." My voice was muffled because I didn't bother

lifting my head to talk around the covers.

"I will not! You're going to thank her yourself when you come to the show." I rolled my eyes.

"I'm not going, Storm." She exhaled getting up out of Nana's chair and coming to sit on the couch with me, forcing me to have to sit up and reposition Eve on my legs to make room for her.

"It's been two weeks, Mon, it's time for you to get up." I exhaled letting my head drop back on my neck, it felt too heavy to hold up.

"You have to rebuild your life!" she said pulling my shoulders, causing my head to jerk back up. "No matter how much you may want to, you can't live in limbo." Tears flooded my eyes causing my vision to become blurry.

"I don't know how." I shrugged. "I've been taking care of Nana for so long, I don't know

what to do now that she's gone."

"I know, baby." She shook her head. "Yah knows I understand what you're talking about. When my grandmother died, I wanted to just lay in the bed and never get up, but unlike you..." Now she was giving me the side-eye.

"I didn't have a husband somewhere paying my bills. I had to get up the next day and try to march forward. Your life is a mess, I ain't gon' lie. But I'll tell you where you can start. You can get up off this couch and show some support for your girls. They've worked hard all summer, and they need their teacher there." She let go of my shoulders.

"And then after that, take it one day at a time. Have faith in Yah. When things happen to us like this, it tests our faith. But believe your way through it, I promise you, troubles don't last always. And for Yah's servants, even less." I grinned one-sided.

"You may not have had a husband somewhere paying your bills, but if my memory serves correct, you had a very rich boyfriend who picked up the stake." She grinned.

"Not at that time. And as I told you, for Yah's servants, trouble last even shorter. Now, I'm going to put up these groceries and then I'm going to take Eve to her dad's. Lay here tonight, but then get up tomorrow. And when you get up, stay up!"

After Stormy and Eve left, I laid there and cried some more. Stormy said I had to rebuild my life without my Nana. The thought of that was terrifying. For the last two weeks, I've gotten up forgetting my grandmother was gone and put on coffee, only to stand there staring at her empty chair and her empty mug. I didn't have to make coffee anymore. When that reality first washed over me, I went down to my knees on the kitchen floor and cried till my throat hurt.

Every night since she died, I've slept in her bed because it still held her scent. I stood in her closet and buried my nose in her clothes, desperate to hold onto her diminishing essence; each day, a little more of her faded away.

Later that night, my phone vibrated on the table. I picked it up and saw that I had a couple of messages from Kaleb. For just a moment, I closed my eyes as I fought my need for him. There was nothing more on earth I wanted than to crawl up in his arms so that he could hold me close and tell me that everything will be okay, but at last, that was not the path for him and me. I clicked on the button to read the message.

It was a picture of him sitting on his couch with Eve in his lap. They were both waving at the camera. *We miss you, Mommy and we love you!* was written underneath. I let the phone fall from my fingers to the floor.

He texted me all the time; in the morning, he would text *good morning.* In the afternoon, he'd text a picture of his bland lunch and then say how much he missed our lunch dates. And at night, he'd text a picture of his chair that he had taken to sleeping in because he couldn't sleep in his bed without me; I never text anything back.

Another thing I had found out the joker had lied about, he still owned his penthouse. Hell, I found out he owned the whole damn building. I shook my head. However, I will never forgive him for lying to me about Man-Man.

Never!

Eventually, I fell asleep. When I woke the next day it took everything I had in me to pull myself up off the couch. Nana would want me to go to the show and support the girls. At one point and time, that center had been her whole life. I couldn't drop the ball. I had to continue her work.

After showering, I went to my Nana's closet and pulled out one of her old costumes. It was a black dress that she had worn to dance the final scene in the *Black Swan, A Tragedy.* It fit my mood perfectly. I pulled my locs back in a tight ponytail giving myself a very severe look.

I had become the Black Swan.

-Narrator-

Madame Queen hurried the next act out to the stage. She had a feeling that this would be the show that would put her on the map. This would be the show that she would always be remembered for. As the show had done the previous seasons before, it had completely sold out. There wasn't even standing room left. She had everyone from the thugs on the street to news reporters in the audience. This was going to be a night everyone would remember.

For the hundredth time, her eyes went to the beautiful young lady that sat off to the side where Stormy had deposited her on the stage steps. Strapped to her back was a beautiful cream guitar. What kept drawing her attention to the little poor soul was how much she reminded her of her Sweet Tart, both of them wore their sadness like a badge.

"Cupcake!" she said catching Stormy who rushed past her shushing the kids, "A moment of your time please."

Looking completely harassed and as stressed out as Madame Queen felt, Stormy stopped to see what she wanted.

"Dear, it's okay to be stressed, but it's never okay to show it! You're too beautiful for that!" She admonished her pupil. Stormy exhaled letting her head fall back on her shoulders, obviously in no mood for advice from Madame.

"Who is that?" Madame cooed, pointing to the young lady with her red French fan. Stormy turned her head to see who it was she was pointing to. Backstage was a very crowded space.

"Who?"

"The beautiful creature with the long brown braids over there." Stormy nodded with recognition.

"Oh! That is Anatiyah, the daughter of my very good friends. I just brought her because she needed to get out of her room. She's beginning to make her parents worry. Is she in the way? I have her sitting there because there is no more room out front."

"She's so sad, isn't she? Kind of reminds me of Sweet Tart," Madame said instead of answering any of Stormy's questions. There was something coming together in her head. She was getting a hunch about the young lady. And she didn't make it this far in her career without following her gut.

"Yeah, she is. Just like Monica, she lost a couple of people that were very close to her."

Stormy went to walk away.

"Tell me, Cupcake, can she play that guitar on her back?" Madame asked, stopping her again. This time when Stormy turned to face her, there was a bright smile on her face.

"Oh, Madame! Her voice is like nothing I can explain with words. It is said that her singing attracts angels. That would be just wonderful if you have room for her in your show. Maybe if she performs, she will feel better." Madame snapped her fan closed.

"Come, Cupcake, introduce us."

Anatiyah sat on the stairs angry her parents forced her to come tonight. She didn't mean to have an attitude with Stormy, but she just wished she would have never run this idea by her mother. She didn't want to be here tonight around all these people. She didn't want to be anywhere he wasn't.

Monroe...

Just the thought of his name brought tears to her eyes. He and Dawid were gone. And her

dad and Gideon weren't even trying to look for them.

"HEY, TY." She looked up when Stormy called her name and then blushed when she saw that she had somehow garnered the attention of Madame Queen, who was famous in the hood for her flamboyance.

She stood to her feet and dusted off her pants as she walked over to the two women.

"Ty, this is Madame Queen. Madame, this is Anatiyah!" "Nice to mee—" Ty began, but Madame cut her off.

"Why are you so sad, Biscuit?" Ty was surprised at the woman's question.

"I—I don't know what you mean?" Madame hit her arm playfully with her fan.

"It's okay, you don't have to tell me, but a talented girl like yourself... I bet you wrote a song about it, huh?" Instantly, Ty thought about the song she had been working on since the night her brother and Monroe walked out of the gym doors. She nodded. Suddenly the need to sing began to burn her soul.

"Yeah, I do." Madame's eyes grew wide with her lust for the performance.

"If I told you I can give you an opportunity tonight to show us all how you feel with your beautiful voice, would you accept it?" Ty didn't have to think about it. The need to sing had taken over her to the point that it left her breathless.

"Yeah, I would."

"Peeerrrrfffect!" Madame cooed. "Come with me, Biscuit!" Stormy wrapped her arm around the girl's shoulders as they followed behind Madame, who glided across the floor to where Monica stood giving her girls a final pep talk before their performance.

"Sweet Tart, can I have a word with you?" Monica turned her head to look at her for only
a second.

"Not now, Madame. I have to get the girls ready for the performance, they're up next."

"I only need a moment of your time, dear." Monica exhaled, knowing there was no use
ignoring Madame. It was an impossible mission.

"I'll be right back," she told her girls, "Try to relax. You guys are going to do great!" "Sweet Tart, meet Biscuit, Biscuit, meet Sweet Tart!" For a moment both, Monica and Anatiyah were at a loss for what to do or say.

"WHAT SHE MEANT TO SAY," Stormy said coming to stand between the two girls. She picked up both of their hands. "Is Monica meet Anatiyah, Anatiyah, meet Monica." The two young women that were very close in age looked into the other's eyes and saw their sadness reflected in the other.

"Sweet Tart, Biscuit here is going to provide the music for your closing performance." "Oh Madame, about that—" Monica began, but Madame cut her right off.

"No, no, no, dear! There is no, *no* about that! Surely you won't open your lips to tell me your thinking about not doing it!" As she talked her voice began to rise as she prepared herself to have one of the grand fits she was legendary for. Monica, who didn't have the will or the energy to try and talk her down off the ledge, grabbed her hand.

"Of course not, Madame, I was just going to say that Anatiyah and I have not practiced anything, so it may be a bit awkward trying to perform on the fly like that." A huge smile came across Madame's face.

"Oh, Sweet Tart, the greatest events that happened in show biz history happened by happenstance. This is going to be the most majestic performance that ever hit the stage, you mark my words. Be ready, you two are up after your little ballerinas." And then she turned and sailed away, leaving Stormy to work out the kinks.

"I think what she saw in you two is that you both share a common sadness. And just maybe, you can come together and express that onstage." After giving their hands one last squeeze, she told them both that she loved them and then rushed off to try and regain order to the little ones who were overexcited to be backstage and were running to and fro.

Feeling like two fish out of water, Monica and Ty both smiled, but neither of their smiles reached their eyes.

"I'm sorry they put you on the spot like this, I guess we can just go out there and wing it." Ty shook her head.

"They didn't put me on the spot. Sometimes, I feel like all I can do is sing. It's the one beautiful thing I have left." Monica swallowed as she looked at her. Their sadness very much mirrored the other. She reached out and took Ty's hand. And for a moment, they just stared at the other, both of their eyes filled with tears that didn't drop. It was as if in that moment, they silently shared their stories.

Monica nodded. "Okay!" she said before she turned and prepared her girls to go out on

stage.

Neither Ty nor Monica knew that this night would seal their fate, and although it will be a while before either of them saw the other after tonight, they would eventually become the best of friends.

Monica

Together, Ty and I walked out onstage. Someone had placed a stool and a microphone up front. We walked out to a standing ovation. When the audience quieted down and settled back into their seats, I approached the mic. Ty smiled encouragingly at me.

"The show tonight is dedicated to my grandmother. She would have loved this. I just want to thank you all for coming out and to say—" Right then the auditorium door opened, casting a little light in the dark space. My words stalled when I saw who it was.

Kaleb.

I hadn't seen him since my Nana's funeral. The sight of him took my breath. He was so handsome and so strong. He carried Eve in one of his strong arms. She clung to her daddy's neck, a luxury no longer allowed to me. I forced my gaze away from him, putting it back on the audience. They all looked up at me with so much expectation. They wanted to be entertained. But I had nothing left in me to give but pain.

"I just wanted to say that... this will be my last dance."

I felt Anatiyah grab my hand. I squeezed hers before slowly walking to take my spot center stage.

I had become the Black Swan.

As if on cue, everything went dark before two spotlights shined down on us.

I stood in the center of the stage and closed my eyes as my pain washed over me. I let it have me completely. And with it came anger. Anger that my life had been such a—

"I call this piece, Tragedy!" Anatiyah said into the mic. My eyes drifted open. It was as if she was in my head, but she wasn't. She sat on her stool in front of the mic with her guitar in her arms. Her fingers began to strum her instrument and a beautifully haunting tune that sung instantly to my soul filled the darkness.

My eyes drifted closed and I began to sway to the tune. I gently moved my neck and shoulders, embodying my tragedy. I thought about Man-Man and who he could have been. I thought about Mika, Ro, Po, Nay and who they will never be. I began to move my arms to the tune. And as my body got more involved in my tragic sway, I thought about Rasheed. I thought about Mama Rita, who had to bury her child. I thought about my Nana, but it was as I was thinking about Kaleb that my hands came up to suddenly clutch my womb.

And just then, Anatiyah's voice filled the room and I was no longer in control of my movements. My body became elegance as I danced to our tragic love story; two souls that could never be because life had made a vicious decree. I went up on my toes causing my body to extend out into an Allongé before lifting my leg straight in back of me in an Arabesque.

Her beautiful voice washed over me and it seemed as if it

caused me to dance like I had never danced before. And I guess it's only fitting that if this is the last dance, then it should be the one they remembered me by.

I danced for Man-Man. I danced for Mika, Ro, Po, and Nay. I dance for Rasheed and Mama Rita. I danced for my Nana. And finally, I danced for me and Kaleb's love story. We all shared one thing in common. We had all been weaved into this tragic pattern that had only left pain in its wake.

Anatiyah's words came to an end at the same time my dance did. And when I opened my eyes, I was amazed to see that I stared at the audience through tears.

They all sat staring at us as if in a trance. Breathing heavily, I welcomed the burning journey of my tears as they ran down my face.

Anatiyah turned to look at me with a smile on her face, this time it reached her eyes. I was not surprised to see that she had been crying as she sang. You could hear the pain in her voice. Somehow, she had made us all feel the pain in her voice. I reached for her hand and together we bowed. Together, she and I had made history. Together, we had managed to make the world see our tragedy.

Madame Queen was the first to snap out of the trance. She stood to her feet and began to applaud as if she had never seen anything like our performance. There were tears in her eyes. Her applause brought everyone else out of whatever hold the presentation had on them. The whole room stood to their feet, and I was even more amazed to see that many of them had tears in their eyes as well.

Chapter 20

ONE LAST DANCE

MONICA

1 year later....

I CAN TRY to explain to you what it is like to be chosen to truly know the Heavenly Father. What it's like to see him changing and molding you into perfect clay. But then I would just be wasting my breath, because some things no matter how skilled you are, cannot be told.

Now, looking back over my life, looking at the way things went down. I realize that certain things had to happen just the way they did. You see, it took me losing nearly everything to truly give my heart completely to the Father.

And I know you say, but Monica, it looked as if you were doing good before. I wasn't. I was occupied with my Nana, my new husband, and the new life we were building here at the boarding house. Never in all that time did I put Yah first. He was always an afterthought; something to get to when I found the time; something to do in my *spare* time.

This is a grave error so easily committed. We get so caught up in life, that the only time we stop and reach for the Father is when our heart is in pain. And he is so loving and so understanding that he's always there when we need him. But my life didn't truly change until I learned to reach for him, for *everything*.

In the morning before I rise out of the bed, I stop and I say, *thank you, Father, for bringing me through the night*. As I walk down the street and feel the sun shining down on my skin, I say, *thank you, Father, for bringing me through the light*. When I look out my window at the rain and how green it makes the grass and trees, I say, *thank you, Father, for the beautiful sight*. I began teaching Eve to do the same.

You see, in the year after my Nana passed, I was in so much pain that I couldn't cope with anybody else because I didn't know how to cope with myself. I felt like I was in limbo, lost and confused, not knowing which way to go. But one thing I knew for sure, the old Monica had died with my Nana, and until I found the new, I was of no use to anybody.

At first, I didn't want to pick up my Bible because in a way, I was angry with Yah. I was angry with him for allowing my life to be ripped to shreds the way it had. But things got so bad that I felt I would suffocate if I didn't go to him. I continued my reading in my scriptures a month after burying Nana and it took me an entire year to finish it.

Oh y'all, I can try to tell you how good he is. How magnificent he is. How he took a fool like me and changed me, molded me, into something he could look at one day and say, *well done, my true and faithful servant*; words my ears long to hear.

During that year, I had to retrain myself to live. I can't begin to explain how painful that time had been for me, but halleluyah he brought me through. And he was so merciful in the way that he did. I'll tell you what I mean.

Although I still couldn't bring myself to get back with Kaleb, my husband insisted on continuing to pay all the boarding house bills that he had changed over into his name well before my grandmother had passed. And he continued to put money on the card he had given me when he first moved in; which meant I didn't have to go back to work.

Of course, I told him he didn't have to, but he stubbornly refused to listen, saying whether I liked it or not, I was still very much his responsibility. I didn't argue, the truth was, I didn't want to go back to work anyway. This freed up my time to spend reading my scriptures and being the mom Eve needed me to be. My relationship with my friends, Keturah and Shante have changed quite a bit.

Just because the Father touched *your* heart, doesn't mean he will touch the heart of your friends and family. They didn't understand the change that was happening to me. Keturah got upset and said she couldn't believe I was falling prey to the white man's religion. And no matter how much I tried to explain to her that it wasn't the white man's religion and that the Bible was black history, she wasn't trying to hear it.

"All I know is... that's the book our slave masters held in their hand as they cracked the

whip over our backs," she'd say.

"But Keturah, if I was the devil and there was a really important truth that I wanted to hide from

a people, what better way to do it? His plan was perfect." She still refused to hear me.

I begged her to just read it for herself, but she wouldn't. And as for Shante... oh my goodness! She is just an outright heathen.

"Dang, Monica, put the bible down and let's go out to the club," she'd whine. I shook my head.

"Naw, Tey, I just ain't feeling it no more."

"Uhhh! Why you have to change? I miss my club buddy.' I looked at her, struggling with the words to tell her. I wanted to try and explain to her what was happening to me, but I knew she wouldn't understand. I knew it would just come across as me trying to preach to her. So, I tried a gentler approach.

"Inside my heart was a hole," I told her putting my hand to my chest. Tears came to my eyes as I spoke.

"I have always felt the need to fill this hole." I wiped away the tears, but more came.

"When I was a kid, I searched on TV for the answer, in music videos and movies. The smiling

faces that stared back at me from that tube told me that if I did certain things, I would be happy. They said if we shopped for clothes and went out partying with friends and caught the eyes of attractive men, it would fill this hole." I patted my chest, looking into her eyes, pleading with her to understand.

"But the smiling faces lied. No matter how many clubs we go to, how much shopping we did, and how many times we hooked up with cute guys only to later get our hearts broken, that hole was still there." I looked down at the floor as I thought about all the years I'd wasted.

"For the first time in my life, I feel as if that hole has finally been filled. And I can't explain to you how good that feels. I can never go back to where I was. I know to you it don't look like I'm living, but for the very first time in my life, that's exactly what I'm doing." I wiped at my tears as I shook my head.

"I can't go back, Shante... I can't go back. Please be a good friend and don't ask me to."

Tears were now in her eyes as she came to me and hugged me close.

"I won't, Mon. I won't ask you to go back anymore." She dried her tears. "I'm happy for you. Maybe one day the hole in my heart will get filled too." Her words made me feel good. Because I thought for just a moment, that she would seek in order to be found. But just like our Master said in the parable of the Sower; there is some soil when the seed falls, the devil comes and snatches it away so that the person cannot be saved.

After that day, I began to see both her and Keturah less and less. And yeah, it hurt, but what could I do? The Word was a dividing sword, whether we liked it or not. However, my friendship with Mika grew. She agreed to read through her scriptures with me from the beginning. We called each other and discussed the amazing things we found in our read. She even went to Stormy and Shelomoh's house with me some Sabbaths.

Now, I know you're all wondering about me and Kaleb's relationship. And surprisingly, it's cordial. I no longer had Stormy dropping Eve off to his shop. I did it myself. I was still uncomfortable with him coming to the house because, well, let's just face it, that's still Kaleb; a very handsome, strong, capable man. And I'm just a flesh and blood woman.

So, you say, why don't you just get back with him already? And the truth was, I was afraid. I was afraid because although I wanted him so badly, oh, my goodness, he looked so good, I just couldn't get past all the things that happened. It is morally wrong to live happily ever after with the man that murdered my brother. I just couldn't bring myself to do it.

And y'all, after a year, he is wearing me down. When I drop Eve off to the shop to him, he always has flowers or some kind of gift. He'd say something like...

"Hey, I was hoping we could grab lunch at Mama Rita's and just talk for a little bit" or " Carlos and Angela has been asking about you and Eve, I told them I'd bring you guys by to have lunch with them."

Let me tell you something, if I make the mistake of letting Kaleb get me alone or even alone at a table in a restaurant, I was a goner. He can be very persuasive when he had a mind to.

Plus, my nights have grown really lonely and cold. And I missed having his strong warm arms wrapped around me. I missed feeling his lips against my skin. I missed feeling his...

Well, you get the point.

Anyhow, we've worked out a little system where I would drop Eve off to him at the shop on Fridays. I will decline his lunch offers or going to his office and talking offers. Once I kid you not, he

347

offered to take me and Eve to Jamaica to visit a good friend of his. And then he would drop her back off to me at the Center on Monday. And so far, it works. Being a joint parent isn't so bad.

I've also worked up enough nerve to begin going through my Nana's belongings.

Slowly at first, but over the last few weeks, I've begun to pass on some of her things that I knew she would have wanted to go into good use. Stormy told me how her grandmother always told her if she died, don't hold on to her things to make a shrine out of them. Of course, that was the first thing I wanted to do, and I did for a few months. I just left everything how Nana had left it.

But after some intense prayer, reading of my scriptures, and just meditating, letting the Father speak to me; I have come to see that my actions although comforting, were not healthy. It was one day while I was going through her little side-stand by her bed that Yah shifted my life yet again. I stumbled upon my Nana's diary. Heck, I hadn't even been aware she kept one.

After making Eve some lunch and laying her down for a nap, I settled back on the couch and began to read it.

March 6, 2007
It's been a while since I wrote in my diary. I got this stupid thing, I should learn to use it more; anyway, I got a doctor's appointment tomorrow. A little afraid of what they are going to find. My throat has been real scratchy, and I've noticed a little lump that's kind of tender to the touch.

March 22, 2007
Well, they say it could be cancer. They want to run more tests, but after thinking about it real hard, I don't think I'm going to let them. Maybe it's cancer, maybe it ain't. I got too much on my plate to add this to it. The city is pulling our free lunch program. The boarding house is falling apart and in need of serious repair.

Hell, if I don't get no more tenants in here, I may just lose this place altogether. And Man-Man... he just breaks my heart the most. No matter how much I beg him to stay out them streets, he's determined to make a name for himself. I'm afraid he's going to hurt somebody or somebody gon' hurt us looking for him. Dear God, he is my grandson, my daughter's only son, but he's wearing my nerves down. I can't keep going like this...

February 3, 2008
Oh hell, I done forgot I had this thing in the drawer. Where do I begin? My grandson stole my last twenty dollars out my purse. Three hours later, he called me from jail needing me to bail him out. I don't know where I'm going to get the money this time. My poor baby Monica is running herself tired overachieving trying to make up for his underachievement. I hate to say this, but sometimes I pray somebody just put that boy out of his misery. Forgive me, Heavenly Father for feeling this way. But he's tearing down all that I have left, and I don't know what to do about it.

May 9, 2012
What a wonderful day. My baby Monica got accepted to Julliard. Her mama would be so proud of her. And get this, she is her class valedictorian. That's my girl. That's my Monica. She the reason I keep fighting. She the reason I'm gon' keep fighting. No matter how big this lump in my throat gets.

May 20, 2012
I think Man-Man killed somebody. Dear God, help us! I think he killed somebody...

May 21, 2012
My grandson is dead! I don't know how I feel about it... please, God, help me, because I think that I just might be... no, I can't write that!

June 3, 2012

Tomorrow is Monica's graduation. She don't know that I know, but she's been throwing up. I found the pregnancy test she threw in the garbage. My baby is having a baby. I pray she don't do nothing stupid like try and have an abortion. I just wish she would come talk to me about it. She always so careful about my feelings, she has no idea how strong her Nana is. She has no idea the things I've survived and the stories I have to tell. That being said, I think it's kind of sweet she babies me like she does; she the only person in the world that ever did. So, I'll wait till she works up enough nerve to come tell me. I've been feeling better these days. And I guess if I'm telling the truth about it, I was afraid of dying knowing that I would be leaving my baby back here to have to deal with her brother, but now, not so much. I just wish we had some more family or somebody that could look out for her. I know Stormy and Shelomoh will be a great help, but I am so tired of leaning on those folks. And I know they are probably good and tired of us. Stormy girl is just too much of a sweetheart to ever admit it. I just wish Monica had somebody of her own. Maybe the baby's father will be there.

June 7, 2012

Well, she finally told me about the baby and that she won't be going to Julliard this year. Instead, she will try and go the following year. When I asked her about the father, her answer broke my heart. I am disappointed in her. I always figured that she would be smart when it came down to men. Ain't no use crying over spilled milk though. She and I got a baby to take care of. And as long as God give us the strength, we gon' get it done.

December 5, 2013

I'm dying. Today for the first time, I spat up blood. I've been feeling weaker and weaker. My poor baby is working two jobs and still managing to take care of me. She so tired. I caught her nodding off as she did the dishes tonight. Please God, if you hear my voice, send us some help. We need some help. My poor baby... she need some help!

August 12, 2014
God is good! He answered my prayer. Today, Eve's daddy walked through my front door. And goodness gracious, what a man! I take back my words. My girl still on point 'cause she picked a hell of a man to sire her child. Fiiiiinnnne! Dripping fine, and he a hard worker; most importantly, he strong, which is a must to deal with my Monica. Can't be no little weak man. No sir, Monica will run all over a weak man. But not Kaleb, there ain't nothing weak about him. It's like my mama would say, he all man! HalleluYah, thank you for answering my prayer!

THE DIARY FELL from between my fingers. I brought my hand to my mouth to hold in my grief. She was dying the whole time and she didn't tell me. I knew it was something wrong with that cough. I begged her to let me take her to the doctor.

Dear Yah, she had done me like she did Stormy. She didn't want to tell me and put any extra weight on my shoulders.

And she knew about Kaleb. She knew who he was from day one. She had prayed for him. If only... a knock on the door interrupted my thoughts. I got up from the couch drying my eyes as I walked to the door. Opening it, I was surprised to see Mika standing there.

"Hey." Smiling, I opened the door to let her in, but she shook her head.

"No, sis, this has to be quick, my taxi is waiting." I looked behind her to see the taxi.

"What's up?"

"I just came by to thank you for everything you did for me." I frowned.

"Why does it sound like you're saying goodbye?" She smiled a beautiful smile.

"Well, because I am. I've decided to move to California with my mom. It's time for me to try and start again. I mean, I know I will never get over my loved ones, but you helped me to see something very important."

"What?" I was confused. What could I have possibly helped her to see that caused this wonderful change in her?

She hesitated before she spoke. Her eyes went down to my bare feet for a moment before they rose back to mine.

"Monica... I know you're Man-Man's sister." I put my hand on my mouth as tears came to my eyes.

"It's alright," she said reaching up to pull it down. Her eyes began to shine with tears as well.

"That's just it... that's what you showed me." I shook my head.

"I don't understand. What did I show you?"

"Love."

"What?"

"You showed me love. Because you loved me and didn't want to hurt me, you didn't tell me who you really were. At first, I didn't know how to feel about it. But then, I realized I was so blessed to have somebody that would be willing to hold on to such a terrible secret, just so they wouldn't hurt me further than I already was." She nodded.

"That's love, Monica. It was your love that helped me to see that life is still happening. And Ro, Po and Nay wouldn't want to see me wasting away, letting it pass me by." She squared her shoulders and took a deep breath.

"I can no longer allow Man-Man to take away my joy. And I pray that you don't either, sista." She reached in and hugged me.

"Don't let him continue to steal your joy." She turned and walk toward the cab, but before she got in, she paused. "My plane leaves in two hours. I'll call you when I get settled in."

"Okay," I said, feeling like I was losing my best friend.

She nodded encouragingly. "You can do this, Mon, I know you can. You're the bravest girl in the whole world!" She slid into the cab that instantly began to drive away. I was feeling so lost at that moment. Mika and I had formed a great bond over the last year. I wanted to stop her, but she needed this. She needed this change.

She looked back at me through the window and the smile of joy on her face pulled at everything inside of me. And then she mouthed, *thank you!*

I don't know how long I stood there looking after her cab. But the only thing I could think about was my Nana's words, how she said Man-Man was draining her and destroying everything she had. My brother was a very bad person. I see that now. I mean. . I saw it then.

But the magnitude of the lives he destroyed didn't really settle in till now. I didn't know Nana felt that way about him. I knew that he was weighing heavily on her, but I didn't know that she sometimes wished him dead. Mika said she would no longer allow him to steal her joy. And here I stood, still allowing him to steal mine.

I walked in and sat back down on the couch. The door opening and closing must have awakened Eve because she slowly made her way down the stairs.

"I woke up," she mumbled as she climbed up in my lap, laying her head on my shoulder. I smiled holding her close. Oh, I loved my baby.

"Did you sleep good?"

She shook her head.

"Why not?" I asked lifting her head so that I could see her little face.

"I want daddy." she whined. For the third time in a matter of minutes, my eyes pooled back up with tears.

"I want daddy too," I admitted quietly. Without blinking an eye, Eve slid off my lap and went to the table to get my phone. She brought it back to me and handed it to me. I took it but I couldn't help but stare at her; sometimes she seemed so much older than just her four years.

"I can't do it, baby." Now it was *me* whining. She nodded her head.

"You can." Picking up my finger she placed it on the screen. I looked down at it and I couldn't remember a time I was more afraid. Mika said I was the bravest girl in the world, but if she only knew the truth.

"Do it, mama!" Eve whined a little louder.

"I'm thinking about it. Goodness, give me a sec, will you?" In a huff, she sat next to me on the couch with her little arms folded. I chewed my bottom lip as I thought overall the information I had in my head.

Talk to me, Father. What should I be doing? My heart and my soul wanted to go back to my husband. I missed him so much I was in physical pain. But is that what you want me to do, Abba? Eve picked up my Nana's diary and opened it.

My Nana had prayed for Kaleb. She felt that he was heaven-sent. She knew about him. She approved of him. What are the odds that I would find her diary today? What are the odds that right after I read her words, Mika showed up to encourage me to not let my brother steal my joy anymore? I looked down at Eve.

"I think the Father has already showed me what he'd have me to do." She smiled. With shaking hands, I started a text.

```
Me: Shalom K, I know it's not Friday. But
Eve just told me she wanted to see you, is
that alright?
```

I sat back on the couch tapping my leg. I was a nervous wreck. He made me a nervous wreck. That gentle unsure, sorry Kaleb was gone. He didn't last long after the funeral. Aggressive mob boss

Kaleb was back with a vengeance. Surprisingly, he didn't force me to come back to him. He kept his word about that; although he didn't keep it a secret that he wanted to.

What would he think of my text? Over the last year, I never deviated from our schedule. I chewed my bottom lip till it hurt. Maybe he was with another woman, but then again, maybe not. Mama Rita told me last week that when he wasn't at the shop, he was at the Lyon's Den. She said she was worried about him because it looked as if he was losing weight.

It did. I tried to ask him about it the last time I dropped Eve off at the shop, but he'd only turned and asked me why I was asking.

"Cause," my mind searched for an answer. He was crowding my space; standing all close to me, causing my mind to turn to mush. I licked my lips looking around at the few people that were there in his shop pretending that they weren't watching us. When I looked back up at him it was to see him staring at my mouth with a look of raw hunger it snatched my breath right out of my lungs.

"Cause what, Mon?" His deep voice... goodness.

"Cause, I still see you as a fri—" I never got the word out my mouth.

"No!" He growled down at me, causing me to jump and take a step back away from him. He took two more steps toward me, really crowding my space.

"I am not your friend. Do you hear me? I am not your friend." He took Eve's bag from me and then gently took her hand and walked away. When I looked up at Miss Keisha, she sat behind her desk fanning herself. The scene had gotten too heated even for her.

The sound of my phone dinging brought me out of my thoughts. Eve looked down at it as if she could read it.

```
Kaleb: You don't even have to ask. Do you
want me to come get her or do you want to
drop her off?
Me: I can drop her off.
Kaleb: I'm not at the shop.
```

```
Me: Where are you?
Kaleb: Home.
```

My hands stalled on my screen keyboard. I was back to chewing my lip.

"What?" Eve asked looking up at me.

"He's at home." She nodded her head.

"K," she said looking back at the screen. When I didn't move, she grabbed my finger to try and get me to text again.

"I'm thinking," I told her. She sat back on the couch in a huff, folding her arms. Okay, if Kaleb gets me behind closed doors it's over. Am I ready for that? Hmmm...

```
Me: That's fine, I can bring her there.
```

I inhaled, looking down at the phone as if it was something strange. Amazingly, Eve stared at it too. Goodness, she was a trip. It seemed like it took his response ages to come, but really, maybe it was a few seconds.

```
Kaleb: Okay, I'm here.
```

I let out my breath, Eve looked up at me and it seemed as if she was still holding hers.

"Let's go get dressed!" She screeched and began jumping up and down in her excitement. After I got her dressed, she sat on my big lonely bed and watched me get dressed. I picked my outfit carefully. I didn't want it to say *desperate*, but I did want it to say *available*. I settled on my long gray skirt and my oversized v-neck white t-shirt that I had to tie in a knot in the back.

After I got out of the shower, I moisturized with my Jasmine body butter. Kaleb loved the smell of it. I moisturized my locs with it too before I pulled them up in a high ponytail. I took the box with my wedding bracelets out of my drawer. When Eve saw what I held, she came and held up her arm for hers.

"Do you think I should put mine on?" I asked her, she nodded.

"Yep, put yours on too, mommy!" She took one of my bracelets out and tried to push it on my arm.

"Here, let me help you," I told her, finishing the job for her. After adding my last few accessories, I stood in front of the mirror and took myself in. I couldn't help but laugh out loud. He was going to know something was going on.

I chewed on my lip. Maybe I could just play it off like I was dropping Eve off there before going out somewhere else.

Yeah...

The whole drive over, I was a nervous wreck. I felt like I was going on a blind date or something. When we got to his building, I was surprised to see that the valet driver knew my name.

"Evening, Mrs. Jacobs," he said as he held the door open for me.

"Evening," I responded, trying to see if I could place his face. But before I could figure it out, the doorman was opening the front door greeting me the same way.

"Evening, Mrs. Jacobs." "Evening."

By the time I stepped off the elevator on the top floor, my nerves were a jumbled mess. The fact that those strangers downstairs knew who I was did not help. What was even more nerve-racking was me remembering the last time I walked down this hall. I was leaving from spending the night with Kaleb right before I called the police on him. A night I will never forget.

I lifted my hand to knock on the door, but then I punked out. But leave it to Eve to get this party on the roll. She lifted her little hand and knocked instead. So, then I had to knock as not to look like a complete coward. I was giving her a look when Kaleb opened the door.

"Hey!" I cried startled looking up at him with a huge unnecessary smile on my face. My smile was so huge and unnecessary that it caught him completely off guard. He stood staring at me as if it was his first time meeting me.

Crap, Monica! Get it together. Dang, you are such a geek.

"Hey," he finally said, stepping back to open the door. "Come in."

Eve didn't wait for the invite. She broke away from me and ran and jumped into her daddy's arms.

"Hey, princess!" he said catching her with a smile on his face. I took that time to check him out.

Like my Nana said in her diary, he is so *fiiinnnee!* It looked as if he hadn't too long before I called come in from work. But it must have been one of his laid-back days because he was in a suit instead of jeans; which meant he hadn't been working on the cars today.

Well, he was in a partial suit. He had gotten rid of his jacket and tie, but he still had on a pair of black slacks with black suspenders. Goodness, this man looked good in suspenders. The first few buttons on his dress shirt were undone, and his sleeves were rolled up over his muscled forearms.

My eyes continued to travel up his sculpted body. Before he and I had separated, Kaleb stayed lined up and always seemed fresh from the barbershop. Since the separation, he started doing something different with his look. Maybe he wasn't going to the barber as often because his beard looked rough as if it hadn't been lined in a few weeks. But it still looked good. Kaleb could rock a full beard as lovely as he rocked the lined up trimmed beard.

My gaze rose to his eyes and I nearly jumped out of my boots. He was watching me check him out. He even wore a little smirk on his face as if he knew my thoughts. It was then I realized he had asked me a question.

Aw hell, I was screwing this up.

"Hmm," I asked trying to play it off.

"I asked if you will be staying for dinner?" By this time, Eve had run off to do whatever it was she did when she came to her dad's house. I mean, she really disappeared like up-the-stairs disappeared, leaving me alone with her father in the foyer.

Thanks, Eve!

"Oh! Umm, I had plans." One of his eyebrows rose as his gaze raked down my body taking me in just as thoroughly as I had done him.

"Plans? You smell really good. Plans with who?"

I bit my lip as I looked away from his heated eyes. He was jealous. Wow! And you know me. I couldn't just end it there. I had to press it a little bit to see just how jealous he was.

"Nobody you know." He shut the door.

"Nobody I know? Well, that's going to be a problem." I frowned up at him, now dedicated to the role I was playing.

"I don't see how that's a problem, surely you must know that you don't know all my friends." He chuckled dryly.

"Oh, but I do. I not only know all your friends. I know everybody you come in contact with *when* you come in contact with them." He was so smug.

"Hmmm, well, aren't you nosy." He chuckled again.

"Naw, I'm just a desperate man in love with my wife and will guard and protect her no matter what..." He paused for just a minute and came to stand so close to me I could smell his delicious cologne, always invading my space this one.

"I am still the man you met in this very place four years ago. Which mean, if another man even think about coming near you in hopes of taking what's mine, I will kill him." He was frowning now. I had to bite my lip to keep from smiling. Okay, maybe it was time to end this. I shrugged.

"Well, if you're going to be such a spoilsport about it, I guess I will stay for dinner." He looked down at me for a minute without speaking with anything but his dark gaze. His eyes searched mine, reading me like a book; reading me in only a way that he could. When he was done and he got whatever answer he sought, he nodded his head before a one-sided grin appeared on his face.

"You're in luck, tonight. I'm preparing my specialty." It was my turn to raise an eyebrow.

"Oh yeah? What's that?"

"Spaghetti-O's ala Kaleb, Eve's favorite."

I found out that Eve ran away to get on her father's PlayStation that she somehow knew how to work. He had to pull her away from it to eat dinner. She opened her mouth as if she was going to have a fit. But he just hit her with one of those bass-filled, "Eve!'s and it died a sudden death.

When we were finished, I told him I would do the dishes while he got Eve ready for bed. I was so nervous. The whole time we ate he watched me in a way that made me feel as if he was starved and I was his only food. His gaze was so heated that all I could do was nibble at my dinner because I had no appetite.

When I was done cleaning the kitchen, I stood leaning against the sink chewing on my bottom lip. I couldn't believe I was here. I couldn't believe it took me so long to get here. I couldn't believe it's been a year. A year that I needed, I reminded myself; a year that I had nothing to focus on but the Heavenly Father. I felt like a new woman. I felt like now I was able to love a man like Kaleb. Now I was able to be the mate a warrior of Yah needs.

"What you thinking about?" his deep voice filled the kitchen causing me to jump.

"I didn't hear you come downstairs," I told him putting my hand on my chest. I forgot that about him. The man moved without making a sound. He turned one of his chairs around and sat in it facing me. His wide legs were so long that they nearly trapped me in. But then he relaxed back in the chair bringing his legs closer when he slouched, folding his hands in his lap and waited.

I waited too. I know he didn't think I was going to be the one to break the ice.

"I've been asking you to dinner damn near every week for a year, dinner wherever you wanted; Paris, Jamaica... Mama Rita's.

After a year of turning me down, you decide to settle on Spaghetti-O's?"

I smiled down at him. "They were very good Spaghetti-O's."

"Yeah, right." The smiled left his face and he got really serious. "What brings you by, Monica?" I exhaled. *Well, I guess the small talk was over.*

"I umm…" As I spoke my voice quivered a bit. "I –" I rubbed my head. Wow! This was a lot of pressure.

"Come on, Mon, be a big girl, spit it out." My shoulders dropped.

"Goodness, Kaleb, you can at least offer me a seat or a cup of tea. You got me standing here like I'm being interrogated. It's a lot of pressure." He sat up in his seat bringing himself closer to me. His face came to my chest.

"I have gone a year without my wife. A year of fluctuating between my living room chair and my office chair to sleep in because I couldn't stand the feel of sleeping in a bed without your warm body next to mine. A year of feeling like my heartbeat was gone." He lifted one side of his mouth in a grin that did not reach his eyes.

"You have no idea what true pressure feels like. I think you can stand in the line of fire for just a few minutes while you help me understand what is going on in that amazing mind of yours." Then he sat back in his chair and waited.

When he told me that I had no idea what true pressure feels like, there was something in his eyes that spoke to me loud and clear. And for the first time, a realization dawned on me. My grandmother prayed that she would get relief from her burden that was my brother. And I'm sure Mama Rita at some point had the same prayer about her son.

Man-Man and Rasheed were two very bad seeds and Yah had used Kaleb to remove them both. I know it may not have been too hard for him to take out Man-Man, but Rasheed was flesh of his flesh and blood of his blood, that must have been devastating. And yet, he did it and still managed to take care of me, Eve, Mama Rita, the restaurant, the body shop and all his other responsibilities. And yes, he had many. There were a lot of people that depended on Kaleb to make a way for them.

I nodded.

"Yeah, you right, I can take the fire for a little while." I traced my hand over my bracelet

"I've been selfish," I began. My voice was just barely over a whisper. "It's funny how that happens to a person." I chuckled with no humor. "You get these images of yourself and like any image, it can tell a lie. I got so caught up in an image that I lost my view of real life. And you was there, forced to fight real-life by yourself. The only thing I could see was my troubles, my grief, my pain... at no point did I stop and look at you. I got so used to seeing you as this powerful figure that I never stopped and saw that you were in pain and that you needed me."

I went down to my knees in front of him, still looking down at my bracelet. "I can understand if you don't want me anymore. I mistook you once and I promised I would never do it again, only to turn and do it again." Tears filled my eyes, I felt so bad.

"I was supposed to be your peace and I've been nothing but your grief." He sat up then, bringing his powerful arms to rest against his legs. This position caused him to corner me in completely, trapping me between his big body and the sink. He brought his hand out and gently lifted my head so that I could look into his eyes.

"Baby, you are my peace. The time I've been without you is the price I had to pay. Every man must pay for their sins and I was no different. I had many. I lied to you and I shouldn't have." I reached up and took his hand.

"Yeah, but how can I get mad at you when all I did was lie when we first met?" He gave me a look that said, yeah, you have a point. But then he shook his head.

"Naw, my lie was pretty big. It's because of me you nearly got killed in a car wreck and then kidnapped. I should have taken care of my brother a long time ago. I should have just washed my hands clean of him and his whole operation. By not shutting him down, all the blood of the people he poisoned with his dope was on my hands. I had the power to end it and I didn't. For that, I had to pay."

"We *both* had to pay," I told him. "But Yah is merciful. It's amazing how he has a way of punishing and restoring those that are his at the same time. Yeah, it was torture being without you over this last year, but something amazing has happened to me. I've developed my own relationship with the Father. I know him personally now. I feel like... if you would have me now, I will make you the perfect wife."

"Are you kidding me, if I will have you? You're asking a man who's lost his heart if he will have it back." He gently grabbed me by my arms pulling me until my lips were inches from his.

"I've been waiting a whole year for you to come back to me. I would have waited as long as you needed." I smiled at him through my tears.

"Let's start over, baby. No more lying, no more pretending. I'm hanging up my acting career. From this day forward, just straight Monica, no tricks." A hesitant look came over his face that frightened me a bit.

"Okay, so when you say no more pretending and acting, does that mean no more chicken costumes or harem dances? 'Cause I kind of like that part about you." I frowned.

"What part?"

"You know, the part of you that get a crazy idea like dressing up like a sexy chicken surprising me at work. When you say straight Monica, you don't mean boring Monica? 'Cause that's not who I married." I laughed because that sounded like music to my ears.

"So, you don't mind that I came to your job covered in feathers?"

"Mind?" He pulled me closer wrapping his arms around me. "I wish you had something stashed up your sleeve right now; the sexy sunflower or the frisky kitty. I've been bored out of my mind this past year without you. There have been no adventures. I need my troublemaker back." I laughed really missing him.

"Well, I don't know, I'm sure I can pull something together if my husband will say he'll have me back. Maybe come back to the boarding house, it's so big and lonely without him." He smiled at me and I couldn't do anything but thank Yah for it.

"I'll come back, but only if you'll let me take you upstairs and make love to you in my bed one more time. Maybe you can dance for me on the terrace and recreate the first night we met." He palmed my face with his big strong hands, gently pulling me so close that as he spoke, his lips gently brushed against mine.

"I think I can do that for—" My words were abruptly cut off by his mouth taking mine. He kissed me with such a fever that the only thing I could do was wrap my arms around his neck and let him have his way.

My body strummed to life as his mouth sipped from mine.

Oh! How I've missed his aggressive touch...

Oh! How I've missed his powerful embrace...

Oh! How I've missed my strong Hebrew Warrior...

Oh! How I've missed my Kaleb...

THANK YOU

Thank you, guys for coming along Kaleb and Monica's journey to finding love for the

Heavenly Father Yah and for each other.

Like them, we all must learn how to put Yah first. And then, ne in his loving commitment will provide our every need.

I am Edwina Fort, The Hebrew Griot...

If you liked this story, please leave me a message letting me know and don't forget to

check out my Hebrew Griot YouTube page for many more stories just like this one...

Hebrew Griot YouTube Channel:
youtube.com/channel/UCN2wo3cuLpM2oSo1SUpyXzA

Facebook Page:
www.facebook.com/hebrewgriot

Edwina Fort Facebook Page:
www.facebook.com/AuthorEdwinaFort

Edwina Fort Twitter:
twitter.com/Edwina_Fort

Edwina Fort Website:
authoredwinafort.com

Edwina Fort YouTube Channel:
www.youtube.com/channel/UCSKCjVKwFB- rWq_uHUuqE4Q

the griot's garden
IS LOOKING FOR AUTHORS.

Do you have a story to tell?

Submit online:

GriotsGardenPublications.com/submissions

ABOUT THE AUTHOR

Author Edwina Fort is a writer who writes with a passion and purpose. She was born and raised in Chicago, but now resides in the South. Although she is new to many, this author has been writing for many years and has given her unique style of writing away freely at no cost to those who would receive. Her passion for writing came about at an early age and developed into what it is today based on her experience and life lessons. With her stories, she wants to redefine all that we've been taught to believe and shed light on our truths and potential. Writing is her calling and she wants to share that gift with you through the pages of her work. Each book will take you on a memorable journey you will find hard to forget.